# The Iconic Warrior

# The Iconic Warrior:
## The Genesis of a Fighting Soldier

*By Gene Klann, Ph.D.*

*Lieutenant Colonel,*
*U.S. Army (Retired)*

*Dedicated with high respect to the gallant and selfless brotherhood of warriors who have experienced the crucible of combat, the ultimate trial by fire, the definitive stimulation of the emotions and senses, and the indestructible bond between all frontline battlefield fighters.*

The Iconic Warrior: The Genesis of a Fighting Soldier

By Gene Klann, Ph.D.
Lieutenant Colonel, US Army (Retired)

ISBN: 978-1956-904-154

Printed in the United States of America

Published by Blacksmith LLC
Fayetteville, North Carolina

www.BlacksmithPublishing.com

Direct inquiries and/or orders to the above web address.

# Acknowledgments

This is the fourth book I have written and had published. That said, I want to thank my precious wife Kathy for her steadfast love, encouragement, and support during each of those challenging writing adventures. Kathy has consistently been the bright shining star that has lifted me toward the successful completion of all these major projects. Thanks Princess!!

My sincere gratitude goes out to several of my highly esteemed friends and colleagues who read and commented on the drafts of this book. They provided valuable and insightful feedback regarding necessary changes and improvements. These associates include my best buddy Drew Whitler in Omaha, mi amigo Ray Critchett in Mexico City, Colonel Greg Laskow (U.S. Army retired), Professor George Liebman, John Fonville, Nancy Geyer, and Marshall *Sonny* White. These are all well read and distinguished scholars in their own right whose words of encouragement were more meaningful than they will ever know. Thank you! Also, the feedback I received from leadership authority and U.S. Army retired Lieutenant General Walt Ulmer was especially inspiring. After reading the draft he said, "That is interesting stuff! History and philosophy on every page!"

Words fail me to adequately and humbly thank the Good Lord. He gave me the vision, skills, insights, wisdom, understanding, time, and the opportunity to write this book. Thank you!

Finally, I would like to thank you dear reader for selecting my book as part of your personal reading plan. My deepest hope is that it provides you as much pleasure reading it as it did for me when I wrote it. May the book always educate, entertain, edify, and encourage! Hoorah and oorah!!

# Praise for The Iconic Warrior

"The Iconic Warrior: Genesis of a Fighting Soldier provides a creative adaptation of American history and personalities through the eyes of a fictitious young hero. Every page gives pleasure and insight." – Walter F. Ulmer, Jr. Lieutenant General, U.S. Army (Retired), Former President and CEO, Center for Creative Leadership

"Dr. Klann's Iconic Warrior book captures the reader's interest, constantly portraying an excellent command of American history and colorful descriptions of what authentic soldiering is all about. He does this brilliantly by stimulating all five senses." – Greg Laskow, Ph.D. Colonel, U.S. Army (Retired)

"As a teacher of United States history at an historic military academy, I found Dr. Klann's book an informative source and an entertaining study of a neglected era of our military history. Gene Klann has given us a gift of heritage as well as history." – George Liebmann, Faculty Oak Ridge Military Academy

"The Iconic Warrior is among the most delightful and historical novels I've ever read. The characters jump off the page, engage you, and inform you! Outstanding!" – Drew Whitler, Senior Faculty Center for Creative Leadership

"The Iconic Warrior is a fast-moving tale of a valiant young man's devotion to duty while remaining true to his core values. A must read!" – Ray Critchett, President and CEO ARTIPAC, Mexico City, Mexico

"This historical military fiction book by Gene Klann is not only fun to read, but more importantly, it reveals critical lessons about life and leadership." – Marshall White, Ph.D. President Emeritus, Midlands Technical College. Retired Division President, Consumer Care, NAFTA, Ciba Specialty Chemicals

"Dr. Klann's Iconic Warrior book provides many key inspirations and also valuable messages for achieving success in life."
– Nancy Geyer, Mental Health Advocate

"This masterfully written page turner is a must for those who hunger for a book that is not only entertaining but also exceptionally instructive."
– Coble Fonville – Financial Controller (Retired)

"Fast paced, historically accurate epic set in a realistic military setting that challenges the reader's values in critical areas such as leadership, ethics, decision-making, and problem solving!"
– Bill McQuiston, NC Law Enforcement Krav Maga/Combatives Instructor 3rd Dan Black Belt in Saeng Jeon Do Martial Arts

# Contents

# Definition of Terms

In the U.S. Army, a lieutenant colonel (O-5) and a full colonel (O-6), are both referred to as colonel in army verbal discussion and conversation.

All four ranks of a general officer, i.e., brigadier general (O-7), major general (O-8), lieutenant general (O-9), and four-star general (O-10), are all referred to as general in army verbal discussion and conversation.

Jean-Paul or J.P. is also known by his nickname of Professor because of his knowledge of military history and his ability to recall history applicable to current situations. He is also sometimes called teenager or Rough Rider.

Herkimer Hanky is also known by his nickname Three-Ring because of his prior work in the circus. Jean-Paul periodically refers to him as Bunkie since they were tent mates in San Antonio and later roomed together when they were assigned to Fort Snelling, Minnesota.

During this period in the army, there were four ranks of non-commissioned officer: corporal, sergeant, first sergeant, and sergeant major. They are also referred to as NCO's or noncoms. A first sergeant was also informally referred to as top sergeant because he was the senior noncommissioned officer in a company-sized unit.

An infantry company generally had a strength of one hundred men. Seldom, however, were they at full strength. Many times, their assigned strength was less than fifty soldiers. In combat, it might have been even less. In the cavalry, a company-sized unit was referred to as a troop. In the artillery, it was called a battery.

Enlisted promotions in the U.S. Army were generally based on merit (although seniority was given some consideration). For example, before he attended the United States Military Academy at West Point, Edgar Allan Poe had achieved the rank of sergeant major in the artillery after being on active duty for only eight months.

AWOL is the army acronym for absent without leave. When a soldier leaves his unit without authorization, he is considered AWOL. After being AWOL for thirty days, he was dropped from the unit rolls (DFR) and was considered a deserter.

## *Note from the Author*

The Iconic Warrior books are a series of historical fiction writings that follow the army career of protagonist Jean-Paul DeBert from the Spanish-American War in 1898 through World War II. That includes his service in the war with Spain in Cuba, the last major battle between the U.S. Army and the American Indians at Leech Lake/Sugar Point, Minnesota, the Philippine Insurrection, the Boxer Rebellion, putting down the Pullman Strike, the relief efforts for the San Francisco Earthquake, and many, many more exciting adventures.

# *Introduction*

The Iconic Warrior is a series of fast moving and informative historical fiction novels describing the combat experiences and exploits of protagonist Jean-Paul DeBert (pronounced duh-bear). From his youth Jean-Paul, or J.P. as he is also known, dreamt about becoming a great battlefield warrior.

In 1898 Jean-Paul was eighteen years old, six-foot one inch tall, handsome, fluent in four languages, an avid runner, educated in a New York Jesuit school, skilled at the French martial art of savate stick fighting, and of French and American Indian descent. His passage from raw civilian recruit to battle hardened veteran began with his 1898 acceptance into the U.S. Army's First Volunteer Cavalry, aka Teddy Roosevelt's Rough Riders.

The objective of the series is to promote and enhance professionalism in the military and specifically, in the United States Army. Readers are leaders and leaders are readers. Reading these Jean-Paul books will educate the reader in military history, foster a grander vison of the way of the warrior, and increase personal combat readiness. They also promote the idea that how an army fights is based on the influence of its past military victories and successes. The books are designed to improve the readers' ability to think critically, motivate them to apply what they read, and broaden their perspective about life, relationships, and the craft of soldiering. It will also assist military readers in becoming refined and sophisticated renaissance men and women so they will be as comfortable at an embassy lawn party as they are on the battlefield. In addition, the books have a balanced and academic approach to war, the military, and soldiering. In that regard, they discuss anti-war, anti-military, and isolationist points of view. The writings are aimed at producing and strengthening military professionals like George Washington, Matthew Ridgway, and Joshua Chamberlain and not the likes of Attila the Hun, Tamerlane, or Genghis Khan.

These books also endorse the notion that the nobility of a constitutional republic are the men and women of its military who are called to ensure its safety, security, and survival. Those who serve in uniform are always ready and willing to sacrifice their lives for others, fight injustice, and destroy tyranny. In doing that, they are indeed the aristocratic class of the nation and deserve the eternal gratitude of their countrymen.

There is also a spiritual component to the series. Jean-Paul believes in an omniscient, omnipresent, and omnipotent God. That is the Being who created the galaxy with only words and who has known the thoughts and actions of every general, commander, and soldier on all the battlefields in history. Jean-Paul believes this Deity is someone he must stay connected with if he is to survive and thrive on the battlefield.

The historical events described in this series are all from primary, original sources. The entire series faithfully follows the actual sequence of the wars, campaigns, and battles it describes. The books are not historically revised or rewritten based on the trends of the current culture. Consequently, they are *not teleological presentism* which looks at the past through the lens of current moral, social, or political judgments.

# 1

## *The Call to Arms*

There was a knock on the front door of the DeBert household. From the kitchen window the family could see the person who had knocked was Pudgy McKenna. He was the dimwitted favorite son of Henry McKenna who ran the local telegraph office. Old man McKenna employed his son to deliver cablegrams. The problem was that Pudgy would read the cables and then share the contents with the entire town. When complaints about that behavior reached old Henry, he would simply dismiss his son's behavior as being harmless and endearing.

Eighteen-year-old Jean-Paul DeBert intuitively sensed the knock on the door was significant. Pudgy McKenna could be carrying the telegram that would make his perpetual musing about becoming a great warrior and a fighting soldier a reality— or not.

As a result of his visit to his ninety-year grandfather Gerard in France when he was five years old, Jean-Paul's goal was to make a heroic name for himself on the battlefield. As a sixteen-year-old, Papa Gerard had joined *Emperor Napoleon's Grand*

*Armée.* He had fought from Russia to Waterloo. During his three years of service, he had been decorated, wounded five times, and promoted to sergeant in the *Young Guard.* During the entire visit, young Jean-Paul sat on the old warrior's knee and listened to his many war stories. What capped it was Gerard's prophecy that someday young Jean-Paul *would be a mighty warrior.* That predication inspired his vision to become a great soldier.

Jean-Paul opened the front door. Pudgy loudly proclaimed, "So you're joinin' da army and going off ta da war!! How dumb is that! Hope those Spaniards doesn't blow you to up like dey did da Maine! Do ya think you'll make it back here alive?" Pudgy stared at Jean-Paul waiting for a response. When there was none, he said, "Well do ya? Do ya think you'll come back alive?" Jean-Paul looked directly at the rotund blob and didn't answer.

After Pudgy passed the cablegram to Jean-Paul and mounted his bicycle he yelled over his shoulder, "Good luck! You'll be needin' it!!! Ha, ha, ha...!" Pudgy also muttered something else inaudible under his breath. It was probably a derogatory reference to either Jean-Paul's American Indian heritage, his French ancestry, or his Jesuit faith. Jean-Paul shook his head as he watched Pudgy cycle away. He never really did care for either Pudgy or old man McKenna....

The telegram was from Lieutenant Colonel Theodore Roosevelt. Jean-Paul read it aloud: *"You are hereby accepted into the lst United States Volunteer Cavalry Regiment. Report immediately to Camp Wood, San Antonio, Texas. Roosevelt, Lieutenant Colonel, Deputy Commander."*

Jean-Paul was elated beyond words. The cable was the response to a telegram he had sent to Roosevelt requesting a slot in that newly organized volunteer cavalry regiment. It was one of many volunteer units being formed to go to war with Spain because America's regular army at the time numbered only twenty-six thousand soldiers.

Sitting at the kitchen table watching his concerned mother preparing dinner, Jean-Paul reflected on the background of the cable he had just received. On the 25th of April, the United States had declared war on Spain following the sinking of its battleship—the USS Maine—in Havana harbor. The sinking had occurred two months prior on the 15th of February, 1898. At the time, Roosevelt surprised everyone by resigning his post as the Assistant Secretary of the Navy to become the deputy commander of a newly formed army cavalry unit. Jean-Paul had hoped his telegram would reach Roosevelt during his transition from the navy to the army. It was now clear it had.

Jean-Paul's father Louie was also sitting at the kitchen table doing what he always did—he was reading. Periodically he would glance at Jean-Paul. Louie knew that ever since the visit to France, his son was constantly fantasizing about becoming a great warrior. For good or bad, Louie knew Jean-Paul was not only motivated by his grandfather but also what he had read and *his own military service.* Louie had survived fighting the Germans in the 1870-71 Franco-Prussian War. Then too, there were the motivating warrior exploits of the Chacopac Indian tribe with whom the DeBert family lived.

As he took a drink of lemonade, Jean-Paul ran the sequence threw his mind regarding how he had met Teddy Roosevelt in New York City in 1896. At the time, *Teddy* was the president of the board of the New York City Police Commissioners. As a police commissioner, he would routinely accompany his New York police officers on foot patrol. Jean-Paul was absolutely convinced Providence had fortuitously scheduled a divine appointment between Commissioner Roosevelt and himself.

He took another sip of the pungent lemonade and continued his reflection. On an oppressively hot and humid New York City summer evening, Jean-Paul and his dad had just finished dining at *Le Tres Maggot,* a renowned French restaurant on West 53rd Street in midtown Manhattan. When the two walked outside they were met with a flurry of commotion and yelling. Men were wildly running towards them. A quick glance made it clear the police were chasing a man who was just out in front of them.

*"Stop him, stop him,"* they yelled. With his natural impulsiveness, Jean-Paul, then age sixteen, tackled the runner and unceremoniously threw him to the ground. Within seconds

the police patrol arrived. It included Police Commissioner Theodore Roosevelt.

Roosevelt kept repeating to Jean-Paul, "Well done; bully, bully—well done. You are a brave lad, a very brave lad. Bully! Well done." Jean-Paul and his dad then walked to the police station with the patrol and the cuffed criminal. Roosevelt, exuberant and full of energy, had his arm around Jean-Paul the entire way. At the station Jean-Paul and his father gave brief statements, were interviewed by a news reporter, and the teenager had his photograph taken.

The next day he was featured as a daring hero on the front page of the New York Times. The headline announced: *"Intrepid Teenager Tackles Criminal."* After reading the article, Jean-Paul was shocked how the article had embellished his action. Considering the exaggerated manner in which it was written, he wasn't sure it was even the same incident. Because of this event, Jean-Paul had hoped Mr. Roosevelt would remember him when he received his cable. About that he was not mistaken.

This episode occurred in August of 1896 when Jean-Paul and his dad had traveled to New York City to pick up several trunks of goods sent by his French grandmother: Monique *Nana* DeBert. Two or three times a year, Nana DeBert, who lived in the Loire River Valley of France with her husband Papa Gerard, would send one or more trunks with books, clothing, chocolates, blocks of hard cheese, bottles of wine, gifts, and generous sums of French francs to the North American DeBert family.

Jean-Paul's dad, Louie, was Monique's very favorite son. Monique was the second wife of Gerard *Papa* DeBert, who had inherited the family vineyard and had become a very prosperous wine producer in the Loire River Valley. It had been a spring-autumn marriage because Monique was thirty years younger than Gerard!

Jean Paul's thoughts then turned to his mother. Stoically, she kept working at the kitchen counter, never looking up. She seldom showed much emotion, but her body language betrayed the distress she was feeling about her oldest son going off to war. Finally, she said, "Now that you are a man, I know going to war is something you want to do. What deeply concerns me is that soldiers are trained to kill, because that's what war is. I know that's what you will have to do and also that you yourself will be exposed to being killed. This is something that I as your mother can barely think about.... I will pray for you every day. My prayers will be that not only that you will come home safe but that your experience will not have too great an effect on you." Her comment left Jean-Paul speechless.

At this time Jean-Paul's younger brother and sister, *Marcel and Arlette,* came storming into the house. Even though they were three years apart in age, eleven and eight, and of different genders, they spent much of their time playing together. Marcel acted as the protector of his younger sister, which was perfectly fine with their parents.

"What was Pudgy McKenna doing here? Did he bring us a telegram?" Marcel inquired breathlessly.

"Yes, he did," their father Louie, answered quietly. "It seems your brother is going to join the army and will probably being going off to Cuba to fight the Spanish Army. Actually, fighting the Spanish is what many of our French ancestors have done. And quite successfully too I might add."

"That's great," Marcel exclaimed. To his brother he shouted, "Will you bring me a Spanish medal or a knife or an army hat?"

"I want you to bring me those things too," Arlette echoed, always emulating her brother's behavior.

"I'll see what I can do but no promises. For sure if I go to Cuba I will bring you something. You can count on that."

Jean-Paul then said, "I am going to tell Abby about the cablegram." Abby or Abigail Bradley was Jean-Paul's best girl and the daughter of the local Methodist preacher, the *Reverend Doctor Amos B. Bradley*.

Unfortunately, Dr. Bradley did not like Jean-Paul on a number of counts. First, J.P. was a Roman Catholic. According to Dr. Bradley, this made him a papist and the offspring of the *godless Inquisition*. Second, his social standing was in question being the son of Louie DeBert, who was an unpaid, volunteer teacher at the Jesuit school on the Chacopac tribal lands. How would the Reverend explain to his socially connected family in Boston the marriage of his daughter to this penniless boy? It was bad enough the Reverend was living in the backwater of upstate New York, but to have his daughter get hooked up with this Jean-Paul half-breed? Never!

Finally, Reverend Bradley simply did not like Jean-Paul for no other reason than he was Jean-Paul. He felt the young man was too immature and impulsive, was too easily angered, and was nothing more than a roughneck with no future prospects. His daughter Abigail could do much better and could probably do no worse. The Reverend didn't know that the majority of times when Abigail left the house, it was to be with Jean-Paul. That included those skinny-dipping episodes at Silver Mountain Lake.

It was now near suppertime. Regardless, Jean-Paul went directly to the front door of the Bradley house and knocked. Within seconds, Reverend Bradley jerked the door open. With a scowl is demanded, "What do you want?" As if he didn't know thought Jean-Paul.

"I would like to see Abby," Jean-Paul said in a firm yet respectful tone. He was always respectful to Reverend Bradley who seldom reciprocated that behavior.

"I said Abigail is not here," the Reverend said loudly. It was his standard line. Jean-Paul was always amazed that here was a highly educated and respected clergyman who had no

11

compunction to lie and say his daughter was not at home. When in fact, she was most probably in her bedroom just above them.

Jean-Paul said, "Sir, I believe you are mistaken. I do believe she is here, and I need to speak to her right away."

"Are you calling me a liar Dee-bert?" Reverend Bradley knew exactly the correct pronunciation of Jean-Paul's last name, but he routinely and purposely mispronounced it.

"Sir, my name is pronounced *duh-bear* and I need to see Abigail since I am leaving to join the Army. And, I will most likely go to Cuba and fight the Spanish."

Ignoring the reason for the visit, the Reverend said, "I told you she is not here and if you don't leave, I will get my shotgun and teach you a thing or two." His face was now beet red, the veins were bulging from his neck, and he was actually starting to shake. Jean-Paul who also struggled with anger when he sensed he was being marginalized, patronized, or treated unjustly, felt the need to push the confrontation. He had taken two steps back after he had knocked on the door. Now he took two steps forward and was within arm's reach of the old clergyman. When angry J.P. always felt a tightening in his chest. It was *the feeling*. His breathing also became faster and heavier, he would clench his fists, and sense a need to go on the attack. That *feeling* was now present and quite strong.

Jean-Paul's weakness had always been his over sensitivity to perceived unjust treatment. His French and Indian heritage and the fact he was a Roman Catholic in a community dominated by Protestants of English ancestry routinely resulted in insensitive comments and biased behaviors from the locals. This always triggered a negative response from Jean-Paul and a scolding from his father for not being more patient and forgiving. His father would routinely remind him of Alexander Pope's quote: *"To become angry is to revenge the faults of the other person onto yourself."*

Jean-Paul noted that Mrs. Bradley was standing a few feet from her husband and trying to stay out of his view behind the door. She was somewhat sympathetic toward J.P. but in deference to her husband, she had never encouraged him. The look on her face was one of total terror.

*"Get the h-ll off of my property now!* I don't ever want to see you here again. A papist has no place in this family. The Romanists unjustly murdered millions of so-called heretics in the Inquisition. Your Jesuit school teaches those poor ignorant natives by conjuring up and employing demonic forces. That's right—demonic forces. *Now get the h-ll out of here!"*

Jean-Paul was startled by the Reverend's outburst. He had been quietly hostile in the past but now he was taking it to a new level. It made him think the Reverend Doctor was going insane. Without thinking he said, "Did you learn that *"h"* word and that ignorant notion about the pope being the anti-Christ in your seminary studies or was it in your Bible college days? And by the way, did you happen to learn anything about *agape love, tolerance, grace, or mercy* in your training to be a preacher? And furthermore, the Jesuits have done ten times more for education and soul saving missions than yours or any other religious group ever thought about doing!"

Then without thinking, he did it. He said, "And, if *you Reverend,* don't accept Jesus Christ as the Lord of your life and your personal Savior, you will not get to heaven."

"That's it! That's it! You are telling me I'm not going to heaven? That's it, I'm getting my gun!" The Reverend turned quickly, stumbled, and almost fell.

Mrs. Bradley came quickly to the door and said, "Go Jean-Paul! Now go quickly before he hurts you! Go! Go now and hurry!"

Out of respect for Abigail's mom, Jean-Paul walked down the steps of the porch and kept backing up not taking his eyes off the door. When he was back far enough, he saw Abigail in the window of her room, which was just above the front door of the Bradley house. She had both hands on her head and was shaking and crying uncontrollably. Apparently, she had been crying the entire time he was at the front door. Seeing that was too much for him. He turned and started running as fast as he could. He was a very good runner because he had habitually run into the town of Good Hope to pick up supplies or complete errands for his parents. He would also run home depending on how much he was carrying. It was a little more than two miles in each direction.

The two-mile route however, was not the shortest. The shortest way was only about a mile and a quarter. The problem was that route passed the *Beckenbauer sawmill.* Julius Beckenbauer and his family came to the United States from East Prussia in 1863. It was said he did so to avoid being drafted into the Prussian Army. He had two sons: Arno and Bruno. One was nineteen and the other eighteen. They were both as rude and obnoxious as their father. When Jean-Paul would run past their sawmill as a young boy, the Beckenbauer boys would throw verbal insults at him. They would pester him about being French, about being Catholic (since they were steadfast German Lutherans), about being part American Indian, and about anything else that came to mind. Once they even sicced their German Shepherd on him. From then on, Jean-Paul's father had forbidden him from using that route and insisted he use the longer road into town and back.

Jean-Paul was still fuming. He now came to the *Y* in the road where he had to decide whether to use the long or short route home. Of course, the short route went by the Beckenbauer sawmill. He stopped for a second but only a second. In his current frame of mind, he decided it was time to go home using the shorter road which passed by the Beckenbauer mill. He knew that was a bad decision and simply an emotional response to his experience with Reverend Bradley. But frankly—he didn't care. He was leaving for the army tomorrow and this was something he felt he needed to do. There was something of a score to be settled with those *thick-necked, crimson-faced sauerkrauts!*

Jean-Paul always carried a large knife that had been given to him by his dad on the occasion of his first communion. His dad called it a *Bowie Knife* after the legendary blade carried by Alamo hero and Louisiana adventurer Jim Bowie. This knife was a total of twelve inches in length with the blade being 7 and 3/4 inches long and two inches wide. The handle was made from hardwood and was shaped to fit the grip of his hand. J.P. kept it incredibly sharp. More times than he could remember he cut himself with this oversized weapon. It was more of a small sword than a knife, but it would be enough to defend himself if the Beckenbauers sicced their German shepherd on him—or so Jean-Paul reasoned.

Just ahead of him off the side of the road was a fallen tree. It had several well-rounded branches. With some urgency he ran to the tree, chopped off a suitable branch, and shaped it into a combination walking stick and slender club. He then began his usual jog that was his trademark when going into New Hope.

Jean-Paul was eager for a fight. For six years he had avoided the road past the Beckenbauer's sawmill. But that would not be the case today. If he could not take his anger out on Reverend Bradley, then perhaps he would find an outlet on this road. Besides, he was going to be a soldier whose job was to fight—and to win!

Jean-Paul strategized as he jogged. As he rounded the large bend in the road, he saw the Beckenbauer place. He was hoping the sawmill had not yet shut down *so he would be seen*. As he came nearer, he knew he was in luck. The mill crew and the Beckenbauers—the father and his two sons—had just finished their work and were washing up at the water trough. They were about thirty yards or so from where he would pass by them.

Bruno was the first to see Jean-Paul. He immediately yelled out, "Ja hey, look vat vee have here!!! It be the half-breed Frenchman!" That slur caused a crescendo of laughter from the all-German sawmill crew. Uneducated buffoons thought J.P. It also caused him to stop running and start walking closer to the sawmill side of the road.

Jean-Paul saw the Beckenbauer's German shepherd. But wait, now there were two shepherd dogs tied up by the mill. Of course, there had to be two thought J.P. Who knows, maybe there was a third or a fourth. No matter. he was going to war tomorrow so why not have a little action today? He gripped his walking stick tighter and opened the guard to the sheath of the Bowie knife.

Old man Beckenbauer was a stocky, bloated faced, overweight man, with almost no neck. He was respected for being an extremely hard worker with a hard-nosed business sense—but not much else. He came to North America with nothing. Through his own industry, energy, and discipline, he built and continually expanded his sawmill. He was now providing lumber not only for Lafayette County but for several of the surrounding counties as well.

He was also in continuous conflict with the Chacopac tribe because he wanted to get lumber from their land. Since the forested portion of their tribal land was not very large, they kept rejecting his offers. Several times Beckenbauer had asked Jean-Paul's dad to intervene and convince the Chacs to let him cut the timber on their land. Louie DeBert would have nothing to do with it. Several times Beckenbauer had covertly sent his loggers onto the tribe's land without permission. In each case they were driven off with little ceremony. The lack of support from Louie DeBert was another reason *The Becks,* as their family was called, had little use for the DeBerts.

The one saving grace of the Beckenbauer family was their youngest daughter Berthold—or Berti as she was called. She had neither the appearance nor character of a Beckenbauer. The family members were short, stocky, round faced with dark hair. Berti however was tall, attractive, well-proportioned, and had blonde hair. The family was assertive and generally mean spirited. Berti on the other hand was reserved with a kind and gentle heart. It was rumored she looked more like *Big Harley Faust,* a former employee at the sawmill, than old man

Beckenbauer. This of course was just a rumor.

Harley unfortunately had met his demise in a dreadful accident at the sawmill. He was essentially cut in half when one of the big saws came undone. This had never happened before and had not happened since. It occurred on the first day Big Harley had been assigned to operate that saw—an unfortunate coincidence.

Berti had taken the initiative to ask Jean-Paul to teach her French. In return she would teach him German. This had surprised him. But always curious and looking for opportunities to learn—he took her up on her offer. At least once a week and sometimes twice they would get together for a couple of hours and speak French and German with one another. It wasn't clear the Beckenbauer family knew this was happening but that didn't matter to him. His only motive was to learn German. Jean-Paul had inherited the gift of languages from his dad. Not only did he quickly pick up German with all its unusual elocutions, but he could easily retain it and recall it. And, he could do that instantly. Since Berti was a friend and classmate of his girlfriend Abigail, Abby was always present at these language sessions. She was there mostly to protect her interests in J.P. Abby recognized Berti was interested in something more than just learning French from him. This was something Jean-Paul also sensed but dismissed because of his feelings about Abby—and *The Becks*. He couldn't imagine having Arno and Bruno Beckenbauer as brothers-in-law. That was an exceedingly dreadful and depressing thought!

True to form, Bruno went to loosen one German shepherd and Arno the other. When unleashed, both dogs took just a couple of steps and then sat on their hind legs never taking their eyes off of Jean-Paul. Even though work hours were over, none of the sawmill crew had left the yard. They apparently wanted to watch the action. There was a nervous excitement in the air. Arno walked over to Bruno and they were quietly having a laughing conversation. "Animals," said J.P. under his breath. Up to this point old man Beckenbauer had said nothing, but he had a huge *Cheshire cat grin* on his face. He was oh so proud of his two boys. In Jean-Paul's world they were the country punks—rough neck bullies. By his standards they both were uneducated, simpletons.

Jean-Paul's dad Louie had observed that the Germans loved to bully others during his experience with them in Europe and in the Franco-Prussian War. They just loved to laugh at people and the misfortune of others. The workers were apparently expecting someone to have a bit of misfortune *here and now*. J.P. agreed that someone was about to have misfortune, but he was *quite convinced* it would not be him.

When Arno and Bruno finished their discussion, the mood changed. Suddenly and without warning Arno yelled out, *"Hansel, Gretel, sic 'im."* Those were the magic words for the two German shepherds. They immediately took off like a shot for

Jean-Paul who was still standing about thirty yards away.

Jean-Paul braced himself and cocked back the branch ready to swing at the dog that came upon him first. That apparently was going to be Gretel.

Out of nowhere the cry rang out, *"Hansel, Gretel, ruhe, still; herkommen, komm."* It was the unmistakable voice of Berti who had raised and trained these dogs and who took care of them. Incredibly both dogs stopped immediately, turned and started trotting obediently toward Berti. Simultaneously Arno and Bruno began yelling in German at Berti and the dogs. Jean-Paul understood what they were saying and none of it was complimentary to either their sister or the dogs. But it was quite clear who controlled the dogs and who did not. Interestingly, old man Beckenbauer told his two boys to relax. He then told Berthold to also settle down as his boys were just having some fun.

In her slightly accented English Berti replied, "Father, ordering dogs to attack a person is not fun but is quite irresponsible. What if I had not been here? They could have killed J.P., and then what? Wirklich, und dann was?" ("Really, and then what?")

Hearing Berti call Jean-Paul by his nickname startled both old man Beckenbauer and his two boys. They had no idea she had been teaching him German.

"So ve are now calling the Frenchman by his buddy namen?

21

Vhen did vee get so friendly mit our Indian lovin' Frenchie neighbor?" Arno asked this with both confusion and contempt in his voice.

Berti did not immediately reply. After a brief pause, she said, "Since we live together in this community, we must learn to get along with one another. We must do better than our German countrymen do with their French neighbors back home." She then said something quietly to the dogs and all three, in complete calm, walked away.

Jean-Paul had never seen Berti interact with her family before. It was quite clear from this exchange that her strong personality extended well beyond his contact with her. She was clearly a force to be reckoned with by both her father and brothers. Jean-Paul remembered what his dad had said: *"In a German home the mother always rules the roost, and the father is almost always passive."* Maybe that's why the Germans were so warlike—the men had to get away from that female control by going off to war. An unusual thought for Jean-Paul only seconds after almost being eaten alive buy two ferocious German Shepherds.

The Beckenbauer men, who were too thick of mind to recognize that an eighteen-year-old female had just embarrassed them publicly, again turned their attention to Jean-Paul. Bruno directed an ethnic slur toward Jean-Paul in German. J.P. understood exactly what he said and *responded in German* by saying, "Are you talking to me or your brother?" His response in their language surprised everyone who heard it to the point that they were speechless. Jean-Paul, still fuming and knowing better, could not let it drop. Now in English he said, "Tomorrow I am leaving to join the army and fight the Spanish in Cuba. Arno and Bruno, are you two going to sign up too or are you going to stay home here in New Hope with the women and children?" He then turned and started walking home. There was some indiscernible talking behind him but he didn't care. It was time to get home and get ready to leave tomorrow on his new adventure.

When Jean-Paul got home it was still light. At this time of April, the sun didn't set until after seven. His anger had subsided and now he had almost completely recovered from his rage. He was also feeling somewhat ashamed of himself because of his behavior with both Reverend Bradley and the Beckenbauers. He knew better and his thoughts and conduct had not been consistent with the belief system he had been taught by the Jesuits. Now he felt the usual internal Jesuit conflict. He had enjoyed with a base and fleshly pleasure what he had just said and done. On the other hand, he now felt *the uncomfortable press of conscience, conviction, and Jesuit guilt—always with the Jesuit guilt!*

Before he had a chance to tell what had happened, Jean-Paul's father said, "Eat your dinner quickly and then get your camping things; we are going to *The Grotto.*

## Thought Questions for Chapter 1:

1. In what way did Jean-Paul's grandfather—Papa Gerard— motivate and inspire him to become a great warrior?

2. Assess and evaluate the comment's Jean-Paul's mother made to him when she learned he would be going off to war? Why did she say what she did?

3. When visiting Revered Bradley, why did Jean-Paul get *that feeling* in his chest? Was it justified? Why or why not?

4. Why did Jean-Paul take the forbidden short route home after his meeting with Reverend Bradley? If you had experienced what he had, would you have taken the short or long route home? Why?

5. What was your biggest learning or take away from this chapter? What can you apply from the information in this chapter? What in it did you find the most interesting? Why?

# 2

## *The Grotto*

The Grotto was the cave where Jean-Paul's dad Louie would go when he wanted to think, make an important decision, solve a problem, or simply enjoy some solitude. The cave was hidden away on hillside that overlooked the entire valley. The ceiling of the cave was about eight feet high, and the cave's length was about thirty feet. It was an *L* shaped cave. This was good because when it rained Louie could locate his sleeping area in the leg of the cave.

Jean-Paul had fond memories of coming to *The Grotto* with his father. During these visits he had been captivated with Louie's thoughts about France, Paris, Nana and Papa DeBert and his visits to his stepsister and her family in London. He would share his thoughts about his studies at the Sorbonne, his early days with the Chacopac tribe, his war service with the French Army, and more. He particularly enjoyed the accounts of his father's priest in France: *Father Alexandre*. He too had ministered in North America with the Chacs. Jean-Paul figured this particular overnight visit, in true French tradition, would be his father's commissioning of him for his journey into the army— the customary *laying of hands* prior to *going out into the world.*

The walk to the cave took about an hour. Jean-Paul was following his swift moving dad along a narrow trail. He revered his father. He was convinced his dad was the most brilliant, kind, and decent man alive. He could speak several languages fluently, had a first-rate education from the Paris-Sorbonne University, had an insightful understanding of people and cultures, and was a prolific reader and writer. His wisdom and knowledge of life's practical issues were bordering on genius.

Louie had given up a prosperous future in France by refusing to take over the family vineyard in the Loire River Valley. Instead, he had moved to New Hope, New York, to teach at the Jesuit school for the Chacopac Indian children. He did this knowing he would not receive any financial compensation in that position.

All twelve years of Jean-Paul's formal schooling had taken place in that Jesuit institution. It had been an excellent and comprehensive education with much memorization and recitation. There had also been a generous emphasis on Greek and Latin classical thinkers. Admittedly, the informal schooling and mentoring he had received from his father Louie had actually been more impactful than the classroom. Plus, his personal readings had added to a very robust learning experience. As much as anything, *they taught him to think.*

In addition to being a student at the Chacopac School, during the past two years Jean-Paul had assisted his dad and the

Jesuits priests in teaching both history and English. He now knew the wisdom of the adage that *the teacher always learns more than the students.*

Currently however, Jean-Paul was finished with school and wanted to get out on his own, experience adventure, and see parts of the world other than upstate New York and southern Ontario. America's recently declared war with Spain would give him that opportunity.

The last few hundred yards to the grotto were the worst as they were on an extremely steep incline. Since it was the end of April, there was a sharp spring chill in the evening air. Jean-Paul often wondered how his father had found this cave. When he had asked him, but his dad simply answered, "Oh, just by exploring the area around New Hope."

Once in the cave Jean-Paul's dad went to make a fire from the firewood left there from a previous visit. The fire was always by the opening of the cave for two reasons. One was for the smoke to escape and the other was to discourage predators—of which there were many. When Louie picked up the first branch, he saw movement among the firewood. He immediately backed up to the far wall and alerted Jean-Paul with a whisper. Out of the firewood slithered a four-foot-long *timber rattler.* Its chunky body, wide head, and long body were quite distinguishable from its New York cousin: the *pygmy rattler.* Almost as if it knew it was not welcome it gracefully slithered out of the grotto. As it disappeared, both Louie and Jean-Paul breathed a sigh of relief.

Jean-Paul didn't like snakes. Each time he saw even a harmless garter or a black snake—which were quite common around New Hope—he would shudder. Father Luc had said the shudder was caused by the curse God had placed on snakes in the Garden of Eden. Curse of not, Jean-Paul didn't like snakes.

The campfire took the chill out of the night air. There was an old loose stump and also a log that would serve as chairs. Louie told Jean-Paul to sit on the stump. He took a bottle of wine from his pack, opened it, and poured two glasses. He stood and handed one glass to Jean-Paul and then returned to his seat on the log. He looked down and said nothing for what seemed to be a very long time. He finally raised his head, looked directly at Jean-Paul, and said quietly, "Well son, tomorrow you are going off to war. Your grandfather, Papa Gerard fought with Napoleon for three years as a teenager. Within a few months after I graduated from the Sorbonne, I fought the Prussians. Now you will carry on the tradition and fight the Spanish in Cuba." With this he raised his glass as a toast to Jean-Paul and said, "*Here is to your safety and may the grace of God go with you.*" Proposing a toast was something his father only did on rare and special occasions.

"Thank you, father," said Jean-Paul as he took a drink of his father's locally produced *pinot noir!* He always referred to Louie as *father* rather than dad or any other familiar name. He totally respected his father. There was no one else he had ever known, even the Catholic priests at the Chacopac School, whom he esteemed more. His dad spent much of his time reading, writing, and preparing his classes for the Chac School. Emulating his father and to keep his favor—Jean-Paul also spent most of his evenings reading and studying.

"You Jean-Paul are headed for a great adventure. Living here with the Chacs was quiet and peaceful. There was very little stress, pressure, or turbulence of any kind. Not much here made life difficult for you. We have everything we need. If you think about it—we lack for nothing. But for you that will all change tomorrow when you get on the train. Your life will be totally different. You will be on your own for the first time." Louie stared at J.P. for a few seconds and then took a small sip of *pino*.

Jean-Paul, waiting to hear the real reason for their meeting was growing impatient. "That's all correct father. But you did take me to New York City many times to pick up the trunks Nana DeBert sent. We must have done that at least ten or twelve times. That was always exciting, with lots to see and many curious sites and interesting people. And of course, we also did go to Ontario, Canada, many delightful times."

With no emotion Louie, still looking down said, "I took you into *the City* to give you a larger world view than you would get from the tribal lands and the village of New Hope. But what you are about to do now is quite different. You will see things and be exposed to things you would never in your wildest imagination have experienced here."

Jean-Paul felt he knew what his father meant but nevertheless asked, "Like what father?"

"Well, for starters you're enlisting in the army. The life of a soldier *is not one of ease and leisure.* It is a hard life—a difficult life—especially in wartime. Even in peacetime a soldier's life is one of hardship and privation. There never seems to be enough food and what the soldier does get to eat is about the same quality that is usually fed to a household pet. Those supplying food to the army are generally thieves—out to make the most money and always at the soldiers' expense. Then too, you will march everywhere. Because of this, you will always be dead tired, your feet will be blistered and bleeding, and you will feel like you can't take another step. And the boredom of the sameness can be overwhelming."

He continued, "Generally uneducated, brutal sergeants and marginally competent, indifferent officers will lead you— generally. You will mean nothing to the majority of them but will be just another body to throw into the caldron of war. And when you become part of the inevitable attrition of those killed or wounded, *there will be a steady stream of anonymous others to be thrown into the fire after you.*"

Louie then added, "If you think about it, war is actually quite irrational: humans killing other humans. It is most curious that humans are irresistibly drawn to war. There is an undeniable allure, a definite attachment to the crucible of combat. It fascinates us and beckons to us. It almost charms us. It is like the beautiful siren Lorelei on the Rhine River who lures sailors to their death on the jagged rocks. It is the eternal paradox of our species that we are so naturally attracted to something so horrific, destructive, and evil. Perhaps that's because war is the ultimate human competition—man against man fighting *to the death*. It is the ultimate means to test and prove a person's manhood. Some mistakenly interpret combat and its hardships as being necessary for individuals and societies to grow, mature, and progress—even flourish. This is very Germanic and is nothing more than incredible nonsense...."

Then with a shrug and a drink of wine he said, *"War is the lesson of history and nature of man.* War seems to be firmly entrenched in the deceitful and wicked heart of all mankind. The Good Book says that as long as the earth remains there will be war. Jesus' brother James wrote that conflict is caused by man's greed for power, wealth, land, and resources. And that, will never change. In addition, the philosophers Plato and George Santayana are both credited with writing, *'Only the dead have seen the end of war.'* I think they both knew what they were talking about."

Louie paused briefly and then continued as if on mission, "Many times you will be totally bored in the army because you will be doing menial and mind-numbing tasks. Even in wartime there is an endless monotony, unless of course you are in battle. *Combat by its nature, is not boring.* It's not tedious because you are fighting for your life and the lives of your comrades. In combat one experiences a bizarre thrill—an inexplicable and most curious rush. I'm sure it is triggered by the possibility of imminent death...."

Here Louie shook his head and added, "Unfortunately, in the army you will find many comrades who are nothing more than scoundrels—people who are extremely difficult to be near. Those persons will be your barracks mates and the ones you will have on your left and right on the battlefield."

Jean-Paul interrupted, "But father, all soldiers aren't reprobates and degenerates, are they? These are certainly not the type of soldiers you befriended when you were in the army. There must be some decent, honest, and god-fearing men in the army, right?" Jean-Paul asked these questions with some bewilderment.

"Of course, but probably not many. But those who are, are the ones you must seek out and befriend. There is an old French proverb about soldiers. It says, '*Just as good iron is not used to make nails so also good men are not made to be soldiers.*' But I think for this current war with Spain, there will be many good men volunteering to fight. Of that I am quite sure." Louis stopped talking and simply watched the fire. In some way he seemed to be communicating with it....

He again began speaking, this time more slowly and softer than before, "Some of my most *vivid life memories* are from my war service in the 1870-71 war with the Prussians. I had just graduated from the university and was in London visiting my stepsister's family. I was working on my English language skills in preparation to go to North America. The war was to be short and an easy victory because France supposedly had the best army in Europe. Instead, it was a complete disaster for the French. Six weeks after war had been declared, French Emperor Napoleon III surrendered himself and the 120,000 soldiers of Marshal MacMahon's *Army of Châlons* to the Prussians. They had been encircled near Metz with no obvious way of escape. France, the nation, was still at war but now her leader was a prisoner of the enemy. That was quite unbelievable."

Louie continued, "At this point I felt I needed to be a patriot and *get into the fight.* I returned to France and joined *General Louis Faidherbe's* newly formed *Army of the North.* We were all amateur recruits, had few supplies, little to eat, and no winter clothing. It was the most miserable and uncomfortable period of my life. More than half of our unit deserted. Incredibly we did win several small victories against the Prussian First Army near the towns of *Ham, Hallue, Pont-Noyelles, and Bapaume.* These were memorable because we were able to seize the Prussian's bread, sausages, cakes, wine, and most important of all—warm clothing."

"That winter Paris was under siege and starving. Out of desperation, France's *Minister of War Leon Gambetta* ordered *General Faidherbe* to attack the Prussians surrounding Paris in an effort to break the siege. We made our assault at St. Quentin on the 10th of January in 1871. It was a total disaster, and we were soundly thrashed—and I mean soundly thrashed." Louie stopped, stared into space and then shook his head.

"But if the personal misery, the combat, the wounds, and France's national humiliation were not enough, then came France's *Civil War*. When the Prussians captured our leader Napoleon III, there was a power vacuum in Paris. And, whenever there is a vacuum there is always something waiting to fill it. In this case it was the revolutionary socialist government known as *The Commune*. It was committed to *radical socialism* and had formed its own military force known as the *National Guard*. The Prussians, who had a monarchy and were threatened by every European socialist movement, demanded the French army eliminate the socialists by any means possible. They were not going to get involved in that dirty work. The remnants of General Faidherbe's *Army of the North* were given that mission by what remained of the French government. We were directed to crush the *Paris Commune*."

Louie sighed deeply and with obvious hesitation said, "Putting down the Commune was yet another horrific experience. I had to fight and kill other Frenchmen. They were so committed to their socialist cause that they simply refused to surrender. Even with multiple wounds—some being mortal—they would keep fighting. If I had not seen it myself, I would not have believed it. It became clear to me that if people are so devoted to a cause that they are willing to die for it—it is next to impossible to defeat them." Louis took another small sip of pino noir and once again stared into space.

With another sigh Louis continued, "Our unit was given orders to take no prisoners. Son, do you know what that means? It means you are to kill any of the enemy you capture or find wounded. That was more than horrific and violated everything I had ever been taught. Such personal conflicts, however, are quite common in war. I know I dispatched a number of Prussians and Communards in the fighting—but neither my squad nor I ever killed anyone we captured. Never. We either sent them back to our headquarters or let them lay wounded where they fell. On a couple of occasions, we even let them go free. Maybe none of those actions were consistent with our orders, but that's what we did. That was humane and in keeping with the *laws of land warfare*. To this day that fighting in Paris gives me recurring nightmares."

Louie poured himself a second glass of wine. Finally, and almost under his breath he said, "There are no words that could describe the experience of fighting the *Communards*. No words.

For me, those images from Paris have never gone away. They seem to be fixed in my mind and have remained as vivid as the day they happened." He was slowly shaking his head as he said this. It continued to move from left to right even after he had finished speaking.

"And of course, Paris surrendered shortly thereafter. To France's eternal humility, the Prussians marched down the Champs-Élysées in a victory parade and then declared a unified German state at Louis the XIV's grand palace in Versailles. That was also unbelievable." At this point Louie spit on the ground...."

He then stood up and walked outside. Jean-Paul could hear him retching and puking. The wafting smell of vomit made him nauseous and caused him to gag. His father had never before shared any of those thoughts.

When Louie returned, he acted as if nothing had happened. He then went through the process of lighting his German style curved pipe. Jean-Paul always enjoyed watching his father follow the ritual of lighting this very European object. He especially enjoyed the smell of the pipe's tobacco smoke. It had a soft and sweet aroma. It was certainly more attractive than the *odor of vomitus.*

Louie continued, "In combat you will be exposed to enemy fire and the risk of being killed or badly wounded. Contrary to what some would have us believe, death on the battlefield *is not glorious.* Union General Billy Sherman said, *'War is hell.'* For certain, he got that right. Few soldiers are killed instantly. The ones that are, are the lucky ones. No, most soldiers die on the battlefield of their wounds. The majority of wounds are so hideous and painful that those receiving them wished they had been fatal. I saw the most heinous, shocking, and indescribable battle injuries. They were the most grievous and horrendous injuries to the human body. In excruciating pain, the soldiers lay there watching their lifeblood drain out of their body and their intestines or body parts lying on the ground. They knew that when enough blood drained out of them, they were done for. They would yell for help or their mother. But many times, that was fruitless because either their comrades had pushed forward and were long gone, or the enemy had driven their friendly units back and they were now laying in enemy territory. And that son, is never a good state of affairs."

"I received two minor wounds and was lucky enough to survive both—and the war. I did so thanks to two of my mates who actually saved my life. That fact convinced me soldiers *fight as much for their comrades* as for any grand cause or for the nation. That is also one truth of war that will probably will never change."

He took another sip of wine and a short puff of his pipe. He then looked directly at Jean-Paul and continued, "There were sights on the battlefield that are beyond human words—beyond description. Man was not made for war in any way, shape, or form. Regardless of how much training or mental preparation a soldier receives from the army—the reality of the battlefield goes well beyond anything experienced in training. Unfortunately, some nations have been forced to send their women into battle. But that was only as a last resort because their state was on the verge of being destroyed. In those cases, the women involved fought with ferocity and represented themselves well—very well."

"The philosopher Narosky was right when he wrote, '*In war there are no unwounded soldiers.*' And that British politician was also correct when he said, '*In war there are no winners.*' Those are two profound thoughts promoted by anti-war pacifists." Louie *yet again shook his head* confirming to himself the truth and veracity of those profound philosophical notions.

Standing up and now almost speaking as if in the classroom, Louie said, "Every combat soldier's most common acquaintance is *fear*. It is his closest companion in battle. When on the front of the fighting line, *it* will be your constant and unshakable colleague. When you are about to go into action, fear will grow and cause you to be scared out of your wits. I saw grown men lose complete control of their body and *wet and soil themselves*. They would throw up. They would shake uncontrollably, sweat like it was raining, and some could not stop weeping. Others would become immobile and actually were not able to move. I saw an officer shoot two affected soldiers for not going forward.

I don't think they were capable of going forward even if they wanted to. Their body was totally locked in fear—totally locked. Many who had talked the loudest about how they would show the enemy a thing or two in battle could not even speak when under fire."

Louie stopped, cleared his throat, and then went on, "Orders are given in battle, but few could hear them because of the deafening noise. It all became quite dreamlike and fairy tale surreal. In my first combat it seemed all my senses were heightened. Colors were more vivid, the noise seemed to be full of incredibly loud cracks, and the bullets flying past me sounded like angry bees. The pungent smells of powder from the weapons made me gag."

After a drag on his pipe he said, "Then too, you will very likely have to end the life of another human being. That's another way of saying you may have to kill someone—someone created in God's own likeness. *Everyone has value* because they were created in God's image. We all have a *unity, a relationship, and a connection* with humanity—past, present, and future. It's one thing to shoot and hit an enemy soldier from a distance—but when you must kill in a hand-to-hand, life and death struggle, it is quite different—really different. If the person who is involved in such a very personal fight survives the war, he will relive that event in his dreams time and time again. That's right, time and again...." Louie had the custom of repeating himself when he wanted to *emphasize the point* he was making.

Louie mused, "It's quite strange. If, as a civilian you kill one person, you are either hung or placed in prison for life. In the wartime army, you can kill a hundred men and they give you a medal and you're a hero. That also doesn't make any sense."

Louie paused and again looked with affection at Jean-Paul. "But I know and sincerely believe that joining the army and going off to war is something most young men want to do—even must do. They've got to see what they are made of and if they can function in combat. Not to join the army when there is a war going on will cause a man to think less of himself for the rest of his days. Shakespeare got it right when he wrote those lines in his *'Henry V'* drama about war."

"Those lines? What lines are those?" asked Jean-Paul knowing full well his father had probably memorized them. He committed to memory almost everything important that he wanted to recall.

"I'm not sure if I will get this exactly right but it goes something like this,

*'Gentlemen in England now-a-bed, shall think themselves accursed they were not here, and hold their man hood cheap whiles any speaks, that fought with us upon Saint Crispin's day.'"*

"That's right—hold their manhood cheap *because they weren't in the fight.* They *were not* part of the brotherhood of warriors—the fraternity of front-line fighters. Shakespeare had incredible insights about life and in this case about humans at war. Rather a gifted fellow considering he was an *Englishman.*" Louie and Jean-Paul both smiled.

There was another short pause in the conversation. Then Jean-Paul, now in a rather confused state asked, "Father, is service in the army and a person's war experience always bad? It seems from what you have said it is always terribly negative."

"No, it's not all bad. Like anything, there are positives. The anti-war crowd may not agree—but there are some positives. As I already mentioned when quoting Shakespeare, there is the brotherhood, a band of brothers that develops among those who experience war together. There is camaraderie, a bonding, a sense of community, and a looking out for one another that inevitably takes place among those who share the hardships of war. A strong connection develops between the men you have depended on and who will have depended on you in life and death situations. Remember what I said earlier, my mates saved my life when I was wounded at Saint Quentin. Next to marriage, there is perhaps no greater or deeper bonding experience than what one experiences in war. That kind of *soldier communion* is sweet, priceless, and lasting. It is almost *spiritual.* For me, it still provides some balance to all the negative memories I mentioned. Routinely in the trunks Nana DeBert sends us are letters from those I served with in the *1870 War.* Those are bonds that can never be broken. Unfortunately, that depth of bonding is something not found in civilian life. Those poor civilian wretches are really missing out in that regard."

Louie continued, "You could say that the other positive advantages of warfare—if you can call them that—are the advances war creates in *medicine, logistics, transportation, communications, commissary,* and *human psychology.* However, many would say these developments are miniscule when compared with the *human suffering* and the *material, property,* and *environmental costs.*"

Now Louie took a baguette, a block of goat cheese, and a small sausage from his bag. He cut these and gave some of them to Jean-Paul. With the wine and the company, it was a great and memorable feast. There was a warmth present that went well beyond the campfire.

Louie now took in a deep breath and said, "Let's shift and talk more about you going into the big, wide world for the first time. There are some things I want you to remember, to think about, and to focus on. It's nothing you haven't heard before, but I just want to emphasize them once again. First of all, never forget *the standards of behavior, values, and morals* you learned from me, your mother, and from your Jesuit education. Always remember that our foundational beliefs and values are the *Ten Commandments.* Those ten commands, which Jehovah God gave to Moses—are the moral code we are to live by. They are actually *imprinted on our conscience* and *tell us the difference between right and wrong.* Some say they are *old-fashioned conventions and only for the ignorant and uneducated.* But really, what is outdated about behavior *that reveres God; respects one's parents; does not lie, cheat, steal, murder, or covet their neighbor's property; or commit adultery?"* Really, what?

"Half of these commandments are essentially summed up in the *Golden Rule,* which is *treat others as you would want them to treat you.* It is a command from Jesus' *Sermon on the Mount* that tells us we should treat everyone with *unconditional love.* We are to do that *because love is the highest human need.* It is also the main attribute of God. That's why the Golden Rule is found in every major religion in the world. It can and should be a key guiding principle for you. As you know, it has always been for me. And remember what the Apostle Paul wrote to the church in Corinth: *'Love never fails.'* This rule applies to our dealings with everyone, and in your case specifically with your leaders and comrades. *There are of course, other Biblical rules that apply to your contacts with the enemy.* But even then, soldiers are never to take the life of an enemy needlessly. Remember that King David was not allowed to build God's temple in Jerusalem because God said he had shed too much blood in war."

He continued, "Closely related is the idea that you are

*always do what you know to be right*. You must again remember what you were taught here in New Hope. When faced with a difficult decision, ask yourself, '*What is the right thing to do?*' If you answer that question honestly, the path you are to take will be clear—or at least clearer."

"Next, remember to *speak as little as possible*. Make a habit of keeping quiet. Solomon, one of the wisest men who ever lived, constantly emphasized that principle in his book of proverbs. God gave us two ears and one mouth for a reason. No one ever got into trouble by listening too much. This is especially true in the army for a new volunteer. *Never pass up an opportunity to keep your mouth shut!* Remember, your ability to speak several languages is a real asset, but the ability to keep your mouth shut in any language is an even bigger asset!"

"Then too, life in the army is full of rumors, gossip, and hearsay. Never, ever fall into the trap of spreading thrash like that. Also, *never talk bad about anyone or hurt anyone with your words*. That is about the highest form of foolishness and ignorance there is. *Words can hurt deeply and can injure forever*. Remember, whatever negative things you say *will always come back to you*. Never waste *your words or your time* because you can get neither back. Don't forget that!" For the first time in the entire discussion Louie shook his finger at Jean-Paul for emphasis. He would also do that in the classroom when he wanted to set something straight or to emphasize a key point.

With an even more serious look Louie said, "Because you are a Roman Catholic, one quarter Chac American Indian, and of French descent, *there are some who will treat you with open prejudice.*" Louie paused briefly to ensure Jean-Paul was listening. He continued speaking but now more slowly, "Pay no attention to them. Ignore them. Forgive them. Don't respond, retaliate, or give them a second thought. Forgive them from your heart and remember what the Apostle Paul wrote: '*Love keeps no record of wrongs.*' It is *agape love* that does good to someone even if they are evil toward you, treat you unjustly, or respond negatively to your kindness. As I have always said, sovereign *Providence* is in charge of our reputation. He will repay those who do us evil. Of that you can be quite sure. And who would want to come under the judgment and wrath of the mighty hand of God? Do you understand all this Jean-Paul?" J.P. nodded....

With a gentler expression Louie then said, "Now I know you have always had a problem with anger. As part of your initial training in the army, you will purposely be treated harshly and even unjustly. This is done to transition you from being a civilian to a soldier. It is also done to see how well you handle stress. How you deal with stressful situations in training will be similar to how you will handle the pressures of combat. And peacetime training demands do not even come close to the stress experienced on the battlefield. If you are wise, you will quietly take whatever treatment they pass out and never respond with anger. If you lose your temper, you will probably be severely punished or worse, be placed in a military prison. I cannot stress enough this idea of remaining calm and silent." Louie stared at Jean-Paul with a look that seemed to know his boy would inevitably get himself into trouble because of his anger.

Louie continued, "Most important of all is to remember to *trust the Good Lord Almighty*. Rely on Him, depend on Him, and hold fast to Him. No matter how difficult or hopeless your situation you must rely on and trust in Him for everything. And I mean *everything*. The Good Lord is always with you and loves you unconditionally and promises to help you. He will always give you the skills and ability to achieve what you are required to do. That may even be *supernatural skills, extraordinary skills, or miraculous skills well beyond your natural abilities*. That's *who our God is. He is a God of the impossible, of wonders, of miracles, and of mighty works*. And remember, *the Good Lord is omniscient, knows all; omnipotent, all powerful; and omnipresent, present everywhere at once*. That means He has been on every battlefield in antiquity and knows the words and thoughts of every commander and soldier on each of those ancient battlefields. He has also influenced all those conflicts *according to His will*. Never forget that He can multiply your ability as a soldier. He can be *an incredible resource and comfort* for you. To appropriate such a blessing, remember to pray, give thanks, and forgive others in all circumstances. Those are imperatives and smart things to do."

He then added in a solemn tone, "And of course, you may be killed in battle. That's always a real possibility. Regardless, do not fear death. As Christians, we know that immediately upon our death, our immortal soul and spirit will be face to face with the Good Lord Himself in heaven. That prospect alone should remove any fear of dying."

After another brief pause Louie said, "Well son, joining the military service is a brave and noble thing to do. Contrary to what some believe, the military is a national necessity because it alone guarantees the *safety, security, and survival of the state.* Patriots, the bold and courageous, are a *cut above* those who did not volunteer. They are totally selfless because they know they may potentially have to give up their lives for their country. They are also admirable since they temporarily sacrifice many personal freedoms while in the service of their nation. They are indeed willing *servants* of the state; that's why they call it *military service.* Those in uniform serve their country, its citizens, its constitution, and *its policies.* In your immediate situation, this means liberating the Cuban rebels from Spanish oppression. I have always asked myself, where do we find such principled and high-minded people who are willing to serve like that? Where? Those who are willing to sacrifice their life for others are indeed *the nobility and aristocracy of the constitutional republic* in which we live."

Then Louis added in French, *"Incroyable!"* (Amazing!)

"Next to service in military life, there is the grand notion of *duty*. First and foremost, you must always do your duty. That means you must successfully accomplish all the tasks you are given regardless of the obstacles or difficulties involved. You may be tired, hungry, frustrated, fed up, and have not one ounce of energy left. That won't matter. You must go on and accomplish the job you were given. That is what *sets the military apart* from the civilian world. Soldiers who serve are trained to accomplish their assigned mission *regardless of the obstacles encountered*. They never, ever give up until they do so and get it done. If they die trying, then so be it. They died a noble death while doing their duty. It is the nature of their military service—*duty above everything else."*

"When you are given a task or an order that seems impossible, always remind yourself, *'With God's help, I can do anything—I can do this.'* Repeat that to yourself as often as necessary."

Those two ideas, *service and doing one's duty* are the two highest callings of the army you are about to join. Without those two noble ideas, the military is nothing more than an armed mob of trained killers and a menace to society. Do you understand that son? Do you have any questions about anything I've shared about *service or duty?"*

Jean-Paul shook his head no, he had no questions; he

understood clearly.

"Oh yes, there is one more thing. It sometimes occurs that after soldiers have experienced intense combat, they experience lasting, negative effects. That of course can be physical, but it also can be emotional and psychological. In literature from as early as 2000 B.C., it was reported that a soldier named *Gilgamese* had recurring nightmares after seeing his best friend *Enkidu* killed in battle. Then too, after the Battle of Marathon in 440 B.C., the Greek historian Herodotus wrote that *Epizelus* went blind after seeing his comrades killed in battle. Regardless of how much training a soldier is given, unless he is a total sociopath, he will be impacted by death and the taking another's life."

"I have a personal theory on how to avoid such after-combat trauma. What my experience and readings inform me is that if a soldier has two related personal codes, he is less likely to suffer serious after-battle damage. First, if a soldier has a strong value system, a personal moral code that clearly defines right and wrong conduct, then the impact of combat may not be as severe as it potentially could be. For you, that would be your Christian values. Second, if a warrior is assigned a warrior code such as the ones the Japanese Samurai or the medieval knights operated under, those too can also *remove much of the guilt, shame, and remorse for killing a fellow human being.* Those warrior codes provide boundaries and limits to what a soldier

49

does on the battlefield. It keeps him from stepping over the line and committing war crimes or obeying unlawful orders. You of course, have a strong personal code and the Army's adherence to the laws of land warfare will hopefully provide the second. For some transcendent reason these codes seem to guard and protect soldier—to some extent at least—from *severe* post-combat trauma. And because *you* have such a strong personal moral values, they should greatly assist in protecting you also. I have had some aftereffects from my war, but I am convinced they could have been much, much worse had I not had such a strong moral foundation. Anyway, that is my personal hypothesis, and I believe I am right."

In the moment, those two ideas were too much for Jean-Paul to process.

Now Louie reached into his pack and took out a holster containing a pistol. He said, "Here is the French revolver I carried in the war with the Prussians. Never really had to fire it at someone but it was good insurance and gave me a feeling of security—real or imagined. I just cleaned and fired it. It works just fine. There are only twenty rounds, but since it is simply for your personal safety, that should be enough. Anyway, I hope you too will never have to use it." Jean-Paul took the pistol and ammunition and automatically said a quiet thank you. He looked at it with some interest because he had never seen it before.

"I'll also give you some money for your trip tomorrow." Jean-Paul nodded. His dad was very generous and neither he nor their family had ever been short of money. In fact, it seemed the more money his father gave away to the church or to help others, the more prosperous the DeBert family became. The generous sums of money sent by Nana DeBert, the wine Louie made and sold from their small family vineyard, and the royalties he received from the books he had written, always provided more money than the family needed.

After a few minutes of silence his father said: "That sums it up for me. What are you thinking? What questions do you have? Is there anything else we need to discuss? Do you need advice about anything else?" Jean-Paul shook his head.

"Your mother and I, and of course your brother and sister, will be praying for you every day. Try to write as often as you can, your mother would like that. And of course, I would too. I don't imagine it will be a very long war. But then one can be grievously injured or killed in a short war as well as a long one." With that Louie stood up, walked over to Jean-Paul who was now also standing, and kissed him on both cheeks and gave him an extended hug. Louie mumbled something under his breadth that Jean-Paul understood to be yet another prayer for his safety. Louie then threw some logs on the fire and then rolled up into his blanket.

Jean-Paul too rolled up in his blanket and through the

crackling fire looked at his dad. What an amazing man his father was. He was going to miss him dearly. He had learned something profound from him almost every day. Louie DeBert could have become quite prosperous and famous in France had he decided to go into business, politics, stayed in the army, or been a wine producer. But he had decided to come to America to live and work with the Chacopac tribe. If only he, Jean-Paul, could live up to his dad's character and his ability to relate to people. Right then he promised himself *again* he would always live as his father had instructed him. He would never let him down. Never—ever! Then he quietly said to himself, *"I can do this because God is my hope and my champion!"*

### *Thought Questions for Chapter 2:*

1. Jean-Paul's father Louie shared extensively about his military service and his thoughts regarding war. What are your impressions and reactions to what he said? Would you have added anything based on your experience?

2. Jean-Paul's father told him to always remember the values, the principles, and the moral compass he had been taught growing up. What are your impressions and opinions about what Louie said? Would you have added anything or changed anything to what he said?

3. Why is there such a special comradery, bonding, and

connection between those members of a military unit that have experienced combat together?

4. What did Louie tell Jean-Paul to do to avoid any lasting psychological effects from being in combat? Do you agree or disagree with Louie's hypothesis? Why? What might you have added?

5. Why did Louie tell Jean-Paul he should not fear death?

6. What was your biggest learning or take away from this chapter? What can you apply from the information in this chapter? What in it did you find most interesting? Why?

# 3

## *Leaving Home*

"Wake up Jean-Paul. It's time to go. You have to be on that noon train to New York City." J.P. knew this train since it was the one he and his father had taken many times to pick up the trunks of goodies sent from France by Nana DeBert.

The sun was just rising over the horizon as Jean-Paul and his dad started the three-mile walk home. The birds were singing joyfully. The New York spring wind was humming through the large oak trees that were barely showing their leaves. The newness of the spring matched the excitement the teenager felt about the advent of his new life. He craved the adventure that undoubtedly lay ahead of him. He was sure it would be the first chapter in the fulfillment of his calling—*his rendezvous with his own personal destiny.*

Both Jean-Paul and his father were silent as they walked— locked in their own thoughts of the changes the day would bring. These were changes that would be for the better, at least for the teenager. His emotions were racing and mixed. He truly loved his family, each and every one of them. His dad was his hero who could do no wrong. His mom was surely an Indian princess in the tradition of Pocahontas and Sacajawea. If only Jean-Paul could find a wife half as beautiful, both inside and outside, to love and marry. And of course, there were his siblings, Marcel and Arlette. They were always happy and full of youthful energy. As these thoughts flowed through his head, he felt tears starting to well in his eyes. At that, he shook his head as if to shake them away. There would be none of that emoting nonsense for a potential warrior who was about to join the U.S. Army's First Volunteer Cavalry Regiment.

Jean-Paul had learned to ride a horse when he was three years old. He was an excellent rider and could ride equally well with or without a saddle. The Chacs were natural riders and in order to be accepted, he had to become proficient in all of the expectations they had of their young men. The tribal rituals that were involved in passing from adolescence to manhood had not changed since their conversion to Christianity. These rites included many tests of skill and courage. While living with the Chacs during the past eighteen years he had learned to wrestle, run and swim distances, play lacrosse, fish in all seasons, track and hunt large and small animals, efficiently use a rifle and a composite bow, and participate in a variety of tribal ceremonies. He could sing and dance with the best of them.

Jean-Paul would routinely compete with his Chacopac contemporaries during the tribe's annual spring and fall festivals. He especially excelled at the wrestling, swimming, lacrosse, and distance running competitions. Distance running was of course his favorite. He was quite comfortable running bare foot. He felt shoes inhibited his speed and hurt his feet. Even with all their stamina and excellent physical condition, Jean-Paul was always able to defeat the tribe's best distance runners in the festival competitions—always!

Jean-Paul had tried to teach the Chacs the art of *Savate,* which was a combined form of stick fighting and kickboxing. He learned savate from his father Louie who had been introduced to that art while a student at the Sorbonne University in Paris. It was very popular with France's aristocratic students who used it to honorably settle disagreements. Savate was considered more dignified than either wrestling or boxing. Boxing was not popular in France because it was considered to be a British creation. And, in the post-Napoleonic period, there had been a strong anti-British sentiment in France. Because a savate stick could also be a walking stick or cane, savate was also an effective method in dealing with robbers or street thugs. Jean-Paul's father referred to his savate stick as a *short-range impact weapon.* The Chacs however, seemed to have little interest.

Overall, it had been a good life living with his family, the tribe, and the Jesuit mission school. It was a lifestyle he would surely miss. Yet, it was clearly time to move on.

The sun was now shining brightly as Jean-Paul and his father approached their house. To their surprise there were at least twenty people gathered at their front door. It was not clear how long they had been waiting, but there was great murmuring when they saw the two approach.

Led by *Alexis Swift Fox,* the supreme leader and chief of the Chacopac tribe, all twelve of the tribe's elders were present. Also present were Father Vincent and the other Jesuit priests, staff, and volunteers who operated the mission church and school.

Jean-Paul was surprised to also see the Chac elder, *François Dancing Bear.* He didn't know where the name Dancing Bear name came from exactly, but one thing was for certain, a *dancing bear* Francois was not. Three years prior Jean-Paul had shown a particular interest in Francois's daughter *Claudine Singing Sparrow.* She was a dark and a strikingly attractive natural beauty. J.P. had become infatuated with her. Unfortunately, Francois Dancing Bear was not infatuated with him. In no uncertain terms he told Jean-Paul to stay away from his daughter. Dancing Bear proceeded to tell Louie DeBert and Father Vincent that was his uncompromising desire. He said he would appreciate their support on the matter. It wasn't at all clear what his exact problem was with Jean-Paul. Gossip alleged he felt Jean-Paul was too *impatient, impulsive, and easily angered.* J.P. agreed with that analysis but did not feel those were reasons for him to be quarantined from beautiful Claudine. He was painfully aware he would become angry when some people in Good Hope treated him in a patronizing, dismissive, or condescending manner. Those reflections raced through his head as he walked toward the crowd of people standing in front of his house.

Francois did not want Jean-Paul shining around his daughter and yesterday it was quite clear the good Doctor Reverend Bradley did not want him hanging around his daughter Abigail. His comments to Reverend Bradley and his negative motivation for walking by the Beckenbauer's sawmill reinforced a pattern of behavior that Jean-Paul frankly did not understand about himself. These behaviors were in complete violation of his Jesuit value system. He certainly knew better. Oh well—*knowing and doing are two completely different things....*

Louie DeBert raised his hand in a greeting wave. He then said in Chacopac, *"Good morning gentlemen! Good morning! What can we do for you?"*

*Alexis Swift Fox,* the Chac's supreme leader and a man of great wisdom responded: "We know that young Jean-Paul, the Chacopacs' friend and teacher, will be leaving to become a warrior for the United States in their war with Spain. There is a Chacopac prayer for all of its warriors before they go into battle. It is a prayer to the Lord of Hosts, the God of Abraham, Isaac, and Jacob, for strength, safety, and courage." Then he motioned to Jean-Paul and said, "Come here young warrior and kneel before us."

*Alexis Swift Fox* had such dignity, presence, and charisma that Jean-Paul immediately obeyed and knelt before him. The trial elders, including *Francois Dancing Bear,* gathered around him and raised their hands over him. Alexis Swift Fox however, put his hand directly on the top of Jean-Paul's head. With his deep, booming voice he said *in the Chacopac language, "Let us pray."* At this the elders began a quiet, murmuring chant, the likes of which Jean-Paul had never heard before. Alexis began in a loud voice: *"Great Father in heaven, creator of all things, we lift up this young warrior to you as he travels the way of all fighters to the battlefields of honor. Bless him, protect him, make your face shine upon him, be gracious to him, place your hand upon him, and give him Your peace. Preserve him from all harm and danger, from the terrors of the night and the arrows that fly by day. Give him your favor as well as the favor of all of his leaders and comrades."*

The chief's voice lowered as he continued, *"Bless your servant Jean-Paul with wisdom, with strength, and with great courage. Preserve him from all misfortune, from illness, from wounds, and all calamities. Keep these far from him, his fellow soldiers, and his leaders. Protect him from the ruses of the devil and his imps. Watch over this mighty man of valor, guard him, and guide him always. We thank you now for what you will do in answer to this prayer. We pray this in the name of your son Jesus the Christ, who is our savior and friend. Thank you, thank you, and Your will be done above everything. Amen and again amen."* Amen was a good ending as it indicated all who said it agreed with what had just been prayed, i.e., so be it. The elders' murmurings turned into a repetition of amens. Since there is no equivalent word for amen in the Chac language, they had appropriated that English word.

The Chief removed his hand from Jean-Paul's head and took a necklace from the large pocket of his deerskin jacket. He gently put it around Jean-Paul's neck. Then speaking in English, he said to the non-Chacs present, "This is the traditional necklace of the Chacopac warrior. It is given to the tribe's young men after they pass the initiation trials of manhood. This young man is the first to receive the warrior's necklace who is not a natural born Chac. The elders decided this unanimously last evening."

Jean-Paul stood up and beamed with pride. This necklace was made of a string of reddish-black garnet gems. Receiving it was a distinctive and unique honor. Apparently, the design of the warrior's necklace had been the same for centuries. Only the gems used had changed since the Chacs had arrived in New York. When the tribe converted to Christianity the necklace had one major addition. It now had a small wooden Christian crucifix attached.

The elders then came by and each gave Jean-Paul the Chacopac version of a hug: securely grabbing him by the shoulders and powerfully pulling him forward. Even an expressionless *Francois Dancing Bear* did this. They all mumbled something when they hugged the teenager. He did not quite understand what they were mumbling but took it to be another Chac blessing.

Not to be outdone *Father Luc, Father Vincent, Deacon Lionel,* and the other school staff and volunteers came by to wish Jean-Paul safety on his upcoming adventure. No hugs here but hearty handshakes were now the order of behavior. Father Luc was the last to offer his good wishes.

The Father was a kind and gentle man who was probably fifty years of age. He had a very peaceful countenance that made him look twenty years younger. His servant's heart was as big as his intellect. There were no guile or self-serving tendencies in him. He would spend the first two hours of each day in prayer. His commitment to the Chacopac tribe, the Jesuit mission school, and of course *the Good Lord* were complete. Also, he sincerely appreciated the entire DeBert family. He routinely sought Louie DeBert's advice and opinion on major school related issues and decisions. Moreover, he had a special gift for listening and discerning the correct action to take on difficult problems. Louie told Jean-Paul that the Father's insights were so very keen because he spent those first hours of each day praying.

Father Luc shook Jean-Paul's hand and did not let it go. He pulled him near to him. He spoke in a low tone, almost in a whisper, as if the others were not to hear. He spoke directly into his ear. "My son, may God go with you. As it is written in Psalm 91, *He* will preserve you from all harm and danger. His angels will keep you from dashing your foot upon a rock—that means from any bodily harm. Don't forget that, believe it, have faith in your Savior and you will return home safely. Also, God hears, and He listens. He promises to hear our prayers. So, pray and He will listen and answer." Then the Father gave Jean-Paul an enormous bear hug. When he let go, Jean-Paul noted a tear in the Father's eye. Good man thought the teenager—a very good man.

When everyone had left, Jean-Paul went into the house. He didn't have much to pack. His only store-bought clothes were the ones Nana DeBert routinely sent from France. Good quality but not the style generally worn in upstate New York. His mother actually made most of his clothing. On this occasion however, he would wear a French outfit for his trip to Texas. In his shoulder bag he would take his Bible, the gun and ammo his dad had given him, one change of clothes, socks, underwear, writing paper and pencils, and of course Colonel Roosevelt's telegram. Then too, his mother would give him a paper bag of ham sandwiches and fried chicken for his trip. He would also take a bottle or two of his father's wine and a flask of water.

For good luck, he would also bring the *knight class of the French Legion of Honor medal* that his grandfather Gerard had given him. It had been Papa Gerard's most prized possession.

Emperor Napoleon had personally awarded him that medal after a battle near Belostock, Russia, in November of 1812. To the family's surprise, Gerard had given the medal to Jean-Paul on his visit to France in 1885 when Gerard was ninety years old, and Jean-Paul was all of five. The occasion was when Louie DeBert had finally decided to return to France to reconcile with his aged father. Papa Gerard wanted Louie to take over the family estate, but Louie's personal vision was to move to America and work with the Chacopac tribe. The reconciliation between the father and son was a complete success. That was in large measure to young Jean-Paul. He and his grandfather had an immediate and total affinity for one another. Years later J.P. was sure the connection was the *kindred spirit that all warriors share.*

Jean-Paul spent almost the entire visit to France sitting on his Papa's lap asking him questions about Napoleon, the wars and battles he had been in, and his life in the Loire River Valley. Papa Gerard was so impressed with young Jean-Paul that at the end of his visit he gave him the coveted medal he had received from Napoleon. The old soldier had been wearing it during the entire visit of Louie and his family. He gave it to Jean-Paul with a prophecy. He said that he himself had been a *good soldier,* but that someday, Jean-Paul would be a *great soldier—a mighty warrior.* This was a prediction J.P. would never forgot. It was actually the turning point of his life. From that moment he purposed to make his grandfather's prophecy become reality. He recalled the event as if it happened yesterday. He now carefully wrapped the *sacred medal* in a handkerchief and placed it is his shoulder bag.

When Jean-Paul and his family arrived at the train station his father moved to purchase his tickets. Many of his friends from the tribe and some of the students from the Jesuit mission school were waiting to see him off. Like most young boys, they were excited at the thought going off to war. In all their youth, idealism, and naiveté they spoke of war as a great adventure. At this moment these boys seemed to be more excited about the idea of going off to war than was Jean-Paul, who was preoccupied with thoughts about leaving home. The Chac boys surrounded him and were chattering loudly in their native language.

Jean-Paul felt a constant tugging on his arm. Thinking it was one of his siblings he paid little attention. Finally, there was a big tug and he heard his name called. Jean-Paul turned and was very surprised to see it was *Berti Beckenbauer* who was doing the tugging. Berti had taught him German and yesterday had saved him from being eaten alive by the Beckenbauer's two German shepherds.

"I need to speak to you right now," she said in a serious tone and with a sense of urgency. Jean-Paul thought it had to be about their mutual friend Abigail who was not present.

She took him by the hand and led him to a small room in

the train station that was being used as a holding room for unclaimed baggage. The door to the room was only a formality, as it had no knob, latch or lock. Berti closed the door as far as it would go. She came right up to him and said in a whisper, "I want to tell you something." With that she gave Jean-Paul a hearty and drawn-out kiss. Jean-Paul's arms were paralyzed at his side. Berti released a stunned Jean-Paul and with a huge smile said, *"That's what will be waiting for you when you return."*

She walked toward the door and then with a smile said in German, *"I love you Jean-Paul."*

Jean-Paul was speechless. He did not see that coming. He sensed Berti cared for him but not that deeply. Perhaps Abigail suspected it, which is why she was always present when he and Berti would have their German language sessions. He had always dismissed it when Abby would refer to that lovely Beckenbauer girl as *flirty Berti.*

Jean-Paul had gone skinny-dipping with Abigail. Abby was thin, slight of build, and small chested. Berti on the other hand, the German fraulein, was bigger boned, had a rounder physique than Abigail, and was more impressive everywhere. My goodness....

As Berti opened the door to leave this now memorable holding room, the whistle of the incoming train echoed through the spring air. That whistle summed up Jean-Paul's experience in the holding room exactly. No sooner had Berti left than Jean-

Paul's siblings came storming into the room and said, "Come on big brother, the train is approaching. The train is approaching."

Jean-Paul stepped outside, his excitement having subsided, and went immediately to his mother. He gave her a heartfelt goodbye hug. She said quietly, "We will pray for you every day—many times over!"

"I know mother and I will pray for you too—all of you." Jean-Paul noted tears rolling down from her mother's beautiful face. That was the first time he ever saw his generally stoic and reserved mother shed tears. That was too much for him, he had to turn to his father Louie.

Jean-Paul's father handed him an envelope. Here are your five train tickets to get you to San Antonio and some dollars for your trip. He then shook Jean-Paul's hand, pulled him close and gave him a strong embrace. Then Louie handed Jean-Paul his favorite walking stick from his Sorbonne days. He was never without it and it was the device he used when practicing the art of savate. Jean-Paul was taken back. He blurted out, "I can't accept this father."

"Of course you can and you will. I have others or better still, I will use yours. Take it. You could probably use it on your trip to Texas. It's doubtful you will need it in Cuba however," he said with a knowing smile. Jean-Paul mumbled a thank you and then hugged both of his siblings. They in turn reminded him he had promised to bring back some war souvenirs.

Jean-Paul, with his shoulder bag and savate stick, boarded the train and found his seat. As the train began to move his family and friends were waving with various degrees of enthusiasm. His sister, brother, and their friends ran along with the train as long as they could. He kept up the waving until everyone at the station was out of sight. About a quarter mile from the station, Jean-Paul was surprised to see Berti Beckenbauer standing on the road staring at the train. He raised his hand in recognition. Berti instantly saw him and raised her hand. It was an odd exchange considering what had just happened in the train station.

Jean-Paul thought, goodness me, how did I miss Berti's feelings toward me? As a farewell, Berti gives me the biggest kiss of my life and Abby—my best girl—didn't even show at the station. There's got to be meaning in that. Then he reconciled that Abigail didn't know exactly when he was leaving. Right, not much chance of that since there is only one train a day coming through the thriving metropolis of Good Hope. Undoubtedly Pudgy McKenna had told just about everyone in town that J.P. had been ordered to leave for the army as soon as possible.

Jean-Paul's head was spinning. A flurry of thoughts raced through his brain. His emotions were all out of sync. He was simultaneously excited, happy, nervous, and of course sad. His safe and secure life with his family and the Jesuit fathers at the Chac mission school were now in the past—at least until he would return from the war. He then had an epiphany. What he was experiencing was not unlike what other young men throughout history had known when they traded, either voluntarily or involuntarily, the safety and security of home for the unknowns and dangers of war. He was now leaving everything that was dear and comfortable in exchange for army life and potentially life-threatening duties. He knew of course that the idea of getting killed or seriously wounded did not apply to him. It might happen to others but no way it would or could happen to him. He reasoned that the *Almighty* would take care of him so no need to worry about that. It never occurred to him from his knowledge of history that many *God-believing soldiers* were either killed or wounded in the various religious wars. This included countless so-called *soldiers of faith* in the eight crusades of the Middle Ages.

Jean-Paul remembered the envelope his father gave him. The only thing he had taken out of it was his ticket from New Hope to New York City. There were four other tickets that his father had purchased for him: New York to Chicago on the *overnight Pullman,* Chicago to St. Louis, St. Louis to Dallas and Dallas to San Antonio.

Jean-Paul reviewed these tickets with some interest. He would be in a sleeping car on the trip from New York City to Chicago. He would be traveling on the very famous New York Central Railroad. That would be a new adventure. It then occurred to him that the army should be paying for these train tickets since he was traveling to fight their war. Since that was probably not going to happen—and he so desperately wanted to join the First Volunteer Cavalry—it didn't matter if he, or his father, paid for the trip. It reminded him of what his father once said, *"If you want something badly enough you must do whatever it takes to get it."* He had been referring to coming to North America against the will of his father Gerard.

Jean Paul then took the money and counted it. He was speechless for the second time today when he realized how much money his dad had given him. It was a combination of one, two, and five-dollar United States notes that totaled sixty dollars. These legal tender notes were commonly known as *greenbacks* because of their color and also as *horse blankets* because of their size. That was a considerable amount of money considering the army's newly enlisted soldiers were paid a whopping thirteen dollars a month. In fact, the sixty dollars was the most money Jean-Paul ever seen. The only cash he previously had was when he went to buy food or supplies for his family in New Hope.

Jean-Paul then reflected that he never really needed any money. He read books from his father's library, the Jesuit school library, and those Nana DeBert had sent from France. The latter were of course in French, leather bound, and very expensive. The DeBert family in New Hope had their own fruit trees, vegetable garden, and vineyard. They owned chickens, cows, sheep, and a couple of horses. There was never a shortage of anything. His mother would make clothes for all the family. Plus, Nana DeBert always sent him shirts, pants, and jackets from France. Louie DeBert had an income from selling the wine from the vineyard, royalties from the children's books he had authored, and of course the generous amounts of money Nana DeBert sent with those trunks two or three times a year. A percentage of the money the DeBert's received was always put into the Jesuit Mission School. But since the Chacopacs now received a sizable income from their tribal wood crafting, they had taken up much of their own support for the mission school. Thus, Louie DeBert did not supply the same amount of money to the school that he had done in its earlier days.

Jean-Paul watched the New York spring countryside rush by train's window. He liked trains and had fond memories of his trips to New York City with his father. For him, trains represented adventure and serendipity. There were always interesting people on trains. Each had a story of where they were going and what they would be doing when they got there. He remembered train travelers his dad had engaged in conversation during their trips. There was a hardened army colonel with his browbeaten enlisted batman, a self-assured businessman, a frenzied family going on vacation, and a dreamy honeymooning couple. Then there was a prince and his entourage from the court of the Austro-Hungarian Empire, or so they said, and a

Frenchmen who was fascinated why Louie DeBert was living in North America.

There was also an *atmosphere* surrounding trains. It was their sights, sounds, and smells. It was unlike anything he had experienced in Good Hope. The engine, or *Iron Horse* as the Chacs called it, was powerful, menacing, and unpretentious. The locomotive sat there spewing forth clouds of white steam, like a horse ready to charge into battle. There was the smell of the steam emanating from this highly lubricated machine; the shrill of the train's melancholy whistle that gave warning and also signaled the train's arrival; the anticipation following the conductor's cry of *"All aboard"*; the piercing sound of the bells alerting everyone the monster was moving; the *chuffing* sound made when the exhaust steam traveled through the blast pipe and out the engine's chimney; and of course, the kind of clicking and clacking sound made by the wheels as they moved over the steel rails. Finally, there was the train's rhythm. There was a tempo to the train's side-to-side movements felt by all its passengers as it raced through the countryside. Jean-Paul nodded his head and pressed his lips together as these thoughts passed through his head. He could not help but conclude that trains were from the good Lord Himself because they were totally magnificent.

**Thought Questions for Chapter 3:**

1. Why didn't François Dancing Bear want Jean-Paul to spend time with or pay attention to his daughter Claudine Singing Sparrow?

2. How was Jean-Paul's grandfather—Papa Gerard— instrumental in the teenager's vision to become a great warrior?

3. What epiphany did Jean-Paul have on the train? Why did he think he would not be killed in combat? How realistic was his belief that he would survive the fighting?

4. Was it a strength or a weakness that Jean-Paul didn't recognize the strong feelings that *Flirti Berti Beckenbauer* had for him? Why?

5. What was savate stick fighting and why was it popular in France?

6. What was your biggest learning or take away from this chapter? What can you apply from the information in this chapter? What in it did you find the most interesting? Why?

# 4

## *The Pullman Car*

It was a seven-hour trip on the *New York Central and Hudson River Railroad* from New Hope to New York. That included eight stops of about ten to fifteen minutes each. Jean-Paul's emotions were still racing. He had fantasized his entire life about going off to war and now he was doing it. He had however, never thought about leaving his family, friends, and everything that was familiar. As he was going through his shoulder bag, he came across the *Legion of Honor medal* his grandfather had given him. He wondered if Papa Gerard had similar feelings when he left home in 1812 to join Napoleon's army at the age of sixteen. He remembered his ninety-year-old Papa telling him all of his war stories, several times over in fact. Each time they were as interesting as the first.

As he looked out of the passing countryside, Jean-Paul continued to reflect on his grandfather. With very little initial training at the district's induction depot, Gerard Papa DeBert was sent to Russia as a replacement in late October 1812. Immediately after his small replacement force of three hundred men and sixteen supply wagons crossed the frontier from the Duchy of Warsaw into Russia, it was harassed by irregular

Cossack cavalry. These Cossacks were filthy individuals armed with lances, firearms, and whips with a weighted end. They rode hardy steppe ponies, made blood curdling war cries when attacking, and excelled at raiding and scouting. Gerard was convinced they were nothing more than looters, criminals, and ignorant savages on horseback.

In one of these engagements sixteen-year-old Gerard DeBert, who was a capable hunter and marksman, genuinely distinguished himself. The Cossack attack evolved into a hand-to-hand struggle, a battle in which Gerard was wounded and credited with personally dispatching at least seven Cossack warriors and wounding several more. Emperor Napoleon and his entourage, who were leading the French Army that was retreating out of Russia, witnessed this entire melee from a nearby hill. After the French replacement convoy had repulsed the Cossacks with heavy losses, Napoleon joined them. On the spot he awarded several of them, including the wounded Gerard, the coveted *Legion of Honor* medal. The Emperor then ordered them to join him on his return journey to France. What was left of the replacements would provide the emperor's headquarters additional security. The supplies they had would ensure all of the material needs of Napoleon's entourage would be met on their trip back to Paris. This move would also provide the wounded French replacements, including Gerard, a chance to exit Russia and not bleed out or freeze to death in the winter snow.

Based on this action in Russia, Gerard was placed in *Napoleon's Young Guard,* a unit in which he would see action in Napoleon's campaigns in 1813, 1814, and finally at Waterloo in 1815. In July of 1815, after Napoleon's final exile to St. Helena, Gerard returned to his parent's farm and vineyard in France. He had been promoted to the rank of sergeant and was now a seasoned war veteran at the tender age of nineteen. He was the recipient of the *Legion of Honor* decoration, had been wounded five times, and possessed a treasure trove of experiences. Some were memorable, some forgettable, and many others very forgettable.

He never talked much about those three years, but it was clear he was extremely proud of his military service. On all major celebrations and festivals, he would wear the *Legion of Honor medal* the Emperor had personally awarded him. The bright red ribbon of that medal included bloodstains from the wound received that day in Russia. It remained his most prized possession.  It also gave him his primary identity in the Loire River Valley community and had been a factor in his wife Monique, aka Nana DeBert, selecting him as her mate! It was a great story to remember. Jean-Paul hoped he could live up to his Papa's legacy!

The train arrived at Grand Central Depot in New York City just as it was getting dark.  The station was just as he remembered. He gazed at the colors of the sunset through the arched ceiling of the massive iron and glass train shed. This structure was an architectural marvel, not something to be seen in New Hope for sure.

Jean-Paul walked quickly and with caution as he crossed the active tracks to get to the passenger waiting area. There was a human mass rushing past him moving to and from the trains. That the trains in this area of the station did not injure more people was surely a miracle. Bumped and jostled and ever conscious of pickpockets, he moved to the passenger waiting area. On their previous trips, Jean-Paul's father had constantly warned him of these bag snatchers, but he never paid much attention because he had previously never carried a bag in this station.

He moved to the area where the printed schedule of train arrivals and departures was located. He verified the departure time and the track of his overnight train to Chicago. He had a ticket for an upper sleeping berth in a Pullman. This was to be another new experience since he had never before been on an overnight train—all part of his current grand adventure. Although he had the sandwiches his mom packed, he decided to get something to eat from one of the vendors outside the station. His favorite was an expensive cheesecake that cost a steep fifteen cents.

Jean-Paul had always been fascinated with the scenes outside the station. First of all, there was the hustle and bustle of train travelers arriving and departing. The majority of the men wore a coat, a tie, and a hat. It was clear there were many nationalities and ethnic groups represented among this mass of travelers. Outside too, there were the conspicuous towers with their massive caps that probed the sky from the various corners of the station. Also impressive were the three enormous clocks on the center tower. They were always illuminated at night.

The street outside this magnificent building was paradoxically unpaved. It was dirty, dusty and was littered with horse droppings. Yuk-oh! This was always problematic for the food vendors. Regardless, Jean-Paul found the seller of cheesecake. He was a Frenchman named *Sebastian*. Daily, he would have only two cheesecakes to sell by the individual slice. These were French-style cheesecakes that were very light, had gelatin as a binding ingredient, were one to two inches high, and had a light texture and flavor from Neufchatel cheese. Sebastian recognized Jean-Paul immediately and came out from behind his booth to give him a kiss on each cheek and a friendly hug. Luckily there was one piece of cheesecake remaining for purchase. Sebastian asked about the health of his father and what the young boy was doing in the city. When J.P. said he would be traveling to San Antonio to join the army in Texas, Sebastian wrapped a small block of cheese, some ham, and half a baguette in a newspaper and gave it to Jean-Paul for his trip. The teenager thanked him graciously, put the ham and cheese in his shoulder bag, gobbled down the cheesecake, and walked back into the train station.

Just before turning to enter the terminal his eye caught a glimpse of a special war edition magazine published by Randolph Hearst's *New York Morning Journal*. Jean-Paul thought this would be good reading material for his lengthy train ride. When he looked up at the newsstand vendor, he experienced a chill over his entire body. He remembered this man from previous visits. That person had always given him the same uneasy feeling. The vendor had long, dirty black hair with a beard spotted with food participles. His clothes, starting with his long black overcoat, were filthy, ill-fitting, and disheveled. He was missing a front tooth and those that remained were crooked, chipped, and dark brown. If Jean-Paul could imagine what the devil looked like, it would be was exactly like this newspaper vendor.

Ginning up all his strength Jean-Paul hesitantly mumbled, "How much for the war magazine?" The vendor also sensed something and acted as if he didn't hear Jean-Paul. So, now in a more confidant tone the teenager asked, "How much for the Hearst war magazine?"

The response was a roughly spoken, "Five cents."

Strange thought Jean-Paul since the Hearst newspapers cost one cent and now this magazine, which was not as large as a daily newspaper, was five cents. But he just wanted to get the magazine and get away from the newsstand. Then, out of the corner of his eye, he noticed an urchin of a figure who was standing to the left of the newspaper stand. He was hunched over, hopelessly ugly, and dressed like the vendor.

"Without thinking Jean-Paul asked the vendor, "And who might that be?"

"The reply was swift and sarcastic, "That be my trusted assistant and colleague Max. Why do you need to know?"

Jean-Paul responded with a shoulder shrug and a quiet, "No reason." He then took out the money envelope in which he also placed the coins he received in change for the cheesecake. He couldn't immediately find the dime, so he took out a fifty-cent piece. He gave it the vendor ensuring he did not actually touch his hand. He did not notice the interest both the vendor and Max, who had now stepped into the light, were taking in the envelope containing the money. The vendor gave Jean-Paul his change and made a point *to touch* his hand when he did so.

Jean-Paul glanced at the change and recognized immediately that he had been short changed. He blurted, "This is not correct. I gave you fifty cents for a five-cent item, and you gave me twenty cents in return. My change should have been forty-five cents."

The vendor gave as short shake of his head and with smirk said, "Sorry boy, you gave me a quarter and I gave you the correct change."

Leaning forward he added, "You got ah problem wit dat?"

With that, Max stepped within an arm's length of Jean–Paul. He actually smelled worse than he looked. He also had his right hand in his jacket pocket.

Jean-Paul felt his anger starting to rise. He strengthened his grip on the savate stick. His immediate thought was, "I haven't been gone from Good Hope for twelve hours and I'm being treated like this?" Now he had choices. He could insist on getting his correct change and push it regardless of where it led, or he could drop it and walk away. In a staring contest with the vendor, his mind raced between the two options. Finally, he simply put the magazine in his shoulder bag, took a couple of steps back, said nothing, and walked toward the entrance of the station.

Once in the station Jean-Paul simply shook his head about the whole experience and congratulated himself on walking away. People were still rushing about the station but not as many as when he had arrived. He had some time before his overnight train left for Chicago. He decided to use the toilet and then go the passenger waiting room and have a sandwich.

He dreaded the notion of going into the public toilet in the train station. The sights, smells, and sounds were totally disgusting. These toilets were filthier than the outhouses where he came from up north. Ugh. He walked into the dimly lit and empty room. The smells did not disappoint. Gosh, what do people eat to leave smells like this? The dead and decaying animals he had come across in the forest did not smell as bad as this toilet. One could probably get a disease just being in here. He hurried to relieve himself holding his breath as best he could.

As he was finishing, he heard a voice behind him that said, "Give me that envelope with your money!" When buttoned up, Jean-Paul turned around to see that revolting little Max from the newsstand. Max was pointing a knife with a six-inch blade at him. "I'm not playing," Max blurted out as he waved the knife in the air at J.P.,'s direction.

Jean-Paul was going to have none of this and yelled, "Get out of my way little man I'm leaving." As he took a step toward the door Max lunged at him with the knife. Without thinking and in self-defense J.P. flung his shoulder bag to take the knife thrust. Then and as if by instinct, in one motion Jean-Paul swung his walking stick and struck Max solidly on the side of his head. The blow put Max on the floor his knife flying across the room. He thought, "Goodness gracious, I hope I haven't killed him!" He bent over the smelly little man and noted he was still breathing. Good, he's not dead.

Jean-Paul. looked at his leather should bag. Of course, there was a hole that Max had made with his knife. Looking in the bag J.P. saw that Max's knife had penetrated one of his mother's ham sandwiches. Darn it. He took the sandwich and thought, "I can't eat this. Max's knife probably included many exotic diseases. He took the sandwich and tossed it at Max who was now moaning. Jean-Paul also picked up the knife and decided he would keep it. Putting it in his bag he walked out of the toilet toward the passenger area. As he was walking, he was trying to get his angry thoughts under control. With all that had happened today, the thought crossed his mind that he should be keeping a journal.

Jean-Paul was about one hundred yards from the toilet when someone began yelling, *"Stop him! Stop him! He stole my money! He stole my money!"*

Jean-Paul turned and saw that it was Max who was running, yelling, and pointing at him. He stopped. Max ran up to him and gesturing wildly, yelled to the crowd that had gathered, "He stole my money. He stole the envelope with my money." He kept up his yelling, continually repeating himself.

In addition to being angry, Jean-Paul was also stunned. He had never been accused of stealing anything in his entire life. The fact was, he had never even thought about stealing anything. Now there were about twenty people who had stopped and were staring at him—an alleged thief.

Max was still screaming hysterically but keeping his distance since Jean-Paul was still holding the walking stick that had knocked him silly.

The crowd opened and out walked a giant of a man. It was a New York City policeman in his long blue coat with a center row of brass buttons, a badge on his left breast, two rank stripes on his upper sleeves, and gold braid around the lower sleeves. Add to that was his high standing police helmet and his nightstick. He was indeed a formidable looking specimen.

"What seems to be the trouble here?" the officer asked calmly.

Max immediately pointed at Jean-Paul and shouted, "He stole my money! He stole my money!"

"Max, my boy, when and where exactly did he do this?" It was clear the police officer knew Max since he called him by name.

Max continued to speak loudly and rapidly, "In the toilet, in the toilet. He took my envelope of money, knocked me silly with that stick, and left me for dead. I just want my money back and I don't care what happens to him. Come on O'Callaghan, for once you gotta help me!"

Officer O'Callaghan looked squarely at Jean-Paul and said sternly, "What do you have to say for yourself boy?"

Jean-Paul was calmly replied, "I was using the toilet and this person," pointing at Max, "came up behind me with a knife and demanded my money. When I told him to get lost, he actually tried to stab me. I blocked his knife thrust with my bag and then hit him with my walking stick. I made sure he wasn't dead and then left to go to the passenger area to wait for my train. And by the way, I picked up Max's knife." J.P. then took the knife out of his bag and handed it to O'Callaghan handle first.

He then showed the officer the hole in his bag.

Officer O'Callaghan took the knife and briefly examined it. He then turned to Max and asked, "Is this your knife?"

Max shook his head and said, "I ain't ever seen that knife before I my life."

O'Callaghan nodded his head. He apparently knew Max from his previous skullduggeries and by his expression, appeared convinced Max *was not* telling the truth. The officer handed the knife back to Jean-Paul. O'Callaghan then stared intently at Jean-Paul. There seemed to be something familiar about him. "He asked, "Have we met before? Do I know you?"

Jean-Paul responded, "I doubt it, I only come to New York two or three times a year with my dad."

The officer's head tilted a bit forward and he arched his eyebrows as if to get a better view of Jean-Paul. After a second or two he said, "You really look familiar. Where are you from?"

"Upstate New York, near the town of New Hope."

"Ah, so you are the one," Officer O'Callaghan enthusiastically exclaimed. "You are the one who tackled that no good Rufus Dregger on West 53rd a couple of years ago. That was the chase with the good Mr. Roosevelt."

"That right, that was me. I recently wired Mr. Roosevelt asking if I could join his newly formed cavalry regiment. He replied yes so I am on my way to San Antonio, Texas, to join the army and fight the Spanish in Cuba."

"Excellent my boy. Just excellent." Then as if he remembered the business at hand he turned to Max whose body had been in constant motion since they had been standing there. O'Callaghan's expression and voice changed as he asked the accuser, "So Max, how much money was stolen from you this time?"

This question caught Max off guard. He stuttered, "I, I, I, don't really know. I can't remember."

"You don't know? How can it be that you can't remember?"

Max's body was now jerking and moving even more rapidly knowing he was caught in a lie. He replied, "It was a lot of money, and it was in a white envelope. This rube put my money in his bag." Max pointed his shaking and dirty finger at Jean-Paul's leather shoulder bag.

"You mean the bag you stuck with a knife? Hmm, well try to remember how much money it was that was taken from you? If you are lying and you in fact assaulted this nice young man with your knife, you will again be sent *up the river* to Sing-Sing prison. And this time for a longer time than before!" O'Callaghan was getting evermore stern in his tone and comments to Max. He also started impatiently tapping his nightstick into his left hand.

Max looked at Jean-Paul and then Officer O'Callaghan. He then bolted and ran as fast as he could toward the closest station exit knocking travelers aside as he ran. Jean-Paul instinctively made a move to go after him. Officer O'Callaghan immediately grabbed his arm and shook his head. He dropped J.P.'s arm, took his whistle, and blew several short bursts. He stopped the whistling and said to Jean-Paul in a fatherly manner, "You can go young man. We all know Max and that he is continually up to these kinds of shenanigans!! Little beggar! My partner who is just outside will take care of him. Now get to your train. May God go with you and keep you safe in the war!" O'Callaghan then broke into a slow trot in the direction of Max's escape.

Several of the onlookers then patted Jean-Paul on the shoulder wishing him good luck on his upcoming venture.

With his anger subsiding as he walked, Jean-Paul did not know quite what to make of his day. It had been an interesting trip. He had bid farewell to everyone he ever loved and then of course there was the Berti Beckenbauer incident. Add to that was the fact he had been cheated out of money by the vendor, lunged at with a knife in a public toilet, and was almost the victim of a premeditated stabbing and robbery. And all of this before he had even left the Empire state of New York. He simply shook his head, said a quiet prayer of thanksgiving, and walked quickly to his assigned overnight Pullman car.

Upon entering the Pullman car, Jean-Paul was greeted by a Black man wearing an immaculate blue uniform and a large kepi with a brass plate inscribed with the words: *Pullman Porter*. He received Jean-Paul with a huge smile and said, *"Welcome to the Pullman Express to Chicago!! My name is George and I'll be*

*your porter for the trip to Chicago. May I see your ticket? Also,*
*I can take that shoulder bag if you like."*

Jean-Paul handed him his ticket but not his leather bag. He
followed him down the center aisle of the train car. There on the
left was his seat. It was directly across a like seat with a high back
and French upholstery. The entire car was carpeted with a plush
green carpet and had expensive looking mahogany side paneling.
It had a peculiar, scented smell. George offered Jean-Paul a glass
of water, which he took to drink with his mom's fried chicken. As
he was enjoying his dinner a dapper looking man came and sat
directly across from him. Jean-Paul pegged him to be a
businessman. He was wearing a dark gray suit coat with a
matching vest, black trousers, a short turnover shirt collar, and
a floppy bow tie. He had a pointed beard, short hair, and his hat
was made of soft felt. Most impressive thought Jean-Paul.

He extended his hand in greeting to Jean-Paul and said,
"So, you will be my traveling companion on our trip to Chicago.
My name is *Sorensen, C. William Sorenson.* You may call me
William. I was here in the city here for a series of meetings. I'm
going back to Chicago where I live and have my business."

Obviously, an extravert, he continued, "Ultimately, my plan
is to move to Hawaii and take advantage of the amazing
agricultural opportunities there in sugar cane and pineapples."
He stopped and then asked, "So, what's your name?"

I am Jean-Paul DeBert from New Hope, New York. I'm

traveling to San Antonio, Texas, to join the First Volunteer Cavalry Regiment. I'm hoping to go to Cuba and fight the Spaniards.

Jean-Paul's objective seemed to spark Sorenson's interest. He now gazed at the teenager with more than casual interest. He nodded as he said, "I was in the army for three years from 1862 to 1865. Ran away from home and joined up when I was seventeen. Told the army I was twenty. I'm sure they didn't believe me, but they were desperate for volunteers because of the *Dakota unrest.*"

"Dakota unrest?"

"It was actually more than unrest. Back in August of 1862 the Dakota Sioux began raiding settler's homes in central Minnesota. They wanted the Whites off their lands and out of the area. They supposedly killed as many as eight hundred White settlers, but I think that number was exaggerated. I went to the fight with Company C of the Fifth Minnesota Infantry. It was a good fighting unit. Joined up at Camp Ridgely with several other volunteers on the 19th of August. They gave me a uniform and some bedding but no weapons. It was a good thing I brought my hunting rifle because the next morning about four hundred extremely angry Sioux attacked us. We held out of course but had five soldiers killed and about fifteen wounded. The next day there was a tremendous thunderstorm. We used that time to strengthen our defenses as best we could. We thought the Sioux had left. That however, was a mistake. On the 22nd of August they attacked again, this time with as many as eight hundred warriors. We fought off their first attack but they kept the pressure on us with constant smaller attacks. Just before sundown they again attacked in full force. That was an incredible thing to see. We again held out—but just barely. Several of their warriors actually breached our perimeter. But that was really the end of the big fighting. From then until August 27, they held us under siege. We couldn't leave the fort, and none of the poor settlers that were trying to get to our camp could get in. On the 27th, Colonel Shelby with a force of 1,400 militiamen arrived. The Sioux thought better of taking on that size force. They left to go after other White civilian settlements. Sometime at the end of September the army captured about four hundred of the Sioux troublemakers. That pretty well ended the fighting."

*C. William* now lit a cigar. He continued, "At that point the army ordered a number of us south to out parent regiment in the *Army of Tennessee.* My unit saw a lot of fighting in the *War of the Rebellion.* We took part in the siege and assault on Vicksburg, the Battle of Nashville, the Battle of Franklin, and many other smaller scrimmages. I was really lucky because I was wounded three times but none of those wounds—thank God— were really serious. When the war ended in April of 1865, our regiment did garrison duty in Montgomery, Alabama. That was worse than the fighting. At least during the war, we had a purpose. Once the war was over, we just wanted to go home. And my oh my, did those civilians in Montgomery ever hate us! There was no love lost for us Yankees down there. They hated us with a vengeance. That was actually the worst period of my time in the army. The women—those refined genteel Southern belles with their parasols and nicely painted faces—would actually spit at us. I also found it interesting that the South started the war and when we defeated them soundly, it all became our fault. Incredible." He shook his head slowly as if in total disbelief.

"Our regiment took a train back to Minnesota. I mustered out at Fort Snelling in St. Paul on the 6th of September. I remember the day exactly because as soon as I got my small severance pay, I went over to the University of Minnesota and enrolled." Sorenson nodded his head in self-approval and opened his newspaper.

A second or so later he looked over the newspaper and concluded by saying, "That's my soldiering story. I survived two wars and three wounds in my three years of soldiering. Actually, I learned quite a bit about life during that experience. Mustered out as a First Sergeant. There isn't a day that goes by in which I don't think about my former comrades—many of them never made it out of the war alive. My life has been quite boring since, and with that, I am okay." He looked at Jean-Paul as if waiting for a question or a response. When none was forthcoming, he went on reading his paper.

Jean-Paul was awestruck and simply stared at this man. He was amazed at the man's memory. He remembered dates and a remarkable amount of detail about events of thirty-five years ago. Mr. Sorenson had done what he was about to do. C. William had survived and seemed to have thrived in combat. He was obviously a man of courage and a person to be reckoned with. He had become a First Sergeant, which undoubtedly was a significant achievement during wartime. My, oh my! Jean-Paul continued to stare at him thinking here was *a real man* in the tradition of his father Louie and his grandfather Papa Gerard. C. William Sorenson was a man of courage, action, and decision. He emanated confidence and was completely sure of himself. Jean-Paul wanted to become like this man. He now sat back and stared at nothing out of the window. He was now more than ever sure that his decision to join the army was the correct one.

The train whistled its departure and like a big behemoth began slowly moving forward.

Jean-Paul had been so enamored with Mr. Sorenson and his stories that he barely noticed the two people who were now sitting across the aisle from him. It was a married couple who were still in the process of getting settled in the Pullman. The man was an average looking middle-aged, gray-haired gentleman, in a black suit and highly polished black shoes.

Jean-Paul took great interest in the woman who was apparently the gray-haired gentleman's wife. The woman was younger than her husband and was the exact image of a *celebrity Gibson Girl*. J.P. recognized the *Gibson Girl* image from the pen and ink drawings of Charles Dana Gibson in the *Harper's Weekly* magazine. Abigail, his girlfriend, was always talking about Gibson Girls. She aspired to look just like them. Huh.... Abby, like many women of the day, thought these female images were the personification and ideal of feminine beauty.

Even though he had been taught never to stare at someone, Jean-Paul watched the woman get settled. He noted that like in the Charles Gibson drawings, this lady was tall, slender, and very conscious of her femininity. She had been wearing a huge, broad brimmed hat that was trimmed with masses of feathers, ribbons, and artificial flowers. Having removed her hat, her hairstyle was characterized by hair piled high on the top of the head and hanging down on the sides. Quite impressive thought Jean-Paul. Apparently, George the porter, thought the same as he was fawning all over the lady as she was getting settled.

Jean-Paul reasoned that based on appearance, the couple was clearly from the upper strata of society. This woman was not like anything he had observed in his small village of New Hope. She was certainly as attractive as any female he had seen on his previous trips to New York. He smiled when his thoughts compared this woman's appearance with that of his mother. His mother was modest, shy, and humble. All the elegant and stylish clothes Nana de Bert had sent his mother from France were securely stored in the trunks in which they had arrived. The only time his mother had worn such clothes was on their trip to France. Even though she looked beautiful in them, Jean-Paul always remembered her saying how uncomfortable she was wearing them.

When the couple finally got settled, extraverted Jean-Paul extended his hand across the aisle and introduced himself with a smile and his name. His father always told him he should smile and give a strong handshake when he introduced himself. The gentleman gave Jean-Paul an indifferent look and responded with a limp handshake. He said his name was *Professor Henry Xavier Tanner.* He added without looking at Jean-Paul, *"Professor of philosophy and logic* at *New York State University. I teach students to think,"* he said as his voice sloped off.

Really thought Jean-Paul. That was an interesting way to introduce oneself. Professor Henry Xavier must be very proud of himself and his job at the university....

Jean-Paul nodded a greeting to the *Gibson Girl* and said, "Hello, I am Jean-Paul."

Unlike her husband she seemed more interested in this handsome young male traveler. She leaned over as she extended her hand and with a smile replied, "My name is *Summer Jewel Tanner.* You may call me Summer."

"Certainly Summer."

Jean-Paul could not help his extraversion as he continued, "I am traveling to San Antonio, Texas, to join the First Volunteer Cavalry. Teddy Roosevelt, the regiment's deputy commander, personally invited me to join. I am quite sure we will be shipped to Cuba to fight the Spanish. That is if Mr. Roosevelt has anything to say about it!" J.P. was so excited as he was saying this he was almost shaking.

Jean-Paul's travel plans caught Professor Tanner's attention. Rather than just being another person of no relevance to the Professor, Jean-Paul's immediate future triggered a level of interest. Unfortunately, it was not a positive interest.

Professor Tanner sat up and with an unpleasant expression said, "I am sorry to hear that. He quietly repeated himself, "I'm really sorry to hear that."

Jean-Paul, somewhat surprised blurted out, "Why is that? Why are you sorry?"

The Professor, put his book aside and with an agitated and twisted look on his face, leaned into the aisle and said to Jean-Paul with some intensity, "The war in Spain is wrong—just wrong I tell you. Why does the United States need to help those Cubans? Why do we need to punish Spain for their so-called ruthless colonial government? Who cares what the Spaniards are doing in Cuba? Who cares really? It is none of our country's business! The Monroe Doctrine does not apply since Spain has been in Cuba since 1492. In that Monroe statement, the United

States pledged it would not interfere with existing European colonies, which includes Cuba. Actually, the Spanish consider Cuba a province of their country and not a colony. So, what are we doing violating our own doctrine and Spain's national sovereignty? No doubt it is our government's desire to replace Spain with a colonial occupation force of our own. You just wait and see, we will be the new occupying force there. That is exactly what we will do—assuming we are actually able to defeat the Spaniards. You'll see."

After this unexpected tirade, Jean-Paul wasn't quite sure how to respond. Finally, he said, "The United States had to do something since the Spanish blew up our battleship, the *USS Maine,* in Havana harbor!"

The professor shook his head slowly and stared at Jean-Paul in complete astonishment. "Did they now? And how do you know it was the Spanish that blew up the Maine? How do you know the explosion wasn't simply an accident because of worn equipment, poor maintenance, or an error of some inept sailor? Were you on the Maine when it blew? Or did you read about it in Randolph Hearst and Joseph Pulitzer's aptly named *yellow press newspapers?* Their editorial practice of fictionalizing and embellishing events for profit is simply deplorable. Sensationalism sells papers and makes money for the newspapers. The more exaggerated and shocking the story—the more papers they believe will be sold. That is simple economics and also an unethical way to do business in my opinion. The news should be reported as truthfully and accurately as possible and not in some overstated or outrageous fashion. Anyway, what was the *USS Maine* doing in the harbor of a land that is in a civil war? When we put our naval vessels in such a situation, we can almost predict that bad things will happen. That explosion is more our country's fault than it was Spains."

Jean-Paul did not appreciate the tone or the arrogance of this professor. He clearly sensed the professor was talking down to him. This was happening because the professor probably thought he was a young, naïve hick. He felt the tightening in his chest that always presented itself when he sensed he was being treated unjustly or discarded. It was *the feeling*.

Jean-Paul simply blurted out and rapidly said, "But the *Good Book* says we are to help those that cannot help themselves. And it goes on to say that if we know what we should do but don't do it, it is a sin against God. It also says we should love one another. To love means to help, serve and assist, even if it costs us. The Apostle John writes, *'No greater love hath a man than to give his life for his friends.'* The Cuban rebels have asked the United States for help. The Spanish in all probability sank our warship and based on what is right or wrong, it is the right thing for the United States to help the Cubans."

The Professor seemed a bit taken back at the aggressive reply from Jean-Paul. Rather than addressing his statements, he began as if lecturing in the classroom, "War of any kind, regardless of the provocation is futile. Wars never accomplish anything. All they do is lay the foundation for the next war. Consider France as a result of their disastrous defeat in the 1870-71 War. They are bent on revenge. As soon as that war was over, they immediately began preparing to again fight the Germans and get back the two provinces they lost: *Alsace and Lorraine.* The Germans know the French are preparing. Their common phrase about that is: *"Der tag kommt"*, which literally means *the day is coming* or more precisely, *another war with the French is inevitable."*

Jean-Paul tried to interject but the Professor raised his voice and kept on speaking. He didn't want to listen, since in his arrogance he apparently knew everything.

The Professor continued, "In war there are never any winners, every nation at war loses. Always. Even the good we do in war is ironical. We liberate or capture a place by destroying it. We liberate people by killing them. The military says, *'Look, we captured this city from the enemy and now it's a pile of rubble.'* That is a big military achievement indeed. It takes decades to build a city and a few hours to destroy it. In 1812 the Russians retreating in front of Napoleon's Grand Armée destroyed every town in its wake so nothing would be left for the French. Where did that leave the people who lived there? Where I ask you?"

As if on mission and without looking at Jean-Paul, the

professor continued, "The United States doesn't need a big army if indeed any army at all. Consider, two weak neighbors to the north and south and two oceans of fish occupy our nation's four borders. We need to isolate ourselves from the world's problems, oppose war in any form, and reduce our military to something of a police force. The optimum army we ever had was after the American War of Independence. It had been reduced to eighty soldiers guarding an ammo bunker at West Point. That is exactly what it would be again if I were the President. We need to keep the government out of our lives as much as possible and that would start with a smaller army. Remember the Caesars of the Roman Empire recruited their *Praetorian Guard* from the ranks of the army. On more than one occasion the *Praetorians* turned on their Emperor. They murdered *Nero* for example. Granted he deserved it, but my point is that a standing army is a threat to any form of democratic government. And I would say it is a very serious threat!"

The professor stared aggressively at Jean-Paul and then Mr. Sorenson for a reaction. Not getting one, he rattled on, "It takes eighteen years to grow a soldier and less than a second to kill him. The military gives a naive young boy a uniform, a gun, and training and for what exactly? So, he can get killed and then someone else replaces him will have the same future and the same fate. Young men are fools. They sign up for the war with bands playing, flowers thrown, parades, big send offs at train stations, and kisses from young girls. They parade around wearing their new uniforms with brass buttons. That is the *side show clown suit* in which they will be killed and buried. Amazing idiocy—simply amazing"

The Professor seemed unable to stop his tirade. "War is nothing more than loss and destruction: loss of lives, loss of material, destruction of property, destruction of the countryside, and the loss of the individual potential of all those who are killed. Who knows how many doctors, inventors, and yes, college professors, are dumped in graves with all their unmet potential? Think of what could have been for the 650,000 young men who died in our nation's civil war some thirty years ago?"

The professor glanced down and just shook his head at that thought. He then looked up and once again continued, this time more slowly and quietly, "If one looks at approximately six thousand years of recorded history, there have been only two-hundred-sixty-eight of those years in which there have been no wars. Like I said, *war is man's eternal destiny.* One could even make a case that man has *a biological war gene.*

It appeared that the businessman, C. William Sorenson, who was sitting across from Jean-Paul and diagonally from the professor, had been totally focused on his newspaper during the professor's harangue. But it now became clear by his demeanor, as he resolutely folded his paper, that he had heard the entire lecturette.

"Sir," said Sorenson to the professor, "I believe your viewpoint of warfare is unfortunately limited." This statement startled Professor Tanner. Clearly, he was not used to being challenged. Certainly, none of his nineteen-year-old university students ever did so.

Sorensen continued: "For all the evil in war, warfare has many positive aspects."

"Name one," challenged the professor.

"Of course. A primary one is the field in which I work: supply and distribution of goods and materials. This system was first developed in ancient times so armies could move away from their military depots and be resupplied. Also, the Persians initially developed the first postal service so their emperor could better communicate with his armies in the field. Ambulances were created to take casualties from the battlefield to hospitals in the rear areas. *Prostheses* devices for those who lost limbs were greatly improved because of war."

"Right," mumbled the professor, "That's an important area. And of course, there would be no major need for improved prostheses if there were no wars."

Sorensen ignored the professor's comment and continued, "Canned foods were first developed for Napoleon's Grand Armée. This was a major development. No longer did armies have to forage for fresh food for the soldiers. They could carry their own food. In the recent civil war here in the U.S., soldiers were issued tinned food goods that contained meat, coffee, condensed milk, and biscuits. It wasn't as good as fresh food, but it was certainly better than nothing at all. "

Sorensen noted that the professor was losing interest and was probably no longer listening. He decided to conclude his argument even if only for Jean-Paul. He said, "As a result of that war there were several other advances. For example, it caused our country to move away from coins and instead print paper money: the *greenback dollars*. War resulted in the transition from pocket watches to wristwatches. The use of sewing machines was greatly expanded. Our infantry regiment had several of these machines to patch our uniforms. Iron rather than wooden ships were created. Because of the volume of military uniforms needed, a variety of different sizes were produced rather than only personally tailored shoes and clothing. And of course, there were many advances in medicine including the triage concept and improved sanitation in military hospitals."

Sorensen took a breadth and then continued, "War also gives soldiers a broader outlook on life. Because of war, they travel to other lands. They see and experience things they would never have back home. Their experience and learnings stimulate ideas for improvements and advancements in their own culture. That can be anything from education, food, medical procedures, health remedies, building and farming techniques, ways people live and work, and a myriad of other things. After the war the soldiers bring these new ideas back home, implement them, and their culture progresses as a result. The returning crusaders brought many new ideas back to Europe from what they learned from the more advanced Middle Eastern cultures. "

The Professor looked directly at Sorensen and in a patronizing tone said, "So you think those so-called advances were worth all the death and destruction? I don't think there were many cultural advances the Union troops brought back to the North as a result of the War of Rebellion!"

Before either Sorenson or Jean-Paul could respond the professor's, wife joined the conversation.

Looking at Sorensen she asked, "So I understand from your comments that you were in the *War of the Rebellion?*

Sorensen nodded in the affirmative.

"Then you must have seen how army life can destroy a young man even if he never experiences battle!"

"I am not sure what you mean. What exactly are you saying?"

Jean-Paul personally sensed he knew where the professor's wife was going with this.

"Army life is destructive simply by its nature. No matter what a person's values are when he joins the army, the other soldiers inevitably drag him down to their level of debauchery. Soldiers are notorious users of alcoholic and tobacco. They are gamblers, thieves, and whoremongers. Women are not safe around soldiers. They impoverish farmers by stealing their animals. They ravage farmers' wives and daughters and burn their buildings. They leave them starving and destitute. What Union General William Tecumseh Sherman did in Georgia and South Carolina in the last war was total barbarism. By any standard, he was a war criminal."

Jean-Paul was struck by the incongruence of the harshness of the content of what she had said with the easy, friendly manner in which she had said it. Interesting....

She paused for a second or two as if to gather her thoughts, and then she continued as aggressively as ever, "Many soldiers are nothing more than delinquents. They are in the army because they had a choice between going to jail for a crime they committed or joining the military. In that regard, the army is just another form of prison. That's right, prison. After the Custer massacre in Montana in 1876, I remember reading that his famous 7th Cavalry had many members who were immigrants from Europe. They could barely speak English and had to be taught to ride a horse *after* they had joined the cavalry. They only joined the army to have a job and avoid poverty and destitution. That is representative of people who join. Those who stay in the army for a career and become sergeants treat new recruits worse than animals. They are ruthless and inhumane. They have no notion of fairness or just treatment. These sergeants are insecure, suffer from an inferiority complex, have low self-esteem, and obviously don't respect themselves very much, otherwise they would not have stayed in the army. Life is even worse in the Navy considering the dreadful conditions on those unheated ships when at sea."

With a sympathetic look she said to Jean-Paul, "So young man," she continued, "that's what you are getting yourself into. You look like a nice, intelligent youngster who has a bright future ahead of him. My advice to you is this. When we get to Chicago you should get on a train and go right back to New York!"

Sorensen was now red faced and could no longer sit still. With a raised voice he responded. "Madam, what you said about life in the army in general and about sergeants specifically, is not accurate, not accurate at all. I was a first sergeant in the last war. Among the best, bravest, and most capable soldiers I served with were career noncommissioned officers, or sergeants as you call them. They were tough, natural leaders who were comfortable with responsibility and taking charge. They could always be trusted to do their duty, conduct themselves with honor, and do what was right. They led and taught by their personal example, were able to deal with any problem, and would not hesitate to make decisions. The sergeants I served under in two wars loved their country and would sacrifice anything for her. They were also fiercely loyal to those they were leading—fiercely loyal. What I always admired was that their experience allowed them to see things the rest of us could not readily see. It was at times astonishing. That ability and their numerous soldering skills kept many of us alive. Think about that—their skill kept others alive. How amazing and valuable is that? The training they put us through was tough and hard because the battlefield is a tough and hard place. The training was difficult because the weak— those not strong enough to do their job in battle—had to be weeded out. If they were not, they could compromise the mission and get their comrades killed. War is a tough business and is not for the weak."

Obviously still agitated, he continued, "That said, the percentage of sergeants that behave as you are suggesting is quite small. It is unfair to suggest all career enlisted soldiers conduct themselves as you have stated, very, very unfair."

Sorensen sat back with a satisfied look on his face after his direct but respectful homily. He was wondering where this woman gained such a negative impression about soldiers and army sergeants anyway. Certainly, she had no first-hand experience with them. It was probably from her arrogant and opinionated husband.

Just then George, the Pullman porter, arrived with a cart containing a pitcher of water, a pot of coffee, a pot of tea, and an assortment of chocolates and cookies. Of course, the Gibson girl was the first to be offered and served the refreshments.

Next Professor Tanner asked for a cup of coffee. When

George was pouring it, the train made a lurch and a drop or two of coffee spilled on the Dr. Tanner's coat sleeve. As if he had but shot with a double barrel goose gun, the Professor screamed fiercely at George. He cussed at him using words the likes of which Jean-Paul had never heard before. George was totally shaken and couldn't stop apologizing. He took a cloth and tried to dab the smidgeon off coffee Tanner's sleeve. The Professor grabbed the cloth and yelled that he didn't want to be touched. He wiped his arm as if the entire pot of coffee had been dumped on him. Both Jean-Paul and Mr. Sorenson were speechless at the Professor's rude behavior.

Without thinking, extraverted Jean-Paul exclaimed, "Sir, you have no right to talk to him that way. He didn't do it on purpose and besides, he apologized more times than was necessary. I think you owe George an apology."

George, still flustered, said, "No sir, no sir, no apology is necessary; none at all. It was entirely my fault. It was my fault completely. I am so sorry, so very sorry."

Professor Tanner, now calmer, said, "I accept your apology." Jean-Paul looked at George who signaled that the teenager from New Hope should drop it. He then looked at Sorenson who shrugged his shoulders and briefly shook his head. J.P. had never quite seen someone be so rude to another person as what he had just witnessed. Even when some people back home would make disparaging remarks about his background or religion it was generally more subtle than overt—generally. Jean-Paul was quite convinced that if the Professor had talked to him like that, he would have used his savate stick.

After taking a sip of coffee, the Professor began again as if nothing had happened. He continued with another anti-war diatribe, "Let's not forget, war does irreparable damage to nature—irreparable damage. Trees grow for years and are destroyed in minutes by shelling. Rivers are lakes are polluted with rotting bodies or by the garbage thrown into them by the army. The wake of an army on the march is one of desolation, litter, and human waste. There is virtually no hygiene or sanitation in armies. Soldiers in the field generally live like animals. In one crusade, the people in Jerusalem could actually smell the filth of the crusader army when they were still fifty miles away. Throughout history sickness and disease has killed twice as many soldiers as has combat. There has always been dysentery, diarrhea, and typhoid fever in military camps. In Cuba, with that god-awful tropical climate, there will undoubtedly be many deaths from malaria and yellow fever."

Looking at no one, *His Rudeness* droned on not seeming to care if anyone was listening, "War destroys families. When the father goes off to war it is never clear he will be coming back alive or in a box! Actually, war is simple: I will attempt to kill you while you try to kill me. After we accomplish that, other young men will be sent to do the same thing to each another. And after they are successful, then other young men come along and will do the same. It is simple attrition and a never-ending cycle. That's why war is insane. Also, war is innately not fair. Brave men who take risks get killed while cowards who hide survive the battle and live on. It is simply not fair, not fair I tell you." The professor was now pale, sweating, and continuously shaking his head. *It seems he was more twisted up about what happens to humans in war than how they should be treated when they spill a couple of drops of coffee.*

As if in a hurry he went on, "The fighting is also horrific. The soldier never forgets what he sees on the battlefield. Soldiers kill and destroy. This experience is with them always and changes them forever. One never forgets or gets over seeing his best friend being killed—ever. If they survive, they come home and potentially become a threat and impairment to society. If they actually were in combat their experiences will have been so intense that they will have a very difficult time adjusting to the routine of civilian life. What are they to do when the war is over and they come back into society? What? Immediately go back to farming or working in a sweatshop? And think about this: what happens when a soldier is wounded in battle? He either bleeds to death, or if he loses a limb, he is a physical cripple for the rest of his life. Undoubtedly, he will also be emotionally damaged. When they come home a cripple, they are no more than half of a man. Life for them is certainly less than what it could have been.

But at least they are alive, but for what purpose? As General Sherman said, *'War is not a playground—war is at its best barbarism. All of its glory is moonshine.'"*

The professor looked directly at Jean-Paul and said, "If you are not killed in battle in Cuba young man, you very likely will be done in by some tropical or jungle disease. That is not the way I would want to die if I were you. You should take my wife's advice and head back home to New York."

Jean-Paul was *still a bit shaken* by the manner that Professor Tanner had treated George the porter. In J.P.'s way of thinking, Tanner's behavior indicated a great deal about his character and world view. For an academic, his character was quite different from those who were teaching at the Jesuit school in New Hope.

Reflecting on what Tanner had just said, Jean-Paul loudly and assertively responded with something he had learned in school: "An army guarantees the nation's *safety, security, and survival*. It must be the first priority of a country's leaders to ensure it is protected and sheltered from external attacks or internal threats. Everything else is secondary. Everything else." J.P. found himself repeating himself, mimicking the example of his father.

Security is the foundational value of any nation. Jean-Paul had learned that from his understanding of Chacopac history. There had been continuous encroachments from White businesspeople, settlers, hunters, fishermen, lumbermen, and mineral hunters on the Chac lands. If the Chacs had not placed considerable emphasis on securing their territory, they most likely would have had the same fate as many of the native tribes in the southern and western United States: living on a reservation in a barren no-man's land.

When there was no response from Tanner, Jean-Paul again began to speak, this time in a slow cadence, "The United States does not have a nobility class. That is true. However, I remember reading that *the nobility of the United States is its military*. They were responsible for winning our independence from the British and preserving it in its second war of independence with Britain in 1812. In both wars Great Britain supposedly had the best army in the world. Each time the United States decisively defeated them. Additionally, in the other conflicts in our brief history, the American military saved many of our countrymen from both Mexican and American Indian violence. And then of course the military sustained the Union in the War of the Rebellion. The sacrifices, courage, honor, and duty displayed by those who served went above and beyond. Therefore, *if there is a class of nobles or aristocrats in the United States, it is its military and those veterans who have served in the military*. Without their efforts in both war and peace, the United States would not exist. They have and continue to guarantee our constitutional republic's peace, liberty, freedom, and democracy. They are all

*American heroes.* Nay, they are all *great American heroes.* They are indeed a *national treasure."* As Jean-Paul finished he gave an *and-that's-the-way-it-is* nod toward the bad-mannered professor and his Gibson girl wife. He wasn't even sure where his words came from, as he had not previously thought much about the ideas he had just shared.

Sorensen pointed to Jean-Paul and said approvingly, "I totally agree. I'd also like to add that soldiering, particularly being a career soldier, is truly an honorable profession. What this person provides society is similar to that of other professionals such as doctors, dentists, or lawyers. West Point and Annapolis do an inordinately great service to our nation by providing it with well trained, professional military leaders. Virtually all of the noteworthy generals on both sides in the War of Rebellion were graduates of West Point. The Europeans said that our civil war was no more than two mobs slugging it out with each other. Well, to that I would say if it hadn't been for the graduates of West Point, that war would have been even more of a chaotic mob fest."

Sorenson took a puff on his cigar and added, "There's something else that needs to be said on this topic. Young man, listen to this very closely because it applies to you. The military teaches one about life—especially during wartime service. War—like life—is hard and is a struggle. Soldiering and the soldier's craft are not easy or for the weak. Napoleon is supposed to have said that the life of a solder is primarily one of *hardship*. It has also been said that courage is the most important trait of a soldier. Not true. The most important soldierly traits are resilience, patience, and perseverance. I think Napoleon also said something similar to that. Those are qualities that cause people to be successful and prosperous in life. And they can be learned in the military."

The professor tried to interrupt but Sorenson talked over him and continued at a quicker pace. "Wartime military service also helps develop *other important characteristics* that will significantly help a person in life. Some key examples would be *accepting responsibility, taking initiative, making decisions, solving problems, doing what is morally right, adapting to constant change, achieving results, accomplishing the mission and, of course, taking charge when needed.* That's called leadership. From my experience, leadership is the key to success in any endeavor. Of course, one could add to this list the traditional notions of *duty, honor, country, service, sacrifice, trust, and courage.* Where else could someone get such an education at such a young age? Really, where else? One can learn Latin, philosophy, and history in a classroom, but the attributes I just mentioned are priceless and can only be learned from experiencing life. Soldering in war provides that life experience."

Sorenson was obviously getting more and more stimulated by this conversation. He said, "One more thing, war service gives men opportunities they could never have in peacetime. It shows individual soldiers what they are capable of doing, tolerating, and becoming. It helps them reach their full potential. It can be the defining experience and highlight of their entire life. It really makes them and defines who they are. And when they come home, they truly appreciate life in their peaceful community and what a wonderful the life they have there. It helps them understand what they were fighting for. If they were not sure about that while serving, it becomes crystal clear once they return home. It certainly did for me." Satisfied with himself, he concluded by saying, "That's all I have to share."

Sorenson looked straight at Jean-Paul and said, "Young man, John is it, remember what I just said. It is truth and absolutely sound wisdom. Remember it because it can put your entire military experience in context and give it meaning"

The professor, who had been chomping at the bit to provide a rebuttal, began by saying to Sorensen, "I don't...."

Sorenson said, "I have heard enough from you *Sir Rudeness* and also from you *Summer Breezy*. I am going to the dining car to have dinner and a drink."

Mrs. Tanner said, "The name is Summer Jewel."

"Yes, I am sure it is...." Looking at Jean-Paul he said, "Young soldier, why don't you come with me. I'll buy you dinner."

Jean-Paul jumped at the opportunity. He said, "I would love

to have dinner with you." Taking his shoulder bag and walking stick, he followed Sorensen who was obviously an experienced train traveler. He never looked back at the Tanners."

   During the time in the dining car, Jean-Paul was fascinated with *C. William Sorensen.* Here was a real man, a man's man. His stories about his war service had no end. Throughout the dinner Sorensen shared one story after another with ever ascending enthusiasm. The more *Pinot Noir* he drank—the more interesting were his stories. Jean-Paul sensed Sorensen was embellishing and exaggerating his yarns, but he didn't care. He was just elated to be in the presence of such a man. Life was good and always seemed to be getting better.

### *Thought Questions for Chapter 4:*

1. What are your impressions and reactions to Dr. Tanner's attitudes about war and military service?

2. What are your impressions and reactions to C. William Sorenson's beliefs about war and military service? What, if anything, would you add?

3. What are your impressions and reactions to what Jean-Paul said about the military and the value of serving in the military during wartime? What, if anything, would you add?

4. Why did Jean-Paul say soldiers and veterans were the nobility and aristocrats in a constitutional republic? Why did he think that?

5. What was your biggest learning or take away from this chapter? What can you apply from the information in this chapter? What in it did you find the most interesting? Why?

# 5

## *The Train Trip to San Antonio*

Jean-Paul woke up with a start as the train's conductor nudged him and asked for his ticket. His train rides from Chicago to St. Louis and St. Louis to Dallas had been uneventful. They were, however, not nearly as interesting as the trip from New York to Chicago. The overnight trip from St. Louis to Dallas was extremely uncomfortable. It was because J.P. did not have a sleeping berth. He had to sit up during the entire trip. Arriving in Dallas, he immediately went to the train leaving for San Antonio, found his seat and fell fast asleep. He didn't even wake up when the train pulled out of the station.

Still half asleep he looked at how this passenger car was configured. The many padded seats in this car were in pairs facing each other. This arrangement was the same on both sides of the aisle. Each seat could hold three people, although with two it would be much more comfortable. Also, there was certainly not much legroom if there would be six riders in each paired section.

The train ride from Dallas to San Antonio was scheduled for six hours with stops in Waco and Austin. It would arrive in San Antonio at 2:15 PM. The brown and mostly flat, barren Texas terrain was not the green rolling hills, plush woodlands, and

116

crystal blue lakes that Jean-Paul was familiar with in upstate New York. He already missed that terrain. He wondered what Cuba would be like. He had read that Cuba had many tropical forests with a very heavy annual rainfall. Jean-Paul's mind continued to wonder. Maybe those jungle forests would be the first place he would come under enemy fire.

Across the aisle from him—and sitting by herself—was a young blonde woman. She was wearing a white bonnet, a navy-blue shawl, and a long yellow dress. She was pale and very thin. For whatever reason she seemed nervous, uncomfortable, and even a bit distressed. Jean-Paul reasoned that perhaps she was not feeling well or traveling from or to a difficult situation. She was always either looking out of the window or down at her hands. Jean-Paul also reasoned that this young girl needed to be eating a good deal more than she had been.

There were two or three children yelling and wildly running up and down the aisle. Jean-Paul observed with interest the total indifference of their parents to that behavior. Such unruly conduct would never have been tolerated in the Chacopac tribe. There, the training and disciplining of children was a major priority. Jean-Paul found it strange that the parents of these screaming tyrants were so oblivious and tolerant of their children's rude and disorderly behavior.

Sitting directly across from Jean-Paul was a strange sight indeed. Here was a little man who was at most, five feet tall. His legs did not touch the floor of the train car. Although short in stature, he was evenly proportioned with a muscular build. His hair was quite long extending below his shoulders. He was wearing an unusual style beret and clothes like those Jean-Paul had never seen before. He had bright alert eyes and was watching the landscape pass by with great interest. Jean-Paul took an immediate liking to him, not being exactly sure why.

Jean-Paul extended his hand to the short man and said, "Hello, my name is Jean-Paul. I am going to San Antonio to join the army and hopefully from there, go to Cuba and fight the Spanish."

The short fellow extending his hand leaned forward with such enthusiasm that he almost fell forward out of his seat. With a strong hand shake he said, "I am called *Three-Ring*. I too am going to San Antonio to join Teddy Roosevelt's First Volunteers. I don't know if I will be accepted, but I know I can ride and shoot with the best of them. It is a pleasure to meet you!"

Three-Ring kept shaking Jean-Paul's hand and acted as if he would not let go.

J.P. couldn't help but ask, "You said your name is *Three-Ring?* Did I hear that right?"

"Yes, you did." The little man smiled. "My given name is *Herkimer Alfonso Hanky*. That's right, Herkimer Alfonso Hanky—Herkimer Alfonso. Those are really dreadful names. That's why I prefer Three-Ring. At the age of nine I ran away from my home and joined the circus." He paused and then said with a smile, "You also heard that right—the circus. That's every kid's dream. For me, it was a reality. Have been with them ever since. The circus people gave me the name *Three-Ring*. Because of my size and nimbleness, the circus folks taught me *acrobatics, trapeze skills, riding, juggling, shooting tricks while on horseback, clown acts, gymnastics,* and much, much more. I met people from all around the world. I learned more talking with them than I ever would have in school. When not performing, circus people are generally laughed at, ridiculed, and mocked by almost everybody. Many are seen as freaks. They are totally misunderstood.... They are, however, very talented, skilled, kind, and hardworking people. With the other children of the circus troupe, they taught me how to read and write, how to take care of the most exotic menagerie of animals, and many other things I would never have learned in Costa Mesa."

"That's amazing. But where's Costa Mesa?"

"It's in southern California about forty miles south of Los Angeles. It was in Los Angeles where I hooked up with the circus. Then it was called *P.T. Barnum's Museum, Menagerie and Circus.* One early morning I left home, went to the train station, and hoboed a ride to the big city. Best and smartest thing I ever did. That was in 1882, sixteen years ago. Had I not done that, I would still be working in the fields in the California heat! Never knew either my real mother of father. Lived with a family who claimed to be my aunt and uncle. Not sure that was true. I'm not even sure what my real last name is. Ring is close enough, you know, as in *Three-Ring*. With this he laughed with a deep and hearty laugh. It was a laugh you would not expect from such a little energized man.

"The circus was planning to travel to Europe. But I was looking for something new, more exciting, and different. Then this here war was declared and that was the signal for me to leave."

He lifted his right arm and with his left pointed to it, "You see my colorful jacket, shirt, pants, and beret? These are the best of the best of my circus clothes." He again laughed heartily. His laugh was so contagious that Jean-Paul also laughed out loud, although he was not really sure what he was laughing about.

Three-Ring continued, "I've one thing to say though, as a kid I did learn to speak Spanish in Costa Mesa. Over the years that has been a big advantage for me. Learning languages has always come easy for me. Over half of the people working in the circus were not from America. There were Rumanians, Chinese, North Africans, people from the Czar's Russia, ..."

At this Jean-Paul interrupted and said, "Russian? You had Russian people working with you in your circus?"

"Yes of course we did. There was this trapeze artist named *Tatiana*. She was the most beautiful woman I ever met. That woman was a pure natural beauty. When she was performing on that trapeze, she was poetry in motion. She could do it all and do it with ease. She had no fear—absolutely no fear. I think I was in love with her, as was everyone else. She had no real interest in me, but I did convince her to teach me Russian. Those Russian lessons were most memorable. She would always ask me if I was listening. Most of the time I really wasn't because I was simply staring at her. But I really worked hard at my Russian because I wanted to impress her and communicate better with her. She said I was quite fluent in speaking her language. To that I said, *'Yippee!'"*

Jean-Paul asked Three-Ring what happened to *Tatiana*. Three-Ring answered with some emotion, "We were in Kansas City. As often happened our leaders were invited to dinner by the higher ups in the communities in which we were performing. And, as also happened, *Tatiana* was also one of the ones our leaders took with them to dinner. I, of course, was never invited to any of those events. Well, the day after that dinner we were to leave to Denver for our next performance. That morning *Tatiana* was nowhere to be found and of course no one knew where she was. No one. I stayed behind to look for her. No one in Kansas City knew anything. Our leaders alleged she had come back to camp with them late that previous evening. I don't know, maybe she did. I just don't know. What I do know is our leaders showed no concern whatsoever that she was missing. This was strange since she was such a big hit and star performer. Maybe she ran off with someone from Kansas? Maybe she was kidnapped? No one knew anything, and no one in the circus seemed to care." Three-Ring shrugged his shoulders.

"I got over it. No problem. But my, was she a rare beauty." With that reflection Three-Ring shook his head.

"Do you still speak Russian?" asked J.P.

"Right, and as I said, I got pretty good at it too. But it is my Spanish that I'm hoping will get me a place in Roosevelt's cavalry. Of course, there are many people in Texas who speak Spanish."

"I am sure speaking Spanish will help you. Mr. Roosevelt is a very reasonable man. I'm sure he will recognize your talents."

"You know Mr. Roosevelt?"

"Yes, I met him once in New York City when he was the city's police commissioner. He was a man of great enthusiasm and energy. I guess exuberance would also be a good word for him. I sent him a telegram asking if I could join his unit. He responded with a yes and instructed me to come to San Antonio."

"Well, I am very impressed. You must be well connected. Perhaps you could help me get signed up?"

"I will do anything I can to help. I wouldn't worry about it. Have faith. It will work out. You'll be able to enlist." Three-Ring extended his hand and shook Jean-Paul's hand again with warmth and approval.

\*          \*          \*          \*          \*

## Chapter 5: The Train Trip to San Antonio

Jean-Paul took writing paper and a lead pencil from his shoulder bag. It was time to write his parents and Abby and tell them about his trip. Just then there was a great commotion at the far end of the car. Jean-Paul leaned over and glanced down the aisle. To his surprise and walking toward him was what appeared to be an old man wearing a tattered and dirty army uniform. He was also carrying what was referred to in the South as a *carpetbag*. It was made of carpeting material and his was unusually dirty and stained. He was speaking loudly and mostly incoherently to the passengers as he was passing them. Arriving near J.P., the smell of alcohol combined with human filth and vomit emanating from him was almost overwhelming. Clearly the old man had been drinking and had not bathed or washed his clothes for some time.

The old man looked at Jean-Paul and Three-Ring and then at the young girl sitting across from the aisle from them. He threw his bag in the luggage rack above the seat and without hesitation plopped himself down next to the young girl. This caused the girl to press herself against the window with an even more distressed look on her face than she had previously.

The old man immediately put his hand on her knee and said, "Hi honey! How we doin' today?" The girl now looked more horrified than timid. She said nothing but made a high-pitched squealing noise indicating her discomfort.

Jean-Paul could not help himself. Without hesitation, and in order to distract the old man, he said, "Good morning, sir. I see you are wearing an army inform. Were you in the army?"

The diversion seemed to work as now the old man leaned away from the young girl and turned to Jean-Paul. He said nothing but simply stared at him. The volume of alcohol on his breadth was bordering on intolerable. The young woman next to him was now slowly opening the window.

Still staring at Jean-Paul, the old man said, "I was in the U.S. Army Cavalry, the Seventh Cavalry mostly, for almost seven years. Made sergeant you know." With this he pointed to the three inverted stripes on his sleeve.

"Didn't just sit around either when I wuz in the army. Did more than just shovel horse manure! Much more." The old soldier was slurring his words and burped intermittently but was still mostly understandable.

"In those seven years I was in three Indian wars. That's right, three campaigns: The *Little Big Horn, the Nez Perces, and the Utes.* Made sergeant you know." He again pointed to the stripes on his shoulder.

Both Jean-Paul and Three-Ring's eyes widened. They were captivated by the old man's comment that he had been in *the Little Big Horn Campaign.* J.P. and Three-Ring looked at each other in disbelief. Really, the Little Big Horn?

Jean-Paul was not sure he believed the old man. Regardless, he couldn't help but ask, "Did you say you were at the Little Big Horn with General Custer?'

"Yes sirree and it was Lieutenant Colonel Custer at the time. He had lost his Civil War temporary rank of Major General by then. I was nineteen years old in 1876. Had been in the army and the Seventh Cav for less than a year. It wasn't a good outfit. Discipline was harsh, very harsh. We had lots of foreigners from Ireland and Germany who could barely speak English. They joined only to get the pittance wage of thirteen dollars a month." The old man stopped talking, closed his eyes and acted like he was about to doze off.

As if startled, he opened his eyes, belched loudly, and continued, "Custer had about seven hundred men when we left Fort Lincoln that summer. When we arrived at the Little Big Horn River we found, I don't know, more teepees than we could count. I guess the Sioux were having some big pow-wow with several other tribes."

In a more serious tone he now said, "Custer's tactic was to divide the Seventh into three battalions. I was in A Troop of Major Reno's battalion. He had been a brevetted brigadier in the War of the Rebellion. With G and M troop we attacked what we thought was only a few hundred or so Indians. When we came within about five hundred yards of the Sioux camp, Reno had us dismount and form a skirmish line. Every fourth man held the other three trooper's horses. I understood the need for that, but it reduced our firepower by a quarter." He shook his head.

He continued, "When attacked in the past, the Indians would always run away. Not this time. No sirree, not this time. They not only didn't run, but they attacked us on our left flank with great strength. And our left was our weakest area. I couldn't believe it. There were so many Indians that they just seemed to rise up out of the ground. I didn't know how many of them we figured there was when we attacked, but it had to be many, many more than we thought. We all ran into the tree line to get some cover. It looked hopeless. Troopers were falling left and right. It was the only time in all my fightin' days that I thought I wuz a goner. It was very obvious to Major Reno and all the rest of us that we were outnumbered, outflanked, and in deep trouble. I was looking right at Major Reno when our Arikara Indian scout, Bloody Knife, was shot square in the head. His blood and brains splattered all over Reno's face. That shock did it for Reno. He gave us the order to remount and make for the nearby bluffs. Of course, the soldier who was holding my horse had been wounded and my horse was nowhere to be seen. But I had trained that horse to respond to my call. It never failed. What I did was pucker my lips together, moderately blow, and then sing '*Wee-ooo.*' I'm convinced it will work with all horses." The old soldier then gave a demonstration that immediately silenced everyone in the train car.

As if he had told the story a thousand times, he was now energized and with his breath as odious as ever, continued, "I mounted up and began riding to those bluffs behind us. It was my worst nightmare to be chased by screaming Sioux Indians. I still get nightmares about that to this day. There were soldiers on foot looking for their horses and the wounded were dropping all around me. Those on foot were pleading to be picked up. I saw my Captain, Captain Moylan, running toward the bluffs. I yelled at him and with one arm picked him up and rode as hard as I could to those bluffs. I have no idea where I got the strength to pick him up and carry him all that way. When we arrived at those exposed bluffs, many of the soldiers shot their horses in order to make a barricade. I was not going to do that to my horse. I just shooed *my Gabriel* away. That was my horse's name, *old Gabriel*. You know, like *Gabriel* the angel. Like me, he survived the fight. Yes, he did. On the bluffs we began digging rifle pits using our knives, eating forks, mess pans, and whatever else we could get our hands on. It would have been nice to have a shovel or two!"

Now the old sergeant just stared straight ahead with a most disturbing stare. After a minute or two he continued. "Our battalion lost a quarter of its men in that fight. We were fortunate we didn't lose more considering the helter-skelter nature of the retreat up to the bluffs. After a short time, Captain Benteen, who was in charge of one of the other two battalions, arrived from the south with companies D, H, and K. That was a godsend. Benteen was a good soldier. You know, he was a soldier from *the old school.* He had served in the Union army for four years in the War of the Rebellion. He finished that war as a colonel, and now the army had reduced him back to captain. Earlier in the battle he received an order from Custer to join him and bring a resupply of ammunition. I'm not exactly sure why he passed by us on the bluffs on his way to Custer. However, Major Reno, outranking him and probably scared, ordered him to stay and reinforce us. Good choice for us but not so much for Custer. I'm sure Benteen and his men are what saved us from being wiped out just like Custer was. Without Benteen's men I am sure we too would have been done for. I credit Major Reno for that. Of course, in all the army's inquiries after the battle, both Reno and Benteen got in a lot of trouble for that move: Reno for ordering Benteen to say with us and Benteen for ignoring Colonel Custer's written order and obeying Major Reno's verbal order."

"We had an officer, Captain Tom Weir I think his name was, who commanded company D in Benteen's battalion. He had been a major in the *big war*. He was an impulsive and impetuous sort of man who always seemed nervous and uneasy. Without orders he took his unit to support Custer. Without orders mind you. He got within a mile or so from Custer and got pinned down. Seeing what he was trying to do, Benteen took some soldiers and went to help him. A short time later Benteen's force also got pinned down. Unfortunately, the hill where Weir was located was completely in the open. There was no cover at all. It was an impossible defensive location. We were getting picked off left and right by the Sioux sharpshooters. As a result, we all fell back to our original position on the bluffs with its firing holes and the barricade of dead horses."

"It was eerie you know. All of the firing had stopped in the area where we knew Custer was. It actually never occurred to us that his force had been wiped out to the last man. That certainly never occurred to me for sure. Never. Although thinking about it later, what else could have happened to cause the firing to stop?"

The sergeant paused briefly and then slowly continued, "Back in our positions on the bluffs, the Indians kept pressure on us. Many of their sharpshooters had Winchester repeating rifles compared to our single shot carbines. They kept us pinned down. They also made several unsuccessful attacks. The Indians were constantly crawling around in the tall grass to get close to our position. Capitan Benteen finally got fed up with this, and with one of his companies counterattacked those crawling varmints. It shocked them considerably and quieted 'em down for quite a spell. They did, however, keep firing at us until it got dark at around nine. None of us got any sleep that night. The Indians were screaming and howling, the wounded were moaning, and the coyotes were shrilling. My goodness it was a god-awful combination of noises. I never spent a night like that before or since. It was hell on earth. The worst possible night a soldier could have, I guess. At least I hadn't been wounded and it wasn't rainin' or snowin'. Then on the next day, the 26th of June, it was again terrible hot. The Sioux Indian scouts saw that another army column under General Terry was coming in fast from the north. This caused them to withdraw to the south. That was the end of the greatest defeat the United States Army ever suffered at the hand of them Indians. Incredible. And I lived to be telling you about it here twenty-two years later. That's right. And it's all true so help me God. By God, it's all true."

The old soldier didn't wait for a response from Jean-Paul or Three-Ring. He continued and was now more charged up than ever. "From a personal point of view there is more to the story. The second day of the battle, June 26th, it was really hot. The wounded were in bad shape and couldn't even swallow for want of water. Major Reno asked for volunteers to go to the Little Bighorn River with canteens and get drinking water for the wounded. That would be a very dangerous mission since the Sioux sharpshooters had them repeating rifles and were excellent shots. Those getting water would be exposed to enemy fire for a sizeable period of time. I volunteered to go. Don't know why, but I did. Those sharpshooters shot at me a considerable amount but never successfully. The bullets cutting the air past my head sounded like bees. The troopers who got water all received a medal from the army. I am not sure I deserved a medal for getting water for the wounded but going to get water was the right thing to do. Of that, I am quite sure. I would volunteer to do it again today if I had too. My medal citation said that I *'brought water for the wounded under a most galling fire.'* Sure, galling fire. What I should have been cited for was saving my Captain during the pell-mell retreat to the bluffs. No one ever mentioned that. But Captain Moylan did say thank you for saving him so that was appreciation enough."

The old soldier paused with a reflective look. He seemed unable to stop talking. He started up again, "After General Terry arrived, we went to see what had happened to old Custer. The hill where Custer made his stand was indescribable. Hell could not look any worse than that hill. We found Custer's body. He had a bullet wound to the head and another just above the heart. He had not been mutilated like them savages had done to the others. I think either one of Custer's two wounds could have killed him. Captain Benteen said the same thing. By the size of the bullet holes, it looked like they were both from rifle fire."

"Now just think about Custer. He was offered two Gatling guns and several additional companies of soldiers from the Second Cavalry Regiment to accompany the Seventh on this mission. He rejected both. He said they would slow us down. Maybe that was so with those Gatling guns, but how would other horse-mounted cavalrymen slow us down? I think he didn't want troopers from the Second Cav because he didn't want to share any of the glory with them. How stupid was that? Really, how stupid? *Stupid always seems to cost."* Jean-Paul and Three-Ring now gave each other a stared look.

"Custer, of course, divided his force of seven hundred men into three battalions. His plan was to attack the Indians from three sides. If you think about it, that too was a foolish plan. Had he kept the Seventh intact rather than dividing it into three battalions, we would have won the battle. Just consider, when Benteen joined Major Reno's force, even with all the casualties Reno had just suffered, the Indians could not take us. And that was after they had destroyed Custer and their entire force came to attack our position. It was said that Custer finished last in his class at West Point. Well, that actually explains a lot. He was successful in the *War of the Rebellion* with one tactic—attack. Regardless of the size of the rebel force, he would always attack. With the surprise and shock effect of that tactic, he was extremely successful. That tactic didn't work as well with the Indians, particularly when our army was threatening their women and chill-ren. Considering all what I just said, there was a reason why Custer finished last in this West Point class, don't ya think?"

"I learned much of this from reading the newspapers later. When you're the lowest rank and in a fight, you just follow orders and keep your mouth shut. And of course, no one tells you nuthin'. What you do hear is rumors and gossip, most of which is not close to being true. Plus, you only see your small part of the battle and do not know what is happening on other parts of the battlefield or what the big brass is up to."

"News of the defeat arrived back East in the papers just as the nation was celebrating its 100th birthday, the 4th of July Centennial in 1876. It was reported that Custer and the entire Seventh Cavalry had been wiped out. That was nonsense because two thirds of Custer's Seventh survived. The talk at all the anniversary celebrations was Custer's defeat. That shocked people because they were used to the Army being victorious in its battles with the Indians. And Custer of course was a big Civil War hero. The army investigated the incident, but like in many things, it didn't do a very good job. The army was trying to protect its reputation, the reputation of the survivors, and especially of the officers involved, to include old *yellow hair Custer*."

Now becoming more reflective, the old soldier said with some emotion, "It's amazing how war affects people. Captain Weir left the army and died of depression within the year. He had served with Custer in the big war and was totally devoted to him. Major Reno turned to drink. He was later court martialed for peeping into the window of his commander's teenage daughter. Don't know exactly how that turned out, but he sure wasn't right after the battle. Benteen was promoted to major in the regulars. In 1887, he was suspended from the army for drunk and disorderly conduct at a post somewhere in Utah. I wasn't affected by the battle at all. I haven't had a drink of whiskey in years. That's right, in years." At that comment, J.P. again glanced at Three-Ring.

As he completed the story he had obviously told many times, he gave up another burp, a deep yawn, broke wind, pulled his slouch hat down over his eyes, folded his arms, and fell fast asleep, snoring almost immediately. He did not ask if Jean-Paul or Three-Ring had questions, but simply went to sleep. The two of them didn't know it at the time, but they had just experienced the oldest of military traditions. That was the tradition of old soldiers telling young soldiers war stories. There are no better storytellers thought Jean-Paul, remembering Mr. Sorensen, than old soldiers.

At this, the young woman with great agility immediately stood up, stepped onto the seat across from her, walked across it, and stepped down clumsily onto the car's center aisle. She looked directly at Jean-Paul and asked if she could sit next to him. Without saying anything, he stood up and let her pass. She sat down and without emotion said to the two of them, "There was not a word of truth to what that smelly old man just said. He is nothing more than a delusional, sad, old dinosaur. I wonder if he has ever even been in the army?"

These critical comments made Jean-Paul remember the

training received from his father and the Jesuit school in New Hope. He recalled being taught to never talk bad about anyone or hurt anyone with your words. He was to treat others, as he would want to be treated—with respect, courtesy, and dignity. He was always to assume the best about people rather than the worst. He was always to do what was right and also to help anyone who couldn't help themselves. Somehow those ideas seemed to apply here.

Without hesitation Jean-Paul responded to the woman's comments. "I think you are being a bit harsh on that old soldier. If you consider the details of his story, his emotions and passion, and even his uniform, I think it is apparent he *was* at the *Battle of the Little Bighorn.* I don't think it is fair to pass judgment on someone based on appearance or personal hygiene. If we judge at all it should be based on what's inside of a person—their character—and not their outward appearance."

Right then the soldier, still fast asleep, loudly and with some force *broke wind.*

The woman now seemingly upset at both the old soldier and Jean-Paul's defense of him, said with some vigor, "Did you hear that? Did you hear that? And look at him. Savage! Barbarian! Philistine! Cretan! He is worse than the natives he said he was fighting. His clothes are filthy. He smells like a goat—actually, like a dead goat. A live goat does not smell as bad as he does. And no gentleman would ever flatulate in public! I am quite sure he is also a hopeless drunk. I can smell him all the way over here! He even put his dirty hands on my new yellow Easter dress. How could you possibly stick up for someone like that? How?"

Jean-Paul knew the woman made a number of valid points. He paused for some seconds and then looking her directly in the eye said, "If he had actually been at the Little Bighorn and other battles with the natives like he said, and I think he was, he couldn't help but be affected by those experiences. We don't know what he saw and what he had to do. I've been told that war affects people in different ways. We shouldn't judge him because we don't know how exactly the wars in which he fought impacted him. To talk critically about him is really unfair—really unfair."

The old soldier, still fast asleep, was making some mumbling noises and his lips were moving as if talking to himself. Jean-Paul also noted that he was drooling out the left side of his mouth.

Turning again to the young woman, he noted she was staring angrily at the old soldier and shaking her head back and forth. At this point, Three-Ring had dozed off and had also begun to snore.

The woman looked at Jean-Paul, then at Three-Ring, and with obvious disgust said, *"Men."*

Jean-Paul realized that nothing he had said had impacted her. He now wondered if she had even listened to what he had said. She apparently didn't care to continue the conversation and had actually pressed herself to the wall of the passenger car. She now had a blank look as she stared at the bleak terrain of the Texas hill country. Jean-Paul reflected that someday she would make some man a very challenging wife. Poor beggar.

After a time, the train conductor came by and announced they would arrive in San Antonio in an hour. That woke the old soldier. He shakily stood up, took his carpetbag, and without fanfare walked out of the car in the same direction he had entered it.

Fifteen minutes before arriving at the train depot in San Antonio, there was a murmur among the passengers in the car. Jean-Paul looked down the aisle and could not believe what he saw. Here approached the old soldier who was completely transformed. He had washed, shaved, and combed his hair. He had changed into a clean army uniform complete with cavalry boots and a new slouch hat. On his uniform jacket, which still included the three inverted sergeant stripes, was a medal. The ribbon was red, white and blue. The medal was a star with an eagle connecting the ribbon with the star. Jean-Paul was speechless. His amazement was not only at the change in the sergeant's appearance, but also at seeing a *Medal of Honor* for the first time. All he could do was stare. He looked at Three-Ring who was now awake and was also staring. His eyes were bigger than Jean-Paul's. When their eyes met, neither said anything. Clearly Three-Ring was just as shocked as was J.P.

The sergeant sat down in his former seat. This time the smell was quite different, as he obviously had splashed himself with some cheap cologne. His entire demeanor was also different. He sat erect and presented a completely different aura.

He immediately noted that Jean-Paul was staring at him. Caught staring, Jean-Paul felt obligated to say something. He blurted, "When we arrive in San Antonio, my friend here and I are going to join the army's volunteer cavalry."

The old sergeant replied, "Very good. That's also where I am going. Don't know if they will take an old soldier like me but I have experience in training new horse cav recruits. And I know they will need that skill. I'm also hoping that some of the veterans will know of me and that should help my chances of joining up."

At this point the young woman for the first time looked over at the sergeant. The sergeant noting this touched the brim of his hat and said, "Good day miss." The lady frowned, made a grunting sound with her throat, and turned again to stare out the window. Both Jean-Paul and Three-Ring noted her behavior and smiled at one another.

The train stopped at the *San Antonio & Arkansas Pass* or

SAAP which was the city's main railroad depot. Jean-Paul noted that it was very plain station compared to the grand train depots he had previously seen on this trip. Its primary feature was a huge steeple on its frontage corner. That and a lunch counter were the only things that caught J.P.'s eye as he and the other the two aspiring cavalry volunteers walked through the station.

Exiting the station Jean-Paul saw a wagon with several uniformed soldiers. The old sergeant approached them and asked if they were part of the First Volunteer Cavalry. The sergeant in charge said they were and would give him a ride back to their camp after they picked up some crates of cargo.

While waiting for the soldiers to complete their errand the old sergeant turned to Jean-Paul and took hold of his forearm. Jean-Paul did not know what to make of this. The Sergeant without emotion said, "Thank you for supporting me against the comments from that unhappy young woman. I appreciated it. It was quite decent of you and for sure, you didn't need to do that. You don't know me and by my behavior, I wouldn't have stuck up for me. But you did and I appreciate that."

Jean-Paul was taken back. He had no idea the old soldier had been awake and listening to their entire conversation.

The old soldier saw Jean-Paul's surprise reaction. "You didn't think I was listening, did you? Well, I was and was quite impressed with what you said. I hope that someday I will be able to return the favor. There were times during my years in the army when I could have used some support from my comrades and leaders—but such support was not forthcoming. Cowards. But not even knowing me, you said some good things on my behalf. By the way, my name is Troxler, *Joshua Gideon Troxler.*" The old soldier then gave J.P.'s arm a squeeze and finally let go.

Obviously feeling compelled to continue, the old sergeant said with some emotion, "And besides, that woman simply confirmed what I believe and know about women. I was married once. Worst decision I ever made. She was a school marm. Nice looking woman who made a wonderful pot roast and apple cobbler. But that didn't make up for the fact that she was vain, deceitful, and an evil manipulator. She left me for a traveling snake oil salesman. After that marriage experience, I prefer to be around men. Men are simple, honest, and down to earth. They might smell bad, belch, and fart a lot, but they don't play the childish games like them females do."

Right then the woman who had just been the topic of conversation walked by them with a short, pale young man in an ill-fitting suit. The old sergeant again tipped his hat to the woman. She looked at the three of them and said curtly as she walked, "This is Clem, my fiancé. He is a gentleman."

Simultaneously the three volunteers burst out in laughter. The woman put her nose up and grasping Clem's arm tighter walked on without a further word. "Poor Clem. The poor unfortunate beggar" was all Jean-Paul could say. The other two had another laugh on that comment.

As they were standing there, Jean-Paul thought briefly about what the old soldier had said about women. He thought of his mother. She was nothing like the women the old sergeant had described, or like the Gibson Girl on the train to Chicago. Jean-Paul then remembered his grandmother Nana DeBert. According to what his father had said about her, she certainly manipulated her husband, Papa Gerard. But then he reflected, Papa loved her so much that he probably knew what she was doing and didn't care!

The old sergeant said, "Come, let's help these soldiers load them crates. The sooner they are loaded the sooner we will get to camp or Camp Wood—as it's now being called.

Once loaded, the wagon with its cargo and crew, which now included the three men from the arriving train, began to move slowly toward the army camp. The 85-degree San Antonio weather felt good on Jean-Paul's face. For sure this was not early May weather in New Hope. Jean-Paul's great adventure was about to begin in earnest.

## *Thought Questions for Chapter 5:*

1. Why did Jean-Paul defend the behavior of the old soldier Troxler? In a similar situation, would you have done so? Why or why not?

2. Why do you think Jean-Paul took an immediate liking to Three-Ring? What was it that attracted him to Jean-Paul?

3. What were your impressions and reactions to Sergeant Troxler's story about the Battle of the Little Big Horn? How would you evaluate Lt. Colonel Custer's actions just before and during the battle?

4. Why did Sergeant Troxler change his appearance and demeanor prior to arriving in San Antonio?

5. What was your biggest learning or take away from this chapter? What can you apply from the information in this chapter? What in it did you find the most interesting? Why?

# 6

## *Camp Wood, Texas*

As Jean-Paul was riding in the back of the wagon to Camp Wood, he was suddenly overcome with fear. He had to cup his hands together to keep from shaking. It had dawned on him that he was just minutes away from joining the United States Army. Until now that had been a distant reality. That reality was now.

Three-Ring looked at Jean-Paul and asked, "Are you all right? Is something wrong?"

Without looking at him J.P. responded with a weak, "Nothing's wrong. Everything's fine."

Jean-Paul thought, what's the matter with me? I have been thinking about an adventure like this for years. Now that the adventure is about to begin I'm all shook up? That's nonsense. He remembered what his father had said on that last night, "Don't forget what you learned here in New Hope." One of the truths constantly reinforced by both his father and the Jesuits priests, was to *trust and have faith in the Good Lord.* That settled it for him. He told himself, I will believe that and live like I believe it. The fear immediately left him. He remembered the old adage, *"Fear knocked on the door. Faith opened the door. Fear was gone."*

Arriving at the army camp, the wagon stopped at the entrance where three armed soldiers were on duty. The sergeant in charge of the wagon detail told Jean-Paul and Three-Ring to get off the wagon and report to the tent near the camp's entrance. Sergeant Troxler was told he could ride into the camp with the wagon.

Jumping off the wagon with his shoulder bag, Jean-Paul viewed the tent. There was a rough sign stuck in the ground at the entrance: *"New recruits report here. Veterans report to regimental HQ."* So, thought Jean-Paul, this is the place to make one's destiny.

There were groups of men dressed in rough civilian clothes standing on each side of the tent's entrance smoking and jesting. As Jean-Paul and Three-Ring drew near, a tall man in filthy clothes, with no front teeth, and chewing on a nasty cigar, said with a smirk to the two of them, "How can we help you boys?"

Jean-Paul replied, "We are here to volunteer for the cavalry."

After a short laugh the tall man said condescendingly, "Well boys, it seems you are just a little late. This here cavalry regiment is all fulled up with volunteers. They don't need nobody else. We all," pointing to the men standing there, "wuz just turned away. And as you can see, we are all full-grown men. And if they turned us away, they sure don't need any young boys or dwarfs." That last comment drew a big laugh from both groups. The man in the dirty clothes now moved to block the tent's entrance.

Three-Ring, after being called a dwarf, had his fists clenched. The thought crossed Jean-Paul's mind that yet again, here was going to be a nasty confrontation. First, it was at the train station in New York City, and now with this filthy fella. Goodness, he thought, why do I draw these kinds of derelicts into my life? With that thought he moved his hand from the top of his walking stick to where his entire hand now encircled the stick. Based on the distance between the two of them, placing a blow to the man's left rib cage would be the best tactic. He hoped that wouldn't be necessary. However, he now felt a swelling of anger in his chest from his old friend and nemesis—*the feeling*. He stared directly at the man and was totally oblivious to Three-Ring's presence. This silence and the stare seemed to last forever. Apparently, the stare and the determined look on J.P.'s face caused the man to move aside as if to let Jean-Paul pass.

Jean-Paul stepped forward toward the entrance. As he passed by, the man purposely bumped Jean-Paul with his shoulder. Without hesitation J.P. swung his walking stick and with as much force as he could muster hit the man squarely on the back of his knees. The man fell face forward on the ground. All the talking and laughter of those present stopped immediately.

The man now totally humiliated struggled to get up while making unintelligible threats. At this, Three-Ring came running by Jean-Paul and with a huge leap kicked the man square on his back with the bottoms of both of his shoes. With a loud groan the man fell forward in a lump onto the ground. Three-Ring then turned to J.P. and with a wide smile said, "Learned that in the circus." Then he looked at the fallen man and said, "Call me a dwarf again will you!"

As they were entering the tent, the man still on the ground yelled out, "I'll get you two for this. I'll get you." The others present were now laughing at the man on the ground as they all started to leave.

Inside the tent there were three soldiers all wearing the army's wool blue jacket tunic. One of those sitting was a sergeant and the other a corporal. Standing was a private with no rank stripes, probably a runner. All were sweating in the San Antonio heat in their heavy blue wool jacket.

The three eyed J.P. and Three-Ring with casual interest. The sergeant was the first to speak. "What can I do for you boys?"

Jean-Paul replied, "We are here to serve our country, join the First Volunteer Cavalry Regiment, and go to Cuba to fight the Spanish."

All three uniformed soldiers responded to Jean-Paul's comment with a belly laugh. The sergeant, with the delight of the uneducated, said, "*Sorry boys, you are a little late for that.* The First Volunteers are all full up. We have all the volunteers we need. Congress gave all volunteer units a limit on how many volunteers they could sign up. We here have met that limit, and yes, we even took a few more in case some don't pass the physical requirements. Colonel Wood, you know, Colonel Leonard Wood, our regimental commander, who earned the Medal of Honor in the Apache wars, told us no more volunteers under any circumstances. No more. But if you really want to join up you can go up north. We heard there are some Yankee states like Ohio, Michigan, and Massachusetts that are raising volunteer infantry units. Those infantry boys are the ones who like to walk everywhere." At that, the three had another robust laugh.

Jean-Paul again felt the tightening in his chest that always occurred when he felt mocked, taken advantage of, or made to look the fool. Without hesitation he reached into his shoulder bag and with great impatience and thrashing around among his belongings, searched for the cable from Colonel Roosevelt. When he found it, he immediately handed it to the sergeant. The sergeant put a set of reading glasses and with indifference read the telegram. He then handed it back to Jean-Paul and said, "Sorry, but Colonel Roosevelt hasn't arrived yet, and even if he was here, he couldn't help you because we are full up with volunteers. Full up. As I told you, Colonel Wood said no more volunteers. Now you two boys can go over to the train station and take a ride up to Ohio or Wisconsin and join up with one of those walking girlie outfits." This resulted in more laughter from the three. Jean-Paul looked at the them and thought how ignorant it was to be laughing at people who were experiencing disappointment or misfortune.

At that point Three-Ring blurted out, "This is not fair. We came a long way to join up and risk our lives on the battlefield and now you are telling us we can't join?"

The sergeant, now with anger and apparent impatience replied, "I said you can't join up here. For the third time, I am sure you could do so up north. That's right, up north where I think it is still snowing. Now please get out of my tent or I will call the provost and have him throw you out. That's all gentlemen. Now get out!" With this he gave a wave of his hand with his fore finger pointed at the tent's entrance.

Jean-Paul was a bit stunned by this turn of events. Being rejected by the army was something he had not anticipated or had even thought about. This was now a crisis. He then remembered what he was taught back at New Hope about dealing with an emergency: pray and get God involved. As he was saying a short prayer for assistance, he was oblivious to Three-Ring pulling on his sleeve. When finished he turned to the little man and asked, "What is it?"

Three-Ring said in a whisper, "Maybe we should just wait until Roosevelt arrives. We can go see him, and I am sure he will remember you. He will help us to join up. He is a fair man and will certainly honor his word in the telegram."

Before Jean-Paul could answer both the sergeant and

corporal stood up. Both of them as well as the private came to the position of attention *and saluted*. J.P. wasn't sure what to do until from behind him he heard someone say, *"At ease, carry on."*

Jean-Paul turned and saw Sergeant Troxler, the old Indian fighter from the train. He was impressed how tall the sergeant was and how martial he now appeared. He had a real soldierly presence, especially with the medal he was wearing.

Troxler said to Jean-Paul and Three-Ring, "There is a custom and courtesy in the Army that soldiers are to salute the Medal of Honor when it is worn by a recipient who earned it. It comes from an Army tradition of having those who have received the Medal taking part in military parades. They would stand with the commanding officer. When that officer would order *pass in review,* both he and the Medal of Honor recipient would return salutes from commanders of the units that passed by. And one more thing. You never call a Medal of Honor *recipient* a Medal of Honor *winner*. *Winner* is a word that is absolutely forbidden. Is always *recipient*. There is no contest for this medal. Those who have earned *The Medal* wear it for their comrades, especially the ones who were killed in action. Understand?"

Both nodded in the affirmative.

The Sergeant continued, "So the salute you saw was a courtesy to *The Medal* and not to me personally."

At this the sergeant who had been in charge in the tent and

was now shaken by the arrival of Sergeant Troxler, blurted out: "No Sergeant Troxler, we saluted you as well as the Medal. You are well known throughout the cavalry for the courage you consistently displayed in the Indian Campaigns. Yes sir, well known." The sergeant was so nervous that he was visibly shaking.

Troxler responded, "I was only doing my duty. Doing one's duty, serving, and obeying the orders of one's leaders are the highest responsibilities of any soldier. A famous general once said, *'Duty is the essence of manhood.'*"

With that Troxler walked up to the desk where the two greeters of new recruits had been sitting. He said calmly, "Sit down gentlemen." Both immediately did so.

"Now, I understand there is a problem here with my two boys signing up for the First U.S. Volunteer Cavalry? Is that right?"

Sergeant Troxler did not wait for an answer. He apparently had been outside the tent and had heard some things the reception sergeant had said. "I understand Congress gave a limit of how many volunteers could join this regiment. Well, as you yourself said sergeant, you have been signing up a few more volunteers in case some do not meet the physical standards. What we need in this regiment, in any regiment for that matter, are *fighters. Fighters.* These two young men are fighters but more important, they are smart fighters and not just bar room brawlers. They are the kind of men we need. Therefore, I think you need to sign them up. If you do, I will be personally grateful. That's right, personally grateful."

That seemed to be all the two soldiers needed to hear. The sergeant said to Troxler, "Sergeant Troxler, have no worries we will get them signed up right away. Our mistake. No worries. We'll take good care of them. That's right, good care of them. Now you two need to go into the next tent to sign some papers."

Before going to sign, Jean-Paul turned to Sergeant Troxler, extended his hand and said, "Thank you Sergeant. We both sincerely appreciate your help." Three-Ring nodded in agreement and grunted.

"Well, you boys have been good to me and I always take care of my friends. Now get yourself signed in and get settled. I'm sure I will see you a little later."

He then turned to the sergeant and corporal and again said, "Take good care of my boys. Take good care of them. I'll remember it if you do."

"Yes Sergeant, we will take care of them, of that you can be sure."

After Troxler left the tent, the sergeant said to the corporal, "That was *Wild Bill Troxler*. You know, *Wild Bill Troxler*. I was telling you about him a couple of days ago. He was one of the heroes that came out of the battle at the Little Bighorn and several other Indian war battles. He is a legend in the cavalry.

When they wanted to make him an officer, but he surprised everyone by getting out of the army. He is a real live hero, a living legend. There's been a dime novel written about him and his exploits. Word was he was in South Africa for a time fighting with the British in the first Boer War. This regiment is really lucky to have him."

Then the sergeant said, "Okay boys. Go through here to the next tent where they will...." Here he stopped and stared at the two of them. "You boys are old enough to join the army, aren't you?"

Jean-Paul's heart froze. The thought never crossed his mind that he wasn't old enough to join up. Without thinking he blurted out, "Well how old do you have to be to join the army?"

The sergeant, still glaring at the two of them said, "Eighteen."

Jean-Paul responded quickly, "Of course I am eighteen."

The sergeant looked at him closely, "Eighteen huh. You don't look eighteen to me. And looking at Three-Ring he asked, "And how about you? How old are you?"

"I am twenty-five years old."

"Really? You look like you're seventeen. Come to think about it, can either of you ride a horse since this is a cavalry regiment?"

Three-Ring replied quickly, "I can ride a horse at full gallop while doing a handstand on the saddle. And that my friend, is the gospel truth."

"Sure you can. That I would like to see."

"You will. I learned that and much more about riding horses when I was with the circus touring these here United States." That seemed to quiet the Sergeant, at least for the time being.

The sergeant then said, "In the next series of tents, you will have the medical folks look at you to see if you are physically fit. You will also sign your enlistment papers. Then you'll draw your supplies and equipment. Not sure when you will take your oath. Heard that Colonel Roosevelt wants to be part of that process. He is supposed to arrive either today or tomorrow. He motioned for Jean-Paul and Three-Ring to go out the back of the tent and into the next tent to officially join up. The great adventure was now really to begin in earnest.

With this Jean-Paul and Three-Ring made their way outside to the adjoining and much larger tent. In the Texas heat and with the high humidity, the smell of the tent canvas was nauseating. J.P. wondered where it had been stored and what it had been previously used for. There were a number of soldiers present, each sitting behind a small table with a chair to its front. The solders at the tables were asking the volunteers questions and writing the answers on army enlistment forms. Everyone in the tent was perspiring freely. Jean-Paul was next in line to be enlisted. Three-Ring was right behind him.

Within a few short minutes Jean-Paul was called to sit in

front of a very old corporal. With complete apathy and in the most mechanical way, the corporal, without looking at Jean-Paul, indifferently wrote down J.P.'s responses to his questions. The teenager thought this was very curious behavior. Here he was totally excited and looking forward to the adventure of a lifetime, while the soldier who was enlisting him, acted completely bored. He decided not to answer the question about his height and weight. The soldier asked it again without looking up. Jean-Paul felt *the feeling* swelling in his chest and again opted not to answer.

With frustration and impatience, the corporal finally looked at Jean-Paul.

"Don't you know your height or weight?"

"I know it."

"Well then, why don't you answer?"

"I just wanted you to look up and see that I am a real person."

"You see that I'm a corporal, don't you?" as he pointed to the stripes on his sleeve.

"You see that I am a real human being, don't you?" as Jean-Paul pointed to his own chest. With furrowed eyebrows the corporal now glared at J.P., not being quite sure what to make of him. Jean-Paul quietly stated, "Six-foot, one inch, or thereabouts. One hundred seventy pounds." For a second the corporal continued to stare at him. Then with the same early indifference, he wrote down the information and continued the questioning. When he finished asking the standard list of required information, he turned the paper to Jean-Paul and said, "Check the information to see it's correct and sign on the bottom of the second page."

Jean-Paul checked it and signed.

"Okay, Dee—bert, go into the next tent and the medical folks will check you to determine if you're fit to join the army. If you aren't, then what you just signed means nothing." The corporal said that with a tone that seemed to hope he didn't pass his physical exam.

"Against his better judgment Jean-Paul asked, "How long have you been in the army?"

Without expression the corporal replied, "Which time?"

"You have been in the army more than once?"

"Yep, in fact three times. The first time I joined the cavalry I was put into the Seventh Cavalry. That was poor old Custer's former outfit. Joined up because I couldn't find steady work and also the law was after me for something I didn't do."

Jean-Paul thought, "Right, for something you didn't do...."

The corporal stopped speaking but then as if he couldn't help himself continued, "In the winter of 1890, just a couple of months before my enlistment was up, we were given a mission in South Dakota to bring some renegade Lakota's back to the *Pine Ridge Reservation*. We had them rounded up but when we tried to take their weapons, they fired on us. What happened then caused me to get out of the army and still gives me the nightmares. I try not to think about it anymore." He looked down as if in troubled thought.

He remained silent for a very short time and then started up again, "Stayed out for a couple of years. I was doing meaningless work, so I joined up again in 1894. Got out last year and now joined up again to fight the Spaniards. So, there you have it—three times in the army. Any more dumb questions?"

"No, no more questions."

"That's surprising."

Bending forward and shaking his forefinger at Jean-Paul he continued, "When you are in the army for more than a day, you will understand what a corporal is and you will be more respectful when you are asked or answer questions, of this I will assure you." The corporal again glared sternly at Jean-Paul.

"Thank you for that advice. I meant no disrespect."

"Right. Right. Neither did I. Now get moving. Take these two forms with you. Give the top one to the doctor who examines you and the other one to the supply sergeant."

Three-Ring was standing by the exit of the tent. He asked, "What took you so long? Is that corporal your new and latest best friend? You seem to have a knack for making friends. And here I thought I was your newest best friend," he said with a big grin.

"You are my newest best friend, but you weren't at the *Battle of Wounded Knee* like the corporal."

Three-Ring stopped and quietly but with a higher pitched voice than usual said, "That corporal was at *the Battle of Wounded Knee?*"

"That's what he said. Said the experience still gives him nightmares."

"It should give him nightmares because it's also called *the Wounded Knee Massacre.*"

"*Wounded Knee Massacre?* Why a massacre?"

"Because there were between two to three hundred Lakota Sioux killed by the Army. The majority of them were unarmed old men, women, and children. There were about thirty or so soldiers killed. According to the Lakotas, friendly fire from other soldiers killed those thirty. Most of the soldiers were fresh recruits who were scared, out of control, and firing wildly. In their inexperience and panic these novices simply opened fire to include those who were manning the rapid-fire Hotchkiss guns. That information was in a newspaper article written by a reporter who interviewed the Lakotas after the fight. It turned into a big scandal. Of course, what the Indians said contradicted the Army's official report. The Army denied the allegations, but one thing is certain, a lot of Lakotas who were not warriors died in that fight. Another bizarre angle of the story is that at least twenty soldiers received the Medal of Honor for that action. Can you imagine? Twenty! That's a huge number for a one-hour battle. Frankly, I think the Lakota story as reported by that newspaper writer makes more sense than the Army's story."

Jean-Paul was taken back by Three-Ring's tale. He then took Three-Ring by the arm, leaned over a bit and said quietly, "Whether that story is true or not, I would not repeat it to anyone in this cavalry regiment. There is no telling who besides the corporal was involved in that battle."

"Good idea. That's actually a really good idea."

The first sight Jean-Paul saw upon entering the medical tent was a short corporal with his hands on his hips and an unhappy look on his face. Jean-Paul immediately thought, *"I don't like corporals."*

The corporal began yelling at a volume that was much louder than was necessary considering the size of the tent. "You two new recruits, take off all your civilian clothes with the exception of your skivvies and stack them neatly so you can take them with you into the next tent. Now get with it. Do it now. The doctors are waiting for you. Hurry up! Now move it. And I said now!"

As they were getting undressed Jean-Paul whispered to Three-Ring, "Why do short people have to act so tough? Is it because they are trying to make up for being short?"

Three-Ring looked at Jean-Paul with wide eyes and did not answer. He made a slight upward motion with his head as if to signal Jean-Paul about something behind him.

Jean-Paul thought, "I'll bet that little corporal is standing right behind me." He turned around and sure enough the little man was standing less than four feet away.

"What did you just say to your short friend?"

I said, "I am tall, but I admire shorter soldiers because in battle they are less of a target and usually fight like tigers. Consider Emperor Napoleon for example. He was short in stature but was huge in courage and intelligence. That's what I said to my friend."

"Right, that's what I thought. What's your name soldier?"

"My name is Jean-Paul DeBert from New Hope, New York. My surname is pronounced *duh-bear*."

"Huh, New York, and a Yankee no less. My daddy told me all about your kind. Did any of your people invade my homeland?' He paused briefly and then shouted, "Well, did they boy?"

Jean-Paul who at this time was undressed and standing in his skivvies replied, "I don't know what you are talking about— my people invaded what homeland? What is that supposed to even mean?"

"Are you stupid or something? I mean did your family members in the Yankee Army invade the Confederate States of

America? It was the Yankee Army that unnecessarily and with great malice ravaged my homeland you dimwit."

Jean-Paul replied vigorously, "No, I am not stupid nor a dimwit. The way I heard it, the Confederate states you just mentioned illegally seceded from the union, started the war by firing on Fort Sumter, and twice invaded the North under the command of General Robert E. Lee. Thus, they deserved the thrashing they got. That's the way I heard it."

Three-Ring who was now standing behind the little corporal was signaling Jean-Paul to shut up.

Just at that time an orderly in a white medical jacket pulled back the curtain to the examination area and said, "Corporal Shauermann, we're ready for the next batch of recruits."

The little corporal shook his head. "You are one lucky son-of –a—.... But make no mistake about it—I'll be keeping my eye on you. Of that, you can be certain."

Jean-Paul took his clothes, shoulder bag, and walking stick and went through the curtain into the next room of the tent. Three-Ring followed him.

Three-Ring said with a serious tone, "My goodness, you are making friends everywhere. Didn't those New York Jesuits teach you any manners—or anything about loving your neighbor?"

That comment got to Jean-Paul. He then reflected for a second. He probably had had more conflict since he had left New Hope than in the eighteen years he had lived there. Are all these people related to Reverend Bradley or the Beckenbauers he wondered? His father would not be pleased if he told him about all the negative encounters he had been having. At least he didn't say to Corporal Shauermann what he was thinking, *"That another word for Yankee is winner."*

"Over here. You," said the orderly pointing to Jean-Paul, "over here with Doctor Brochette. Put your personal things down and report to the doctor. Be sure to give him that top form."

Jean-Paul did as he was told. The doctor who had been sitting down writing something now stood up. He walked over to Jean-Paul, took the form from he was carrying and asked, "Where are from young man?"

"New Hope, New York, sir."

"Is it cold up there? Lots of snow in winter?"

"Generally that's the case, but one gets used to it. It makes the spring all the more welcome."

The doctor put his stethoscope on J.P.'s heart.

"Strong heart. Sounds healthy."

The doctor visually examined J.P.'s body. "Got any scars?"

"There is a one on my outer left thigh. It got a deep scrape once when I fell while rock climbing." The doctor nodded and made a note.

The doctor looked at his left leg and bent down and touched two bright pinhole sized scars on his right leg just above Jean-Paul's ankle. "What are these from?" he asked.

"Oh, those are from a snakebite."

"A snakebite? What kind of snake."

"We think it was a timber rattler."

"A rattlesnake? How old were you when that happened?"

"I was about five years old."

"You were very lucky. At that age the amount of poison from a rattler of any size could have killed you."

"That's what the Chacopac medicine doctor said. I do remember him saying that."

"Chacopac? As in the Chacopac Indian tribe?"

"That's correct. My family lives on the border of the Chac tribal lands. My dad teaches at the Jesuit school there."

"Really. And what did they do to treat the snakebite?"

"The tribe's medicine doctor fixed up an ointment made out of a variety of herbs, spices, and greens. He wrapped it tightly over the bite and also did some sort of a native chant over it. Then too, the Jesuits priests came and laid hands on me and prayed. Within forty-eight hours I was running around barefoot and playing outside. I didn't even know I had had a bite. It hasn't changed in appearance since that day."

"That's an incredible story. Do you have any after effects from that bite, like a limp, loss of strength, any numbness, anything at all? "

"Nope, nothing at all."

"You were a lucky young man. Normally there is some permanent damage from a rattlesnake bite."

"I think the proper word is blessed and not lucky. The entire Chac tribe was praying for me. How could I not be completely healed?"

"Completely healed? You're saying you think it was *a divine healing?*"

"That's right, *a divine healing.* Some call that *spontaneous remission.* What else could it have been?"

"I know that kind of thing is possible, but I don't hear of it very often nor have I personally experienced it."

Jean-Paul responded, "I am sure at some point in your medical career you will experience it. It's just a matter of time."

The doctor gave Jean-Paul a disbelieving look and went back to his table. He took a pen and asked him if he had had any of a number of diseases listed on the form. Jean-Paul assured him he had not. He laughed out loud when the doctor asked him if he ever had syphilis or gonorrhea. The doctor finished the form and said, "You are done here. Get dressed and go through that exit to the supply tent. There you will draw your equipment.

After that you will report to your unit, which according to the paper is Troop A. Good luck and stay safe."

They had no sooner entered the regimental supply tent than there was a great commotion outside. There was shouting, cheering, and clapping. Everyone in the tent moved outside to see what the noise was all about.

It was quite a sight. Walking down the roadway in front of the tent was none other than Lieutenant Colonel Theodore Roosevelt himself. T.R.'s enlisted batman followed him with some other soldiers who were carrying the Colonel's personal trunks. Roosevelt looked resplendent in his newly tailored khaki uniform. Periodically he would briefly stop and shake hands with a soldier or two whom he recognized. Those stops were much to the chagrin of the soldiers carrying his personal trunks since they had to also stop and wait until Colonel Roosevelt was again ready to proceed.

He was alternately saluting and waving as if on political campaign. His grin was as wide as it could possibly be. He was clearly reveling in this warm and boisterous welcome.

When Colonel Roosevelt saw Jean-Paul, he stopped dead in his tracks and stared. He clearly recognized Jean-Paul but was obviously trying to figure out when and how he knew him. Suddenly Roosevelt burst forth and again with a huge grin grabbed J.P. by both shoulders, shook him mercilessly, and boomed out, "Jean-Paul DeBert! Jean-Paul DeBert! Our young hero in New York City! How are you? How are you? Glad to see you got my telegram, by Godfrey! Glad you're here young man. Bully! Your courage will set an excellent example for these other men to follow. Glad you are here Jean-Paul." With that he gave him a couple of more shakes, then let go, and proceeded on.

Three-Ring had observed the entire incident. He said, "My goodness amigo, apparently you know the Colonel quite well. I am really impressed," adding a mock salute to his comment. "Yet another new best friend!"

"Don't be impressed. But you know, if I hadn't met him in New York City, I wouldn't be standing here right now." Jean-Paul gave Three-Ring a condensed version of the New York street incident as they walked back into the supply tent.

When he finished, Three-Ring grabbed him by both shoulders and said, "By Godfrey, glad you are here young man, by Godfrey. Glad you are here! Bully! Bully!" He shook J.P. unmercifully as he spoke. Everyone who had seen both incidents laughed with great delight at Three-Ring's antics.

Jean-Paul went back in line to draw his military equipment. The soldiers passing out the equipment were doing it mindlessly and in slow motion. He thought to himself, there is a reason why these specific individuals are performing this necessary but very tedious task. He remembered what he was taught by both his father and the Jesuits: *everything you do should be done with all of your might and to the best of your ability—as if you are working for the Good Lord Himself!* One should never do work halfway or at half speed. Clearly, these supply clerks did not have the same training or point of view.

As he went down the line, the first supply clerk issued him a heavy wool blanket with a protective rubber cover, both of which were to be rolled over one's shoulder when marching. Then there was a half of a pup tent, a haversack with three days of hardtack, a tin cup that was to be attached to the haversack, a canteen, a mess kit, eating utensils, a cartridge belt, a small axe, and a pick and shovel. Jean-Paul looked closely at the shovel. He thought to himself, "I'll bet these are now being issued because of the Seventh Cav's experience at the Little Big Horn.

The uniform issue followed. As items were given to them, the issuing clerks, without enthusiasm, announced the nomenclature of the item. There was the M1898 campaign or slouch hat, two M1898 uniforms with wool blue shirts, two M1884 fatigue uniforms of brown duck material that were to be worn while performing fatigue duties, leggings, campaign shoes, *blue polka dotted neck handkerchief,* pajamas, and underclothing. Jean-Paul reflected that wearing these uniform parts would make him look just like *a wild-west cowboy.*

The supply clerk issuing clothing asked Jean-Paul what size shirt, pants, and shoes he wore. After he was handed these items, he checked the sizes on all of the items. The shirt was size medium, but he usually wore a large. "Excuse me, but this shirt will be too small for me. I'll be needing a larger size."

With obvious impatience, the soldier replied, "Too bad. We don't have many large size shirts left, and in any event, the one's we do have are being saved for the officers, sergeants, and any prior service enlistees."

Jean-Paul looked at this clerk again sensing *the feeling* in his chest. The clerk was defiantly staring back at him. The teenager realized he had two choices. He could say nothing, take the smaller shirts, and move on, or he could press the issue. He reflected that he already had run-ins with two other soldiers and a civilian during this induction process. He noted that Three-Ring was also staring at him in anticipation of what he might do.

Jean-Paul intuitively sensed that he should forget it and move along. He said, "Never mind, these will do fine."

No sooner did he finish that sentence than another volunteer walked up to the counter and laid down two blue uniform shirts. These are too big for me. They are large, and I take a medium. What are the chances of exchanging them?"

In one motion, Jean-Paul picked up the two large shirts and handed the two medium sized shirts to the soldier. "Here these are medium and too small for me; I need a large so this will be a good trade." The soldier looked at the size, mumbled a thank you, and moved out smartly. All this happened in a matter of seconds, so the slow-motion supply clerk was not able to get involved. He was still trying to figure out how to respond as J.P. moved to the next table.

Arriving at the next station, and while they were waiting, Jean-Paul felt the material of the shirts. He turned to Three-Ring and said, "We are going to Cuba where the tropical temperature in May will be in the mid 80's with high humidity. And here the army is giving us one hundred percent wool shirts. That doesn't make any sense."

The soldier waiting in front of him was a grizzled prior service veteran who laughed out loud at Jean-Paul's comment. "That doesn't make any sense. Really? Is that what you said? Wait till you are in the army for a time and getting a wool shirt for the tropics will be the least of the things that don't make any sense. Of that you can be sure." He turned away from J.P. and continued laughing while also shaking his head.

Three-Ring said with some astonishment, "I'm still thinking about the shirts you were issued that were too small. You were going to live with it and then, through nothing less than a miracle, that other soldier showed up with two large shirts. That was incredibly good luck."

"Nah, it wasn't good fortune. You have got to have faith Three-Ring. You have got to have faith and expect good things to happen. You must always be *optimistic* and anticipate the positive. That's called *serendipity*. It seems to me that in life *you almost always seem to get what you think you will get.* If you expect bad things, then you will get them. If you expect good things, well you know.... Life has a way of doing that. You just have to believe."

Jean-Paul's comments caught Three-Ring off guard. "I'll have to think about that one. I'm not sure what you said is true. Where did you learn that anyway? You are not old enough to have that kind of life experience!"

"I learned it mostly from my father. But that said—my limited experience on this earth has convinced me it's true. So far it has been that way. So far."

Three-Ring still unsure—shrugged an okay.

### *Thought Questions for Chapter 6:*

1. In this chapter, Jean-Paul used the term *spontaneous remission* and later the word *serendipity*. What do each of those words mean and is there any connection between the two?

2. The U.S. Army and the American Indians fought each other in the Battle of Pine Ridge. Each had a completely different version of what happened at that battle. Considering what they both said, *what do you think really happened there?* Why?

3. There is an old proverb that says, "It's not what you know, but who you know." When Jean-Paul and Three-Ring arrived at the First Volunteer Cavalry's enlistment

tent, they were told there were no more openings. What changed and why that they were allowed to enlist? What are the lessons that can be learned from that event?

4. Why did Jean-Paul experience so much conflict in this chapter? Was it because of a series of unusual circumstances or was he partially responsible for those encounters?

5. What was your biggest learning or take away from this chapter? What can you apply from the information in this chapter? What in it did you find the most interesting? Why?

# 7

## *Colonel Teddy and the Rough Riders*

Ignoring Three-Ring, Jean-Paul now took note of what he was to receive at the next station. Here the reality of being in the Army really hit him. First, he was issued a M1872 Colt single action Army revolver with a holster. It had the refurbished 5.6-inch barrel that the soldiers called the artillery model. Several rounds of ammunition were supplied with the revolver. J.P. felt the revolver in his hand. It actually felt good and fit his hand perfectly. It was a much better fit than the small French pistol his dad had given him. His thoughts now turned negative. This is a device that is used to kill others. It is a machine made to destroy other human beings made in the image of God. That was not a pleasant thought. Then again, it could also be used to save lives, relieve the oppressed, and promote peace and justice. He finished staring at the empty revolver and put it in its holster and moved on to the next station.

The soldier who was issuing the rifles was much more energetic than his predecessors. He took and rifle and with enthusiasm gave Jean-Paul and Three-Ring what amounted to a short class on the weapon. Holding the rifle gingerly he began, "Here is the Norwegian designed regular army cavalry carbine: the 1898 *Krag-Jorgensen* 30-.40 repeating bolt action rifle. It is affectionately known as *The Krag*. It's known for its smooth operation and the fact that it is the *smokeless model*. It is the U.S. Army's first smokeless rifle. It replaces the army's *Trapdoor Springfield rifle* that uses black powder cartridges. The Springfield was and still is unpopular with the soldiers because the black smoke from its discharge gives the firer's position away to enemy snipers, artillery, and infantry. Thanks to Colonel Wood's efforts, the First Volunteer Cavalry Regiment is getting the *Krag*. All the other volunteer units are still being issued the Springfield. Poor beggars. It will get a lot of them killed. The Krag is loaded from the right side through a hinged loading gate. The soldier demonstrated. It can fire five rounds without reloading. It has a blade-type front sight and this canvas breech cover to protect it during foul weather. You will be issued one hundred rounds of ammunition with the *Krag*. Got any questions?"

"No questions." Three-Ring also shook his head indicating he was good.

Jean-Paul walked out of the supply tent and looked for a place to lay this mountain of equipment on the ground so he could organize it for the trek to Company A. He placed it down gently on the sandy ground ensuring the rubber blanket was on the bottom. He took off his shoulder bag and laid it on the ground also. He leaned his carbine against the pile. No sooner had he done this he heard someone yelling, "Hey there new recruit, you never put your weapon on the ground. You always keep it as clean as possible and you do that by keeping it off the ground. In combat your rifle is your life, your best friend, and your lover. It will keep you alive. You must never let it out of your sight. You eat with it, sleep with it, and go the latrine with it. It has to become part of you just like an arm or your middle leg. You should keep it cleaner than you keep yourself. Got that, cleaner than you keep yourself. Remember, it is your life. Do you understand that soldier? Well do you?"

"Yes sir. I understand."

"Don't call me sir. I am not a sir, I am a sergeant and I work for a living."

"Yes sergeant. Thank you, sergeant."

"What unit are you two greenhorns assigned?"

"Troop A sergeant."

"A Troop? Really? I thought A Troop was only for those Arizona cowboys that Bucky O'Neil brought with him. Huh! You boys must be connected. Must be some of Teddy's Harvard boys, right?"

"No Sergeant, not Harvard, but from the East. New York to be exact." Jean-Paul immediately stopped talking as he remembered the tirade he triggered from the Southern born corporal.

"I'm originally from California," added Three-Ring.

"New York and California. Well, we'll see how Cuba and bullets whistling by your head will agree with you. Gather up your gear and follow me since I'm also going to Troop A."

Carrying all that military gear in the heat and for all that distance brought both Jean-Paul and Three-Ring to the point of exhaustion. Sweat was pouring down both of them when the sergeant stopped and said, "Okay, here we are. Let me get the First Sergeant and we'll see where you two geniuses will be put up." The two of them gently laid their equipment on the ground, making sure their rifle rested on the top of the pile and did not touch the ground.

Suddenly they heard a familiar voice. "Here are my two new soldiers ready to make their country proud." It was Sergeant Troxler who was now wearing the three stripes and a diamond of a first sergeant. Absent from his uniform was his Medal of Honor.

Jean-Paul looked at him and then his new rank and said, "Golly, First Sergeant that was a quick promotion. But I am sure it is very well deserved."

"Welcome boys! Welcome to Troop A, which is and will continue to be the best unit in the regiment. I know you boys have the character to be outstanding cavalry troopers. Let me take you over to where you two can *set up* your tent. Get into those uniforms because just before chow Colonel Roosevelt is going to speak to the regiment. We will then we will be taking our oath to support the Constitution of these here United States."

First Sergeant Troxler continued to share as they walked. J.P. and Three-Ring were again sweating in sheets. Troxler said, "Troop A is made up mostly of cowboys, lawmen, miners, and ruffians from Arizona. Our troop commander is none other than the very famous *Captain Bucky O'Neill*. I met Captain O'Neill back in 1885 when I was traveling through the Arizona Territory. Their territorial militia, or home guard as some calls it, had just been established. Bucky, I mean Captain O'Neill, was their commander. The unit was also known as the *1st Arizona Infantry* or the *Prescott Grays* for short. We had snappy gray uniforms with a large *PG* on our caps. We looked like good old confederate boys in those gray uniforms. As I said, Bucky was our commander. Got to know him and his wife Pauline very, very well. There was lots of mutual respect between Bucky and myself—lots of respect. He was the bravest man I ever met. He had no fear. None whatsoever. He was totally fearless. When I heard he was coming here, I knew I had to come and join up with him. Seems he heard I was coming and had this first sergeant jacket waiting for me. What do you think?" as he lifted his right arm and showed the two of them his first sergeant stripes with the diamond in its center.

"Looks very good," Jean-Paul exclaimed. Three-Ring nodded in agreement.

"Captain O'Neill is what a man should be. Fearless, focused, no nonsense, good family man, and a man of honor and integrity. He has it all and has done it all. He's been a county sheriff, a town mayor, a successful miner, a newspaper editor, a short story writer, and the captain of militia. He was also the best shot in the entire Arizona Territory. He was best friends with the Earp brothers: *Virgil, Morgan, and of course Wyatt*. Everybody down there is still talking about how in March of '89, Bucky and his posse tracked down and captured the four men who robbed the Atlantic and Pacific Railroad train in Diablo Canyon. After a friendly firefight," here Troxler paused and smiled at the notion of a friendly firefight, "the posse captured all four men with no casualties on their part except for Bucky's horse, which unfortunately had been shot dead."

First Sergeant Troxler continued, "His friends call him Bucky. That's because in card games of chance like *faro,* he always plays contrary to the odds. I am sure you know that in card playing parlance, that tactic is referred to as *bucking the tiger.* Hence, he was given the nickname *Bucky.* By the way, if I were you, I would never call the Captain Bucky. You will refer to him as either *sir* or *Captain O'Neil.* Never address him as Bucky, or only by his rank, or only by his last name. To do any of *those last three things* is considered disrespectful in the army and is not in keeping with proper military courtesy. You boys got that?"

Both Jean-Paul and Three-Ring answered vigorously, "Yes First Sergeant!"

"Good. Now get your tent set up and get into your uniforms. Colonel Roosevelt is going to address the entire regiment at four. Then as a regiment, we are going to take our enlistment oath. Since most of our boys have never served under the colors before, we are forming up with rifles on the field behind us at 2:30 to do some practice close order drill. Now get with it gentlemen." First Sergeant Troxler turned to walk away.

Jean-Paul, against his better judgment, said, "Excuse me First Sergeant Troxler, but I have a question."

Troxler stopped and turned, "What's your question? And make it quick, I have lots to do before 2:30."

"Back on the train when we first met, you were unshaven and unwashed, your clothes had apparently not been cleaned for some time, and you smelled of spirits." Upon hearing Jean-Paul's comment Three-Ring's eyes became as big as saucers. He slowly shook his head as if to say, *"Will this boy Jean-Paul never learn?"*

First Sergeant Troxler frowned, shook his head slightly, and took a couple of steps closer to Jean-Paul and asked, "So what? What about it?"

Jean-Paul, now even less sure of himself than before and almost stuttering continued, "Well..., well..., you left your seat, got cleaned up, changed your uniform and came back to your seat a different man. Like now, you are nothing like the first time we saw you on the train. So, what happened? How come the almost total transformation?" Three-Ring's eyes got even bigger still in anticipation of something really bad occurring. In fact, he took a few steps back from the other two in anticipation.

Troxler stared at Jean-Paul for what seemed like an eternity. He then took a deep breath, put his hands on his hips, and stared at the ground. He looked up and replied, "Okay, Private DeBert, okay, since you asked here it is." (This time he had pronounced DeBert as *dee-bert* and not *duh-bear*.) "And I am expecting you not to repeat this. My daddy was the town drunk. I learned the bottle from him at a very young age. That habit only became worse after the Little Bighorn. I loved the Army and was a natural fit. But my affection for the bottle was stronger and got me in lots of trouble. That's why I left the army after seven years. I wondered around some, continued hitting the jug, and getting in constant trouble. One morning I woke up in a pigsty, for true, a pigsty. Didn't even know how I got there, what day it was, what time it was, or where I was. That was it. I vowed to clean myself up. I got religion and with that I changed. You can ask Captain McNeill about it. He will tell you. In Arizona he saw the *new Troxler*. But I also learned that if people think you are a sorry drunk, they would stay away from you, which I liked. Also, they would say what was really on their mind because they believed you are too liquored up to understand what they were saying. A good example of that was on the train with that little prissy in the yellow dress. Now I admit that when I'm bored, I still have a stiff drink or two, kind of like General Grant. He too would hit the bottle when bored. But like our former president, when I have something worthwhile to do, I stay quite sober. So that's the story Dee-Bert. That's the story. Does that satisfy your curiosity?"

"Yes, it does First Sergeant. Thanks for taking the time to answer. Three-Ring now began to breathe easier and took a step closer to them.

"One other thing Dee-Bert, the only reason I answered your really inappropriate and ill-timed question was because you stuck up for me with Miss Prissy. Seldom, if ever, has anyone done that for me. I appreciated it on the train and still do. That, by the way, is why you and your short pal here are in A Troop. I asked for both of you by name to be assigned to my unit. I can tell from by watching you, you both have the potential to make outstanding soldiers. I'm committing myself to bring out the best side of you, that being the martial side. Now get to work and get your sorry selves ready for our 2:30 formation."

"Yes, First Sergeant Troxler, we'll get right on it."

For the first time Jean-Paul noted that all these Arizona men who were tented around him and Three-Ring were staring at the two of them as the First Sergeant walked away. Great, thought J.P. He was sure they all thought the First Sergeant was chewing on them for something they had done wrong. He looked around again. His fellow troopers in Troop A looked hard, mean, and tough. At that moment, he was glad he was not a Spanish soldier posted in Cuba.

As Three-Ring was sorting through his kit to find his half of the pup tent, he said under his breath, "You know Dee-Bert, you really need to learn to keep your mouth shut. At some point that tongue of yours is going to get you into real trouble in this man's Army."

"It's interesting you should say that. My father gave me the same advice before I left home."

"Your father is a wise man—a truly wise man."

With their pup tent erected and now in complete uniform, Jean-Paul turned to Three-Ring and asked, "How do I look?"

"You look like a real soldier—a real soldier. How does it feel?"

"It feels good, almost natural as if it was made for me."

Three-Ring nodded, "It looks that way. I think you may have a future in that uniform."

Jean-Paul nodded. He hoped the little guy was right.

Three-Ring asked, "Okay, how do I look? Let's hear it. How do I look in this army get up?"

Both Three-Ring's shirt and pants were too large for him, he was about the same height as his rifle, and his hat was a bit too small for his head. But he had asked Jean-Paul how he looked. Now J.P. had a choice. He could be honest and tell the truth or he could dishonest and tell the little soldier that he was not looking very military in that uniform.

"You look like a real soldier. That uniform is a bit large but it's quite clear a soldier to be reckoned with is wearing it. How does it feel on you?

"I feel like I am wearing a burlap bag. It feels way too large, the wool shirt is hot and itchy, my shoes are tight, and my hat feels like it would blow away with the first breeze. This is not like my tight-fitting circus outfits for sure. Nope, not like them at all."

\*　　　　　\*　　　　　\*　　　　　\*　　　　　\*

At 2:30 PM, Jean-Paul, Three-Ring, and the rest of the enlisted men of Troop A got to meet yet another veteran, a Sergeant Truscott P. Graham, Jr. Graham was a veteran of the Sixth Cavalry and the Apache War of 1885-86. He was tall and thin with weather-beaten tan skin. He had a huge scar straight across his right cheek, which was apparently received in a hand-to-hand melee with one of Geronimo's warriors. His job was to teach the new volunteers of the First Volunteer Cavalry how to drill, march, and form up. It seemed that between 2:30 and four o'clock, he was constantly screaming, yelling, and demonstrating. Jean-Paul and Three-Ring didn't have a problem learning or remembering. However, for several of the bull legged cowboys from Arizona, it was a different story. There was a short broncobuster named McDougal. He apparently had never walked a hundred yards if there was any possibility to make that trip on horseback. He seemed not to know his left from his right and found it next to impossible to keep in step. He received a great deal of personal attention from Sergeant Graham. Once formed up, the only three things the troops of the regiment needed to do at 4 PM with their weapons was to come to the position of attention, stand at-ease, and salute. In ninety minutes, Graham, the Apache war veteran, was generally successful in teaching Troop A's troopers those three tasks—generally....

Troop A formed up on the right of the line with all the other troops of the regiment to their left. After it had formed up, First Sergeant Troxler turned it over to its commander, Captain O'Neill. Captain Bucky O'Neill was of medium height, thin boned, and of slight build. He stood ramrod straight with short, well-groomed hair, a neatly trimmed moustache and penetrating eyes. His eyes communicated he was focused, a quick study, and a man to be reckoned with.

Jean-Paul's attention now passed from Captain O'Neill to Lieutenant Colonel Roosevelt. Roosevelt was again looking resplendent standing before the formation. He looked taller and bigger than he remembered. His expertly tailored Brooks Brothers army uniform did not adequately hide his good-sized paunch. Regardless, everyone in the formation knew his reputation as a man of courage, energy, and high intellect. Even though he had previously only served in the *New York* Army *National Guard and not the regular army,* Jean-Paul was sure all of the troopers in the First United States Volunteer Cavalry were quite comfortable with him being the regiment's deputy commander.

With Roosevelt, Captain O'Neill, First Sergeant Troxler, and Colonel Leonard Wood, the regimental commander, Jean-Paul was positive he was in the hands of outstanding leaders.

He then reflected on what he knew about Colonel Wood. Being a medical doctor, Leonard Wood had signed on as a contract surgeon with the Army in 1885. He became a legend in the campaign against Geronimo and his Apache band in 1886. He once carried dispatches one hundred miles through enemy territory. Also, despite being a doctor, he had commanded an infantry company whose officers had all been killed in a hand-to-hand fight with the Apaches. For this he was awarded the Medal of Honor and became a national hero. There was also a dime novel that had been written about him. Jean-Paul later found out it was the same combat in which Sergeant Graham received his face wound and a Citation Star for gallantry.

Jean-Paul now focused again on Colonel Roosevelt. Finishing eyeballing the regiment, Roosevelt, with his booming voice and boundless energy, began his address to the regiment. "Gentlemen, I am Lieutenant Colonel Theodore Roosevelt, the deputy commander of this outstanding regiment—*the First*

*Volunteer Cavalry.* Your regimental commander, Colonel Leonard Wood, is not with us just yet. He is still in Washington D.C. insuring we get the best and latest Army equipment and supplies. You will note that the equipment you have already received is the same that is being issued to the regular army. That's because of the efforts of Colonel Wood. For this we all owe him our thanks, particularly for the Krag rifles you are holding. With these Krags, Colonel Wood has already saved many of our lives. Bully for him." Roosevelt clapped his hands and almost seemed surprised that the troopers, who were at ease and holding their rifles, weren't also clapping.

He continued, "We are the First Volunteer Cavalry. A newspaper reporter asked me to describe the type of man who would join this regiment. Among other things, I said they would be tough and rough riding men. Well from that, the journalist published a story that has been printed across the country. He wrote that we are the *Rough Rider Regiment* with no mention of the First United States Volunteer Cavalry. We will be *putting a stop to that* so people will know us by our official regimental title and not some made up nonsense. We won't want people to think we came from Buffalo Bill Cody's Wild West Show. You will remember that it was and still is called, *'Buffalo Bill's Wild West and Congress of Rough Riders of the World.'* "

Roosevelt paused and then said, "Now before we take our oath of enlistment, I wanted to gather you together to explain a couple of things. I know you boys have joined up to have some adventure, travel to an exotic island in the Caribbean Sea, and experience glory on the field of battle. For this I commend and admire you. You will have your opportunity for glory in battle— of that there is no doubt. But there is more to soldiering than experiencing combat. You must be prepared not only to fight *but also* to perform the monotonous, ordinary, routine daily duties of a soldier. Also, Cuba has a miserable climate, and you will be facing a variety of tropical fevers as well as Spanish bullets."

Colonel Roosevelt stopped and looked for a reaction. When there wasn't one, he continued. "Soon you will be taking the oath to join the Army. That means you must obey orders without question and must always be ready to do your duty when called upon no matter how disagreeable or dangerous it might be. Your work will at times be irksome, mundane, and tedious. And when that is the case, no complaint is expected from you or should be made. In the next short weeks, we will train hard for battle. Colonel Wood has put me in charge of this training. I expect you all to avail yourself of this opportunity since what you will learn during our training *will save your life in Cuba*. I further expect you to take pride in your regiment and therefore put your whole heart into soldiering. Now, if anyone feels they cannot or will not do what is expected of him, you may fall out of this formation, turn in your gear, and go on your way with no questions asked.

If you have any reservations about what will be required of you, now is your opportunity to leave."

All the men stood fast. Not one of the thousand men moved. Lieutenant Colonel Roosevelt waited for what seemed forever before he said, "Bully! Colonel Wood and I will be proud and honored to lead you brave men on the field of honor. Regiment, Ah-ten-shun! Regimental adjutant, administer the oath to the members of the First Volunteer Cavalry."

When the oath was completed, there was a great celebratory and spirited shout. When the regiment was dismissed for evening chow, Jean-Paul, Three-Ring, and the other members of Troop A were giving each other vigorous handshakes and words of congratulations.

It was actually the first time Jean-Paul took note of comrades in his unit. As his father would say, *"They looked like the salt of the earth."* They had tough open faces, honest eyes, and were modest in speech. By the appearance of their leathery skin, they were obviously comfortable being outside for extended periods. Because of past adventures, they displayed a notable confidence and a swagger that Jean-Paul appreciated and respected. These were men whom Jean-Paul sensed he could count on in a tough situation and whom he believed could also count on him.

The members of A Troop went through the line at the mess tent. Then, in various sized groups they sat on the ground to eat their dinner. They were issued hardtack, coffee, and salt horse. Salt horse was pork that had been lightly flavored in salt water. Also, there were cases of oranges purchased in the local community for those who were interested in a healthier fare. It was certainly boring and monotonous food, but in that moment, it tasted like steak to Jean-Paul, Three-Ring, and the other troopers.

Jean-Paul looked around at the seven other Rough Riders who were chowing down in an informal circle. First, there was Trooper Cox. He shared with the group that he had prior army service but said nothing about seeing action. Jean-Paul was to learn later that omission meant *he had not seen combat*. He was bragging that he was the A Troop company clerk and would be working directly for First Sergeant Troxler. In that position, he implied jokingly, he would be *running the company*. Therefore, all the troops better treat him with respect. Sure thing thought Jean-Paul. That comment and the body movements that went with it caused Jean-Paul to take a closer look at Cox. He had a light red complexion, which was unusual for someone with dark brown hair. He would also slur his words on occasion and his hands were a bit shaky. That was slight but nonetheless noticeable. Jean-Paul wondered what his physical aliment was and with that, how he passed the physical to rejoin the army. He reconciled that whatever Cox's physical issue was, it was probably nothing.

Then there was Preacher Wilson. Wilson said he had been a clergyman in a church in the mining boomtown of Douglas in the Arizona territory. He was quite casual in relating that in the space of ten months his wife ran off with the choir director, the senior deacon absconded with all of the church's funds, and the church burned down after a lightning strike. He chuckled when he indicated he had interpreted that combination of events as a sign from God to seek another career. Everyone who heard that story nodded in agreement, including Jean-Paul and Three-Ring.

At this point an orderly from the mess came by with a pot of fresh coffee and filled everyone's canteen cup.

Next to tell his story was a common-looking man named Delaney. When he had finished eating, trooper Delaney took out a deck of cards and was constantly shuffling and cutting them. This seemed unusual to Jean-Paul. It was not so unusual when Delaney shared that he made his living as a professional gambler. He said he started his profession as a young man out East. After one very prosperous poker game, he was accused of cheating. This resulted in him being chased by his fellow card players who were bent on doing him serious bodily harm. Fortune smiled on him as a train was just leaving town and as if written in a dime thriller, he just caught the safety rail of the rear platform of the moving caboose. When he finally gained his balance, he made a finger gesture at those who had now given up chasing him. This he said was a mistake for now those with pistols began firing at him in earnest. He laughed that fortunately for him, they were no better shots than they were poker players.

His said his next stop was St Louis. There he began a gambling career on Mississippi River boats. This apparently turned sour again after yet another very successful game of poker. Returning to his room to retire for the evening, two of the other players accosted him with pistols and demanded the money he had won. Delaney distracted the two by looking behind them and yelling for help. When the two looked to see who was behind them, Delaney jumped over the side of the boat into the Mississippi. He stayed submerged for as long as he could. By the time he surfaced, the boat was well on its way although the two were still firing wildly in his direction. Delaney said that since he had been fired at twice unsuccessfully, he reasoned he should try soldiering. He was sure his luck would continue to hold when and if he would be fired on by the Spaniards.

Jean-Paul, always inquisitive, could not help himself but asked Delaney if in fact he had been cheating in those card games. Three-Ring shook his head. He said under his breath, *"Here we go again."*

As all eyes rested on Delaney who stared quizzically at Jean-Paul. Then he said, "Let's you and me play one hand and then you tell me whether you think I was cheating. Let's turn our mess tins upside down and I will deal each of us a hand. Jean-Paul agreed, not exactly sure what to expect.

Delaney shuffled the cards with such speed and quickness of hand that Jean-Paul could not follow it with his eyes. Delaney dealt both himself and the teenager five cards. When J.P. picked them up and to his surprise, he had four aces. He looked at Delaney who had a sly smile on his face. Jean-Paul turned the cards face up and laid them on the upside-down mess tin. Everyone in the circle make some sort of noise in amazement.

"How did you do that?"

"Anyone can do that if all you do is play with cards and your hands have any dexterity at all. It just takes time and practice. I can deal just about any hand I want to anyone at the table at any time." This left the rest of the group speechless.

"Does that answer your question young man?"

"I think it does, thanks," stuttered Jean-Paul.

Three-Ring was the next to share his story. Everyone had a hearty laugh when he said he had worked in the circus. Preacher Wilson pointed out that it is every young boy's dream to run off and join the circus. Three-Ring listed all the things he had learned to do in the circus. Cox then asked him to demonstrate something. Three-Ring stood up and asked the troopers to toss him the oranges they had picked up in the dinner line. When he had four of them, he began a juggling act that was worth a price for admission. He juggled those oranges behind his back, under his leg, one hand at a time, and bouncing them off of his forehead. Three-Ring was obviously in hog heaven doing this. The whole time he wore the biggest smile. To close his act, he tossed an orange to each of its original owners. He received a loud ovation, not only from the small group in the circle, but also from the other troopers who had seen his act. Three-Ring sat down with a profound look of satisfaction on his face.

Next to tell his story was Juan-Julio Soto Mendoza. He was a short, stocky man with a strong accent and a friendly smile. He had worked with cattle his entire life and also had done some bronco busting. According to him, cattle ranching was dying. With sadness he pointed out that the vitality of the land had limits and that the acreage in Arizona had been badly overgrazed. This had resulted in the original grass not growing back because of topsoil erosion. Added to that had been a couple of major droughts. Mendoza said all these circumstances made him decide it was time for him to move on and try something different.

Jean-Paul asked him if he was fluent in Spanish. This brought laughter from several members of the group who felt the answer to that question was obvious. Mendoza replied he was indeed fluent. To that J.P. asked if he could teach the rest of them some Spanish since that was the language of their rebel allies and the enemy in Cuba. Mendoza said he would be willing but that he had never taught before. Jean-Paul replied that would not be a problem as all anyone needed were some key words and phrases. Mendoza nodded in agreement and added, *"That's really all I got."*

The next person to share was Elijah Smith. He began by saying, "People call me *'Lij.'* I was a Texas Ranger." He was a tall slender man with graying hair, which did not match his youthful appearance. "Did that ranger work for almost eight years. Had a wide variety of experiences, some good and some not so good. I was involved in rounding up renegade *Comanches* and taking them back to the reservation; captured a couple of bank robbers; had a firefight or two with some Mexican border bandits; and broke up, well, I don't know how many saloon fights. But I guess the one thing I was involved in that you might have heard about was the big prizefight in Dallas in 1896 between *Fitzsimmons and Maher*. The governor wanted it to be stopped because of the rioting and civil unrest that was anticipated. He sent almost all the rangers and their captains there to stop the fight. In that we succeeded. *Danny Boy Stuart* was the fight's organizer, and he eventually took the bout to a border town in Mexico. But the initial fight became widely publicized over a phrase by *Ranger Captain Bill McDonald*. When he got off the train in Dallas, a city official asked McDonald where were all the other rangers? McDonald is reported to have said, *"One riot, one ranger."* At least that's the way it got reported in the papers. What he told us was that he had said something like, "Hell, ain't one enough?

There's only one prize-fight!" But that's not the way it was reported. That *one riot, one ranger,* line certainly gave the Rangers a lot of positive publicity. The upshot for the city of Dallas was that there was no riot, prizefight, or not much else happening for that matter." Smith paused, as if he wanted to share more.

He then looked up and said, "So that's my story. I joined up for the war because things were really slowing down for me with always more of the same. That's right, always more of the same old thing—same old, same old. That was boring, so I decided to try the army to shake things up a bit. That's about it."

Jean-Paul felt like clapping. He wasn't sure why, but he had read dime novels about the adventures of the Texas Rangers. He had always been impressed with their exploits. Of course, his dad had said what he was reading probably wasn't true and had been greatly exaggerated. The Texas Rangers were the United States' equivalent to Canada's red-jacketed *Northwest Mounted Police.* Jean-Paul had seen Mounties a number of times when he and his dad had traveled the twenty miles from New Hope, New York, to Canada. He was always impressed with the size, appearance, and demeanor of these law enforcers just like he was now with Ranger Smith. J.P. thought, *"Wow, serving in the same troop with a former Texas Ranger. That was almost too good to be true. This is indeed going to be an adventure."*

Jean-Paul couldn't help himself. He blurted out, *"I'll share."* As he said this, he glanced at Three-Ring who had raised his eyebrows at Jean-Paul. He recognized it was the little guy's way of saying, *"Keep it short."* He also remembered what his father had said, *"Always be brief."*

Jean-Paul began, "My name is Jean-Paul DeBert. My last name is pronounced duh-bear and not dee-bert like it's spelled. It's the French pronunciation you know. I was born and raised in New Hope, New York. We lived on the edge of the Chacopac tribal lands. My father taught at the Jesuit school there. I went to that school for twelve years and also taught there for the past couple of years, history and English mostly. My biggest hobby is to read, mostly military history books."

That last comment brought a murmuring among the group. In amazement, Trooper Cox said, "Twelve years of school and your hobby is reading? You poor beggar! That's ten more years of school than I ever had. Everyone, including Preacher Wilson nodded in agreement that twelve years was an awful long time to be in school.

Trooper Delaney said, *"With all that schoolin' and readin', I think we need to be callin' you 'Professor.' What do you think fellas?"*

Everyone mumbled and nodded in approval.

Jean-Paul unphased continued, "I joined the army to begin my own life and get experiences I could never have gotten teaching at the Jesuit School or living in New Hope. I have traveled to New York City several dozen times with my father and also to Canada on a number of occasions. In terms of fighting, I know the French way of savate, which is the art of defending yourself with a walking stick. I am also quite good with handling a traditional Bowie knife. I've hunted and killed a black bear, a mountain lion, and any number of coyotes. I just turned eighteen and in addition to English I can speak the French, German, and Chacopac. Also, there were two Pawnee braves who came to live with the Chacs. From them I learned the sign language of the plains Indians."

Upon saying this, the only trooper who had not shared yet, made a series of signs with his hands. Jean-Paul easily interpreted what he said. He signed that his name was Cherokee Willy and was from the Cherokee tribe. He continued, the plains Indians learned to sign from the tribes in the Southern United States. Thus, the plains Indians should not be credited for creating signing. The southern tribes, and specifically the Cherokee, should be credited with that art. Jean-Paul signed back that he understood and was sorry for not crediting the Southern tribes and especially the Cherokee. Cherokee Bill signed that he accepted his apology. Everyone observing this exchange looked confused.

Three-Ring then chimed in, "What do we have here, an Indian signing club? It would be nice and also courteous for you all to share what you are signing!"

Cherokee Willy joined the conversation. In excellent English he explained to the assembled troopers what he had signed to Jean-Paul. He went on the say that he had been educated in the *Carlisle Indian School* at the U.S. Army post in Carlisle, Pennsylvania. After that, he went back to the tribe but found it wasn't the same. He didn't feel he fit in with American society and now, he no longer seemed to fit in with his tribe. Thus, when war with Spain was declared, he felt it was his opportunity to break away and essentially start his life over. Everyone grunted and nodded in understanding.

At this time Captain O'Neill with Sergeant Graham walked up to the group. Corporal Cox leaped to his feet and came to the position of attention. Sergeant Graham, at the top of his lungs yelled at the troopers on the ground, "On your feet and come to the position of attention. That is what you will always do when an officer comes into your area. And furthermore, you don't move from the position of attention until that officer gives you *at ease or rest.* Do you understand?" He yelled again, "Do you understand?"

Not waiting for anyone to respond, Sergeant Graham, in a quieter and more civil voice, said to Captain McNeill, "We have got some work to do sir, turning these greenhorns into soldiers."

Captain O'Neill, ignoring Sergeant Graham's comment, said to the troopers, "Stand at ease." He then said, "Gentlemen, you need to get some rest. Tomorrow will be a big day. Sergeant Graham here will give you more instruction on close order drill and military discipline. The First Volunteer Cavalry, of which you are now proud members, has been issued regular army uniforms and equipment. The reason is that we will undoubtedly be one of the first units to deploy and see combat, with everything that implies. We will train hard before we ship out because when we get to Cuba, we must be combat ready. To be less than 100% combat effective will cost lives. And that is not going to happen in my troop or in our regiment. Any questions gentlemen?"

Jean-Paul acted as if he was going to ask a question, but Three-Ring poked him. J.P. got the message.

"Well, if there are no questions, then carry on gentlemen. Have a good evening." Sergeant Graham called them to attention and touched his hat in a salute to Captain O'Neill. The captain returned the salute.

Sergeant Graham then turned to the group and told them where to form up in morning and what uniform to wear. They were to be in their M1884 fatigue uniform. This was the issued shirt made of distinctive brown duck material and was intended for fatigue duty. It was to be worn because in the Texas heat it would be cooler and more comfortable than the blue wool service shirt. It would also save the more expensive wool uniform from wear and tear. They were also to bring their rifle.

When Graham left, the group shook hands with one another and went off to their tents. Both Jean-Paul and Three-Ring were both absorbed in their thoughts as they walked. Once arriving at their tent, the two laid out their sleeping blanket, its canvas cover, and the issued pajamas. As on the trip down to San Antonio, Jean-Paul decided to use his shoulder bag as his pillow.

Once settled for a good night's rest, Jean-Paul noticed Three-Ring was snoring. Three-Ring sounded like a wounded bull elephant. My goodness but that little man could make some noise when asleep.

Jean-Paul smiled to himself. The past few days were just great. This is going to be the adventure of a lifetime. The train ride from New York, the people, and experiences on the train, his first day in camp, and his new mates with their amazing stories— all of this was simply outstanding. *It was the good Lord's grace in action.* Jean-Paul said a brief prayer of thanks and then fell fast asleep like a dead man.

### *Thought Questions for Chapter 7:*

1.  Why did First Sergeant Troxler tell Jean-Paul and Three-Ring *never* to address Captain O'Neill a.) by only by his rank, b.) by only his last name, or 3.) by his nickname Bucky?
2.  Jean-Paul sensed he could count on his comrades in A Troop in a tough situation. Considering the stories each told about

their lives and why they joined the Army, do you agree or disagree with Jean-Paul's assessment? Why or why not?

3. What are your impressions and reactions to the qualifications and character of Jean-Paul's leaders in the First Volunteer Cavalry Regiment and A Troop? How confident would you be if they were the leaders who would be leading you into combat?

4. Why was Jean-Paul inclined to ask questions and say things that sometimes seemed to be inappropriate and out of place? Why would Three-Ring be an asset to J.P. to overcoming that tendency?

5. How and why did Jean-Paul get the nickname *Professor?*

6. What was your biggest learning or take away from this chapter? What can you apply from the information in this chapter? What in it did you find the most interesting? Why?

# 8

## *Training in Texas*

Jean-Paul awoke just seconds before the bugler played reveille. It was a beautiful sound and once again confirmed to Jean-Paul that he was a soldier in the United States Army and no longer a schoolteacher in New Hope, New York.

After breakfast, Troop A gathered around in the open field behind the tent city. Sergeant Graham was nowhere to be seen. Everyone was simply milling around in a gaggle. Corporal Cox, the prior service company clerk, yelled, "Alright, let's quit the gaggle and get in formation. Now form up. If the Captain or First Sergeant sees us, or worse Sergeant Graham, you know the trouble we will be in."

At that point, Three-Ring said quietly to Jean-Paul, "Look at that guy. He has the look of someone who was up all-night drinking!" Three-Ring was right. Corporal Cox's face was beet red, he had huge bags under his eyes, his wrinkled uniform looked like he had slept in it, and his hat was on sideways and at the back of his head.

"He certainly doesn't look good, but at least he has taken the initiative to get us formed up and looking military," said

Jean-Paul. Three-Ring nodded and said nothing since Cox was now looking directly at the two of them.

Once they were formed up and standing at rest, First Sergeant Troxler and Sergeant Graham made their appearance. They were marching with two strapping large corporals. These were two of the biggest and ugliest men Jean-Paul had ever seen. They reminded him of some of the lumberjacks the Beckenbauers had employed back home.

Corporal Cox was standing in front of the formation. When approached by First Sergeant Troxler, he called the troops to attention and reported. Troxler returned the salute and Cox fell back into the formation. Troxler ordered the troopers to stand at ease. He proceeded to give a speech to the troop that would not be soon forgotten.

He began quietly, "Gentlemen. I know that many of you have had some experiences involving danger and adventure. That's all well and good—all well and good. But busting broncos, working in a mining camp, riding shotgun on a stagecoach, or working a cattle drive is not the same as soldiering. I am sure you all think you are very tough and ready for anything. Well, let me assure you *that you are not*. Let me say that again—*you are not*. Being in bar room brawl is quite different from going up against a well-trained professional army, all the members of which are committed to sending you straight to hell! Be assured the two are very different experiences. There are over 250,000 Spanish regulars and militia soldiers in Cuba. That's right, over 250,000. When this war started, the entire United States Army totaled 26,000 soldiers. Last month Congress passed mobilization legislation that will increase the size of our army by another 200,000 soldiers. But unlike our regiment, it will take a long time for all those new units to become combat ready. Because of Colonel Wood and Colonel Roosevelt, our volunteer cavalry regiment has the same equipment as the regular army. That will result in us deploying with the regular forces. That means we have no time to lose, to prepare, to get ready, or to become proficient for battle."

Troxler stopped and looked over the formation and then began again, this time with more volume, "Now, there are several things we need to do to change you from a disorganized mob of rabble and individuals, to an efficient team and professional fighting machine. And if some of you don't know what a machine is—don't worry about it. The things that must be done to get you hombres ready for battle are the same that have been done to make civilians into soldiers for centuries. We will instill military discipline in you. You will learn military courtesy. You will be trained to obey orders instantly and without hesitation. And finally, you will be trained to proficiently handle all the weapons of war. I know you think you understand weapons, but not to the degree necessary for what we will be doing. We will also teach you open and close order drill as well as getting you in better physical condition. Since you all seem to be in top notch condition," the First Sergeant paused and grinned, "well, most of you, the primary emphasis will be on discipline and drill. Marching and drill not only instills discipline but also teaches instant obedience to orders. This will transfer you from a street mob of self-seeking individuals into a well-organized team and an effective fighting organization. Now, what are your questions?"

To their eternal credit, no one on Troop A, including Jean-Paul, asked a question.

"One more thing, I have with me Sergeant Graham whom you all had the good fortune of meeting yesterday. Also, with me are Corporal's Osborne and Beaufort. Besides previously serving in the United States Army, they have had other operational military experience. Corporal Beaufort saw action with the French Army in Tonkin and Southern China. Corporal Osborne formerly served as an officer in the *New South Wales Mounted Rifles*. Both have experience in training new recruits. Therefore, they will be assisting Sergeant Graham with your training."

Troxler turned to Sergeant Graham and said, "Sergeant, they are all yours." They returned salutes and the First Sergeant moved off to the side to watch the show. Both Jean-Paul and Three–Ring had an ominous feeling about what was about to happen....

    *        *        *        *        *

That night after dinner, an exhausted Jean-Paul went to his tent and fell flat onto his blanket. Practicing dismounted drill all day in the hot Texas sun had completely drained this eighteen-year-old. Since he was actually too tired to go to sleep, he decided to write a letter home. The letter began:

Dearest Father, Mother, Marcel and Arlette,

I am getting along very well as a soldier in this cavalry regiment. Today we learned various commands, saluting, the manual of arms, formations, and marching movements. Tomorrow we are to do more of the same. I had no problem with any of it, but I must say many of the cowboys in Troop A can't march a lick. I suppose they rode their horses most of the time and seldom walked anywhere. It really shows. These troopers received a lot of special attention from our drill instructors. This was attention that I am pleased to report I did not receive. We each have been issued quite a lot of army equipment. I can't imagine how we will be able to carry it all. Our rifle is the *Krag-Jorgenson*. It is smokeless so it will not give away our position to the enemy when it is fired. I think that is a good thing. We normally wear our fatigue shirt during the day and not the standard army woolen shirt. The food is always the same and not very good. Some of the soldiers have actually gotten sick from it, but that has not happened to me. The men in A Troop are an interesting group. They come mostly from America's far Western territories. They have wonderful stories of past adventures. These stories must be true because they are too amazing to be made up. I have become good friends with a short gentleman who has previously worked in the circus. His name is Herkimer Hankey which is why he prefers to be called *Three-Ring*. How funny and interesting is that? We are still training and have not gotten word about when we might travel east. For the next couple of weeks, we are to do more training. We are supposed to fire our weapons soon, but from what I know, most of these troopers have quite a lot of experience handling weapons. What I am really looking forward to is the training with the horses. We are to do squad, troop, and squadron cavalry formation training. I was told that half of the horses are not broken in for riders. Considering the caliber of men in our unit, I think the unbroken horses don't stand a chance. The leaders in Troop A are Captain Bucky O'Neill and First Sergeant Joshua Troxler. Like you father, they are real heroes in my book. I hope that when I get into action I will conduct myself with honor like you and the two of them have done. I am enjoying the soldier's life very much. It seems to agree with me. I'm actually looking forward to sentry duty, kitchen police (K.P.) duty in the mess hall, and all those other soldier fatigue duties. Colonel Roosevelt said those tasks would be tedious and boring. Maybe so, but they are things a soldier experiences and *I am a soldier!* Thank you for your prayers. I miss the four of you and home very much. Don't worry about me. I am safe and being well taken care of. God bless you all!!!

Your loving son and brother, Jean-Paul

\*        \*        \*        \*        \*

After a few days of dismounted drill, the training focus shifted to the horses. The fact that half of the horses purchased had not yet broken for riders was a point of concern for the regiment's leaders. However, that was nothing less than pure joy for many of the Rough Riders.   Countless of these ruffians had spent their entire life busting broncos out West. Bronco busting was not something for a weak or timid soul. It was dangerous, difficult, and even when successful, it would take a toll on the rider. Those that could do it and do it well, were quite proud of their skill. It was indeed a manly occupation.

After forming up, First Sergeant Troxler marched Troop A to the stable area. Once there, he gave the order to rest in place, as each member of the unit was to be assigned a horse.

It was quite a sight for Jean-Paul to see all the regiment's horses for the first time. The noises and smells of the horses as well as the sight of their graceful movements was absolutely breathtaking. His family in New Hope had a couple of horses, but they were old nags. They were not the regiment's superb animals that were about to become warhorses.

## Chapter 8: Training in Texas

Jean-Paul could not help but stare. There was something about the beauty, grandeur, and physical splendor of a horse. The mass of rippled muscles, their power combined with their gentleness and dignified intelligence—were all something to behold.

He remembered reading that a man is never freer than when he rides a horse. To ride is like having wings and soaring like a hawk. Riding a horse is climbing the sky and racing with the wind. A horse is poetry in motion and God's special gift to mankind. Whoever said, *"If God made anything more beautiful than a horse, He kept it for Himself,"* got it exactly right.

"Smelly and noisy, don't you think?" asked Three-Ring.

Startled away from his thoughts, Jean-Paul said, *"What do you mean?"*

"Well look at them. They are always snorting, coughing, neighing, whinnying, squealing, swishing their tail, tossing their mane, clearing their throats, and pounding their hooves. My goodness but they are noisy. And they smell bad too. No matter how clean you try to keep both them and their stables, they always managed to smell like fresh poop, sweat, and really bad breadth. Whatever circus costume I wore when I was working with horses, it always took on the smell of the horse. Sometimes it wouldn't go away even after it was washed." He was shaking his head the entire time he was talking.

Somehow what Three-Ring had said, had taken the glow off

Jean-Paul's idealistic thoughts about the *majesty of the horse*.

Three-Ring continued, "Just make sure good buddy you get a horse that is somewhat broken in and sociable. Otherwise, you may get hurt before we even get out of these here United States."

Jean-Paul couldn't help himself and responded, "Why are you always so pessimistic and negative? Really? Why? Why can't you *just once* look on the bright side of things?"

"I am very positive, but I like the way you look when I am negative. In those moments your expressions are quite humorous. You really need to get over yourself," said Three-Ring to Jean-Paul with a big smile.

"You know little one, you are really a funny guy—a real funny guy."

"I know, but so are you in a different sort of way, especially when you don't know when to keep quiet!"

Ignoring that remark Jean-Paul said, "Keep in mind, the war horse never had or never will have it easy. Just like soldiers, over the centuries they have *not been* treated very well. Army horses have traditionally been used for essential military functions like cavalry attacks, raids, reconnaissance, intelligence gathering, couriering, and transporting materials. With such functions they were often mismanaged, neglected, cruelly abused, or forced to work under the most wretched conditions. They suffered through disease, starvation, exhaustion, and lousy-to-no veterinary care. Then too, there was the exposure to severe injuries or death in battle. The army has been a terrible life for that animal, a creature that has contributed more than any other to man's success in warfare."

"Well, that's not the way we treated our horses in the circus. From what I saw, they received better food and care than some of the performers!"

At this point First Sergeant Troxler approached Jean-Paul. With a smile he said, "Dee-bert, do you see that brown beauty over there?" He pointed to an animal that had obviously had some years on it. The animal had a severely swayed back and was not the most impressive mount in the stable.

"Right, First Sergeant, I see him."

"Good, because that's your horse."

Jean-Paul grimaced at the sight of his newly assigned steed. Noticing his frown, the First Sergeant responded with a question, "Why the face? What's wrong with old *Applejack?*"

"The horse's name is Applejack?"

"Right, is there a problem?"

Three-Ring, under his breadth said, "I think his name should be old *Appleglue* instead of Applejack."

Troxler asked, "What did you say little one?"

"Nothing First Sergeant. Nothing at all."

"Good, because your horse is that chestnut stallion over yonder."

Both Three-Ring and Jean-Paul gasped as they saw this

large horse who was snorting and prancing about more than most of the horses.

Three-Ring asked, "First Sergeant, if I may ask, why was I assigned that particular horse?"

"You, little one, were assigned that horse because he is mostly broken—mostly. And since you are a big circus horseman, you get frisky old *Sparky.*"

Jean-Paul looked at Three-Ring with a wry smile and repeated the horse's name, *"Sparky—Three-Ring on Sparky.* That actually sounds like a Buffalo Bill Cody wild west act."

Three-Ring's expression indicated he did not think that was very funny.

First Sergeant Troxler went on to assign horses to the other troopers in the unit.

Jean-Paul said, "Just think about it Three-Ring—we are going to be cavalryman. We're joining that long line of warriors who went into battle on horseback."

"And that's important because...?"

"For goodness sakes guy, don't you have any sense of history? We will be joining the tradition of all the horse soldiers who ever served under the colors! My grandfather, who fought in the Battle of Waterloo, told me the French cavalry was so compressed during Marshal Ney's charge that the horses in the center of the formation were actually lifted off their legs and carried along with the attack. Of course, the British infantry were very clever in meeting a cavalry attack. Their soldiers formed squares that were about twenty yards on each side. Even though these squares were exposed to artillery fire, they would generally be very effective against cavalry. The soldiers in the outer row of the square would fix bayonets. They would then take a knee and then plant the toe of their musket stock firmly on the ground with their bayonets pointing up at about a sixty-degree angle. The second rank would be standing with fixed bayonets immediately behind those kneeling. Their bayonets would be held at a ninety-degree angle. Ney's cavalry could not break these squares because the horses simply would not charge into a hedgerow of bayonets. How about that for your daily history lesson."

"Okay Professor, if these squares were so vulnerable to artillery fire, why didn't the French just blast them to smithereens?"

"Good thought Three-Ring. The problem was really poor coordination and communication between the French infantry, cavalry, and artillery. There were many reasons why the French were defeated at Waterloo, but that lack of coordination was a key one."

At this point First Sergeant Troxler moved everyone to the horses and the real fun began. The rest of the day was spent becoming familiar with their steeds. This became great theatre because some of them were barely broken. Several of the horses bucked off their assigned rider with ease. These horses were then turned over to Trooper's *Darnell* and *Wood*. They were reputed to be able to successfully break any horse ever born. They lived up to their reputation and were able to *subdue all* of the rebellious stallions. Jean-Paul had never really observed men who were so skilled at such a difficult task. Their bronco busting performance that day was something he would once again have paid good money to observe. Some of the Harvard men also did a credible job at this undertaking much to the surprise of everyone present.

     *          *          *          *          *

After dinner and with Corporal Cox in charge, Jean-Paul, Three-Ring and several other troopers rode their stallions from the camp to the San Antonio River to wash them. On the ride Jean-Paul stopped and bought some apples. Applejack, his horse, knew exactly what his new master had done and why. Arriving at the river, Jean-Paul gave his horse an apple and then another. Generally, it takes some time for a horse and rider to bond. But it was quite clear to J.P. that the apples had sealed the deal with him and old Applejack. He and his horse were now one. Even as he was washing his mount Applejack kept turning around and gently nudged Jean-Paul. Jean-Paul thought everything about his army experience was only getting better.

Finished with washing their horses, all the troopers mounted up for the ride back to camp. After a short distance, the group came upon the *Menger Hotel,* a hotel that was famous for its bar. At this point, Corporal Cox signaled the group to stop. He said, "Fellas, since we are going to move out from San Antonio sooner than later, I think we need to stop here for a cold one."

Jean-Paul was immediately uncomfortable—immediately. He was not sure this was the right thing to do even though his immediate superior, in this case Corporal Cox, was telling him to do it.

Three-Ring sensed his discomfort and said, "Come on Professor, one drink. What can it hurt? And besides, if you don't want a beer or whiskey, you can get lemonade, a sarsaparilla, a root beer, or maybe even a glass of French wine. At least be part of the group. Come on, be a sport!"

Three-Ring's reasoning convinced Jean-Paul to join. Preacher Wilson said he didn't frequent bars and would stay outside and watch the horses.

This bar, a part of the grand *Menger Hotel,* was a boisterous place. It was magnificent with large paintings, wood pillars with elaborate carvings, and a very ornate bar. There was a piano player, women in fancy dresses carrying drinks, card playing, and lots of noise. Jean-Paul had never seen or even imagined such a place. The group moved up to the bar and everyone ordered a drink. Jean-Paul was not fond of beer but to go along with the crowd, he ordered a beer. And of course, these

Rough Riders were the only soldiers in the bar and being in uniform, they really stood out.

When everyone had their mug of beer, they all toasted one another. That first sip of cold beer in the warm San Antonio climate actually tasted good to Jean-Paul. His Jesuit guilt was beginning to quiet down.

Suddenly Three-Ring's face took on a look of horror. He said to Jean-Paul, "Don't look behind you because that big buffoon who you put down with your cane at the enlistment tent is standing at the bar behind us. He and his pals are looking this way."

In a booming voice that could be heard over all the noise in the bar, the big buffoon yelled, "Is that you green horn soldier boy with the cane? Is that you? My god it is. Hey boys, it is my young friend with the walking stick. I see you don't have your walking stick tonight—too bad for you. And look, there's your little runt dwarf buddy who enjoys kicking people when they are down. What amazing luck! Don't you remember what I told you two the last time I saw you? I told you I would have somethin' special for each of you the next time we met! Remember that? Well, this is the next time." The drunk took a swig of beer, slammed the beer glass down on the bar, and began to laugh hysterically.

Jean-Paul had since turned to face this loudmouth. He had not yet said anything. The rogue was still unshaven, wearing the same filthy clothes as before, and was nursing a nasty wet cigar. Probably it was the same cigar he had in his mouth the last time they met thought Jean-Paul.

By this time the piano player stopped playing, the entire saloon had become strangely quiet. All eyes were now on the drama at the bar.

The buffoon continued, "Here young pup and little one, this is what I have for you two." He put his cigar on the bar and then pulled out a rather sinister looking hunting knife. With an evil glare, he was making a circle as he pointed it at Jean-Paul and Three-Ring.

Jean-Paul noted he *had no rising feeling* in his chest like encounters such as this had previously triggered. He was quite calm and not because his *very quiet army comrades* were with him.

Three-Ring, standing next to Jean-Paul asked quietly, "What do you think we should do?"

Jean-Paul equally quietly said, "Not to worry, I'll take care of this. This jackass reminds me of some clowns I used to know back home in New Hope." Jean-Paul was thinking about the Beckenbauer twins.

Jean-Paul looking right into the eyes of the drunk said, "You are right. I don't have my walking stick. But this is what I do have."

At this point he casually leaned down and slowly pulled the

huge Bowie knife from his right boot. The Bowie's blade was almost twice the size of the buffoon's knife. The eyes of the drunk became large as saucers when he saw the size of Jean-Paul's blade. He obviously had not expected this and now was not sure what to do.

Jean-Paul's readings of military history informed him that *if you want to control a situation, you must always take the initiative.* That is how one influences events whether on the battlefield or in a bar brawl. He held the Bowie with his right hand with the point of the blade pointed up. There was a brief silence. The thought came to Jean-Paul that now was a time for a ruse. He took two *quick steps* toward the man as if he was going to attack him. After the two steps he stopped abruptly. The buffoon, assuming he was being attacked, stepped back quickly. In doing so he stepped on the boot of one his pals who was standing behind him. This, and the large amount of alcohol he had consumed, caused him to lose his balance and fall flat on his back. He dropped his knife, and it clanked loudly on the floor. Almost everyone in the bar laughed loudly at the fallen down drunk. Clearly not wanting to mix it up with J.P.'s Bowie knife, the drunk made no effort to get up.

Jean-Paul with knife still in hand, picked up his beer and took a long pull. He then put the beer down on the bar, reached in his pocket for a silver dollar, and placed it on the on the bar. He then said to Three-Ring, "Let's go and now" Backing towards the door, he and Three-Ring walked out onto the street. No one followed them. The piano again began playing and the bar noise resumed.

Once outside, Preacher Wilson asked, "Where's everybody else?"

Jean-Paul responded, "They'll be coming soon."

Back at the camp, Three-Ring said, "Partner, you did great back in that bar. I was quite impressed. You are a natural in a fight. You didn't seem at all nervous."

"Don't be impressed at something like that. And I'm not sure how much of a natural I am in a fight. I really don't like being in those situations, but they have occurred to me quite often in the days since I have left New Hope. They could stop anytime now."

"They probably will," said Three-Ring. "And then we will get to Cuba, and it will start anew with the Spanish."

"You are always full of optimism and good news, aren't you?" They both laughed and turned in after a long and eventful day. Three-Ring ended his day by beginning his horribly loud snoring. Jean-Paul's custom was to write home and then read some King James by candlelight before he would go to sleep— but not tonight. He ended his day with a prayer of thanks and also a prayer for the protection for his family and friends.

The next day training continued in the Texas heat. At the end of the day, First Sergeant Troxler held a formation of the troop. He didn't seem to be at all happy as he said, "Alright. It seems last evening some troopers, allegedly from our regiment, were in the city drinking alcoholic beverages and were also engaged in an altercation at the bar in the Menger Hotel. Regiment wants to know who they were. Apparently, the trooper who did the threatening was described as young, tall and lanky, and he had a short ugly, soldier friend with him. The tall trooper apparently threatened some upright San Antonio citizen with a large knife. This upstanding citizen is the one who filed the complaint. Now *I am sure it was none of you all,* to include the group who washed their horses in the river yesterday. But if anyone knows anything about this, I need to know as soon as possible so I can report it to regiment. By the way, I need to see Dee-Bert and Hankey. Everyone else is dismissed."

Delaney came by and patted Jean-Paul on the shoulder, "Sorry Professor, you are in for it now. You'll probably see more of the inside of a Texas jail than the inners of Cuba. Maybe now you could tell the First Sergeant some war story you've read." He and several other troopers had a hearty laugh at the expense of Jean-Paul and Three-Ring as they walked away.

Three-Ring said, "What are we going to tell the First Sergeant? If we tell him the truth we will probably go to jail! And, just as that dog Delaney said—we will never see Cuba!"

"Let's not panic. We are not even sure if that's why the First Sergeant wants to see us. Besides, he is a fair man and I am sure he would understand our side of the story."

As they approached Troxler, he simply stood and stared at the two of them.

Finally he said, "Well gentlemen, I was just wondering if you know anything about a tall, young soldier and short, ugly one being in a bar room brawl last night."

Jean-Paul began to speak, "Well First Sergeant...." At this point Three-Ring interrupted.

Three-Ring said, "No First Sergeant, we don't know anything about that. The only thing we bought were apples for our horses. We don't know anything about a bar fight. Isn't that right Professor?"

Before Jean-Paul could answer the First Sergeant said, "I didn't think you upstanding young soldiers would know anything about that. I will report to regimental headquarters that whoever those two troopers were, they were not from A Troop. They must have been some yahoos from *F Troop*. You two are dismissed. Good evening gentlemen."

Not believing their good fortune, both Jean-Paul and Three-Ring simultaneously saluted Troxler. This was a salute motivated by gratitude and not by rank or regulation. He returned their salute. When they had walked two or three steps, Frist Sergeant Troxler said with a smile, "And by the way, Dee-Bert, always remember that a silver dollar is way too much to pay for a beer in any bar."

Jean-Paul said, "I am sure that's right First Sergeant. Thanks for sharing that information." With that exchange both Jean-Paul and Three-Ring turned and walked away a little faster.

When they arrived at their tent, Jean-Paul couldn't help but ask Three-Ring, "Why did you say we didn't know anything about that incident when in fact we were the ones he was talking about? And the First Sergeant knew it was us too you know."

"Well good buddy, I was looking toward our goal which is getting to Cuba and the fighting. If I would have told the truth we both, especially you, would probably been put in jail, and we would have missed the entire war. That's why I said what I did. If one must stretch the truth to achieve one's greater goal then that's what one must do." Three-Ring shrugged his shoulders as he finished talking.

"I'm not sure I agree. I was taught the best policy is to always tell the truth no matter what. If it jeopardizes one's greater goal, as you suggest, then maybe the greater goal is something that isn't worth achieving. My thinking is that *one should always tell the truth.* Providence will reward honesty with some sort of advantage or benefit for the truth teller. I believe that's right."

"Wonderful. You believe that and I will stick with what I believe. But I will tell you for certain—if you would have told the truth the negative possibilities were endless. For example, you would have been put in a stink-rot Texas jail and missed deploying to Cuba. In the court case that would have followed, all of that drunken buffoon's pals would have sworn on the *King James* that you pulled a knife and actually lunged forward to attack him. Other than me, assuming I would have been there in court with you, no one else would verify your story. No one. It would be your New York soldier's word against the drunk and five or six of his Texas buddies. You wouldn't have stood a chance with those odds. You probably would have been sent to the Texas state prison in Huntsville for twenty years. You might even have been hanged for attempted murder. So, let's not be too holy here. How I handled that saved us for the war."

"All good thoughts. But I am not yet convinced. I still think one should always tell the truth. That is the right thing to do in every situation. Tell the truth and good things will happen."

"Right," said Three-Ring, "the good things will be twenty years as a guest of the great state of Texas or at the end of a rope."

Jean-Paul ignored that last statement and settled down to write a letter home and then do some *scripture* reading by candlelight. As he was writing he paused and thought, maybe there are times when it is wiser not to tell the exact or whole truth, maybe....

## Thought Questions for Chapter 8:

1. What were your impressions and reactions to the motivational speech First Sergeant Troxler gave to A

Troop prior to their drill and ceremonies training? What would you have added? Left out?

2. Jean-Paul was taught that if you want to control a situation, you must take the initiative and act. Do you agree or disagree with him? Why? In what way is being proactive and taking the initiative related to leadership and being a leader?

3. Evaluate how Jean-Paul handled the altercation in the bar at the *Menger Hotel?* How would you have handled it? Should have those troopers been in that bar in the first place? Why or why not?

4. Three-Ring believed that if a person must stretch the truth in order to achieve his greater goals, then that is what one should do. Do you agree or disagree with that philosophy? Who or why not? Why didn't Jean-Paul agree with it?

5. What was one of the reasons Jean-Paul gave why Napoleon and the French lost the Battle of Waterloo? Does that principle have any relevance in today's military? Why?

6. What was your biggest learning or take away from this chapter? What can you apply from the information in this chapter? What in it did you find the most interesting? Why?

# 9

## *The Trip to the Alamo*

First Sergeant Troxler announced that Sunday would be a less intense training day. The emphasis would be on cleaning equipment, washing clothes, getting haircuts, and attending to the horses. He also indicated the regimental Chaplain Henry Brown would be leading a 9:00 AM chapel service. Those electing to attend were to form up on the street in front of Troop A's bivouac area. Everyone of Jean-Paul's circle of new friends attended the service including Cherokee Willie and Delaney the gambler. Jean-Paul reasoned that when facing possible death some people might tend to get religion. Perhaps....

The chapel service was held outdoors in a large open field. From what Jean-Paul could tell there were as many as six hundred Rough Riders in attendance. It began with the singing of several hymns including *Onward Christian Soldiers, Amazing Grace,* and *How Great Thou Art.* Jean-Paul was familiar with all of them and sang with gusto, earning the stares of Three-Ring and Preacher Wilson on more than one occasion.

Chaplain Brown officiated the service. He had been the rector of a church in Prescott, Arizona, and had joined the Rough Riders at the request of Colonel Roosevelt. He was dressed simply in a gray shirt and overalls. Apparently, he did not yet have *the surplice,* which was a loose white linen hip-length vestment that an army chaplain normally wore when leading a service in uniform. After the singing, he led the Rough Riders in the Lord's Prayer. Then he preached a sermon on the 91st Psalm. He explained how that Psalm is an assurance of God's protection in times of danger. It was a message in which everyone seemed to take great interest. He closed out the service with a lengthy prayer for the Lord's guidance and blessing on their upcoming campaign in Cuba. When the meeting ended, Jean-Paul felt refreshed and peaceful. As they were moving back to the bivouac area, he shared this feeling with his comrades. Preacher Wilson and Three-Ring said they had a similar feeling. In that exact moment, life was good.

After lunch, Corporal Cox came by and said that there would be a wagon leaving to tour the Alamo—a key battle site during the Texas Revolution. It would be first come first served and when the wagon was full it would be leaving. Three-Ring, always ready for something new and different looked at Jean-Paul. Knowing the look, he nodded. They quickly stored their gear and walked hastily to the wagon. It was just about full with First Sergeant Troxler sitting up front with the driver. When J.P. and Three-Ring got on board and got settled, Troxler told the driver to move out. He noted that several troopers were still walking toward the wagon. J.P. then shook his head because *their procrastination had cost them a great opportunity.* In that, there was an important life lesson.

After what seemed that they had been riding forever in the hot Texas sun, the wagon pulled up in front of what looked like an old Spanish mission. No sooner had they all gotten off the wagon when a middle-aged man of Mexican descent came up to them. In accented English he offered to give the group a briefing and tour of the Alamo. The cost he said would $3.00 for the entire group. The First Sergeant waved him off with his hand, *"No tour."*

Then the guide said, "My name is Paco Guerrero; I will give you tour for only two dollars." Troxler again said, "No tour. Get lost."

The guide not easily deterred said, "My grandfather *Brigido Guerrero* fought for the Americans in the Texas Revolution. He survived the battle here and told me about it when I was a little boy. I know the best and true story about the battle. I give you the best tour for only two dollars."

Troxler was clearly going to dismiss him again when John-Paul interceded.

"First sergeant, I will pay the two dollars for this man to be our guide. What do you say?"

Troxler stared at the Professor for a moment. He then shrugged his shoulders and said, "No problem, it's your money."

Three-Ring gave Jean-Paul a dollar and said, "Here, I'll pay half."

With great excitement, Paco took the money and started to speak so rapidly that almost the entire group in concert said, "Slow down."

That seemed to settle Paco and he began again. "My grandfather was Brigido Guerrero. He had deserted from the Mexican Army in December 1835 and was spared at the Alamo after convincing the Mexican soldiers he was a prisoner of the *Texians*. A *Texian* is what a resident of Mexican Texas was called in those days. My grandfather later fought for the Americans at the great Texian victory over Santa Anna at the Battle of San Jacinto."

Paco continued, "The battle took place here at the Alamo on the 6th of March 1836, during the Texas Revolution. At that time Texas was a province in Mexico and was trying to secede and become an independent country. Their reasoning was simple. The Texians were angry because Mexico's new president, *Antonio Lopez de Santa Anna*, was trying to transform Mexico from a democracy into a dictatorship. In doing so, he was taking many rights and freedoms from the people. Being very independent, the Texians did not approve. So, in 1835 they rose up and successfully drove all of the Mexican Army out of Texas."

"Santa Anna responded to the expulsion of his army from Texas as expected. He immediately launched a military campaign to reoccupy it. He had given himself the nickname of *The Eagle*. He fancied himself a great general and a powerful military leader. There is no doubt he was a brave and very experienced soldier. He had been wounded several times in battle to include losing his left leg in a fight with the French. He had received a battlefield promotion to lieutenant fighting with the colonial Spanish army against the Mexican independence fighters. Being an opportunist, he changed sides and joined the Mexican revolutionaries and then fought against Spain. His combat experience was extensive. He had fought successfully against Native American tribes, the invading French in the *1839 Pastry War,* and against the Mexican provinces that on occasion had rebelled against the central government. His survival and success in these battles made him extremely confident and an intolerable egotist. He was completely full of himself and believed God had anointed him to do great things. As a result of this belief, and his mostly successful military adventures, he gave himself another nickname, *The Napoleon of the West."*

"Despite of all these campaigns, Santa Anna did not understand logistics or what Clausewitz, the German military writer, called *'The fog of war.'"*

Jean-Paul whispered to Three-Ring, "This guy knows Clausewitz? I wonder where he learned that? Apparently, Clausewitz has been translated into Spanish." To this Three-Ring frowned but said nothing.

"For example, Santa Anna's march to San Antonio was a nightmare for his soldiers. They experienced attacks by Comanche raiders, sixteen inches of snow on the 13th of February, an epidemic of dysentery, and scarce supplies resulting in partial rations. Also, the teamsters driving the supply wagons walked away because they did not receive the pay that had been promised."

Paco, now in overdrive continued, "Earlier, when the Mexican troops had been kicked out of San Antonio, Texian soldiers took over the Mexican quarters here at the Alamo mission. This was a former Spanish religious outpost that had been converted into a military fort by the Mexicans."

"Santa Anna's Mexican Army actually arrived in San Antonio on February 23rd, with 1,500 soldiers. They were mostly raw, untrained recruits. Morale was very low. The majority had been forcibly conscripted and included ex-convicts, homeless derelicts, and even some Indians who did not understand Spanish. With the reinforcements that arrived later, Santa Anna's army would eventually number over three thousand men."

"The Texian garrison totaled fewer than two hundred militia men. Colonel *James Neill,* who was the commander, left to round up more men and supplies. He transferred command to a regular army cavalry officer, *Lieutenant Colonel William B. Travis.* However, the volunteer adventurers who comprised much of the Alamo, refused to accept Travis as their leader. This was primarily because he was regular army and not roustabouts or adventurers like they were. They elected Jim Bowie as their leader. He had a nationwide reputation as a vicious knife fighter and brawler. Nevertheless, to remove hard feelings, Bowie agreed to share command with Travis. During the siege Bowie fell deathly ill. It was only under those circumstances that Travis took command."

As Paco continued, the Rough Riders became more and more impressed with his knowledge of the battle and his English vocabulary. Clearly, he had an excellent education.

Paco continued, "At that time, the Alamo was a makeshift fort primarily designed to withstand raids from the Comanche. The Texians however, did not make any arrangements for a siege. The entire complex totaled about three acres with approximately four hundred plus yards of perimeter. This was quite a large border to be defended by fewer than two hundred men. Santa Anna said the Alamo was nothing more than a *'totally irregular fortification hardly worthy of the name.'*"

When the Mexican Army marched into the city in February, the Texian members of the garrison who had been living in town immediately reported to the Alamo. Some brought their families with them. A few members of the garrison failed to report. Most of the militia men who had been living in San Antonio did not try to slip through the Mexican lines. Instead, they tried to mix with the local population."

To that comment several of the Rough Riders shouted, *"Cowards!"*

"On that same afternoon the Mexican troops raised a *blood-red flag* signifying *no quarter would be given to the Alamo defenders.* Colonel Travis responded with a blast from one of the Alamo's cannons. Believing that Travis had acted hastily, Bowie sent emissaries to ask for terms for an honorable surrender. They were informed that any surrender *must be unconditional.* On learning this, both Bowie and Colonel Travis jointly agreed to fire the cannon once again."

Paco now had the complete attention of all the Rough Riders. Seeing their increased interest, he continued speaking with a calm, deliberate pace. "For the next week and a half, the two armies engaged in several minor skirmishes. These did not amount to much and there were few casualties on either side. Meanwhile, Colonel Travis wrote multiple letters to his leaders frantically asking for more soldiers and supplies. It is not clear that any of his messages ever got through. Travis knew that being outnumbered over ten to one and with their dwindling supplies, his force had little chance of victory." At this point in the presentation, many of the twenty-three Rough Rider tourists began mumbling. They could clearly sense the plight of Travis and his men.

"Each night during the siege the Mexican artillery batteries moved closer and closer to the Alamo walls. They fired over two hundred cannonballs into the Alamo Plaza. Reusing the Mexican cannonballs, the Texians matched the Mexican artillery fire. On February 26th, Travis ordered the artillery to no longer return fire in order to conserve both powder and shot."

"On the 5th of March Santa Anna also ordered his artillery to cease firing. Now safe to do so, Colonel Travis assembled the entire garrison and confirmed for them what they already knew: *the situation was dire with not much chance of either success or survival.* Travis gave all his men the option to escape or to stay and fight. All agreed to stay but one—Moses Rose. He stole out of the Alamo that night and was never heard of again."

"Santa Anna, the Mexican Army's commander, was of course very clever. He anticipated that the exhausted Texians would soon fall asleep when his artillery ceased firing. That indeed happened, since it was their first uninterrupted sleep since the siege began. Knowing the Texians would be in a deep, fatigued sleep, he ordered his forces to move forward as silently as possible. This was on the morning of the 6th of March. At 5:30 AM, two thousand Mexican soldiers quietly advanced on the Alamo in four columns. Despite the extreme cold, the soldiers were ordered to remove their overcoats so their movement would not be hindered. The clouds were concealing the moon, so the Mexicans were not initially detected. The Texian sentinels stationed outside the walls were all killed in their sleep. When the Mexicans came within musket range, they now blew their bugles and rushed forward, yelling, '*Viva Santa Anna!*'"

"In the initial moments of the assault, the poorly trained Mexican recruits fired their muskets blindly, injuring or killing many of their own troops to their front. The tight formation of troops also offered an excellent target for the Texian artillery. Lacking canister shot, the Texians had filled their cannons with any metal they could find. Nails, door hinges, chopped-up horseshoes and small, sharp stones turned the cannons into giant shotguns. A single cannon volley effectively eliminated most of a troop of company of chasseurs from the Mexican city of *Toluca.*" At that comment, the Rough Rider cavalrymen groaned in mass since they automatically placed themselves in the chasseurs' situation.

"Colonel Travis, the Alamo's commander was one of the first to be killed. He was shot dead while firing his shotgun into the Mexicans below him. The few Mexican soldiers who were able to climb the ladders to the top of the Alamo's walls were quickly killed or pushed back. After the Texians discharged their rifles, however, they found it increasingly difficult to reload and keep the Mexican soldiers off the walls."

Pointing to the north wall, Paco continued, "Over there, the Mexican soldiers realized that the crude, makeshift wall contained many gaps. The Texians had repulsed the first and second wave of attacks. Now the third attack was stalling at that makeshift wall."

"Santa Anna was getting very worried—and impatient. He decided to commit his reserves to reinforce the attack on the north wall. What broke it open for the Mexicans was not the reinforcements, but the bravery of *General Juan Amador*. He fought off several Texians and personally opened the gate at the north wall. Once open, the Mexican soldiers rushed into the Alamo like a horde of locusts. Immediately the Texian defenders were forced to abandon the north wall as well as a section of the west wall."

"Seeing what was happening, the Texian gunners at the south end of the mission," Paco again pointing, "turned their cannon towards the north and fired directly into the advancing Mexican soldiers. This action now left the south end of the mission completely unprotected. Consequently, and within a matter of minutes, the Mexican soldiers came over the south wall behind the Texian gunners and methodically killed all of them in vicious hand-to-hand fighting. The Mexican veterans among these solders seized the opportunity and turned the 18-pounder on the Texians. By this time General Amador's men had also taken the east wall of the Alamo compound and were rushing through the cattle pens. In keeping with the Texian plan, the majority of them then fell back to the barracks and the chapel."

"The last Texian group to remain in the open was Davey

Crockett and his men. They were too far away to make it to shelter. Unable to reload because of the many Mexican soldiers pressuring them, they used their rifles as clubs, their knives to slash, and anything else they could get their hands on to defend themselves. Crockett fell mortally wounded after killing many of the enemy. Ben, a former American slave who acted as cook for one of Santa Anna's officers, saw the battleground immediately after the fight. He was the one who reported there were about sixteen Mexican corpses surrounding Crockett's body. But who knows if that's really true?"

First Sergeant Troxler immediately blurted out, "Of course it's true. It was Davey Crockett for crying out loud. Of course, it was true." All the Rough Riders muttered in agreement.

"Texian Robert Evans had been given the task of keeping the gunpowder magazine from falling into Mexican hands. Seriously wounded and bleeding out, he courageously crawled towards the powder magazine fully intending to blow it. Unfortunately, a musket ball killed him when his torch was only a few inches from the powder. Had he been successful, the blast would have destroyed the Alamo chapel and killed all the women and children who were hiding inside."

"The Mexican army now controlled all of the outer walls and the interior of the Alamo compound except for some rooms along the east and west walls and the chapel."

"Now there was the incident with the flags. At this point, the Mexican soldiers turned their attention on the despised flag of the Texas Revolution that was waving from the roof of one of the buildings. Like the Mexican flag, it had three vertical stripes of green, white, and red. But unlike the Mexican flag, it had the year 1824 in the center of the middle white stripe. At least four Mexicans were shot dead before the flag of Mexico was finally raised in its place."

"For the next hour, the Mexican army fought to gain total control of the Alamo. The few remaining Texian defenders were firing from the various barracks rooms. The 18-pounder the Mexican soldiers had captured was now aimed at the barracks. Methodically the door was blown off each room. The Mexican soldiers would then fire a volley of muskets into the room, charge with fixed bayonets, and in bloody hand-to-hand combat, eliminate the Texian defenders."

"Too sick to participate in the battle, the fevered Jim Bowie could not move from his bed. When the Mexican soldiers entered his room, he fired a brace of pistols and then slashed at them with his famous knife. He met his end with several mortal bayonet thrusts."

"The last Texians to be killed were Captain Dickinson's eleven men manning the two 12-pounder cannons in front of the chapel. A shot from the Mexican's 18-pounder completely destroyed the crude barricade they were using for cover. As was their tactic, The Mexican soldiers fired a musket volley and then charged with fixed bayonets. Dickinson's crew fired their cannons into the charging Mexican soldiers. Not having time to reload, the Texians fought hand to hand before being overwhelmed and bayoneted to death.

"After the battle, the Alamo was a horrific sight. Dead bodies, body parts, arms, legs, intestines, pieces of flesh and blood were everywhere. The entire inside of the Alamo was red with human blood. It was as if someone had painted it red. The smell was overwhelming. It was worse than any slaughterhouse."

"The fighting and the scene within the Alamo must have completely crazed the greenhorn Mexican soldiers. Even after the resistance had ceased, they continued firing at and bayoneting the dead or wounded Texian bodies. The officers tried to stop this insane behavior *but could not.* Santa Anna arrived inside the Alamo and saw the ongoing madness. In response, he had the buglers sound retreat, but that too accomplished nothing. The Mexican soldiers kept firing and bayoneting, firing and bayoneting, for another fifteen minutes. It was war at its worst. Undoubtedly some of the wounded Texians could have survived their battle wounds, but the insanity after the battle insured that did not happen." To this comment, many of the Rough Riders shook their heads in disgust.

"The Battle of the Alamo lasted about ninety minutes. The numbers of Mexican casualties at the Alamo were about six hundred killed or wounded. That was over one-third of the Mexican soldiers involved in the assault. It was an extremely high casualty rate by any standard. The estimate is that somewhere between *182 and 189* Texians were killed. It is hard to say exactly, because Santa Anna ordered his men to take the dead bodies, stack them with wood, and burn them to ashes."

With some emotion and looking to the ground Paco said, "My father personally witnessed all of this." He then paused for several seconds, continuing to look at the ground.

More quietly and with less energy he said, "Surviving the battle by hiding in the church, were Susan Dickinson, her infant daughter, and Joe, Colonel Travis's batman. Ben, a former slave, escorted the Dickinson's to Gonzales. Santa Anna personally instructed them to relate the events of the battle and to report to other Texian forces that his army was *invincible*. That of course was nonsense, and nothing more than worthless propaganda."

"People around the world remember the Alamo as a place where a small freedom-loving force fought bravely and fiercely against impossible odds. It is a place of honor, courage, and sacrifice. For these reasons, the Alamo is sacred ground and a hallowed memorial to Texas liberty."

Here a couple of Rough Riders began to applaud. Everyone in the group soon joined them.

"The story does not end here," Paco said calmly after the applause died off. "Do you want to hear what happened next?" The Rough Riders nodded.

"Well, Santa Anna now knew that he had to move quickly and engage Texian General Sam Houston before Houston could recruit more troops. With 1,500 men and all his artillery, he left the Alamo to find Houston's militia. Approximately six weeks later, on the afternoon of the 21st of April, General Houston with his militia of nine hundred Texians, attacked Santa Anna's camp at *San Jacinto, Texas*. That was the decisive battle of the 1836 Texas Revolution. In this encounter the Mexican army was taken completely by surprise. It seems they were taking their afternoon siesta, to include enjoying the pleasures of their wives and many camp followers. They were so engaged in this activity and so contemptuous of Houston's Texians, that they did not put out any security. The Mexican Army was camped on a *high-grass* plain. Hidden by that grass, Houston's militia moved quietly until they were only a few yards from Santa Anna's camp. At that point they charged yelling, *'Remember the Alamo!'* and *'Remember Goliad!'* Goliad was where the Mexicans massacred 445 Texian prisoners who had been captured at the battles of

Refugio and Coleto." That last comment shocked the Rough Riders speechless!

"The Battle of San Jacinto was over in less than twenty minutes. Approximately 630 of the Mexican soldiers were killed and 730 captured, while only nine Texians were killed. It was a very bloody affair as most of the Mexicans who died were bayoneted or knifed in hand-to-hand fighting. At that time my father was still with the Mexican army. When he heard the Americans attack, he stripped himself of his Mexican army uniform and killed several of the Mexican officers."

"The Rough Riders snorted and nodded in approval."

"When captured, Santa Anna was hiding in marsh grass and was dressed in a private's uniform. My father was present when he, with great arrogance, said to General Houston, 'The man who has conquered the *Napoleon of the West* was born to no common destiny. And now it remains for that man to be generous to those he has vanquished.'"

My father said General Houston replied, '*You should have remembered that at the Alamo.*'"

"The Battle of San Jacinto forced Santa Anna to order all of his troops out of Texas. This ended Mexico's control and gave legitimacy to the new *Texas Republic*. Three weeks later, Santa Anna signed the peace treaty that formalized the Mexican army leaving the region. This allowed the Republic of Texas to become an independent nation. General Sam Houston of course became a national hero and the Texians' rallying cry, *'Remember the Alamo!' became* an international slogan for freedom, liberty, and democracy."

Paco then said, "Now mi amigos, you may walk around the Alamo grounds. Please go into the chapel and look at the artifacts. I will remain here to answer questions." The Rough Riders gave him a nice round of applause and broke into small groups to walk around the Alamo grounds.

First Sergeant Troxler came over to Jean-Paul, Three-Ring, and Corporal Cox. "Well boys, what do you think? Was it worth $2.00 and your time to come here today to see and hear this?"

Jean-Paul, never at a loss for words said, "It was extremely worthwhile. There is always something a soldier can learn when he visits a former battlefield. He can learn about the leaders, the terrain, the tactics, the reasons why the battle was won or lost, and the like. That is the value of military history. One can learn what other soldiers and leaders did and with that, avoid their mistakes and copy their successes. By applying those learnings, the bloodletting of our soldiers in future battles can be significantly reduced."

For a moment Troxler, Cox, and Three-Ring stared at Jean-Paul. Corporal Cox said, "Where the heck did you get that from? Where did you get so bloody smart? You are just a young slick-sleeve private who is still wet behind the ears?" Cox's breadth was so heavy with the smell of alcohol that it almost knocked the other three of them down. For some reason First Sergeant Troxler didn't seem to notice—or at least he acted like he didn't notice.

To Cox's comment Jean-Paul replied, "Where did I get so smart? I read. Reading is the source of much wisdom. It's that simple. I learned that fact from my dad. When he was not teaching at the Jesuit school or working in our vineyard, he was reading. He would always be reading into the night, every night."

First Sergeant Troxler stared at Jean-Paul as if deep in thought. Then he said, "Dee-bert, you obviously can read, but can you write?"

Jean-Paul thought this to be a strange question. He said, "Of course I can write. I first learned to write when I was four years old. I can write very well in English, French, Chacopac, and even some German"

"Okay then, Mr. Reader and Writer. I have been looking for someone to assist Corporal Cox with his duties as the Troop A company clerk. And you just volunteered. Cox, I want you to teach Trooper Dee-bert here all the army administration you know. You got that?"

Cox looked at Jean-Paul as he replied, "First Sergeant, I will most certainly teach him everything I know and more." With that he punched the teenager on the arm with some force and a big laugh. He and the First Sergeant then walked away to look at more of the Alamo grounds. For some reason Jean-Paul had developed a strong dislike for Corporal Cox.

Three-Ring now shaking his head, said to Jean-Paul, "You just don't' know when to keep your mouth shut, do you Dee-Bert!"

Jean-Paul said, "What do you mean," being totally confused by Three-Ring's comment.

"You had to say you could read and write, and now while we are training for war, you are going to be sitting in the A Troop headquarters tent shuffling papers and filling out army forms. Wonderful." Three-Ring couldn't stop shaking his head in disbelief.

"You my friend, are simply jealous. That's all, just jealous. You had better be careful, *envy* is one of the *seven deadly sins*." He said this with a laugh as now he punched Three-Ring on the arm. "Come on circus boy, let's go look around."

After walking the grounds Three-Ring pointed to a number of vendors hawking their items in an open field across the street from the Alamo. He started walking quickly and beckoned to Jean-Paul to follow him. The vendors were selling just about anything you could imagine from fruit, to souvenir trinkets, to clothing items, and even some hot food. The hot, fried food items looked very tasty. When Three-Ring asked what they were, he was told they were *empanadas*. They were a fried pastry containing beef, cheese, potatoes, and seasoning. Three-Ring bought two and gave one to J.P. They tasted really good. Three-Ring was about to buy another for himself when Trooper Juan-Julio Soto Mendoza arrived on the scene.

Mendoza said, "I wouldn't eat those if I were you."

"Why not," asked Three-Ring, "we already had one."

"Why not? Well take a look at what that pastry was fried in." Mendoza pointed to the tub of boiling fat that had numerous things floating in it, was multiple colors, and was making an unusual gurgling noise. "When do you think was the last time that tub was cleaned? I'd say it was just before the battle of the Alamo. You eat another one and *Montezuma* will get you!

Confused, Jean-Paul asked, "Montezuma *will get us?* What does that mean?"

"Gringo, you are really a little simple. *Montezuma the Second* was the ruler of the Aztec nation. He was known for sacrificing humans as a way of appeasing the gods. Hernan Cortes, the Spanish explorer, defeated the Aztec nation of two hundred thousand with five hundred Spanish soldiers and several thousand locals from rival tribes. The Spaniards then enslaved and virtually annihilated all of the Aztecs. In revenge for this atrocity, it is said that the spirit of Montezuma gives all *White* travelers to Mexico violent and explosive diarrhea. When this happens, we say that the person is suffering from *Montezuma's Revenge.*"

"Yes, but we are not in Mexico," Three-Ring protested. "We are in Texas."

"Si, but don't forget Texas was part of Mexico for a very long time. Many Mexicans still consider Texas to be part of Mexico. So, beware of *Montezuma.*" With that Trooper Mendoza walked away laughing with great merriment.

"Well," said Jean-Paul, "so much for another one of those empanada pastries."

A cleanly dressed Mexican man now approached Jean-Paul and Three-Ring. In English that was quite a bit rougher than Pacos, he said, "*Come, I take your picture. Very cheap. Good picture of soldier in army suit. Come.*"

"How much, asked Jean-Paul.

"Two pictures, three dollars."

Jean-Paul instinctively said, "How about two pictures for two dollars."

"Okay for two dollars—two pictures, two dollars."

"But wait," said Three-Ring, "how will we get them? This sounds like a rip-off Professor."

"No rip-off game, I bring them to camp in three days—in three days."

"Come on Three-Ring. I will pay and you can have one of the two photos."

"Right, I can have one of the two photos, assuming they will show up at camp." Three-Ring was again shaking his head as he looked at Jean-Paul.

There was a festive spirit among the group as they rode the wagon back to camp. Someone started singing: *"It'll be a hot time in the old time tonight."* Then they broke into *"Sweet Rosie O'Grady."* The group sang with lusty vigor. Jean-Paul and Three-Ring joined in the singing with reckless abandon.

Not far from camp the troopers seemed to be worn down from the singing and the ninety-degree weather. Breaking the silence, Trooper Delaney the poker player mused, "I find it most difficult to understand why those men in the Alamo didn't pack up and leave in order to live and fight another day. Why on God's green earth did they stay and fight knowing full well they would all be killed. Why? That makes no sense to me. They wasted their life and for what? Nothing I'd say. They really achieved nothing. The only smart one of the entire bunch was good old *Moses Rose*. He took the opportunity to leave and live to fight another day."

The Rough Riders in the wagon were surprised by Delaney's comments. It was as if the thoughts Delaney was sharing about the defenders possibly abandoning the Alamo had never crossed their minds.

Jean-Paul peered at Delaney who had an expression of confusion on his face. The expression communicated to Jean-Paul that his question was not rhetorical and that he was actually looking for someone to answer it.

Jean-Paul began, "I can understand why they stayed to

fight." This comment caught everyone's interest. He continued, "Some things, some of the beliefs and values people have, are more important to them than their life. They would actually lose their life rather than compromise what they value and believe."

Delaney stared at him in unbelief. He said, "Really Professor? And just what might those values and beliefs be that are more important than a person's life? Give us an example or two." Delaney said that in a condescending tone.

"Sure. Consider the Christians during the early days of the Roman Empire. They would rather be thrown to the lions than give up their faith. Also, consider the Spartan King Leonidas and his 1,400 men that included his three hundred Spartan warriors. They were up against approximately two hundred thousand *Persians* under King Xerxes. In 480 BC Leonidas's forces blocked the Persian's primary invasion route into Greece at *Thermopylae*. Leonidas and his men held out for two days and then were totally annihilated on the third day of fighting. The three hundred Spartans knew their plight was hopeless and that they would ultimately be defeated and killed. Nonetheless, their sense of honor and in order to buy time for the other Greek states to mobilize, demanded they fight to the death. And so, that is what they did. There are other examples of accepting death rather than compromising one's beliefs, but those are the two that readily come to mind."

Delaney sighed and said, "That's all well and good but I

can't think of anything I believe in so deeply that would cause me to intentionally give up my life."

Jean-Paul quietly but forcefully said, "It seems to me you may very well be sacrificing your life by going to Cuba and fighting so that the Cubans can be free from Spanish oppression."

This notion caught Delaney off guard. Now glaring at Jean-Paul with furrowed eyebrows, he said, "That idea never crossed my mind. I joined up to avoid being hunted down and shot. That's why I joined. I certainly did not join to help the Cubans. By the way, how old are Professor?"

"I'm eighteen."

"You talk pretty smart for someone that young."

Jean-Paul replied, "I had some really good teachers, one of which I think may very well be the best teacher in all of the United States of America."

At that statement almost all the troopers laughed out loud.

"Really," said a smiling Delaney. "And who might that be, you know, the best teacher in the entire country—Thomas Jefferson?"

"That would be my father, *Monsieur Louie DeBert*. He is a French veteran of the 1870-71 war with Prussia, a graduate of the Sorbonne University in Paris, a man of faith, and the most well-read and wisest man I have ever met."

"And I am sure with your eighteen long years on this earth

you have met many, many, wise and learned people." That brought yet another laugh from many of the troopers.

Jean-Paul sensed Delaney and the others were mocking him and *that tightening feeling* was beginning to rise in his chest. Three-Ring saw his friends facial expression understanding full well what was happening. He poked J.P. in order to settle him down. The Professor got the message and decided he would not respond the Delaney's last comment.

Getting close to camp, Three-Ring turned to Jean-Paul and in a concerned tone said, "My stomach ain't just feeling so very good. I think I might be having *a gastric incident.*"

Jean-Paul agreed, "My tummy isn't doing so well either. But not to worry, we are almost at the camp."

"Well the driver better hurry up or I will have a troubled event in my pants."

Mendoza heard this and began laughing uncontrollably. *"Remember, I toe you!! I toe you! Montezuma! Montezuma!"*

The wagon entered the camp and was closing in on A Troop's area. Jean-Paul said to Three-Ring who was in obvious agony, "Hang on, we're almost there."

Jean-Paul, whose stomach was also feeling worse by the minute, could not believe his eyes. At the place where the wagon was going to stop stood Captain O'Neil. He was talking with Colonel Wood and Colonel Roosevelt. It was the first time any of the Rough Riders had seen Colonel Wood. He was a broad shouldered, wide chested man with extremely thin legs. He certainly did not appear very well proportioned in his uniform nor did he look the part of a Medal of Honor hero.

When all the Rough Riders exited the wagon, First Sergeant Troxler called the group to attention and saluted the three officers. Colonel Wood told them to stand at ease. He then asked, "Well boys, how was your trip to the most revered site of the great state of Texas?"

The Rough Riders responded with a variety of accolades: *great, good, outstanding, and so on.*

Colonel Wood then asked, "What did learn from the visit?"

This resulted in silence from the Rough Riders.

Trooper Delaney spoke up and said, "Colonel Wood, we are fortunate to have in our midst a highly educated professor. I am quite convinced sir, that he garnered many wonderful learnin's from our Alamo visit and that he would be more than happy to share. Isn't that right Trooper Dee-Bert?" Delaney made that last comment with absolute snideness and contempt.

First Sergeant Troxler joined in, "Come on Dee-Bert, share with us what you learned today!"

At this point Three-Ring who was agonizing from horrific cramps and serious anal pressure said to Jean-Paul under his breath, "Hurry up and talk before I fill my pants. And make it quick."

Undaunted, Jean-Paul confidently took one step forward.

He began, "Well sirs, I learned at least two things of significance. At the Alamo I saw the value of courage. Disciplined men in an organized force, who fight with a furious courage, can take on a much larger force and to a point anyway, hold their own. Even if they are not ultimately victorious, they can inflict what amounts to unacceptable casualties on the enemy."

Three-Ring was fidgeting badly and said to Jean-Paul under his breath, "Will you please hurry up?"

Jean-Paul glanced at Three-Ring, shook his head slightly and continued, "Second, our guide also told us about the Battle of San Jacinto. General Sam Houston's militia conducted a surprise attack and won a decisive victory. What I learned *again* today is that the element of surprise is one of the keys to victory when attacking. And when in a defensive position, one must always put out security and be on guard against a surprise attack. The majority of the decisive land victories in history were because the attacking force employed the element of surprise."

Now Three-Ring was fidgeting worse than ever. When Jean-Paul finished he muttered under his breath, "Thank god, finally."

Other than Three-Ring's almost indiscernible comment, all was quiet. None of the Rough Riders were laughing at Jean-Paul now, especially Delaney. They were all staring at him in a sort of bewildered amazement.

Colonel Wood broke the silence and said pensively, "That's

very good young soldier, very good. That is the way to think about military history. One should always ask what are the lessons it teaches, what can one learn from it, and how can those lessons be applied. One can learn a great deal from walking the terrain of former battlefields. Anytime one has the opportunity to visit such a place, particularly those of our country's civil war, the soldier should do it."

At this point Colonel Roosevelt interjected himself into the conversation. Speaking to Colonel Wood he said, "Sir, this young man has already shown himself to be a hero. That's why I approved his request to join our regiment. When I was on patrol with my New York City policemen, we took chase with a dangerous and armed criminal. This young man saw what was happening and without hesitation tackled the desperado and brought him down hard. If he hadn't done it, *by Godfrey*, I am not sure we would have caught up with him. It was a brave act by this young lad especially since the criminal was armed with both a handgun and a dagger. Bully!!" Seeming not to be able to control himself he, with a huge grin, once again grabbed Jean-Paul by both shoulders and shook him.

All this attention was making Jean-Paul very uncomfortable. He glanced at Three-Ring who nodded and mimicked saying, "Bully."

For the first time, Captain O'Neil joined the conversation. He said, "Colonel Wood sir, I want you to meet the first sergeant of Troop A. Sir, this is First Sergeant Joshua Gideon Troxler. We served together in the Arizona militia. He fought with the Seventh Cavalry and Major Reno at the Little Big Horn. In that action he earned the Medal of Honor."

Colonel Wood took a couple of steps toward Troxler and extended his hand. "Congratulations First Sergeant. Congratulations on receiving *The Medal* and surviving a very nasty battle."

First Sergeant Troxler still pumping Colonel Wood's hand said, "Congratulations to you too, sir, for your receipt of *The Medal* in the Apache War. And to your comment earlier that we should walk the battlefields of the past, I hope I never see that cursed ground at the Little Bighorn River ever again." Troxler had still not let go of Colonel Wood's hand but now he was shaking his head instead of Wood's hand.

All three officers laughed heartily at First Sergeant's comments about not wanting to see the Little Big Horn battlefield again. Jean-Paul noted from the look on Troxler's face that he was serious and did not think his comment was funny.

Colonel Wood, whose hand Troxler had now released said, "All right men, carry on. Enjoy the rest of your Sunday. Take advantage of the time because tomorrow we will again be training in earnest. We don't have much time to get ready for combat. As soon as we get word of our rail transportation, we will depart San Antonio for Tampa, Florida, and from there to

Santiago, Cuba. So, train hard and get ready. Carry on."

Without waiting for any other orders or instruction, Three-Ring, buttock cheeks tight, duck walked to the nearest latrine. Jean-Paul followed but fortunately his stomach was not as angry as Three-Ring's tummy. Arriving at the latrine, Three-Ring got settled and let out a yell celebrating the high velocity exit of the empanada. By the time J.P. arrived, Three-Ring was self-congratulating himself for not soiling his pants. Small victories can be the best....

### Thought Questions for Chapter 9:

1. What is Montezuma's revenge? What relevance can or does it have to soldiers?

2. According to Jean-Paul and Colonel Wood, what is the value of visiting a former battlefield?

3. Why was Santa Anna unsuccessful in stopping his soldiers from shooting and bayoneting the Texian dead and wounded after the battle was over? What can be learned from that event?

4. How did Jean-Paul respond to Trooper Delaney's question asking why the Alamo defenders stayed and fought even though they knew they were vastly outnumbered and probably would not survive? Do you agree or disagree with Jean-Paul? Why?

5. What was your biggest learning or take away from this chapter? What can you apply from the information in this chapter? What in it did you find the most interesting? Why?

# 10

## The Train Trip to Florida

After Monday morning formation, Jean-Paul reported to the headquarters tent of A Troop. He was not sure learning the duties of the company clerk would be a good job. He wanted to be a fighting soldier and not a paper-pusher.

Upon his arrival and as if the First Sergeant had been reading his mind, Troxler said, "I know you are probably thinking you want to do some soldierin' and not be pushin' papers. Well, Dee-bert, there's more to soldierin' than screaming up a hill with a fixed bayonet. There are a lot of things that go on behind the scenes that support the boys charging up that hill. One of those things is *administration*. The army cannot be run without good *administration*.' And you young soldier—are going to learn all there is to know about company administration. While the troopers are out shooting their weapons today, Corporal Cox here will be teaching you about morning reports and the other essential paperwork required by the regimental headquarters and the United States Army. Do you have any questions about that and what is expected of you?"

"No First Sergeant. I've got it. I am sure Corporal Cox will do an excellent job getting me up to speed on *army administration."*

Troxler looked at Corporal Cox and said in a low tone, "I am sure he will. Isn't that right Cox?"

Cox replied, "That's right First Sergeant. That's absolutely right."

"Okay then, get on it. Start with the morning report. When that's completed take Dee-bert up to regimental headquarters and introduce him around. Think you can handle that Corporal?"

Cox replied, "Yes First Sergeant, I got it. I'll take good care of young Dee-bert here. Of that there is no doubt." The smell of alcohol was again strong coming off of Corporal Cox.

After Cox had explained the morning report, Jean-Paul couldn't help himself and asked the Corporal, "Where do you get the alcohol that you always seem to be drinking?"

Cox was a completely surprised by the question. "What's that to you Dee-bert? What's it to you anyway?"

"Well, it seems we were told we were not to be drinking alcohol in camp. And you never seem to leave camp, but you always smell of liquor."

It was clear Jean-Paul had struck a nerve. Corporal Cox stood up, leaned forward and shook his finger angrily at the private. He shouted, "You need to mind your own business. If you continue to ask me or talk about drinking alcohol in the camp, I will tell both Colonel Wood and Colonel Roosevelt that it was you who threatened an upstanding San Antonio citizen in that bar incident. We'll see if that will get you to Cuba." He paused and then said quietly, "Have I made myself clear enough private?"

"Absolutely. No problem. Forget that I ever asked the question. And thanks for teaching me the morning report." said Jean-Paul. Cox grunted and said, "Come on, let's go to regiment. We will turn in the morning report and I will introduce you around."

Walking to regiment Corporal Cox said, "Our primary contact at regiment is their admin sergeant—*Sergeant LaCombe*. He is no one to trifle with. He previously served in the U.S. Navy. He has always been in administration and actually worked for Colonel Roosevelt when the Colonel was the Assistant Secretary of the Navy. I think the last horse he rode was at a country club foxhunt. He knows military admin inside out and is tight with Colonel Roosevelt—which is probably why he is here in the first place. Always stay on his good side and never try to nonsense him. He will see right through it. Got that?"

"Yes Corporal Cox. I got that."

The regimental headquarters of the First United States Volunteer Cavalry was a bundle of activity. Everyone greeted Corporal Cox and seemed happy to see him. He must have done something right to impress all these people thought Jean-Paul.

Cox stopped at the field desk of a huge, strapping sergeant. This sergeant's hair was totally white. However, his face or posture did not peg him as being as old as the color of his hair was suggesting. Corporal Cox introduced Jean-Paul to Sergeant LaCombe.

"Welcome to Army administration young soldier. It is not as efficient as Navy admin, but for what we have to do it will suit. Tell me your last name again?

"It's DeBert and is pronounced Duh-bear. It's French."

In perfect French Sergeant Lacombe said, "Oui, I am French also. My name is LaCombe. Do you speak French?"

Responding in French Jean-Paul said, "Oui, fluently and also some German. My father is from France and all his people still live there."

Continuing in French LaCombe said, "Excellent, excellent. I love speaking French. I was born in Quebec City, in Canada. Both of my parents are French. They moved From Brittany to Quebec and then to the United States. Wonderful DeBert, I look forward to working with you and speaking French with you."

"Likewise."

Corporal Cox chimed in with a touch of envy in his voice, "Well then Private, we need to get going. Thanks Sergeant LaCombe. I am sure one of us will be seeing you soon."

"I am sure one of you will."

\*          \*          \*          \*          \*

Working as the assistant company clerk turned out to be better duty than Jean-Paul had expected. It seemed Corporal

Cox always found excuses to go here or there or on sick call. The result was that he was seldom around. When he was present, he didn't seem to have much time for Jean-Paul. He sensed Cox was envious of him and felt he was angling in on his power and position with the First Sergeant. That attitude did not bother the Professor in the least. He simply wanted to do the best job possible.

Because of Corporal Cox's absences, the First Sergeant took it upon himself to be Jean-Paul's primary teacher. He would sit with him and review all the documents and requests that came from regiment. Using preprinted army forms, the First Sergeant would tell Jean-Paul what to write in response to regiment's various inquiries about training, supplies on hand, shortages, equipment readiness, and so on. He would routinely explain to Jean-Paul why he responded as he did. Time after time he reinforced with Jean-Paul to never *fall into to the trap of thinking higher headquarters didn't know what they were doing.* That he said, is the *thinking of fools.* He explained that headquarters may be inept, but being the higher headquarters, *they are always right* and will win any argument with their subordinate units. And it was a *fool's errand* to challenge headquarters unless there was an ethical issue involved. And even that could be a very dangerous move. You may be right but you probably wouldn't win. Interesting advice thought Jean-Paul.

Captain McNeill may have been the troop commander, but it was clear First Sergeant Troxler was running the unit. Jean-Paul found it interesting that Troxler would make decisions and then tell Captain O'Neill what he did. He would never ask him what to do, he would just tell him what he had done after the fact. Jean-Paul thought this army way of doing business was very curious indeed.

With his new job, Jean-Paul was no longer required to pull guard duty, kitchen police (K.P.) duty in the mess hall, camp police call, or the cleaning of latrines. No problem, he had gotten quite proficient at all these the first time he did them.

Just prior to Thursday's lunch, all of the administrative work was complete. First Sergeant Troxler said to Cox and Jean-Paul, "Gentlemen, since we are caught up, this afternoon we will be joining the rest of the troop for some training on horseback."

Jean-Paul thought that they would only be doing cavalry drills with the members of the A Troop. However, that afternoon the drills were planned for the entire regiment. It was great fun. Jean-Paul's horse performed flawlessly in the open terrain. This was not the case with many of the other recently broken stallions. Many wanted nothing to do with the cavalry formations or the other horses. Because of the horsemanship of their riders, these rebellious steeds were generally managed, but only with a great deal of difficulty.

First, the regiment did essential movements to form a line

and then a column. When in line they first moved in a trot and then at a gallop. They then did skirmish drills in order to get accustomed to advancing in open order. When in skirmish formation, the troopers would advance on foot while one trooper held his own horse and the horses of three other soldiers. Jean-Paul noted that the correct intervals were seldom kept. They, however, did all the movements—as Colonel Roosevelt described it—*with great dash*. Also, they did not have traditional cavalry sabers, which took just a bit of the excitement out of the training.

Early on Sunday morning, the 29th of May, the order came down to transfer the regiment to the rail yard for movement to Tampa, Florida. There was a whirlwind of activity, excitement, and energy throughout the camp. The First Sergeant had previously told Jean-Paul that when orders for movement came, he was to first pack up his personal gear. Then he was to assist Corporal Cox in taking down the A Troop headquarters tent and box up the Troop's admin materials.

After finishing with his gear, Jean-Paul went looking for Corporal Cox. Apparently, he had gone into San Antonio on Saturday night and had not yet returned to camp. Jean-Paul concluded that if the company's tent and admin materials were to be prepared for movement, he would have to do it himself.

While in the middle of this project, First Sergeant Troxler, who seemed to be everywhere at once, stopped and asked, "Deebert, where's that little runt Cox?"

"Sorry First Sergeant, but I don't know. Rumor is he went into town last night and hasn't returned to camp just yet."

"Just yet? That little...."

The First Sergeant then used a string of words in describing Corporal Cox that Jean-Paul had never heard before. They were extremely creative, blue, and insulting. And the cadence and rhythm with which the First Sergeant had expressed himself was equally impressive. Jean-Paul smiled and just kept packing.

Troop A later formed up on their horses. They then rode out of the hot, dusty, and windy camp that had been home for the past several weeks. When they arrived at the rail yard it was clear there were no obvious facilities to load the horses into the box cars. The First Sergeant had told Jean-Paul to stay with him in case he needed a runner. Being with the First Sergeant, Jean-Paul overheard several conversations with the other troop leaders, the railway officials, and also Colonel Roosevelt.

It was the most disorganized and confusing situation Jean-Paul had ever seen. He observed with great interest how everyone was dealing with the stress of the situation while also attempting to solve the problems at hand. He knew if his father Louie were here, he would have gotten all this confusion quickly sorted out. Better still, being the planner that he was, his father would never have let this become the problem it obviously had. *Louie always anticipated.* He told Jean-Paul that one could avoid many headaches if proper planning was done before hand.

He firmly believed planning was one of the keys to success for just about everything.

Because of the obvious limits on space, Colonel Wood decreed that the troopers could only bring what they could carry on their backs. That troubled Jean-Paul for a moment, since he was concerned that would rule out the shoulder bag he had brought from home. But First Sergeant Troxler put him at ease when he told him bringing his leather bag would not be a problem.

At dusk in the station yard, every man unsaddled his horse. Each left his bridle, saddle, and all of his individual property that he did not immediately need in a freight car. A guard was posted, and the horses were then taken to be fed and watered. When they had eaten and drunk their fill, they were loaded on cattle cars. This was no easy effort since those half-broken creatures were fresh from the open range and simply did not want to go up those make-shift chutes. Jean-Paul and Three-Ring watched the loading of the horses with great interest. Those gallant warhorses did not look so gallant during that process. Like First Sergeant Troxler, Colonel Roosevelt seemed to be everywhere at once. Jean-Paul was amazed at the energy of this forty-year-old, somewhat overweight officer.

Despite the electricity in the air, everything remained chaotic and confused. In addition to one thousand soldiers and their mounts, there were over one hundred fifty pack mules as well as the other necessary *going to war* supplies. The troop units were all mixed together and everyone seemed to be yelling or shouting about something. In the mass confusion, some of the troopers slipped away to get one last drink at the saloons near the rail yard.

Well past midnight, when almost everything was loaded, the buglers sounded assembly to get an account of the men. Troop A was all accounted for with the exception of Corporal Cox.

To everyone's surprise and disappointment, the passenger cars had not yet arrived. First Sergeant Troxler told his troopers to stay close and lay on the ground and get some sleep. About this time, Private Dusty Rhodes, who was a runner for Sergeant LaCombe and regimental headquarters, came running and was yelling First Sergeant Troxler's name. Out of breadth, he told the First Sergeant that the San Antonio police had come to the camp. They indicated they had a Corporal Cox from Troop A in the city jail. He had been thrown in jail on Saturday night for being drunk and disorderly. They threatened that if someone from the Army didn't come to get him, he would be prosecuted to the full extent of Texas law and would remain in jail.

Almost all of Troop A's soldiers heard Private Rhodes's report. What they didn't expect was the First Sergeant's response. Troxler, in his first sergeant's voice, said for all to hear, "That little hopeless drunk can stay in jail forever as far as I am concerned. He has been in the army a long time and he knows better than to behave like this. That kind of conduct is why he couldn't keep his sergeant's stripes. I've covered for his drunken butt long enough. If he wants to act like an undisciplined recruit, then he can suffer the consequences—that's right, suffer the consequences. He can rot in a boiling Texas jail forever as far as I am concerned. Since he missed formation tonight, we will just report him absent without authorization and that will be the end of him in Troop A, and for the Army too for that matter."

Troxler then turned around and said, "Where's Private Dee-bert?'

"Right here First Sergeant." A feeling of terror flashed across Jean-Paul's entire body.

"Dee-Bert, you are no longer the assistant company admin clerk—you are now Troop A's company admin clerk. You are also promoted to corporal. And you can thank that drunken Cox for your promotion."

With that announcement Jean-Paul received a nice round of applause from the other troopers. That quite frankly surprised him since many of them had been giving him the raspberries about both his reading and his transfer to cushy duty at the company headquarters.

Three-Ring looked at him and said, "Dee-bert, you sure are one lucky duck. I am going to stay close to you. It seems you can fall into a pile of dog doo and come up smelling like a rose."

With a big smile Jean-Paul said, "You are just jealous circus boy. Just too bad for you *Private* Hankey." The new corporal purposely placed emphasis on the word *private!*

"Three-Ring simply grunted as he then tried to find an unoccupied place on the grass on which to spend the San Antonio evening.

At dawn, the passenger cars arrived. With great enthusiasm the Rough Riders rose and prepared for the trip. Colonel Roosevelt had divided the regiment into four sections. He rode with the section that included Troop F and Troop L. With L being commanded by Captain Allyn Capron.

Jean-Paul had never personally seen or met Captain Capron. He was however, cut from the same hero mold as was Captain O'Neill. After only a couple of weeks Capron had earned the reputation of being an energetic leader, a natural teacher, and someone who was extremely knowledgeable in battlefield tactics and the military art. Most evenings he would conduct classes for the regimental officers on the modernized English version of the *1791 French Drill Manual*. The first time Jean-Paul had seen Capron was when he was organizing his troop for deployment. He was quite impressed since the captain looked and acted like a fighting man. He had an aura about him and there was a natural grace to all his movements. Jean-Paul had heard that the soldiers in Troop L not only respected and admired him but also *liked him*. That combination thought Jean-

Paul, was truly remarkable!

Troop A was assigned three passenger cars. With a sense of urgency that he effectively transmitted to his troopers, First Sergeant Troxler assigned them by squads to the various cars. Just as Jean-Paul was about to step up into his allotted passenger car, he heard someone yelling his name. He turned, and there to his surprise was the photographer who had taken Three-Ring and his photograph at the Alamo. He was waving an envelope over his head and came running toward Jean-Paul. Jean-Paul had forgotten all about those photos. This photographer obviously was a very honest and responsible individual. How unusual thought the Professor.

Finally, all of A Troop's personnel, horses, and equipment were on the train. As the train blew its whistle and started to move, the troopers let out a great cheer. There was a celebratory and festive mood throughout. The war was now closer than it had been before. If anyone was concerned about that fact, it certainly didn't show.

Jean-Paul was sitting with Three-Ring. Directly across from them were troopers Mendoza and Wilson. After all the celebration and yelling had died out, everyone in the car settled down to get some sleep. The movement of the train always seemed conducive for sleeping. J.P. however was on an emotional high and wasn't in a state to go to sleep. Trooper Mendoza was sitting across from him. Since he too did not appear to be in the mood for sleeping, Jean-Paul saw an opportunity for some Spanish language lessons.

"Juan-Julio, perhaps this would be a good time for you to help me learn some basic Spanish phrases?"

"Not really, I want to get some sleep. That ground by the railroad tracks last night was pretty hard."

"Well, it doesn't seem like you are just in the state to go to sleep right now. So, until you get in the mood, maybe you can give me some phrases in Spanish that could be helpful."

"Sure," said Mendoza, "How about, 'I surrender, which is *'Me rindo!'*"

"I don't think I'll be needing that one. How about, *'Hello, how are you'* for a start?"

"Don't you know any Spanish at all?"

"No, but I do know French. And since French and Spanish are both Romance languages, I am sure there are many similarities."

"Maybe, but I don't know that for sure. However, I am sure that you know some Spanish. How do you say, *thank you* in Spanish?"

Jean-Paul replied, "I think it is *gracias.*"

"See I told you that you knew some Spanish. There are many words in Spanish that are the same as English. They just have a slightly different pronunciation."

"Interesting. Give me some examples."

"Sure, how about these: *similar, doctor, hospital, hotel, animal, menu, color, idea, tomate, and posible.* Notice how I said them. Even when they are pronounced with a Spanish accent, one can understand what is meant."

"Understood, I got that."

"Here are some other Spanish words you probably know: wine is pronounced vino; cerveza is beer; siesta is for a nap; fiesta is for a party; casa is for house; documento is for a document, and especially for you young one, *professor* is for *professor.*"

Then Mendoza said, "Here are some common phrases in Spanish. You repeat after me. Say it exactly as I say it:"

"Hello is: *hola*, pronounced oh-lah."

"How are you? is: *Como esta usted?*"

"I'm fine, thanks, and you? is spoken as: bien gracias; y usted? Y is pronounced 'EE' in Spanish and means *and.* It is written simply as *y.*"

Jean-Paul was simultaneously repeating, writing, and concentrating.

"My name is: *Mi nombre es....*"

"Good morning is: *buenos dias.*"

"Good afternoon or early evening is: *buenas tardes.*"

"Good night is: *buenas noches.*"

"Goodbye is: *adios* or *hasta luego.*"

"Good luck is: *buena suerte.*"

"Cheers is: *salud.*"

"I don't understand is: *no comprendo.*"

"Do you speak English is: *Habla usted Ingles?*"

"How much is this, is: *cuanto cuesta* or *cuanto cuesta esto?*"

"It's all good is: *todo bien* or *esta bien.*"

"I don't know is: *yo no sae. Sae is pronounced say.*"

"The response to thank you or gracias is: *de nada.* That is: *It's nothing at all.*"

I love you is: *Te amo chica.*"

Jean-Paul now piped in, "Right, I love you. I'm sure I will need that in Cuba." Mendoza smiled.

"*Alto* is *stop, fuego* is *fire, and socorro* is *help.*" These are pronounced just as they look and the way they are spelled.

The more interest Jean-Paul showed in Mendoza, the more Juan-Julio became energized. Preacher Wilson was now listening and also repeating after Mendoza. Three-Ring was also listening to the goings on with passive interest.

By 7:00 PM the train was coming to a halt. By then Jean-Paul had filled almost all of his twelve pages of writing paper. He generally could remember the words and pronunciations of a new language after hearing them once. At the end of his ten-plus-hour language session, he was communicating with Trooper Mendoza in simple and mostly correct Spanish—well, mostly.

Jean-Paul was both startled and impressed with the

reception the local population gave the Rough Riders at their *Lake Charles, Louisiana,* stop. There was a huge crowd of locals present to greet and cheer the Rough Riders. They brought flowers, fruit, watermelons, water, and containers of milk. Young girls were there in their Sunday finery asking for cartridges and any other mementos they could beg from willing Rough Riders. It was like a 4th of July celebration.

Old Glory was flying and draped everywhere. Mixed silently between the Stars and Stripes was an occasional Confederate battle flag—*the Stars and Bars.* That was noticed by everyone and sent a quiet message of Confederate pride!

There was also a small band present that apparently didn't know any song other than *Dixie.* They played it over and over again as the soldiers unloaded their horses for a drink of water and some hay. Jean-Paul remembered reading that Abraham Lincoln said *Dixie* was his favorite song and that he missed hearing it during the war.

Never having seen a spectacle such as this, Jean-Paul stared at the crowd as he waited for his gallant steed Applejack to finish his dinner. Looking past the girls and young boys, he noticed a most unusual scene. Standing quietly in the background were a number of older women dressed completely in black. He couldn't help but think that these were war widows. The looks on their faces spoke volumes. They had experienced war, and it had not been an experience of bands playing and the eating of watermelons. Also, in the background were some older men missing limbs. Jean-Paul began counting them. When he got to twenty-two he stopped. They also were not smiling. It struck Jean-Paul that it must have stirred many emotions, most of them unpleasant, for these invalid confederate war veterans to once again see all these blue uniformed Federal soldiers.

There were also young men with harsh, bitter faces mixed among the widows and invalids. It took a second for Jean-Paul to realize that these young men had not been born or were even old enough to have served in the War of the Rebellion. However, they were undoubtedly raised on *stories of Southern glory and Northern aggression.* Certainly the city's war veterans had told endless tales of their service with Bobby Lee, Stonewall Jackson, and the horse cavalry of John Singleton Mosby, J.E.B. Stuart, and Nathan Bedford Forrest. Jean-Paul noticed that some of those young men were carrying holstered pistols. The thought of what had motivated them do so, made him urge Applejack to eat and drink a little faster.

Back on the train Jean-Paul fell into a deep and uninterrupted sleep. He dreamt about home, his mother and father, the Chacs, and of course Abby and Berti. Good dreams!

"Wake up Jean-Paul, we are stopping again. We are in Mobile, Alabama." said Three-Ring. It was three o'clock in the afternoon. The Professor was obviously more tired than he thought. He had slept soundly for almost eighteen hours. First things first, he needed to go to the car's toilet.

As they were moving to take Sparky and Applejack for water, hay, and a short walk, Three-Ring said, "The First Sergeant said we will probably be pulling out again sometime after nine tonight."

"Sounds good to me. I really had a good sleep. I think I slept for almost eighteen hours. Unbelievable. That's a first."

"I thought you were dead. It's a good thing you snore otherwise I was sure you were gone."

"Are you serious? I don't snore!"

"No, of course you don't. Those noises coming from your nose and open mouth are undoubtedly from someone else. Probably from the leprechaun that lives in your head."

Jean-Paul shook his head and made a conscious decision to ignore Three-Ring. The little guy was always pulling his leg about something.

The welcoming crowd in Mobile was even larger than the one in Louisiana. There was a also band playing. It seemed to Jean-Paul they were playing *Dixie* over and over again just like the band in Lake Charles.

"Don't these bands down here in the South know any songs other than *Dixie*," Jean-Paul rhetorically asked Three-Ring.

"I like the way that song sounds. It stirs up the emotions which is what all good songs are supposed to do."

Jean-Paul simply shook his head and asked, "All songs?

Perhaps, but I am not so sure. I'd have to think about that one."

"Right. Right. You have to think about it. It seems to me you think about way too many things—way too many things. I'll bet your head hurts a lot from all that thinking." Jean-Paul again ignored that comment.

Jean-Paul and Three-Ring were walking through the crowd of well-wishers toward the train car that was carrying Applejack and Sparky. Over the din of the band and the crowd, Jean-Paul heard his name called. He turned and saw First Sergeant Troxler beckoning him. Captain O'Neill was standing next to him.

Witnessing this of course, was Three-Ring. True to form, he said to Jean-Paul, "Okay Professor, now what did you do? "

"Nothing that I know of. But if I did do something, I am sure I will find out about it in a second." Jean-Paul turned and walked quickly through the crowd. Arriving where the troop commander and first sergeant were standing, he stopped, came to attention and saluted Captain O'Neill.

"At ease trooper," said the Captain. "Since you are now a corporal and Troop A's company clerk, the First Sergeant and I felt you need to be official. That means you need to be wearing the insignia of you rank. So here are corporal stripes for all of your uniform shirts. Congratulations son. I have been watching you and agree with the First Sergeant that *you have a natural talent for soldering*. I am sure before this campaign is over, we will be giving you sergeant's stripes."

Captain O'Neill gave Jean-Paul a handful of cloth corporal's rank insignia. He then offered his hand for a congratulatory handshake.

Jean-Paul shook the captain's hand and then automatically saluted.

First Sergeant Troxler also stepped forward and also offered his hand in congratulations.

He then said, "Now Corporal, to make you official, I am ordering you to go into Mobile and get those stripes sewn onto your uniform. Keep in mind army regulations do not authorize the wearing of enlisted rank insignia on the campaign uniform, but unofficially we have always been doing it. How else will anyone know that a soldier is a noncommissioned officer?"

"But First Sergeant, I really need to take care of my horse."

"That's not a problem. I'll make sure old Applejack is fed and watered. You go and get your rank sewn on. Furthermore, you can take your little circus buddy with you. That way you can keep an eye on each other and ensure you both get back here by nine tonight. The stationmaster said we should be approved to move out tonight somewhere between nine and ten. Make sure you are back in plenty of time. Don't be another Trooper Cox who missed movement and will have a great future hammering rocks in Texas. I don't want to break in another company clerk."

"No problem First Sergeant. We'll be back in plenty of time."

Jean-Paul saluted Captain O'Neill one more time. The Captain smiled as he returned a casual salute.

Walking away, Jean-Paul said, "Stick with me Three-Ring and we will go places together."

"Sure we will. I have been in more fights in the three weeks I have known you than I was in all my years in the circus."

Jean-Paul responded, "Right and just remember, you aren't dealing with clowns, lion tamers, or bearded ladies anymore either."

With a smile Three-Ring said, "Don't make fun of all my old friends. I would prefer them to living in a tribe and going to school with an overzealous bunch of Jesuits!"

Not smiling, Jean-Paul said, "You had better stop now. You are starting to give me *that feeling...!*"

"Okay, okay, we certainly don't want to be doing that," Three-Ring said holding up his hands and with a half-smile.

After getting his other uniform shirts and asking some of the locals where the closest tailor shop was located, the two Rough Riders headed off.

After about a half an hour of walking and receiving many stares, they came to the address of the recommended tailor. Inside was an older woman dressed entirely in black. The shop had garments of every description hanging and lying everywhere. It had a strong, musty, and disagreeable smell of old, dirty clothes. Actually, it had the aroma of a full clothes hamper.

The woman looked up at them and said nothing. She simply continued on with her work.

"Excuse us ma'am, but we would need help with some sewing."

The old woman said nothing and continued working. Jean-Paul and Three-Ring gave each other a puzzled look.

Jean-Paul repeated his request, but the lady again did not look up.

Jean-Paul began the third time, but the woman now jumped up with *scissors* in hand. She yelled, "We don't serve Yankee thrash in here. If you are smart you will turn around and *get the h-ll out of here and now.*"

Neither of the stunned Rough Riders knew what to make of the woman's comments.

"Why do you call us Yankees? I don't understand," asked a confused Jean-Paul.

"Why? Why you ask? Because you are soldiers in the federal army and are wearing their Yankee blue uniform, that's why."

Now even more confused, Jean-Paul in his naivety asked, "Are you equating us with the Union army in the War of the Rebellion?"

"What? What? The War of the Rebellion? That's typical Yankee talk. It was the *War for Southern Independence.* That's right—the War for Southern Independence. General Bobby Lee surrendered way too soon—way too soon in my way of thinkin'."

Jean-Paul and Three-Ring looked at one another, now recognizing what was happening. This woman had deep bitterness and *was still fighting the war*. She was a poor, misguided old lady.

Three-Ring grabbed Jean-Paul's arm and said, "Let's go. We can find another tailor."

Jean-Paul shook Three-Ring's hand off of his arm and asked the woman, "Why are you still fighting a war that ended over thirty years ago?"

Three-ring shook his head and said under his breath, *"Here we go again."*

The woman seemed to have aged several years since their conversation began. With a raised voice and menacingly waving those *scissors*, she began, "My husband was in the war. Left me here with five children and no means of support. Two of my children starved to death—starved to death mind you. Do you know what that's like? For a mother to see her children starve to death? Can you even imagine? The rest of us would have starved too if it hadn't been for meager handouts from the church."

"My husband was shot in the leg at Vicksburg. It wasn't a bad enough wound for those army butchers to cut off his leg, although he said they wanted to. It was bad enough, however, for him to be discharged and sent back here to Alabama after

Vicksburg surrendered. All he brought home with him was a really bad limp and some crazy stories. And of course, he wasn't the same man that left." The old woman just shook her head and stared into space for what seemed like minutes.

Gathering herself, she began again, "Then in 1865 the Yankees came marching toward Mobile. Of course, my dumb husband had to join up once again—gimp and all. This time he took my sixteen-year-old son with him. My husband was killed at the *Battle of Spanish Fort*. My sixteen-year-old, who was as crazy as his father, was killed by the Yankees in *the Battle of Fort Blakely*. Two months later the ammunition depot the Yankees had set up here on Beauregard Street in Mobile blew up. It killed over three hundred people to include my other two children. It sank the ships docked on the Mobile River and destroyed the entire northern part of the city that included my house. Now ask me your question again. You know, the question about why I am still fighting the war?"

Backing up toward the door and grabbing Three-Ring, Jean-Paul said, "Ma'am, I am really sorry but neither one of us soldiers were even born when that war was going on. You really need to drop the bitterness and move on."

To that statement the woman threw her scissors at Jean-Paul but missed badly. But that was enough for the two troopers to rush out of the store and run for a block or two without stopping.

"Who would have believed that—having a scissors thrown at us by a deranged old woman?" asked Jean-Paul.

"Human nature is really strange—really strange," said Three-Ring, shaking his head.

### *Thought Questions for Chapter 10:*

1. What pieces of advice did First Sergeant Troxler give about dealing with higher headquarters? Do you agree with him? Would you have added anything?

2. How did Jean-Paul think his father Louie would have handled the confused gaggle at the train station when the regiment was about to move to Florida?

3. Why was Jean-Paul impressed with Captain Capron? Would the Captain's characteristics have impressed you? Why or why not?

4. Why did the tailor in Mobile, Alabama, throw her scissors at Jean-Paul? Do you think that was justified? Why or why not?

5. What was your biggest learning or take away from this chapter? What can you apply from the information in this chapter? What in it did you find the most interesting? Why?

# 11

## *Meeting Desiree*

Looking for another tailor shop, the two Rough Riders heard catcalls. They turned to see if they were the objects of those calls. What they saw was quite unbelievable. Walking toward them was a magnificently dressed, highly perfumed, and perfectly made-up woman. The low-cut nature of her dress left little to the imagination. She was carrying an open parasol and was walking tall and proud, totally indifferent to the catcalls.

As she approached them, she said in an enticing voice, "Well hello there cowboys. Is there anything I can help you with? Something that might put a smile on your face?"

Jean-Paul, not recognizing this woman for who or what she was, politely (and naïvely) said, "Well ma'am, what I need help with is getting these corporal stripes sewn onto my uniform shirts." He lifted the shirts and then showed the lady the stripes.

"Well, come on with me gentlemen, I think I can help you with that. Considering how you boys smell, you could probably use a bath too."

Neither Jean-Paul nor Three-Ring realized they stunk. Jean-Paul was embarrassed that his personal hygiene was now so bad that others could actually smell him, particularly *a lady.*

"Well, my first priority is to get these stripes sewed on and a bath sounds like a really good idea. What do you think Three-Ring?"

"I think it sounds like a wonderful idea," said Three-Ring with a big smile. Worldlier than Jean-Paul, he knew exactly what the lady represented.

"Wonderful boys, simply wonderful. You won't be disappointed. By the way, my name is Lee Ann. Walk with me. My place is just down the street," she said with the biggest smile either of the Rough Riders had seen lately.

After walking a short distance, they came upon an old, stooped woman dressed in a faded black dress. The three passed by her as she was slowly shuffling along.

Within seconds of passing her she began yelling loudly in a very unpleasant high and squeaky voice, "Look! Look! Here are two fools who are like oxen going to the butcher...like birds flying into a snare...like sheep going to the slaughterhouse. No one who cavorts with wanton women will ever see heaven. Noooo, they will never get to heaven. They will never see heaven!" The old lady totally out of breadth now stopped yelling and was leaning against the wall of a shop they had just passed. Her breathing was loud, heavy, and heaving.

Three-Ring, confused by the incident, asked, "What was that all about?'

Jean-Paul, remembering his Jesuit training said, "She was

quoting verses by King Solomon from the seventh chapter of the book of Proverbs in the *King James*. It talks about the fool or simple person getting involved with a prostitute. But I can't imagine why in the world she would be yelling that to us?" As soon as he said this, it came to him. Perhaps Lee Ann was running more than a sewing shop or a bathhouse. He could have kicked himself for being so simple.

As they were walking in silence, they came upon what looked to be a general store. Outside the store and on the sidewalk was a tall can that contained several walking canes. This caused Jean-Paul to stop and briefly examine them. With one exception, they all had curved handles. Only one was a walking stick like the one Jean-Paul had learned to use as a savate stick. It had an ornate silver head and was painted black. Jean-Paul took it from the can and closely examined it. "I am going to go in here and find out how much this stick costs because I'm not sure I can live without it," he said with a smile.

Followed by Three-Ring and also Lee Ann, Jean-Paul entered the store. Like all general stores it had an odd and unique smell. It was a combination of new clothing, denim, cooking spices, health potions, oils, and God only knows what else. The smell was not particularly pleasant. It was certainly more practical than attractive.

Jean-Paul walked to the counter where there was a thin, balding man dressed in a white shirt, bow tie, armbands, and suspenders. He put the walking stick on the counter and asked, "How much for this cane?'

Completely ignoring Jean-Paul, the old gentleman said, "Good afternoon, Miss Lee Ann. And how are we today?" He was acting like a childish little boy who had just seen his favorite girl.

Lee Ann, again with a great big smile replied, "Why Mr. Gabriel, I am just fine, just fine on this lovely day. And how are you Mr. Gabriel? I hope you are doing well."

Almost giddy, Mr. Gabriel replied, "Oh Miss Lee Ann, I am doing wonderful, just wonderful.  It is always a pleasure to see you. What can I do for you today?"

Jean-Paul looked at Three-Ring who raised his eyebrows and shrugged his shoulders.

"I would like you to assist my two new friends. Could you please help this young man with the walking stick?"

"Oh yes, the walking stick. For you young solder, the stick is fifty cents. It normally would be a bit more, but for you...." Before he finished a very large and *formidable mustached woman* came out of the back room. She had a face that reflected years of unhappiness—many years. She also appeared to have tobacco spittle of her apron.

When she saw the two soldiers and Lee Ann, she halted abruptly. Both Three-Ring and Jean-Paul anticipated that what she was about to say would be very unpleasant. The large woman with the moustache did not disappoint.

"Well, well, just look what we have here." Looking at Lee Ann with apparent disgust, she continued, "I see you have some new clients. With the Yankee army in town business must be good...."

Mr. Gabriel, no longer the giddy schoolboy said, "Now Hildegard, let's show some courtesy to our customers. You know, we are here to serve our customers."

Hildegard looked at her husband and with complete contempt said, "There are some customers we don't need in here because they drive decent folks away."

"Now Hildy..."

"Don't '*now Hildy me.*'" She gave one last evil eye to Lee Ann, turned, and left the room.

The embarrassed old man said, "Don't mind her, she is having a bad day."

Jean-Paul gave Mr. Gabriel the fifty cents for the walking sick and started for the door.

As the three were leaving, Lee Ann turned to Mr. Gabriel and in somewhat of a whisper said, *"Now don't be a stranger Walter."*

Hmmm, thought Jean-Paul, that also explains something. Of course, if I were married to Hildy, I wouldn't be a stranger to Lee Ann's *house* either. It was clear from Three-Ring's expression he was thinking the same thing.

After a short walk they arrived at Lee Ann's *house*. From the outside it looked like a well-maintained hotel. The name above the door was in bold red letters. It read: *THIS IS IT!* Written just below it in smaller letters was the same sentence in French: *C'EST ELLE!*

What Jean-Paul saw when he entered confirmed to him what kind of establishment it really was. He felt an immediate and almost overwhelming uneasiness that made him want to run away. The smell of cheap perfume and fresh cut flowers was exceptionally strong. There were couches, sofas, settees, and loveseats everywhere. Huge paintings of the most unusual and bizarre scenes were hanging on the walls. There were dancing satyrs, centaurs, fleeing nymphs, images of Pan, unicorns, and numerous other nude figures. Many of those large naked female figures should have kept their clothes on thought Jean-Paul. Some *naked* can clearly be more disagreeable than attractive. To the left of the large room was a small whiskey bar with a male bartender who looked totally lost and out of place. There was also a piano player who was playing what sounded like a Johann Strauss waltz. Directly ahead there was a huge circular staircase at the base of which stood two of the largest Black men Jean-Paul had ever seen. He couldn't help but stare. To this Lee Ann said, "They're our security. You understand. It's just in case someone becomes too frisky." Once again there was that huge smile on Lee Ann's face.

Around the room were lounging some very beautiful, young

women. All were dressed in what Jean-Paul interpreted as not very substantial sleeping garb. That is not what a woman would wear at night in upstate New York—even in the summer thought Jean-Paul.

Lee Ann, in a moderate tone told the girls to gather around. She began, "Girls, we have here two of the very famous *U.S. Army Rough Riders*. They are going to Florida and ultimately to Cuba to liberate those poor unfortunate Cubans. They need a hot bath and some female companionship."

With that she turned to the two troopers and asked, "See anyone whom you would like to help you with that bath and perhaps scrub your back?'

There was one young beauty that was about five feet tall. Three-Ring, upon spotting her pointed and said, "She can scrub my back." With that, the young girl giggling at her good fortune, took him by the arm and hurried up the staircase.

How about you young soldier? See anyone interesting?" Lee Ann asked to a very uncomfortable Jean-Paul.

Almost stuttering Jean-Paul blurted out, "Actually, actually, all I..., all I want is to get these stripes sewn on these uniforms." That caused *all the girls to giggle.*

In one swift movement, Lee Ann grabbed the uniforms, stripes falling to the floor, and said, "No worries, I'll see this is taken care of. Now, is there anyone..."

Before she finished Jean-Paul noticed a tall, slender young

girl standing behind all the other girls. Without thinking he said, "How about that tall girl back there." He immediately felt embarrassed. The thought of *what am I even doing in here* kept crossing his mind.

All the women clapped and shouted approval. One said, "Come on up here *Desiree,* here is your first customer."

Jean-Paul did not know what to make of this entire situation or his behavior. This is something his parents and the Jesuit fathers back home would certainly not approve. Loud in his mind were the King James verses, *"It is adultery just to look at a woman lustfully"* and also *"adulterers will not inherit the Kingdom of God."*

The young girl took Jean-Paul's hand and led him up the staircase. She did not look at him or say anything. It seemed her comfort level with this situation was about the same as Jean-Paul's.

From the top of the stairs, they walked down a long hallway. With the walls painted in a deep red color, it was quite dark considering it was still daylight outside. They came to a room and Desiree opened the door for Jean-Paul. Here was a large bright room. Among other furnishings, there was a large bed, a sofa, and bathtub. A heavy Black woman was pouring buckets of steaming hot water into the tub. The soap bubbles in the tub were running over onto the floor.

"That should be enough Lucy," said Desiree to the woman.

"Now soldier, please take off all of your clothes so we can get them cleaned and those stripes sewn on that shirt you're wearing." After she said this, she dropped her flimsy nightwear and undergarments. She then faced Jean-Paul in her birthday suit.

Jean-Paul's mind was still trying to process this series of events. A ridiculous thought kept crossing his mind: this girl should have posed for some of those paintings on the wall downstairs instead of those plump older women who had posed.

Jean-Paul still confused and startled, obediently stripped himself down to his skivvies.

"Don't be bashful we'll being needing those too. They clearly need a washing. Men...! What would you all do without a woman to look after you?"

"But if you wash these clothes, will they be dry in a reasonable time?"

"Well, if you keep talking and not stripping, they won't be, now hurry up and then get in the tub for a scrubbing."

Jean-Paul dropped his drawers and got into the tub. The water was hot enough to scald the feathers off a chicken. But the Professor didn't mind. It felt great. He could feel the weeks of dirt peel off of him.

With a sponge and rough washcloth Desiree scrubbed him down as if on a mission: feet, legs, chest, back, face, and even his hair. At one-point Jean-Paul was completely covered with soap bubbles.

After what seemed like only a short time, Desiree said, "Okay soldier, stand up and get rinsed off." She then dumped a huge pail of cold water over him to get rid of the soap bubbles. It was so cold that it gave him goose bumps.

"Up and out to get dried off." She picked up a huge towel and waited for him.

Almost falling, he slowly got out of the tub. Expertly using the towel, Desiree slowly and methodically dried Jean-Paul.

Relieved and now a bit more at peace with the world, Jean-Paul sat on the couch—still completely undressed. Desiree, using a smaller towel, dried herself and then sat next to him. The teenager couldn't believe the scene. This was nothing he had ever been taught in the Jesuit school. The voice of Jesuit guilt was now barely audible—barely. He slowly took one of the pillows that was lying on the couch and placed it over his groin.

"Would you like a glass of French wine?" she asked.

"I would like that. My father is French and makes wine. I have always enjoyed a good glass of wine."

Handing Jean-Paul a large glass of red wine, Desiree said, "Tell me what you think?"

Jean-Paul took a sip and almost spit it out. *Straight vinegar with razor blades* would have tasted better than what was in that glass.

"You made a face. You didn't like it did you?"

Coughing, Jean-Paul replied, "No, no, it was very good. What kind of wine did you say this was?"

"It's a kind of merlot, I think."

No merlot that Jean-Paul had ever tasted like what was in this glass. "Oh yes, a merlot. Sure, I could tell that's what it is."

Jean-Paul of course couldn't help himself and now asked Desiree, *"How did you get into this line of work anyway?"*

"It's a long and boring story. I am sure you would not care to hear it. Besides we are supposed to talk about you and not me."

"I am sure it is not a boring story. Since my clothes are not back yet, go ahead and bore me and tell me about yourself."

"You asked for it soldier so here it is." She picked up a nail file and worked her nails as she spoke.

"I don't remember my mother at all. My first memories are of my father and that ugly wagon we traveled around in. We would go from town-to-town and sell two kinds of tonic. One was an elixir that my father made out stream water, cocaine powder, sugar, and brown coloring. The other was made out of pure grain alcohol and was one hundred proof. He said that elixir was a tonic, which would cure whatever ailed you. The second tonic was mainly for women. He said it would cure whatever *female issues* a woman had. It was actually our best seller. He had other stimulant formulas. Each had varying amounts of *cocaine powder, morphine, heroin, or alcohol.* These were all items anyone could buy in their local drug store. My father would sell this medicine as well as sing and dance, play the banjo, read newspaper stories from around the country, and even preach some gospel. He was a masterful storyteller. We would stay in a town until something would happen that would cause us to move on. And of course, there was always something that would happen. Most times we pulled out in the dead of night."

"When I was around eight years old, I began to sing, dance, and recite poetry to the crowds. They loved me...or maybe felt sorry for me. But they did throw lots of money. Some time when I was eleven years old, I'm not exactly sure, we came here to Mobile. At that time a young woman joined us. My father was smitten with her—the poor old fool. When we were getting ready to leave, my father told me to go and buy some apples. I walked back into town and bought the apples. When I returned, the wagon was gone. I am sure the young witch that had joined up with us influenced my father—that low life beggar. So, I walked back into town and sat down on the steps of this building. Madam Lee Ann saw me and took me in. I have lived here with her and the girls ever since. I have cooked, cleaned, washed customer clothes, filled tubs with hot water, and listened to the girls talk about their work." Desiree nodded her head and stared straight ahead.

"That's an interesting story, but when did you start, well you know...?"

"Start pleasing men? I just started. Ever since I was living here, even as a little girl, men were always asking about me. Madam Lee Ann would not let them come near me. She has been quite protective. In fact, she has discouraged me from starting. She actually wanted me to get more schooling. She hoped I would become a teacher or something other than working *here*. She wanted a different life for me. She taught me to read and write, play the piano, appreciate literature and art, and interact socially. I started school here in Mobile, but those ratty little local kids would make fun of me and actually beat me. She wouldn't tolerate that. She took me out of school and along with everything else—Lee Ann was also my teacher. She did that for a lot of girls. After a time, she found them jobs, mostly in Montgomery, Birmingham, or Tuscaloosa. She even found husbands for many of them. She has been better than a mother for all of us. I am still here because I want to help out with the income. I convinced her, but it wasn't easy. You are my first customer because Lee Ann said she would only let me work if she picked my customers. And you are the first lucky winner," Desiree said with a huge smile.

Jean-Paul didn't know how to respond.

Then she said, "We still have some time, are you sure there is nothing else I can do for you?" There was another big smile.

"You know, I was taught by my parents and the Jesuit brothers that even to look at a woman with lustful thoughts is a serious sin. And now here I am sitting on a couch without clothes next to a beautiful woman who is also not wearing clothes. What's worse is I am having some really lustful thoughts right now. Forgive me for saying this but I think you really are beautiful."

Jean-Paul caught himself and then said, "What do I owe you for the bath and the drying?"

"Twenty-five cents for the bath. It's normally one dollar for the pleasuring but since...."

"Here are two dollars. You may keep all of it, and I would just like to talk for the rest of the time I'm here if that's okay with you. And please, tell me it is."

"You know soldier, you are really a nice, decent young man. I hope you don't have to go to Cuba and if you do—that you don't get hurt."

"I also hope I don't get hurt. Do you think we could check on my uniforms? I haven't sat with no clothes on this long ever, at least not since I was old enough to remember."

"Let me check." Desire walked to the door and opened it. Jean-Paul was a bit shocked that it had been unlocked all this time. For security purposes he reasoned. Just outside the door was one of those large Black men. He was holding Jean-Paul's folded uniform. He handed the uniform to Desiree making no notice of the fact that she was completely undressed.

"Here are your clothes. Before you put them on, are you sure there is nothing else I can do for you?"

"There are many things you could probably do for me, but not today. But thanks for the offer." Jean-Paul's clothes were still really damp. Regardless, he dressed as fast as he could. He took his walking stick and headed for the door. Desiree, now also dressed, moved in front of him and said, "How about a kiss to remember me by."

"We can do the kiss, but believe me, kiss or not I will never forget you or this afternoon...."

Moving into the hallway, the noise from downstairs could only be described as raucous. It seems that after the horses were tended, Colonel Wood agreed to Colonel Roosevelt's request to allow the troopers go into town—all under the supervision of a sergeant or corporal. Walking down the large staircase, Jean-Paul saw an unbelievable sight. There were Rough Riders everywhere. They were also lined up outside the door. The whiskey bar was six deep and there was so much noise that one could not hear the piano player. When the troopers saw Desiree, they flocked toward the stairs. Out of nowhere Lee Ann appeared at the bottom of the staircase and shooed them all away.

Reaching the bottom of the stairs Lee Ann turned to Jean-Paul and said, "Well young soldier, are you clean all around?"

"Yes ma'am, I sure am."

"Wonderful. Now come with me and we will get the rest of your corporal shirts."

Jean-Paul noticed that not only were the corporal stripes

sewn on correctly, but the shirts had also been cleaned. "How much do I owe you for the sewing and cleaning?"

Not answering Jean-Paul but turning to Desiree, Lee Ann, with some seriousness, asked her, "Did this young man treat you as a lady should be treated?"

"Most certainly *Mom*. Most certainly."

Jean-Paul noted the *Mom*. That motivated him to say, "Miss Lee Ann, you were right in encouraging Desiree to get more schooling or even go to college. I think that would be good choice for her future."

For the first time the big smile on Lee Ann's face left. Jean-Paul remembered a verse from the King James that said, *"Her countenance fell."*

She responded in an angry tone, "And why would you say that? Are you suggesting this line of work is not good enough for her? Is that it?"

Jean-Paul was startled at her abrupt change in attitude and demeanor.

"No, no, not at all." Jean-Paul knew he was not being honest or truthful. Prostitution was not a wholesome line of work for anyone. He remembered what Father Vincent had said, *"Prostitution was a sin and for a woman, it was nothing more than a slow and horrible death."*

"Well then what are saying? Help me to understand? What did you mean by that?"

Confused by the abrupt change in the conversation, Jean-Paul wisely said, "I have a good education and I think everyone should get as much education as possible regardless of their line of work. That's all."

"Are you suggesting that Desiree is uneducated? Is that what you are saying?"

"No, not at all. No matter how much education one has, he, or in this case she, should always be seeking more—you know, more knowledge. That's all. I meant nothing offensive at all and I apologize if I did not make myself clear." Jean-Paul looked at Desiree whose facial expression was completely blank. She had said nothing in Jean-Paul's defense or in support of the notion she should get more schooling.

Wanting to change the uncomfortable subject, Jean-Paul did not give Lee Ann a chance to respond. He quickly followed his last comment by saying, "By the way, how much for the sewing and cleaning of the uniform shirts?"

"Nothing at all. It's our gift to you for serving." Lee Ann was still not smiling. Jean-Paul looked at Desiree and then Lee Ann. It was quite clear where he stood in this conversation. Strange he thought, since according to Desiree it was Lee Ann who brought up the idea of her getting more schooling or even going to college. Maybe he misunderstood, or more likely—it was Desiree who misunderstood.

Fortunately, Three-Ring then appeared with his short

girlfriend in tow. All smiles he said, *"Are you ready to go Professor?"*

"Corporal Professor to you," said Jean-Paul pointing to his newly sewn corporal's stripes. "I am definitely ready, are you?"

"I am, but after this war I am certainly returning to Mobile." His short girlfriend was glowing and still hanging all over him.

"Well then," said Jean-Paul, "Ladies it has been wonderful. Thanks for the bath, sewing, clean clothes, good conversation, and everything else...."

Inexplicably, Lee Ann was still not smiling. Jean-Paul thought to say something about that but decided it would not be wise to do so. He reasoned there must be some sort of *mother hen* situation going on here that he obviously did not understand.

As he walked toward the door, Desiree caught up with him, grabbed him, gave him another kiss and whispered, *"I hope I will be seeing you after the war."* Jean-Paul had no idea how to respond. Finally, he stuttered out, "Right, that would be my desire too. Goodbye Desiree."

Walking out the front door, he saw about fifty Rough Riders *waiting their turn to enter.* On the street they were drinking whiskey, beer, and even wine. The smell of alcohol and human dirt hung heavy in the humid Alabama air. Even the new lieutenant in A Troop, *T.C. Nicolson,* was waiting there. Jean-

Paul shook his head at that. That was quite an example for an officer to be setting. Then he caught himself as he realized that as a corporal, he was now a noncommissioned officer. As such, he also had to be conscious of his behavior and the example he was setting. Now he too, a corporal, was coming out of *a house of ill repute!* This was his first action as a non-commissioned officer...! Ugh!

Walking quickly, Jean-Paul couldn't even begin to process what had just happened. With his short legs, Three-Ring finally caught up with him. He said with great glee, "I'm in love with sweet Lucinda. That's right, in love. After the war I'm coming back here to marry that girl. She is the woman I have been longing for. She is so very, very wonderful!"

"Are you kidding me? You know this girl for a couple of hours and now you are smitten? How much did you drink anyway?"

"What does *smitten* mean?"

"Smitten is an old English term meaning to be positively struck or overcome by something. It is generally used to describe someone who has fallen in love so deeply that they act like they have been struck by lightning. That's smitten."

"Well, if that's smitten, then that's me. Yippee!! I'm smitten. And yes, I have been drinking. I had some of the best red wine I ever had."

"Really, the best red wine you ever had. Well, that explains a lot. For you, it probably *was* the best you have ever had."

"What is that supposed to mean?"

"Nothing, nothing at all. What do you say we get some dinner at that eatery we passed on way here?"

"I'm up for that."

\*           \*           \*           \*           \*

Entering the restaurant, he saw that other Rough Riders who were doing the town had the same idea. The place was buzzing with soldiers. Looking around Jean-Paul noticed a table that had a couple of free chairs. He and Three-Ring moved to the table. There sat an old soldier with a huge, droopy all-white mustache who was wearing a U.S. Army uniform with sergeant's stripes. It was a cavalry uniform just like theirs.

Jean-Paul asked, "Do you mind if we join you?"

The old soldier simply grunted and pointed to the open chairs. The two troopers interpreted this as an invitation to sit.

After being seated Jean-Paul asked the old soldier, "How's the steak?"

The old man nodded and snorted.

Jean-Paul couldn't help himself and said to the sergeant, "I see you are a sergeant in the First Volunteer Cavalry. Had you served in the army before?"

The sergeant put down his fork, sat up, and for the first time actually looked at Jean-Paul and Three Ring. He replied, "I served in the United States Army in *the War of the Rebellion*. I joined in 1863 when I was eighteen years old. I fought in the East with General Meade and General Grant. Fought at *Spotsylvania, Cold Harbor, Yellow Tavern, and Petersburg,* and several other lesser skirmishes. Made sergeant in less than a year and was wounded four times. Left my wife on the farm with my folks. When the war was over, I got off the train in Columbus and walked to our farm. There I took off my uniform, put on my farming clothes—which were hanging exactly where I left them— and went out to work with my dad. It was like I never left. Does that answer your question?"

"Certainly does. Thanks."

"Now I've joined up again thirty-three years later. They made me a sergeant once more as well as the regiment's color bearer. They also assigned me to the dynamite gun. Colonel Roosevelt said I was tougher than *woodpecker lips*. How's about that for a recommendation?"

"But why did you join up again? You certainly would not have had to."

"Why? Well, why not? My kids are all grown and gone and my wife passed three years ago. I was sitting there by myself on the farm waiting to die. If I am going to go out, I might as well do it with some style don't you think? So, I signed up again. The doctor said I was in better condition than many of those youngsters who were signing up. That's what the farm life will do for you. You boys should try it when this here shooting war is over."

Jean-Paul looked at Three-Ring. It was clear from how they had glanced at one another that farming was not in their future.

The two ordered steak and potatoes and a bottle of wine. Their steaks were huge and hanging over the side of the plate. They were cooked exactly right, medium rare—a man's red meat steak. And unbelievably, the bottle of burgundy did not taste like it was from a *horse that needed to see a veterinarian!*

When the sergeant finished, he got up to leave. "Well boys, good luck. Hope you all survive the fighting. I really don't care if I do or not since I have nothing to go back to in Ohio but an empty farmhouse. By the way, my name is Guitilias, Nevin P. Guitilias to be exact. It's pronounced *gee-ti-lee-as*. You'll remember me because I'll be carrying the regimental colors. Yes sir—that would be me. See you back at the train."

With him and several of the other troopers in the eatery leaving, the two started to get nervous. They paid for their dinner and with a flow of other Rough Riders began walking back to the rail yard. Jean-Paul stopped to buy some apples for the horses.

There was a still lot of energy and activity at the Rough Rider's train. After giving their horses the apples Jean-Paul and Three-Ring found their car and took their seats.

"What a day," said Jean-Paul.

"You can certainly say that again," said Three-Ring. "It was a day to be remembered...."

### Thought Questions for Chapter 11:

1. Why did Sergeant Guitilias rejoin the Army after being out for thirty-three years?

2. Why did Madam Lee Ann have such a negative reaction when Jean-Paul said Desiree should get more education?

3. Why was Jean-Paul concerned that Lieutenant T.C. Nicolson and he, as a corporal, had been at Lee Ann's house?

4. Describe Jean-Paul's attitude and behavior toward Desiree. Do you find it in any way unusual? Why or why not?

5. What was your biggest learning or take away from this chapter? What can you apply from the information in this chapter? What in it did you find the most interesting? Why?

# 12

## *The French Attaché's Party*

It was two more days and a stop near Tallahassee before the Rough Riders arrived in Tampa. Jean-Paul, Three-Ring, and the rest of Troop A had enough of train travel by the time they reached Florida. The warm reception, the refreshments that had been provided, and all the pretty girls begging for souvenirs did not make the trip any more agreeable. By the time the Rough Riders arrived in Tampa they were ornery enough to fight anyone.

The situation at the rail yard in Tampa could once again be described as mass confusion. There was a one-track railroad that ended in the sandy, pine-covered, and generally desolate area called Tampa. Jean-Paul couldn't believe the chaotic sight. Soldiers were running or marching everywhere. Horses were being led and ridden in all directions. People were yelling and shouting unintelligibly. There were large groups of soldiers standing around idle—*never a good thing*. The temperature was over ninety degrees with humidity to match. The Rough Riders were now wearing their brown fatigue shirt. The majority of the soldiers from other regiments in the rail area were wearing their army blue woolen shirt. Jean-Paul couldn't imagine how hot, miserable, and sweaty they must have been. Of course, he would find this out for himself once in Cuba.

First Sergeant Troxler came by and said, "Dee-Bert come with me. I may need a runner. *The little one* can watch your rifle and gear."

Troxler was moving like a man possessed asking all the officers and sergeants he saw if they knew who was in charge of this rail yard and where the army's reception area was. That was one thing about the First Sergeant thought Jean-Paul. He would see a problem and would then take the initiative to solve it. There was no waiting around for Top Sergeant Troxler. Despite his age, he was full of energy and a go-getting, self-starter. This impressed Jean-Paul. *Taking the initiative when in charge was a priceless lesson he was learning about leadership.*

Just ahead of them were Colonel Roosevelt, Captain O'Neill, and several of the other Rough Rider troop commanders. The First Sergeant and Jean-Paul walked up and saluted as Colonel Roosevelt was speaking.

He was saying, "As you know men, we will be shipping out to Cuba from here—Tampa. It seems that some thirty thousand soldiers have arrived here in Tampa in the past few days. Neither the Army nor the railroad officials were prepared for that size force. Before the war, the United States Army numbered about 26,000 men. They did little more than keep the Native Indians in line out West. Mobilizing and deploying such a large force as this is clearly beyond the current expertise of the Army staff and its logistics bureau. This certainly is not the federal army of Grant, Sherman, and Sheridan."

Roosevelt paused for a moment and then with a new enthusiasm almost shouted, "But by Godfrey, that will not hinder us in any way, shape, or form! Bully!! By Godfrey there's no one here to greet us, there's no food, no place to set up camp, and no wagons to get us there even if we knew where to go. But we will overcome and bully, we'll make the best of it." At that he pounded his fist into his other hand.

Jean-Paul liked to hear Colonel Roosevelt use the word *bully*. It was an adjective and meant, *"first-rate, grand, or awesome."* In this case it probably meant, *"We will successfully work through this."* *Bully* thought Jean-Paul; *we can do this.*


"Gentlemen, since there are no rations here, we officers need to buy food and coffee for the men," said Roosevelt. "And I need to find Colonel Wood. Do we have a runner here? I think the Colonel must be somewhere up ahead."

First Sergeant Troxler spoke up, "I have a runner here. He'll find Colonel Wood. Are there any other instructions?"

"Yes, tell him I will have my ad hoc headquarters set up under those three trees over yonder.' With that he pointed to a clump of trees. "We will also be buying food and drink for the men locally. And, we will persevere to find out where we are to set up our camp. In the meantime, we'll be commandeering wagons for transport."

"Got that Professor?" asked Troxler?

"Yes, First Sergeant, I got all of it."

"Now get going."

Jean-Paul saluted in the general direction of Colonel Roosevelt and the other Rough Rider officers and started off at a slow trot toward the front of the train. The heat, the humidity, and not having run for several weeks made him begin breathing heavily and almost immediately. My oh my, but that's not good thought Jean-Paul.

After what seemed like a half a mile, he saw a large group of men. There was a mix of uniforms. There were black suited railroad officials, officers in the army blue uniforms, and others wearing the brown fatigue uniform. Among these he saw Colonel Wood. Success thought the Professor.

He moved behind Colonel Wood. When there was a break in the conversation, Jean-Paul saluted and said, "Colonel Wood, sir, I have a message from Colonel Roosevelt."

Colonel Wood automatically returned a natural and very sharp salute. He looked closely at Jean-Paul with narrowed eyes. Clearly, he was trying to process where he had previously seen him. After a second or two he said, "Right, you're the Alamo history professor. What do you have for me young soldier?"

After Jean-Paul reported the message, Colonel Wood said,

"Tell Colonel Roosevelt to continue to do all he is doing, particularly regarding the food and getting the wagons. I will find out in an hour or so where we are supposed to set up our camp. When I have that information, I'll come down to his location."

Jean-Paul saluted and began jogging back to Colonel Roosevelt's location. Arriving out of breath, he saluted and gave his report. The Colonel's response was, "Bully, good job young soldier." I have found my headquarters staff—including my runners—so you can go back to your troop. That's A Troop, correct?"

"Yes sir, Troop A." Jean-Paul saluted and turned to find his unit.

Only a short distance away he found his comrades. They were lined up on the ground in a very loose formation. Here was Three-Ring with his as well as Jean-Paul's gear.

"Well, well," said Three-Ring, "look here folks, *the anointed one* has returned."

Mimicking the First Sergeant, he said, "'Come with me professor, I need a runner. Let *the little one* take care of your gear.' Sure, let *the little one* take care of your gear. Please, please Professor, can I be your batman, you know, your personal valet and striker?"

Jean-Paul smiled wryly and said, "You are just jealous. Get over it *little one*. Jealousy and envy are not becoming a highly trained circus performer like yourself. By the way, could you do some *monkey flips* for the boys here?" The troopers always seemed to enjoy with great glee the repartee between Jean-Paul and Three-Ring. Jean-Paul always fed back what Three-Ring shoveled at him, but he did not like those kinds of exchanges. He believed that when someone jokes about another person—*he really means it.* The message actually was what the sender was really thinking and feeling. The joking was just a cover to make it less offensive.

After they had received sandwiches, fruit, and coffee that had been personally paid for by Colonel Roosevelt and the other officers, wagons began arriving for the regiment's equipment. Jean-Paul helped load the Troop A boxes and then went to get Applejack. He gave him two apples, saddled him, and with the rest of A Troop followed the wagons to the troop's camp area. Colonel Wood and Colonel Roosevelt had worked around the system *yet again.* Jean-Paul wondered if that was the Army way—in order to get things done one must do *work arounds?* Hmmm....

Arriving at the cantonment area, Colonel Wood directed how the camp should be set up. The tents were to be lined up perfectly on each side of the main street. The officers' tents were at the upper end and the mess hall was to be at the opposite end. Strict rules were given about the police of the area, sanitation, and personal hygiene.

The horses were given thirty-six hours of rest. The Rough

Riders spent that time drilling on foot with their weapons. After resting the horses, the mounted drill began in earnest. The troops formed in columns of four and then joined the other units to do squadron drill. The biggest challenge was to get some of the marginally trained horses to follow and respond to the *movement of the guidons.*

Jean-Paul participated as much as he could in the training. First Sergeant Troxler had him filling out forms, running to regimental headquarters with messages, and doing odds and ends around the Troop A's headquarters. Attending to this administrative work did not seem to bother Jean-Paul. What bothered him was that this work might keep him out of the fighting once they arrived in Cuba.

The Rough Riders continued to wear their brown fatigue shirts because they were much cooler and loose fitting than the woolen dark blue shirts the regular army soldiers wore. Thus, one could always tell the regulars from the First Volunteer Cavalry. The Fifth Corps regulars in their dark blue shirts were from the Third, Sixth, Ninth, and Tenth Cavalry Regiments. Also present were the all-Black Twenty-Fourth and Twenty-Fifth Infantry Regiments.

Just after lunch of the third day in Tampa, Jean-Paul went back to Troop A headquarters to finish some paperwork. While there, First Sergeant Troxler appeared with the company barber. In a serious tone, the First Sergeant said, "Professor, how well do you speak French? Can you really speak it or is it mostly bar room French?"

"I am quite fluent. But I don't really know what exactly is bar room French, First Sergeant?"

"All right, assuming you can actually speak French, we are going to get you a haircut and then you get you washed up *so you don't smell like a goat*. Then we are going to go to regimental supply and get you fitted into an officer's uniform, with no rank insignia of course. You need to be at regiment at 6 PM to go to the *Tampa Bay Hotel* for a *soiree* being put on by the French army attaché, *Colonel Davout*. He will be accompanying our little war expedition as an observer and in typical French fashion, he is sponsoring a grand dinner. You are going as the personal French language interpreter for Colonel Wood and Colonel Roosevelt. I find that interesting because I am quite sure I once heard that Colonel Teddy speaks excellent French. Get yourself cleaned up real good trooper since all of our generals will be there to include the Fifth Corps commander, *Major General Pecos Bill Shafter* himself."

Jean-Paul incredulously said, "General Shafter our corps commander?"

"That's right professor, General Shafter himself. Pecos Bill earned his Medal of Honor in 1862 at the Battle of Fair Oaks. He later campaigned against the Cheyenne, Comanche, Kickapoo, and Kiowa's, and God only knows how many other tribes. Heard he got himself in some trouble at Fort Davis in Texas when he court-martialed *Lieutenant Henry O. Flipper*. Flipper was the first Black man to graduate from West Point. Old Bill's judgment was called into question on that one. I guess he must be well over sixty years of age now and last heard he is weighing in at about 300 pounds and has some serious health problems. Can't imagine why he was selected to be our corps commander other than the fact he never had a political bone in his very large body."

Jean-Paul didn't know what to say about all this. Almost unconsciously he had his haircut, washed himself, and then walked with the First Sergeant to regimental supply.

Entering regimental supply, everyone stood when they caught sight of the legendary First Sergeant Troxler. Generally, one only stood when an officer entered. But there was such respect for the First Sergeant and his warrior reputation that they also stood for him.

"What can I do for you First Sergeant?" asked the supply sergeant.

"This young soldier is going to the big party at the Tampa Bay Hotel tonight to interpret and translate for our colonels. He needs an officer's uniform with no rank insignia. Can you fix him up? We are kind of in a hurry here. Remember, no rank insignia."

Jean-Paul was squared away in no time. The officer's uniform with polished officer boots fit him perfectly.

The First Sergeant stared him up and down. He then said,

"You know Professor, you even look the part of an officer. That said, don't take it to your head. And don't screw up anything tonight. If I hear even the slightest negative comment about you from the Colonels' or anyone else for that matter, you will be shoveling horse manure for the rest of your time in the Army. Is that clear soldier?"

"Yes, First Sergeant. Perfectly clear."

"Good. Now, let's get you hooked up with Colonel Wood." The First Sergeant wasn't smiling.

Riding in the coach with Colonel Wood and Colonel Roosevelt to the Tampa Bay Hotel was extremely uncomfortable for Jean-Paul. The two colonels were engaged in deep discussion and behaved as though he wasn't present. He concluded that must be the way of senior officers—and for good reason....

Arriving at the Tampa Bay Hotel, Colonel Wood finally acknowledged Jean-Paul and said, "Old Pecos Bill, ah, I mean General Shafter, advised us that our host tonight, the French attaché Colonel Hercule Davout, who is also accompanying us to Cuba as an observer, is noted for his *egotism and arrogance*. He likes to speak French to American officers solely to embarrass them and highlight the fact they don't speak his language. That is why the General spread the word for all attendees to bring a French language interpreter. Depending how many French speakers we have, which I don't think will be very many, you may be interpreting for several of our generals and colonels tonight.

So, stay close but out of the way and as invisible as possible. We are not sure if you will be eating with us or simply sitting behind Pecos Bill interpreting. Any questions?"

"No sir, no questions."

Colonel Wood gave Jean-Paul a patronal pat on the shoulder and in automatic fashion said, *"Good, good."*

Colonel Roosevelt added a hardy back slap with an enthusiastic *"Bully!"*

Jean-Paul was impressed with everything about the Tampa Bay Hotel. A huge, covered veranda encircled it. There were many rocking chairs occupied by army and navy officers and attractively coifed women—all drinking lemonade or iced tea. There were news reporters scurrying in and out of the hotel and *hangers-on* everywhere. Electricity and excitement were in the air. It was quite clear everyone was feeling it and thriving on it. Jean-Paul remembered reading many historical accounts of how a nation's population was generally overjoyed and excited when their government declared war. However, when the casualty reports and the coffins started coming home, the excitement seemed to taper off. It was interesting that when men are going off to kill and be killed everyone seems to get excited. That made absolutely no sense!

One of the uniformed doormen escorted the two Rough Rider colonels to the salon where the banquet was being held. Jean-Paul was quietly bringing up the rear. On the way they stopped to greet Clara Barton, the seventy-seven-year-old Civil War *Angel of the Battlefield*. She was the founder of the American Red Cross. She was preparing to take a team of nurses to Cuba to work in the army hospitals. Jean-Paul noted that she was short, homely, and looked every year of her age.

Colonel Roosevelt made a point to introduce Frederick Remington to Colonel Wood. Roosevelt had apparently met Remington years before on one his trips to the Western United States. Remington was going to Cuba as a war correspondent and illustrator for William Randolph Hearst's *New York Journal*. Jean-Paul noticed Remington was a portly man, looking nothing like the slender cowboys or cavalry soldiers in his paintings and sculptures.

Passing them as if in a great hurry was a young man with a woman who was dressed in a very revealing fashion. Colonel Roosevelt stopped him and said, *"Crane, is that you?"*

The man stopped and, in a manner indicating he had been nipping said, *"Yes sir, Colonel, yes sir, Stephen Crane, famous and award-winning author at your service sir."* At that he made a very low and awkward bow, almost falling in the process.

Colonel Roosevelt said to Colonel Wood, "Sir, this is Stephen Crane the author of the best-selling novel, *'The Red Badge of Courage.'*"

"Great book young man. It is the most vivid portrayal of men in battle that I have ever read. Very well done," said Colonel

Wood.

"Thank you, thank you most honorable colonel." Turning to the woman he was escorting he said, "May I introduce you to...to...ah, what was your name again?"

"My name is *dummy* for hanging around with you. Now let's go, our coach is waiting."

"Well, gentlemen, I am going to wonderful Jacksonville, Florida, to catch a steamer to Cuba. Can't wait around here any longer. I am in the employ, for a generous stipend I might add, of the *Bacheller-Johnson Syndicate* to work as a war correspondent in Cuba. Adieu fine gentlemen. Adieu. I will see you in Cuba. I will be there waiting for you while drinking large carafes of rum and pineapple juice." With that he raised his arm in a farewell salute. Then he was almost yanked out of the hotel by his consort.

Colonel Wood said shaking his head, "He is a talented and gifted writer but certainly leads a degenerate and reprobate lifestyle. Poor clod." The group moved on to the banquet room.

This was an opulent room, with chandeliers, small potted trees, flowers, and numerous French flags of varying sizes everywhere. Jean-Paul was awestruck at the number of generals and colonels present. Some of them were actually wearing their *mess dress uniform.* Now why would they bring their most formal army uniform when they were going off to war? Then Jean-Paul reasoned that was a good decision since they were able to wear it tonight. It was something to remember in the future about being prepared for every occasion and circumstance.

Both Wood and Roosevelt seemed surprised there was a receiving line. Colonel Davout the French military attaché, his wife and daughter as well as the French *Conseiller des Affaires Étrangères* and his wife from the French consulate in New Orleans were doing the receiving.

A junior French army officer, Jean-Paul could not determine his rank, probably a captain, asked the two colonels their name and rank. Speaking French, the officer introduced Colonel Wood to Colonel Davout. In French Colonel Davout said, "Welcome Colonel Wood. It is indeed a great honor and privilege to have such a distinguished warrior with us this evening."

Without waiting for any signal Jean-Paul automatically translated Colonel Davout's comments to Colonel Wood. Colonel Wood responded with an equally courteous greeting, which Jean-Paul promptly shared with Davout in French.

There was a similar exchange with Colonel Roosevelt and the attaché.

Before Davout introduced Colonel Roosevelt to his wife, he asked Jean-Paul in French, "You speak excellent and well-accented French for an American. In fact, it is so correct that I suppose you are originally from France."

Without hesitation he responded, "No sir. I am an

317

American who was born in the United States. My father was from France. He is a graduate of the Sorbonne and fought for France in the 1870-1871 War. Also, my grandfather was in the Grand Armée for three years and was personally decorated with the Legion of Honor by Emperor Napoleon himself."

Colonel Davout gave Jean-Paul an incredulous look. It was quite clear the Colonel did not believe the part about the Emperor awarding a medal to Papa Gerard. Jean-Paul now carried that Legion of Honor medal wrapped in a handkerchief in his pocket. He felt the biggest urge to pull it out and show it to Davout but then thought better of it since Colonel Roosevelt was staring at him. He responded to that look by quickly sharing with Roosevelt what Davout had asked him and his response.

Jean-Paul was still carrying his savate walking stick he had purchased in Mobile. He had not had time to put it down when he and the two Rough Rider Colonels had entered the banquet salon. Colonel Davout noted the walking stick and said in French with a smile, *"Is that your savate stick?"*

"Actually, it is. My father taught me the art from his experience at the Sorbonne."

"Really, I too have my *stick* with me tonight. I am rated *a master* of the art of savate. Perhaps we could put on a demonstration for the group later?" Davout said this with a devious grin.

Jean-Paul immediately panicked, and his expression must

have betrayed him. He weakly replied, "Perhaps we could." His only thought now was, I certainly hope not, I do not want to take on a *master of the art* and get myself soundly thrashed in front of all these generals and my two commanders.

Next to Colonel Davout's wife in the receiving line was a strikingly beautiful young woman in a most exquisite gown. Mrs. Davout reached out and pulled Jean-Paul forward, so he was standing equal with those going through the receiving line. Up until that time, he was standing behind his two colonels. With some fanfare she introduced Jean-Paul to her daughter whose name was *Bridgette*. J.P. almost went speechless when she greeted him in French and offered him her hand. Gathering himself together he took her gloved hand and following appropriate social protocol, gave the top of her hand *a dry kiss*. She then said she too was quite impressed with Jean-Paul's French language skills. She indicated it would be wonderful if they could talk further after the receiving line had ended. Jean-Paul, still a bit stunned at her natural beauty and the possible savate match, answered that would also be his wish. Before he could back out of the receiving line, Bridgette introduced him to the French conseiller from the French consulate in New Orleans. He was a thin, pale, balding, and sad looking man. His verbal greeting was very soft and his handshake was equally frail. The conseiller's wife on the other hand was well preserved for her age with exquisitely coiffed hair. Her American English accent was perfect which made Jean-Paul think she had some link to the United States in her background.

That concluded the receiving line. Jean-Paul looked at his two colonels who had just been served a glass of wine. They were both staring at their interpreter corporal who had joined the receiving line for the guests. He responded to their stare with a shrug of his shoulders and a discreet open-handed gesture. This caused them to look away and made Jean-Paul feel like a fool.

As he was gently shaking his head at what had just happened, there was a great commotion at the entrance to the salon. Jean-Paul looked and saw the arrival of the Fifth Corps commander, Major General Pecos Bill Shafter. The appearance of Major General Shafter actually shocked Jean-Paul. The general was probably the heaviest man Jean-Paul had ever seen. The only person J.P. had seen who had greater girth had been in a circus sideshow. Shafter's bulk actually caused him to waddle when he walked. However, the general *was wearing* the Medal of Honor awarded him in the War of the Rebellion. That thought Jean-Paul, was indeed impressive but did not fit with the General's appearance.

The General was breathing heavily as he walked up to the receiving line. Jean-Paul noted he did not have anyone with him who appeared to be an interpreter. On his own initiative, Jean-Paul walked to the front of the receiving line. He arrived just as the general was giving his name to the young French army captain. In French, Colonel Davout greeted General Shafter warmly. Jean-Paul interpreted. General Shafter, with obvious diplomatic experience in Washington D.C., never looked at Jean-Paul and shared a warm greeting and some words of appreciation for the invitation. J.P. interpreted.

Colonel Davout in French then said to General Shafter, "The United States has a considerable challenge ahead of it. I am going to observe with great interest how your country will manage this expedition. America has not had a major military operation since your great Civil War. France on the other hand, *has since* campaigned in Tonkin, Dahomey, Madagascar, Algeria, Morocco, and Tunisia." After saying this and without looking down, he lightly touched the five full-sized medals he was wearing. He had obviously participated in several of those campaigns. Jean-Paul translated.

General Shafter responded by gently patting the Medal of Honor he was wearing and said, "America has the best human material in the world for soldiering. The great Civil War as you just called it—combined with all the campaigns against the American Indian—has given us all the experience we need for this campaign." Jean-Paul translated.

Then Davout calmly said, "But fighting against a volunteer army or native tribesmen is not the same as fighting a professional army from Europe. Spain has over 200,000 well-trained soldiers in Cuba. They are battle hardened since they have been fighting the Cuban insurrectionists for several years. Your country has but 26,000 regulars and a number of volunteers. I think you will have a tough fight on your hands." Jean-Paul again translated.

To his credit, Shafter was intimidated by this haughty French Colonel. He said, "I have great faith in the officers and soldiers of my expedition Colonel. If you will remember the United States—with almost all volunteers—defeated the British in both our War of Independence and again in the War of 1812. The British army we defeated in the Battle of New Orleans in 1815 was, I believe, the same army that defeated Napoleon and the French army at the Battle of Waterloo." General Shafter paused to wait for a response from Colonel Davout. When there was none, he said, "I look forward to seeing you in Cuba Colonel." General Shafter then moved on to Madam Davout without waiting for Jean-Paul to translate.

There was not much translation required for the remainder of the receiving line. Jean-Paul followed his two colonels who now began *working the room*. The other senior American army officers seemed overjoyed to see them. The exuberance of these officers seemed excessive and phony to J.P. He wondered *how sincere they actually were* about having these two popular and well-known personalities as part of the expedition. He again recalled that the Jesuits taught that *envy* was one of the *seven deadly sins*.

## Chapter 12: The French Attaché's Party

The two colonels made a point to introduce Jean-Paul to all of the V Corps division and brigade commanders. Their response to the introduction was mostly indifference mixed with a few casual grunts. Jean-Paul stepped off the side since there was clearly no need for French interpretation in that group.

A waiter—dressed in a Tuxedo and looking like a penguin—came by carrying a tray of glasses filled with French champagne. He offered a glass to Jean-Paul who politely refused. The thought of *no drinking while on the job* had briefly crossed his mind.

Then he could not help but hear a discussion in a language other than either English or French. He slowly turned and saw the Russian and German military observers huddled together speaking German. Interesting. Jean-Paul was astounded at how much of the discussion he understood considering his only training in German was from his sessions with *flirty Berti Beckenbauer*. But then too, he had read the military writings of both *Carl von Clausewitz* and *Prussian Field Marshal Freiherr von der Goltz Pasha*—*in German*. These had certainly helped him understand some German military terminology and strategic theories.

The German officer, Oberstleutnant von Geisler, who was also accompanying the expedition to Cuba as an observer, seemed to be doing all the talking. Jean-Paul, knowing *it was rude to be listening,* couldn't help but overhear the nonsense he was spouting. In fact, what he heard caused *that feeling* in his

323

chest....

Against his better judgment and knowing he would regret doing it, extraverted Jean-Paul turned and joined the conversation. To Lieutenant Colonel von Geisler in English he said, "You made a comment that the two American armies in our civil war, or *burger-krieg* as you Germans call it, were nothing more than two unsophisticated mobs simply bashing out one another's brains. I would disagree. There is sufficient evidence to support the belief that the Confederate army had some of the best infantry soldiers the world had ever seen, and the Union army had some of the best artillery cannoneers in the world. We here in America believe that together they could have, and still could, easily defeat any army in the world. We will prove this to be true in Cuba."

The German officer, as well as the Russian officer, did not know exactly what to make of Jean-Paul since he was not wearing rank insignia on his uniform. Jean-Paul continued intermixing English words for the German words he did not know. "The leadership of both The Northern and Southern armies has since been studied by war colleges and staff colleges around the world. Consider General's Robert E. Lee brilliance in 1863 at Chancellorsville. He soundly defeated an enemy force twice the size of his own by violating the principles of war and dividing his force. Then too there were General's Grant and Sherman. Both understood total war, or *totler-kreig* as you

Germans call it, and were generations ahead of other military thinkers. They not only understood modern war but actually put their theories into practice. Also, consider how effectively both armies utilized the new technologies of the day such as the telegraph, railroads, observation balloons, repeating rifles, ironclad ships, and submarines. Then too, the majority of the senior officers on both sides were West Point graduates who had previous combat experience. Many had fought with distinction in the War with Mexico and also the wars with the Seminole and Blackhawk Indians. No sir, the American Civil War was certainly more than a war of attrition with two amateur armies simply slugging it out."

The two foreign observers were caught speechless. It was mainly because they did not know exactly who this young man was with no rank insignia and who could also speak German.

Their response—or lack of it—caused Jean-Paul to lose the angry feeling in his chest. He then said to the stunned group, "Now gentlemen, if you will excuse me." He then turned and walked away in no particular direction.

A waiter walked by Jean-Paul with another tray of champagne. Without thinking the corporal took a glass, chugged it, and set it back on the tray. He thought, "I deserve that for defending my country and its fighting soldiers."

Jean-Paul then walked by one of the full-length wall mirrors that were in the room. He stopped to admire his army officer's uniform. It felt good and he looked good. Then the champagne made him remember the New York Metropolitan Police Department. In the mid 1850's they threatened to go on strike because the police commissioner directed they were all to wear a standard uniform. Up until that time, they had worn civilian clothes and carried only a badge for identification. They felt a uniform was beneath them and something only a butler or a servant would wear. Silly people thought Jean-Paul.

He then reflected on what his father has told him before he left New Hope, "Keep your mouth shut and speak as little as possible." Good advice thought Jean-Paul. He wished he had remembered that before getting involved in that just completed conversation.

At this point all the guests were invited to take their seats. There were some chairs positioned along the wall. Jean-Paul walked up to Colonel Wood and said, "Sir, I will be sitting there along the wall. If you need me during the dinner, just give a gesture. I will come right over. Colonel Wood said nothing but acknowledged with a nod.

Jean-Paul reached the wall and a chair fully anticipating a boring, lonely evening without food. Out of the commotion of everyone finding their assigned seat Jean-Paul noted that at the head table were Colonel Davout and his wife, the French Conseiller and his wife from New Orleans, Major General Shafter, and the three division commanders: Brigadier Kent,

Brigadier Lawton, and the cavalry division commander, Major General Wheeler.

Jean-Paul had read about General Wheeler, the flamboyant cavalry commander of the Confederate's *Army of Tennessee*. It was said he was given command of the cavalry division for this Cuban expedition because the government in Washington wanted a general from the former Confederate States of America to hold a high-level command. Wheeler was the one chosen. His nickname was *Fightin' Joe*, which he earned fighting Indians in the New Mexico territory before the Civil War.

In combat with the Union Army, Wheeler had been wounded three times, supposedly had more than fifteen horses shot from under him and had a reputation of being a cavalry leader equal to *Nathan Bedford Forest*. He was purported to be well over sixty years of age. His totally white hair, beard, and moustache, however, did not match his youthful gait or obvious energy. Jean-Paul had read about him and now here this legendary cavalry officer was, only a few feet from him. Incredible!

Jean-Paul stood waiting for everyone to be seated so he too could sit. He noticed Bridgette talking vigorously with her father and pointing at Jean-Paul. After some discussion Colonel Davout motioned for Jean-Paul to come to him.

He said to Jean-Paul in French, "Corporal DeBert, I want

you to sit behind me and General Shafter and interpret as necessary." He then instructed one of the penguins to bring a small table and chair so Jean-Paul could also have dinner. In no time a small table with chair showed up with plates, glasses, utensils, and most noteworthy, a full bottle of champagne. He glanced at Bridgette who was staring intently at him with a huge smile for what she had just pulled off on his behalf. He acknowledged with a return smile.

When everyone was finally seated Colonel Davout stood and asked Jean-Paul to interpret for him. Jean-Paul immediately stood. The colonel opened with glowing comments about the American army and their crusade against the evil, oppressive Spaniards in Cuba. The Americans in the true spirit of *Liberté, Égalité, and Fraternité, (freedom, equality, and brotherhood),* were going to free the oppressed Cubans. The Colonel had obviously worked with interpreters before because he paused appropriately after each sentence or two so the interpreter could speak and did not have too much to remember. At the end of his speech, he lifted his glass for a toast to the American Army and its upcoming victory. Everyone stood and said the very British response of approval for a good toast, *"Hear, hear."*

The dinner was very French with eight courses, each served with its own unique alcoholic drink. And of course, before the dinner a light champagne had been served as an aperitif. The first course was soup, then appetizers or hors d'oeuvres, then the fish course, followed in turn by the main or principal course, the salad course, the cheese plate, and the sweet desert course. This was followed by the refreshing fruit course.

Jean-Paul did some translation for Colonel Davout and his wife but, as the various courses were served with the appropriate alcohol, the Colonel began speaking more English and less French. This was fine with J.P. as it gave him the opportunity to eat his dinner. During the entire dinner Bridgette would stare at Jean-Paul and smile like a moonstruck child. He would smile back but did not understand her interest in him. He concluded that she must be very lonely and needed badly to speak to a young male in her own language. Who knows? Yet another mystery!

After dinner Colonel Davout invited all the men onto the veranda for cognac and cigars. When Jean-Paul stood he realized how much alcohol he had consumed. He even noted that the champagne bottle that he was given at the beginning of the dinner was almost empty. On the way out to the veranda Bridgette intercepted him. Standing only a foot or two away she said, "Jean-Paul, you must come visit me while I am staying here in this lonely hotel. There are many people here but none my age who speak French. I long to have company of a handsome young man who speaks French so well." With this she stood even closer and was squeezing his left forearm.

Jean-Paul did not know what to say or make of this. He did notice that Bridgette's perfume was remarkably appealing and agreeable. He changed the subject by asking, "What are you planning to do after your father's leaves with us to Cuba?"

"My mother and I will travel back to Washington D.C. In the fall I will most probably start school at Georgetown, your nation's oldest catholic university. I will study diplomacy and English. I don't know if it will be as difficult as a French University, but I will meet some young people and that will make the time pass quickly. When you return from Cuba, you must come visit me."

Jean-Paul noted that the men were all on the veranda now and he may be needed. He said, "I would love to come visit you in Washington D.C. I am sure the Jesuits at Georgetown will give you an excellent education. Most of my education in New York was from the Jesuit brothers. I learned an amazing amount, as I am sure you will too at Georgetown. Now if you will excuse me I must join my leaders."

Without warning Bridgette kissed J.P. on the cheek. She said, "You must come visit me here in the hotel. I am in room 327."

"I would like that," said Jean-Paul. As he walked to the veranda he thought, "Humph, a good Catholic girl inviting me to her hotel room. That's not an invitation I will be accepting anytime soon." He did not understand that entire exchange.

Stepping out onto the veranda, Jean-Paul realized once again how oppressively hot and humid it was in Tampa. He quietly stood behind Colonel Davout and a sweating General Shafter. The waiters were walking around with boxes of cigars. Jean-Paul overheard Colonel Davout say they were cigars from Cuba which he had procured from the embassy of Spain in Washington D.C. Jean-Paul reflected that the next time this group of American army officers would be getting Cuban cigars would be in Cuba.

There were various sizes of cigars in the wooden box the waiter presented to Jean-Paul. Jean-Paul selected a long thin cigar that was clipped at both ends. The waiter said it was a good choice. He went on to say the cheroot's aroma stuck to the smoker's skin, thus hiding the smell of sweat. The smell of perspiration draws mosquitoes. Thus, the cheroot smoker would be less of a target for being bitten and the victim of an insect borne disease.

The waiter lit the cigar for Jean-Paul. Innocently, he took a deep draw that took his breath away. He coughed slightly trying to regain his breadth. This drew the unwanted attention and smiles of a few of the senior officers standing nearby.

The waiters also offered the officers the choice of a cup of coffee or a snifter of cognac. Jean-Paul asked the server what kind of brandy it was. With great pride he was told it was from France made by the Camus family. Its name was *Camus Cognac*

*Cuvee 3.128.* Jean-Paul was not familiar with it but hearing it was a vintage cognac from France, he knew it would be good.

Since there was alcohol served with every course of the evening's meal, Jean-Paul was feeling *quite merry.* He decided to pass on the cognac. He had since lost any inhibition about being the lowest ranking individual present and in an officer's uniform with no rank insignia. He was sincerely enjoying the moment. He couldn't wait to write home and tell his father and mother about this experience.

Unfortunately, the moment was rudely interrupted. Out of nowhere Colonel Davout called for everyone's attention. He beckoned Jean-Paul to join him. He asked Jean-Paul to translate for him. In a loud voice and speaking French he said, "In France we have a gentleman's sport known as savate. It is a combination of stick fighting and kickboxing. Our young interpreter here has learned that art from his father who is originally from France. Therefore, I propose the two of us put on a brief demonstration in the garden." All the American generals and colonels applauded at the prospect. One of the waiters brought J.P.'s and Colonel Davout's walking sticks as they were stepping down from the veranda into the hotel's extensive garden. Jean-Paul was horrified at this turn of events and actually stumbled going down the steps.

Once in the garden Colonel Davout gave a brief overview to the group of the art of savate, including some basic rules and protocols. Interestingly, he did this in English. He then turned to Jean-Paul and asked him if he was ready. Jean-Paul said he was, although he really wasn't.... Colonel Davout raised his stick in front of his face in a salute to Jean-Paul. The scared teenager returned the salute. This salute was a variation of the military command of present arms that originated sometime during the sixteenth century. After the salute Colonel Davout shouted something unintelligible but what sounded to Jean-Paul like *en garde*. Then he yelled *ready* in English and proceeded to attack Jean-Paul.

The young corporal was not quite sure what to expect and in particular, how aggressive Colonel Davout would be. Davout seemed to be attacking at half speed. He was placing blows to the arms and legs and not to the head. Jean-Paul easily parried those blows. He also tried to kick him, but the teenager—alcohol and all—was able to avoid the Colonel's efforts. After several minutes of attacking and maneuvering, Davout paused and gazed intently at Jean-Paul.

The Rough Rider interpreted this as the Colonel evaluating his skills and how he should proceed. Jean-Paul reasoned that since the Colonel recognized his opponent had reasonable savate skills, he would now ratchet it up and be more aggressive. Sure enough, the next attack was swifter and with many more attempted blows, this time some to the head. J.P. was able to parry off all of them until the Colonel, successfully kicked him just below the right knee. This really hurt and for a brief moment caused Jean-Paul to lose his concentration. It was then that Colonel Davout struck a blow to the left side of Jean-Paul's head. While he was able to block it, the momentum of Davout's stick forced Jean-Paul's stick directly against his head. It was with a force that somewhat stunned him and caused him to stumble back.

Colonel Davout paused and again stared at Jean-Paul, once more evaluating his opponent. The Colonel being the host of the party and a gentleman, recognized he might have been a bit too aggressive. *It is never in good form to injure a guest at your dinner party.* He dropped his stick and asked the group to applaud Jean-Paul for being a worthy opponent. Everyone gave him a rousing and hearty round of applause. Colonel Davout came over to Jean-Paul, put his arm around him and in almost gushy French told him what a wonderful adversary he had been, how incredibly skillful he was, and that his performance had certainly promoted the art of savate. J.P. thanked the Colonel for his comments and almost fell down when the Colonel removed his arm from him. At this point Colonel's Wood and Roosevelt came over to Jean-Paul and praised his courage, skill, and gumption. He thanked them and then said he was going inside and sit down.

Jean-Paul had just entered the dining hall when a U.S.

Army lieutenant came rushing toward him. This officer was sweating liberally, and his uniform and his face were covered with dust. The lieutenant asked for Major General Shafter. Jean-Paul stepped outside and pointed at the obese general. The officer rushed over to the General, saluted and gave him a piece of paper from his shoulder bag. J.P. watched the entire process and noted the General's entire demeanor changed when he read the cable the lieutenant had just given him. The general immediately took his three division commanders aside and briefed them, undoubtedly based on the content of the telegram. The division commanders then did the same with their brigade commanders. Whatever the message was, it didn't take long to pass it down the chain of command.

At that point General Shafter beckoned Jean-Paul. He took him to say farewell to Colonel Davout, thanking him for his grand hospitality, and a wonderful evening. The Colonel was equally gracious in thanking the General for accepting his invitation and being such a wonderful guest. He also apologized for the short notice of the invitation and how that had hindered him being a more affable host. Jean-Paul translated for all the generals and colonels as they said goodbye to the Colonel.

Once all the American officers had paid their farewell to Colonel Davout, Jean-Paul turned to leave. Colonel Davout called him back and said, "Young man, I am quite impressed

335

with you. Your French is excellent, you have very good skills in the art of savate, and you are socially quite skilled. I am extremely pleased to have met you and am looking forward to seeing you again during the expedition." Jean-Paul thanked him for his hospitality and shook the Colonel's hand. He then took one step back and saluted. He then hurried to catch up with the two Rough Rider colonels.

When he walked out of the front door of the hotel, Colonel's Wood and Roosevelt were just getting into the coach. Jean-Paul hurried down the steps and jumped in right after Colonel Roosevelt and closed the door.

Both of the colonels stared at him but said nothing. Finally, Colonel Wood spoke, "Well corporal you had quite an evening."

"Yes sir, that I did."

"General Shatner wants to have you transferred to his headquarters. I told him no way. If he needs you, we will send you to translate for him, but we are keeping you with us. We need talented soldiers like you. I understand from Oberstleutnant von Geisler that your German is also quite good. Is that right?"

"I seem to get by sir."

"Good. I know your French is excellent but how about your Spanish? How is your Spanish?"

"I have been learning it sir, but I would say I am only a

novice at Spanish."

"No problem. After observing you this evening, Colonel Roosevelt and I have decided to bring you up to regiment. You will be working with Sergeant LaCombe, and will also be used as an orderly, a runner, and, of course, a language specialist. You will report first thing in the morning. How does that fit for you?"

Jean-Paul didn't know what to say, so he simply said, "Thank you sir, I look forward to coming to work at regiment." He thought to himself, Captain, O'Neil, First Sergeant Troxler, and Three-Ring *will not like this*. The First Sergeant will think *that I somehow worked this transfer*.

At that point Jean-Paul again became invisible to the two Colonels. They began discussing the content of the General Shafter's cable. The teenager was astonished by what he heard. Fifth Corps was to leave for Cuba *immediately!* Since there was not time to get more transport ships, *the cavalry would not be taking their horses*. Because there was also limited space for soldiers, the Rough Riders would only be taking eight troops of seventy men each. That meant that *almost half of the regiment would not be deploying*. It seemed the two Colonels were as surprised about this turn of events as Jean-Paul was to overhear them talking about it.

When the coach arrived back at the camp, Jean-Paul went directly to his tent. Three-Ring couldn't stop making wise remarks about his uniform and him hob-knobbing with the bigwigs. He ignored him and went directly to sleep—no reading the Scriptures or writing home tonight. The alcohol, the upcoming deployment, and all the other information of the day put him into a restless and somewhat confused sleep. This adventure was now going to continue in earnest.

### *Thought Questions for Chapter 12*:

1. Why was Jean-Paul impressed on how First Sergeant Troxler approached and dealt with problems?

2. Why did Jean-Paul love it when Colonel Roosevelt used the word *Bully*? Considering the context in which Roosevelt would use it, what does the word *Bully* even mean?

3. Why does a nation's population get so excited and energized when its government declares war? When and why does that excitement die down?

4. Why did Jean-Paul say the armies of the North and the South in the American Civil War were *not* simply mobs of armed men slugging it out? Do you agree or disagree with him? Why?

5. Why was Jean-Paul transferred to regimental headquarters? From knowing Jean-Paul, what was his primary concern about being transferred?

6. What was your biggest learning or take away from this chapter? What can you apply from the information in this chapter? What in it did you find the most interesting? Why?

# 13

## *Transferring to Regimental Headquarters*

The next morning after the first formation, Jean-Paul went to Troop A headquarters, raised up all the sides of the tent and began his work. He wasn't sure how he should tell First Sergeant Troxler what had happened the night before. He was quite sure the First Sergeant would be really angry about the news of his transfer.

Then there was the business of the order to move out immediately and without horses. It would take at least twenty-four hours to take down the camp and pack it up for movement. Apparently, the order had not yet been officially passed down, as things were business as usual. Eventually First Sergeant Troxler came into the tent. He tossed his hat, sat down putting his boots on a field desk, leaned back, and cupped his hands behind his head. "Well Dee-Bert, how was your time last night at the Frenchie's fes-tivitiees?"

"It was all good First Sergeant. Had the opportunity to interpret for General Shafter as well as our colonels. Colonel Davout, the French attaché, was a wonderful host. Got to meet his eighteen-year-old daughter Bridgette who was more than gorgeous. Drank some excellent French champagne. It was really a good time."

"Did you hear any rumors about when we will be shipping out?"

Now Jean-Paul had a choice. He could be honest and tell the First Sergeant what he had heard or he could say nothing and let that information come down through the chain of command.

As Jean-Paul was thinking of how to respond, Sergeant LaCombe from the regimental adjunct's section walked into the tent with another trooper. He handed the First Sergeant two pieces of paper. They were handwritten orders. One was reassigning Jean-Paul to regimental headquarters and the other assigning the soldier with LaCombe to Troop A.

When First Sergeant Troxler read the first order, he let a line of cuss words that would have made any army veteran proud. He never read the second order and threw the papers on the field desk. He turned to Jean-Paul and actually yelled, "*Did you have anything to do with this? Did you know about this? Did you work this with your French buddy Sergeant LaCombe here? Well??*"

"First Sergeant, I..."

Sergeant LaCombe swiftly interrupted. "He had nothing to do with it. This is by order of Colonel Wood himself. He wants DeBert at regiment primarily to do translation and interpretation. Actually, General Shafter wanted him at corps headquarters, but Colonel Wood insisted he stay at regiment. In exchange for DeBert here is Trooper Cornwallis. He is a Harvard man, is an expert in polo and horsemanship, and is a quick study. He has rapidly picked up Army admin procedures while at regiment and will be a more than adequate replacement for Corporal DeBert."

Sergeant LaCombe's comments seemed to settle the First Sergeant. He picked up the two orders again and this time actually read them. He looked at Jean-Paul and shook his head. Then he said to Sergeant LaCombe, "Well, I suppose I have no choice in the matter, but I am not happy about this nor will Captain O'Neill be pleased. I hate to admit it, but you are taking one of our best soldiers in *Dee-bert*. Trooper Cornwallis, you will have big boots to fill. Okay, Dee-bert, get your gear and get along with your new boss."

About this time Captain O'Neill, somewhat out of breath, came into the headquarters tent. "First Sergeant, I need to see you right away."

Captain O'Neill then noticed Sergeant Lacombe and the other trooper. Sensing something, he asked no one in particular, "And what do we have going on here?"

The First Sergeant with some reluctance said, "Dee-bert here is being transferred to regiment. Apparently, Colonel Wood wants him for his amazing linguistic skills. In exchange, they are giving us Trooper Cornwallis here, a Harvard man."

Captain O'Neill glanced at everyone in the tent. He nodded his head once or twice and then said, "Well, if it weren't for our immediate problem, I would fight this. But right now, we have other more pressing issues, so Dee-bert you are getting a pass. Get your gear and get going. We have deployment issues to deal with." The Captain and First Sergeant then walked outside the tent discussing the details of breaking down the bivouac area and moving the unit to the docks.

Jean-Paul half-heartedly picked up his shoulder bag and left with Sergeant LaCombe.

As they were walking, he was feeling really low. He felt he had let down Captain O'Neill and the First Sergeant. He had nothing to do with the transfer but felt he was being blamed for it.

Sergeant LaCombe sensed Jean-Paul's mood. He said, "Don't let this bother you. In the military people come and go and are transferred in and out all of the time. It's part of military life. Think about combat. Every day, good soldiers as well as bad ones are killed or wounded and replacements are assigned. Yet the Army goes on. O'Neil and Troxler are old soldiers; they know how the system works. You can consider it a feather in your cap that they both were upset about you leaving. If you had been a second-rater, they would not have had that response and could have cared less. *To be respected by good soldiers is something to which we all aspire. It is one of the few rewards we get in the Army, being respected by our peers and our betters."*

Jean-Paul appreciated Sergeant LaCombe's efforts to set his mind at rest, but his words did nothing to change how he was feeling. This was *not the way* he wanted to leave his first Army unit. Oh well...

Sergeant LaCombe was a tall man with broad shoulders, a long torso, and something of a pigeon chest. He had thin, athletic legs and an overall physique not unlike Colonel Wood. He also had a rather large head with a stylish handlebar moustache. His graying hair did not fit his youthful and unwrinkled face. Overall, his appearance was dignified and that was also how he carried himself. Jean Paul concluded that his family probably had money and was socially connected.

Sergeant LaCombe walked with Jean-Paul to get his gear and also return the officer's uniform he had worn last evening. Three-Ring and the other members of A Troop were training and nowhere to be seen. It was a good thing thought J.P. They would soon be coming back and tearing down their bivouac area. He couldn't imagine the kidding they would give him when they found he was being transferred to regiment. Three-Ring would never let him live it down. They stopped at regimental supply, and he turned in the officer's uniform. Jean-Paul liked the way it felt and how he looked when he wore it. The thought briefly crossed his mind that maybe someday...

Back at regimental headquarters, Jean-Paul helped pack up the admin materials and field equipment. With only the tents left to take down and pack, Sergeant LaCombe said to J.P., "Let's you and me take a short break and go to the mess hall. Maybe they still have some coffee. LaCombe said nothing during the walk to the mess hall, which was also being torn down. There was a large canister filled with black coffee steaming over a small fire. Sergeant Lacombe quietly poured himself and Jean-Paul a cup. He then said, *"Come, let's sit in the shade under that tree."*

Jean-Paul was not sure what this was all about but regardless, he knew enough to keep quiet and listen.

"This morning both Colonel Wood and Colonel Roosevelt said they wanted you transferred up to regiment. That was partially because Trooper Cornwallis, the Harvard polo player, wanted to get out of the headquarters and get back down *to the line*. He had been pestering everybody about that ever since we formed up in San Antonio. So, the trade was good all around."

"You don't have any problem being assigned to regiment, do you?"

Jean-Paul wasn't exactly sure how honest he should be in his response. He knew he had to choose his words carefully.

"Well, like Trooper Cornwallis, I joined up to see combat and find out what I am made of...."

Sergeant LaCombe immediately interrupted him. "Well, I wouldn't worry about that. You know Colonel Wood and Colonel

Roosevelt. They are not going to sit in the headquarters while there is fighting going on. They will be in the thick of things and believe you me, you and I will be right there with them."

Without expression and in monotone Sergeant Lacombe continued, "Don't be surprised by that—it's true. By the way, why do you think you were transferred up to regiment?"

"I suppose it's because I speak French."

"That's what I thought you would say. But that's not all of it—not at all. The language skills you displayed last evening played only a small part. Colonel Roosevelt favors you because of what you did that night in New York City. He told me the story when I worked for him and he was the *Assistant Secretary of the Navy*. He said how you, unarmed, didn't hesitate to tackle a crazed criminal, who had two pistols and a butcher knife. He sees you as a man of courage—and more than anything else—that is what the Colonel respects in a man. You also impressed him with your knowledge of military history, especially when you told the stories of the battles at the Alamo and San Jacinto."

Sergeant LaCombe now stared at Jean-Paul and without emotion and said, *"Quite a hero."* He shook his head and looked away. J.P. detected a tone of sarcasm in the Sergeant's voice.

LaCombe continued. "Your speaking French last evening only brought you to Colonel Roosevelt's attention once again. You seem to have a knack for making yourself visible. That's very clever. Of course, such a tendency toward *politics* may upset some people and make others jealous. They might think you are *showboating,* or even worse, trying to show them up. Do you understand what I am getting at?"

Jean-Paul wasn't totally sure but thought it wise to say, "Yes Sergeant."

"Good. Now this is how we do things at our headquarters and what I am expecting of you." Here Sergeant LaCombe seemed to become even more serious. He said, "Do what you are told. Don't second-guess. Don't cause trouble. Stay in the background. Do your job and keep your mouth *mostly shut.* If you do those things, we will get along fine. I don't think there will be many opportunities to do translation so you will be used mostly as an orderly, a foot messenger, and a runner. When you are not out doing those things, you will have some minor admin duties. You will also be expected to keep the headquarters area policed and clean. That includes when we get to Cuba. If you can do these simple things, again, we will get along just fine. If you don't, we will have to remove those corporal stripes and send you to the toughest, meanest first sergeant in the entire regiment. Now, did I make myself clear enough for you Professor?"

"Yes Sergeant, perfectly clear. Perfectly clear." Jean—Paul was taken back that the Sergeant had called him Professor. He was also puzzled at this meeting. He didn't understand why the Sergeant had been so tough and threatening. Perhaps thought J.P., it was because he too was suffering from a bit of envy regarding the incidents in New York City and the hotel party. No problem. The teenager had decided weeks ago he was going to do his best regardless of the attitude and personality of his leaders.

As they were walking back to regimental headquarters the entire area was buzzing with activity. Because of the proximity of the deployment, there was an unmistakable energy and excitement in the air. Jean-Paul noticed that even Sergeant LaCombe was walking at a faster pace than before.

Not thinking, Jean-Paul blurted out, "Sergeant, how did you come to sign up for the Rough Riders?"

Sergeant LaCombe stopped and glared at him.

"Why would you ask me such a question, particularly after I just told you to keep your mouth *mostly shut?*"

"Well, I just want to learn. It seems to me you are an educated man and I assume you have an interesting background. I am always curious to learn from such people. But if you don't want to share, that's perfectly fine." Jean-Paul was feeling extremely awkward.

"Alright. I will tell you, but we need to keep walking."

After a few steps the Sergeant began, "I was born and raised in Marblehead, Massachusetts. It was on the ocean, and I learned to sail before I could walk. My brothers and I were always on the water. My father was in the merchant marines and was gone much of the time. When I was fourteen, I joined the merchant fleet and for the next four years made several voyages with my dad. It was an awesome experience. Saw most of Northern and Western Europe, the Mediterranean, and North Africa. Traveling was an education unto itself. However, my dad wanted me to get a formal education, so I took the exam for Harvard, which was not far from my home in Marblehead. I spent two years there. Compared to being at sea, college was boring. Harvard had no female students, and of course our sister college, Radcliffe, had no men. The Radcliffe girls were from money and seemed to be only interested in marrying money. Thus, they paid little attention to me. Being bored, I dropped out of college and joined the Navy. Because I had been in college, the navy trained me in administration."

The Sergeant paused reflectively and then continued. "I went out to sea again but this time on a battleship, the *USS Texas*. It was a magnificent vessel that was designed after the British Majestic Class of battleships. It was protected by hardened steel armor, had batteries of both heavy and light guns, and was powered by large, coal-fueled steam engines. It was a marvelous seagoing vessel—simply marvelous. We sailed around Cape Horn in very ugly weather and traveled all over the Far East. That was yet another great adventure. I was working in administration on the *Texas* and was actually promoted to chief petty officer. It was a great disappointment when I was reassigned from fleet to duty to the office of the *Secretary of the*

*Navy* in Washington DC. But there was also a positive side to that. It was there I worked directly for Mr. Roosevelt, who at the time was the Assistant Secretary of the Navy. We connected immediately. My enlistment in the Navy expired simultaneously with the advent of this war and Mr. Roosevelt's resignation as the assistant secretary. When he was commissioned as an officer in the First Volunteer Cavalry, he asked me to join him. He wanted to give me an officer's commission, but I didn't need or want that. I figured I could give him better support by working admin for him. Fortunately, he never asked if I could ride a horse. I could of course, but not as well as the rest of these cowboys. So that's my story. Did you learn anything from what I said?" It was evident that cynicism was aimed at Jean-Paul's comment that he asked questions to learn.

"Yes, I did. But I have one more question if that's okay."

"Probably not, but what's the question?

"You were in the navy and apparently liked it. Spain has a big naval fleet in both the Philippines and in Cuba. There will certainly be some big naval battles. Why didn't you join the navy instead of the army's cavalry?"

"Perhaps you weren't listening Professor. I told you earlier, I joined the army to be with Secretary Roosevelt. That's the whole of it. I don't think I ever respected someone more than I do him. He is the ideal man—a man's man—as some would say.

I'm here to support and assist him. That's the reason I am in the army! Any more questions?"

"No Sergeant, no more questions."

"Let me add something here. I think the United States Navy is vastly superior to the ridiculously small and inefficient frontier United States Army—vastly superior. Superior in technology, tactics, leadership, and God only knows what else. There are no Navy admirals that are one hundred pounds overweight like General Shafter." With that comment Sergeant LaCombe raised his eyebrows and glanced at Jean-Paul for a reaction.

Jean-Paul thought it best to say nothing and gave no expression.

LaCombe continued, "There is nothing like being at sea and out on the water. And I'm not talking about a river or a lake. I am talking about *God's great seas—the oceans*. Standing on the deck of a majestic iron warship with the wind blowing saltwater in your face, moving your body at one with the motion of the ship, and watching the angry waves pick up and drop that monster ship like a child's toy, is a breathtaking experience that is never to be forgotten. Never. Navy life is manifestly better than marching in the dust or the mud. It is a significantly better military life than the Army by any standard."

Sergeant LaCombe, who had almost been in a sort of romantic daze, now caught himself. "Alright Professor, this is what I want you to do. And, you must do this quickly because I don't want you to miss movement like several soldiers did when we left San Antonio. Go to the stable and see Corporal Belcher and check out a horse to make a courier run. I need you to take these documents and messages to Fifth Corps headquarters at the Tampa Bay Hotel. They should also have some items for you in return."

Being assigned to the regimental headquarters, thought Jean-Paul, might not be such bad duty after all.

Arriving at the hotel Jean-Paul was again impressed at the outer porch of reporters, officer's wives, and hangers-on. He noted that those he thought to be officers' wives were simply beautiful in their long flowing dresses. Even in the Florida heat and with all those clothes, they did not appear to be uncomfortable.

Leaving his horse with an attendant, Jean-Paul walked up the steps leading to the porch and the main entrance. Suddenly he heard his name called out and by a woman's voice. It was Bridgette, the daughter of Colonel Davout, the French attaché. She, her mother, and the Colonel were having afternoon tea in the shade of the hotel's porch.

Bridgette literally came running and almost knocked him down when she gave him a big hug. She then pulled him toward their table exclaiming in French, "Come join us, come join my parents for some tea. You simply must join us."

Jean-Paul tried to protest but to no avail. As he was being pulled, he noted that Bridgette looked even more beautiful than she did last night. Jean-Paul tried not to stare, but that was very difficult....

Once at the table he said, "I have some important messages for General Shafter and Fifth Corps headquarters. I really must get to delivering them."

Completely ignoring what he had just said, Colonel Davout asked him in French, "So young soldier, what are your plans after the war? Will you be staying in the Army?"

Jean-Paul thought that an unusual question. He responded, "Well sir, I haven't really thought that far in advance. I was teaching at the Jesuit school back home in New York. My family lives there and the Jesuit brothers want me to come back to continue teaching. I really loved studying and teaching history. I have kind of a gift for that. However, there was no pay and not much of a future."

Jean-Paul casually glanced at Bridgette. She simply radiated beauty. Abigail and Berti were attractive, but Bridgette was at a higher level of elegance, style, charm, and natural beauty. She was actually holding his right hand with both resting on his knee. Odd thought Jean-Paul, very odd, particularly with her parents sitting there. The Colonel and his wife seemed indifferent to their daughter's behavior. Very French all-around thought Jean-Paul.

Colonel Davout then said, "I have just learned *this morning* that my assignment next summer will be to command a regiment in the *Légion Étrangère* or the *French Foreign Legion* as it is called here in the United States. It will be in Sidi-bel-Abbès in Algeria. Madam Davout and perhaps Bridgette will be accompanying me. You must consider coming to Algeria and joining the Legion. With your fluent French language skills and you war experience, I will make you a sergeant immediately. In the Legion, the sergeants are all-powerful and run the regiment. You would be the perfect candidate for such a responsibility. What do you say?"

Jean-Paul noticed that Bridgette was now holding his hand with both of her hands and was squeezing it tighter as her father was speaking to him about joining the Legion.

"I have read about the Legion, but I never actually thought about joining."

"You would be perfect. You speak French fluently. You are physically fit. You understand the culture and are a natural leader. You would be an ideal candidate for the Legion."

"Perhaps sir, but first I must survive this war and also deliver these messages." Bridgette gave his hand another hard squeeze.

Again, ignoring what Jean-Paul had just said, Colonel Davout continued, "The Legion is probably the toughest fighting force in the world. They can withstand any hardship and no mission is too difficult. They have no fear of wounds or death. They simply want to fight and fight some more. The Legion is a military organization that has no equal. You would be an excellent addition."

Then the Colonel added in English, "You simply must consider joining." It seemed to Jean-Paul it was at least the third time he said that. Bridgette gave his hand yet another squeeze. That was actually beginning to hurt. Jean-Paul thought to himself, if my hand is to have pain, well then, this is the way to have it!

"I will consider it of course. But now I really must get on with my duties and deliver this pouch of documents to Fifth Corps headquarters."

Bridgette held Jean-Paul's hand tight and did not let go as he stood up. With some force Jean-Paul awkwardly pulled his hand away. Putting on his hat he saluted Colonel Davout who responded by simply raising his right hand. He then glanced toward Madam Davout and touched the brim of his hat.

Bridgette put her arm through his and said, "I will walk with you."

Once inside the hotel door she stopped and gave him a really big kiss!

"That is how we do it in France," said Bridgette with a huge, satisfied smile." Please consider what my father said to you. If you join, I will leave Georgetown University and be in Algeria waiting for you!"

"That was a very nice kiss," said Jean-Paul uneasily. He looked around and almost everyone in the lobby was staring at them. That included several field grade U.S. army officers.

Bridgette added with great energy, "You must join us for dinner tonight, you simply must."

"I would like to, but I have my duties and don't think it will be possible. We are getting very close to sailing for Cuba, and I don't think I will be able to get away."

Still speaking in French Bridgette again said, "You really must join us for dinner. Try to join us for dinner, won't you? Please? Please?"

"Certainly, I will try but I can't promise. Now really, I must deliver these messages."

Bridgette kissed him on the cheek and with a longing look turned and walked away glancing back as she walked out the door.

Puzzled at the entire encounter with the Davout family, Jean-Paul started toward the rooms where Fifth Corps headquarters was located. Almost immediately an old, worn army Lieutenant Colonel stopped him and gruffly asked, "Where are you assigned soldier? "

Somewhat startled, Jean-Paul responded, "Sir, I am assigned to the headquarters of the *First Volunteer Cavalry Regiment.*"

The Lieutenant Colonel shook his head and replied, "I have heard about your unit—*the Rough Riders.* They are Leonard Wood and Teddy Roosevelt's privileged ones. So privileged that you think you can come into this headquarters and have a sexual display with any young woman you see? Isn't that right corporal?"

Jean-Paul immediately had *that tightening feeling* in his chest. He wanted to say what he was thinking, but he knew that would be disrespectful and a huge military mistake.

The Lt. Colonel condescendingly continued, "Well, isn't it soldier?"

"No sir, it isn't. That young woman is the daughter of Colonel Davout the French Army attaché. Colonel Davout is accompanying Fifth Corps as an observer. I met her last evening when I attended Colonel Davout's party serving as a French language interpreter for General Shafter, Colonel Wood, and Colonel Roosevelt."

Jean-Paul, now almost shaking with anger, said in French, *"Vous sentez comme du boeuf et le fromage."* The sour old colonel didn't know he had just been told he smelled *like beef and cheese.*

Jean-Paul's response seemed to stop the Lt. Colonel in his tracks. It was also clear he was now not sure how to respond to J.P. Realizing he may be dealing with someone who was more connected than he was, he grunted and said, *"Get on with your business and get back to your unit where you belong. And you had better be quick about it."*

Jean-Paul said, "Yes Sir," and moved out smartly. He had not experienced such an officer during his entire time with the Rough Riders. All of their officers were men to be looked up to and respected and not some detestable, stale, old has-been. This poor excuse of a soldier was a staff officer who had probably not *served with troops of the line for years.* Contemptible lout!

Dropping off his pouch of documents, he picked up another to deliver back to the regiment. There was much to think about. Bridgette said she would be waiting for him. Berti said the same. Desiree said she wanted to see him after the war. It would have been great if Abigail had also said that, but....

Moving quickly through the lobby, Jean-Paul was stopped by a most elegantly dressed and coiffed middle-aged woman.

"Excuse me soldier, but I understand you are assigned to the First Volunteer Cavalry. Is that correct?".

"Yes ma'am it is."

"Excellent. I am Edith Roosevelt, wife of Colonel Theodore Roosevelt. Would you please give this package to the Colonel? It contains the extra pairs of eyeglasses he requested. Fortunately, they arrived from New York this morning. I would sincerely appreciate it if you would insure he gets them."

"Yes ma'am, I will be sure that he does. You can count on it."

"Thank you young soldier. What is your name?"

"Ma'am, my name is Corporal DeBert, Jean-Paul DeBert."

"Jean-Paul DeBert. I remember a French name similar to that from a street incident my husband was involved in when he was the police commissioner of New York City. That DeBert was quite a hero. Per chance was that you?"

"Yes ma'am it was and still is." Amazing thought Jean-Paul. What a memory.

"Wonderful. My husband talked for days about what you did. He quite respected your courageous behavior."

"Thank you ma'am."

"And thank you for delivering the glasses."

"No problem." Jean-Paul touched the brim of his hat and walked out onto the hotel's large porch. Fortunately, Colonel Davout and his family were no longer sitting there.

Back at Rough Riders headquarters, he helped put the tents, trunks, and field desks on the transport wagons. Sergeant LaCombe said the order to start moving to the rail tracks was expected at any moment.

After eating hardtack and beef jerky for dinner, Jean-Paul walked back to his old bivouac area to get his half of pup tent he had been sharing with Three-Ring. Then a trooper named Bell caught up to him and began walking with him. Like Jean-Paul, today was also Bell's first day assigned to regimental headquarters. When assigned to F Troop, Trooper Bell was regarded as a bit dim-witted and apparently could not do anything right. Why he was then assigned to regimental headquarters was something J.P. could not understand. The ways of the Army were at times befuddling to this young man from up-state New York. For whatever reason, now Trooper Bell seemed to be shadowing him.

As they were walking Jean-Paul heard someone yell, "Dee-Bert." He turned to see Trooper's Three-Ring, Mendoza, and Delaney from Troop A. He was overjoyed and started running toward them. He yelled, "Hola mi amigos! Hello!"

There was no response from the three but blank stares.

Jean-Paul stopped within a few feet of them. He was startled by their non-response. "What's wrong?" he asked.

"What's wrong?" responded Three-Ring. "You abandoned us once again for a soft, cozy job at headquarters, that's what's wrong. You deserted all your friends for safe and secure work with the brass. That's exactly what's wrong."

Jean-Paul blurted out, "Come on now, I had nothing to do with that. I was ordered to report to regiment."

Delaney responded, "First you get invited to the Frenchie's big soiree last night, and now you go get yourself transferred so you can hob-nob with the big brass. I always heard that's what people from New York are like. They'll hang around with you until they find someone better. Then they'll drop you like a hot potato."

Julio Mendoza added, "Amigo, how am I going to teach you any more Spanish with you at headquarters. And how is Delaney going to teach you to play poker now that you are up there?"

For once Jean-Paul was at a loss for words. He had no idea what to say. Suddenly all three broke of laughing. Delaney said, "We had you going there for a while Professor. We were just playing with you. We came over to congratulate you on your good fortune. Somebody is really looking out for you. You certainly have the *Midas touch* or as my people would say, *'The luck of the Irish.'*"

"My goodness, you guys had me there for a moment, no question about that."

The three huddled around Jean-Paul and patted him on the arm and shoulder. Three-Ring had brought him his half of the pup tent.

Suddenly there was a lot of yelling, "We are moving out! We are moving out!" We're moving to the tracks to take the train to the docks.

Delaney said, "Come on guys, we need to go. Adios Professor, take care."

"See you on board Professor," said Three-Ring as he saluted and turned.

Jean-Paul returned his courtesy salute and said, "You can count on it. See you on board."

| \* | \* | \* | \* | \* |

The next thirty-six hours were a whirlwind of activity and chaos for Jean-Paul and the Rough Riders. First, they had been ordered to move to a location where a train would take them the nine miles to the port. They were further told that if they were not aboard the transport ship by daybreak of the following morning, they would not be going to Cuba. This put everyone in the headquarters in a state of agitation and significant panic.

The Rough Riders moved themselves and their equipment to the appointed railroad track by midnight. When they arrived, there was no train present. Jean-Paul exhausted from the heat and the day's activities slept on the ground. Around 6:00 AM a train pulling empty coal cars came by. The racket it made woke everyone. Like a leader should, Lt. Colonel Roosevelt *took the initiative* and with some difficulty convinced the engineer to take the regiment to the port in the coal cars. The engineer reluctantly agreed, not being able to stand up to the Teddy's persuasive personality.

Jean-Paul rode in the coal car with Colonel Roosevelt, Sergeant LaCombe, Trooper Bell, and several of the regiment's staff officers. Roosevelt said with resolution that since the number of transports available was known, and the number of regiments deploying was also known, it should be simple work to get their regiment onto the appropriate vessel. J.P. wondered if that would be the case....

The regiment arrived at the port with all its belongings and covered in coal dust. No matter, they were where they were supposed to be and on time. Sergeant LaCombe directed that Jean-Paul follow Colonel Roosevelt since he was now serving as the Colonel's runner.

Colonel Roosevelt's assumption that there was a plan to put certain regiments on certain transports was a myth. There of course, was no plan. The dock area was yet another area of chaos and anarchy. Jean-Paul had seen this spectacle before. It was indeed déjà vu! There were ten thousand soldiers milling around with their leaders generally working at cross-purposes. Apparently, the depot quartermaster, Colonel Humphrey, had the master-loading plan. He was however, nowhere to be found. His assistant thought the good Colonel *was sleeping*. Hearing this, Colonel Roosevelt blurted out, *"For what's going on here he might as well be asleep."*

After an hour Colonel Humphrey appeared. Jean-Paul was once again startled at this officer's appearance. Humphrey was overweight and wore an ill-fitting and discolored uniform. He had gray hair, large eye bags, was a bit stooped, and appeared to be ninety years old if he was a day. He told Roosevelt the Rough Riders had been allotted to the transport *Yucatan*.

Hearing this, Colonel Wood immediately commandeered a stray launch and left to board that transport which was located in the bay. The Yucatan's captain said he had been told there were two regiments allotted to his ship. They were the Second Regular Infantry and the Seventy-first New York Volunteers. That was a problem since the Seventy-first alone had more men assigned than the capacity of the *Yucatan*. The ship docked at the same time that Colonel Wood's launch reached shore.

Colonel Wood told Roosevelt he needed to get the regiment on board this transport as quickly as possible or they might *miss the war!* It seemed all the regiment's staff officers and even Sergeant LaCombe were away running some sort of errand. The only ones left from the regiment at the dock by the Yucatan's gang plank were Jean-Paul and Trooper Bell—the supposed dimwit.

Lt. Colonel Roosevelt turned to Jean-Paul and in a high-pitched voice and with a great sense of urgency said, "Young soldier, I am going to fetch the regiment. You are to stand here ensure that no other regiment boards this ship. That is your mission. Do you understand?"

"Yes sir, I understand."

"Good. You have a revolver. If some unit wants to board this transport and bullies you, draw your weapon and tell them you are under my orders not to let them board. Do you understand?"

"Yes sir, I understand." Good grief thought Jean-Paul immediately, I sure hope I won't have to draw my pistol on another American army unit!

"Good, Trooper Bell, you're coming with me. Let's go." Then they took off running through a maze of soldiers in the direction of the regiment.

Jean-Paul was both confused and worried. He had just received an order to draw his revolver on any unit that wanted to board the *Yucatan*. Certainly, if a unit did show up, the ranking person would undoubtedly rank higher than J.P.'s corporal stripes. He would then probably be drawing his pistol on an officer. Wonderful. Jean-Paul was not sure that was the way things were to work in the Army. But this was war and as he had read in Clausewitz, *war is not business as usual.*

Thirty minutes passed and it seemed to Jean-Paul he would be able to avoid any sort of confrontation. No sooner had that thought crossed his mind when a unit in full formation marched up to the Yucatan's gangplank and stopped. A colonel, probably the regimental commander, began giving orders for the unit to board the ship. Instinctively Jean-Paul drew his weapon keeping the barrel pointed to the ground.

A Lieutenant Colonel walked toward the gangplank totally ignoring the corporal standing there. It startled him when Jean-

Paul stepped directly in front of him. Jean-Paul transferred the pistol to his left hand and saluted. As forcefully as he could muster, he said, "Sir I'm sorry, but this transport has been allotted to the First Volunteer Cavalry. They will be here to board directly. I have been tasked by Lt. Colonel Roosevelt, the deputy commander of the First Volunteers, to ensure no other unit boards before they arrive."

The Lieutenant Colonel was completely speechless at this unexpected encounter. He took a step back and stared at Jean-Paul. Then his faced changed. His look was a combination of anger, contempt, and arrogance.

"Soldier, I am *Lieutenant Colonel Ralph Gordon Howell III*. I am the deputy commander of the United States Second Infantry Regiment. These are regular army infantry soldiers mind you and not novice, amateur volunteers. By virtue of my rank and position I am ordering you to step aside and also to put that revolver back in its holster. I don't care if the good Lord Himself gave you your orders soldier, my regiment will be boarding this ship. Now step aside, and that Corporal, is a direct order."

"Sir, I can't do that. I am already under orders from my regiment's deputy commander." With this statement Jean-Paul automatically raised the pistol equal with his right shoulder, barrel pointed up, *and then he cocked the pistol.*

Simultaneously the Second Infantry's regimental commander, a full bird colonel, with a herd of staff officers and sergeants in tow approached.

"What seems to be the problem here Ralph?" asked the Colonel.

"Well, it seems the Corporal here thinks he has been ordered to keep all other units from boarding this vessel other than his own unit—the First Volunteer Cavalry. Apparently, he has not been particularly well trained and doesn't understand military rank or what a direct order means."

"Ah yes," said the Colonel, "the First Volunteer Cavalry. The unit of cowboys commanded by celebrities: Wood and Roosevelt." The Colonel then looked at Jean-Paul and shook his head in disgust.

"Sirs," said Jean-Paul, "I have been very well trained and know military ranks and the meaning of a direct order. That is why I am standing here." Jean-Paul wanted to add something in response to the colonel's comment that celebrity cowboys commanded the First Volunteers. Wisely, he reflected that would not be a good idea.

The Colonel again looked at Jean-Paul. He then turned and said, "Sergeant Major, go find the nearest military policeman. We are going to put this soldier under arrest and ensure he is court-martialed and imprisoned in the military prison at Fort Leavenworth. Considering what he will experience in prison, he will have wished he had let us board this ship. Having gone to war would have been much better than what is in store for him in that Kansas hell hole."

The Sergeant Major said, "Yes sir," saluted, and took off at the double time.

His cocked pistol still raised Jean-Paul felt he looked resolute, but inside he was not feeling very resolute. Goodness gracious, now I am going to prison instead of to Cuba. Just a few days ago I was going to prison in Texas. This is not how things are supposed work.

Out of nowhere Colonel Wood and Lieutenant Colonel Roosevelt appeared. Intuitively they recognized what was taking place. Roosevelt immediately said to Jean-Paul. "Good work Professor. Now go and join the unit and prepare to board."

Jean-Paul did not have to be told twice. He holstered his now uncocked weapon, saluted, and ran as fast as he could toward the Rough Riders formation, brushing past the two officers of the Second Infantry regulars in the process.

Jean-Paul quickly joined the rear of the formation of the headquarters troop. Once in the formation he closely observed the exchange between his two colonels and the two colonels of the infantry regiment. He knew part of their conversation must have been about him. But shortly Wood, Roosevelt, and the Second Infantry's commander were all laughing and shaking hands. With Roosevelt's booming voice, J.P. was sure he heard him say the Second Infantry could put some of their troops on the transport, as there probably would be room.

Jean-Paul noticed that Lt. Colonel Howell was not paying attention to the Colonels' conversation but was simply staring at him. It was an *evil eyed stare* to be sure. It wasn't hard to comprehend what that colonel was thinking, and for certain, it wasn't good. His father always said to *not worry about things over which you have no control.* And this was a situation over which he had absolutely no control. Jean-Paul would probably never run across him again, even in Cuba. He simply stared back at the colonel, expressionless.

### *Thought Questions for Chapter 13:*

1. When Jean-Paul was transferred to regimental headquarters, Sergeant LaCombe said that to be respected by good soldiers is something to which all aspire. Why is that the case and how does someone achieve it?

2. What was it about Jean-Paul's behavior that made Sergeant LaCombe say to him it might appear he was showboating and even trying to show others up? Why did he say that and from what you know about Jean-Paul, do you agree with LaCombe?

3. Why did Sergeant LaCombe think military life in the Navy was better than the Army? Do you think he was right? Why or why not?

4. Colonel Roosevelt gave Corporal DeBert an order not to allow any Army units board the *Yucatan* while he went to bring the regiment to the ship. Evaluate that order and the situation in which it placed Jean-Paul?

5. What was your biggest learning or take away from this chapter? What can you apply from the information in this chapter? What in it did you find the most interesting? Why?

# 14

## *Traveling to Cuba*

Once on board the ship, Jean-Paul's quarters were in deck cabin #4. It was a room exclusively for the non-commissioned officers assigned to regimental headquarters. It contained several flimsy foldout cots. By smell and appearance, the room had previously been used by the ship's crew for recreation. It reeked badly of tobacco smoke and spittle sputum that had missed its mark. At least there were portholes and a door that could be left open for ventilation and fresh air. It yet again reminded Jean-Paul that he was no longer in New Hope, New York.

The cabin door faced the water and opened to a railed walkway. Jean-Paul's cabin was next to the cabins of Colonel Wood and Colonel Roosevelt and Regimental Sergeant Major Sacker. Deck cabin #5 was reserved for the regiment's first sergeants. All the junior noncommissioned officers (NCO's) were staying in the large bays in the bottom deck with the troops

With great commotion, the NCOs from the headquarters section arrived and got settled. There were Sergeant Lacombe from admin; Guitilias and Wright, the two flag bearers; Douthett the quartermaster; Kansky the saddle sergeant; Clay

Pratt the regimental trumpeter; the Colonels' two batmen; and finally, Jean-Paul's counterpart, Corporal Scarborough. He was the runner for the regimental commander. The room was clearly not large enough for ten people, but no worries thought Jean-Paul. At least he would be sleeping under cover and near his leaders. In his short time in the army, he knew being near the leaders is where things were *happening,* and the information he would hear from their conversations would not be gossip or rumor.

After getting settled, Sergeant LaCombe told Jean-Paul to check on Trooper Bell who was in Bay #1 below deck with the other enlisted members of headquarters troop. Walking down the ladder of steps into the bay, he felt he was entering a twilight zone. The conditions could only be described as wretched. The temperature was about 85 degrees outside, but in this bay, it must have been at least 110 degrees with stifling humidity. It was dimly lit, there was no ventilation, and the floor was absolutely wet and filthy. The air was nauseating with the foul smell of coal, smoke, grime, seasick vomit, and unwashed men. With all their equipment, the troopers were cramped beyond reason with barely room to move. Jean-Paul felt like throwing up just entering the place.

Barely into the bay he heard someone call out, "Corporal DeBert, over here." It was Trooper Bell.

As if in a maize, Jean-Paul snaked his way over to Bell.

"Well Trooper Bell, how are we doing?"

"Doing just great Corporal. It is a little warm and cramped down here but considering the adventure we are about to go on, it's tolerable. We were told that when the ship starts moving, it will create some ventilation. Can't wait until that happens, but in the meantime it's great to be here. Just think—we be going to war!"

Jean-Paul liked Bell's attitude. It seemed that people could put up with a lot if the reason for the discomfort was worthwhile. At least it seemed so in this case.

"I'll come by every day to check on you. Sergeant LaCombe and I are in Stateroom #4 on the main deck. Remember that, main deck, room #4."

"Okay Corporal—main deck, room #4. And just think, only six more days, and we will be in Cuba fighting the Spanish Army—just six more days." There seemed to be a tone of anxiety in Bell's bravado.

"That's right, so let's make sure we are ready." Jean-Paul patted Bell on the shoulder.

"Right, be ready—ready for anything and everything," Bell replied with an obvious reserve.

"Now I am going to see my old mates in Troop A," said Jean-Paul.

Loudly he asked to no one in particular, "Does anyone know the location of Troop A?" Someone grunted and pointed toward the back of the bay. After an obstacle-ridden trip, Jean-Paul saw a familiar face. There, amidst all the laughing, smoking, cussing, and chattering sat Three-Ring and several of the A Troop gang.

"Hey, Three-Ring! Hello fellows!" Jean-Paul noticed Delaney was in a poker game, Preacher was reading his Bible, and Mendoza was fast asleep in a twisted and very uncomfortable position.

"Hello Professor," said Three-Ring casually. How is life upstairs with all the big shots?"

"It's wonderful. I'm in an overcrowded room that smells like dirty feet. How is life down here?"

"Well, you can see for yourself. It's hot, crowded, and smells like elephant droppings. I would prefer the dirty feet.... Sooo, that's how life is down here. Somehow, I think your overcrowded and smelly accommodations are not as bad as ours."

"Perhaps, but not by much. What's new?"

"Nothing. It was quite a circus getting here from camp. But I am used to being in a circus, so it was no problem."

Jean-Paul replied, "After being in the Army for about six weeks, I think there are quite a few times when it could be compared favorably with the circus."

From right behind him Jean-Paul heard a familiar voice say, "That's right Professor; the army can sometimes be likened to a circus. Here is what I have to say about that, having spent some of the best years of my life in the army?"

Jean-Paul was elated to see it was First Sergeant Troxler who was doing the talking. He not only respected the First Sergeant, but he also liked him. *He always learned something when he was around Troxler.* To the First Sergeant's question, Jean-Paul—with a touch of uneasiness for being overheard—said, "I would really be interested in hearing what you have to say about your years in the Army First Sergeant?"

"All right, like with everything in life, including work and money paying jobs, there is the good and the bad. Got that—there is good and bad. Agreed the Army can be like a circus, but it can also be the best and most honorable profession to which a person can aspire. Army life for sure is one of service, sacrifice, misery, and discomfort. Preachers say they have a calling. Well, being a soldier is also *a calling* of sorts. To be a good soldier, one has to go beyond the misery, discomfort, and the circus atmosphere of the present and not lose sight of their *higher calling.* The soldier must focus on the honorable service he is doing for the country and his fellow man. It is no longer just about him; it is about *duty and serving*—many times at the cost of life or limb. You got that young soldiers?"

Jean-Paul, Three-Ring, and the other troopers who heard the First Sergeant's commentary on army life were silent but did nod in agreement. After a brief pause Jean-Paul started clapping and said, "That was great First Sergeant, simply great. Thanks for that." The others—with some hesitation—also started clapping—however weakly.

Encouraged by the response, the First Sergeant continued, "There will be many times when army life will get you down, particularly when you are in a combat zone. But if you remember the bigger picture, the greater good, and the higher ground, those will carry you. Never forget that. If you do, the danger and pettiness of army life *will not wear you down*." The First Sergeant paused as if waiting for a response. None was forthcoming.

"Now about the clapping Professor, that was unnecessary and could be interpreted that you are ingratiating yourself, you know, kissing up to me. I would be cautious about doing that with someone who ranks you."

"You are right First Sergeant. Thank you." The others mumbled in agreement.

Jean-Paul then turned to Three-Ring and said quietly, "I'll come around again. In the meantime, enjoy *the calling*."

"Right professor, you too enjoy *the calling*," said the little guy with a big smile.

*      *      *      *      *

The food and water served on the ship ranged from disgusting to totally inedible. It could truthfully be described as nauseating, worse than *gruel or swill*. The meat was canned beef with no salt. It was stringy and tasteless. It had obviously come from either the lips or the rear end of some kind of an alien cloved-foot animal. The drinking water on board was warm, was not clear, and had an off taste. And of course, there was no ice to cool it or anything else that was fresh, including fruit, vegetables, or meat. Eating the hardtack biscuit with this disgusting beef and dirty water made Jean-Paul think about what the First Sergeant had said. There are times when one must look at the bigger picture, overlook the unpleasantness of the moment, and remember the soldier's *higher calling*. Nice idea reflected Jean-Paul, but easier said than done.

Sergeant LaCombe, somewhat out of breath, came into the stateroom and said, "DeBert and Scarborough (Colonel Wood's enlisted orderly), you must go and see Colonel Wood and Colonel Roosevelt right now."

Seconds later they came upon the two colonels. Both had a very concerned look. Roosevelt spoke first. "I want you two to go and find the eight troop commanders and tell them to meet us in the ship's mess hall, or galley as the navy calls it, in one hour. In one hour, got that."

"Yes sir." Jean-Paul and Corporal Scarborough had no idea where all these officers were exactly. No problem. J.P. had already learned that just because you didn't know exactly how to carry out an order did not mean you wouldn't try to comply or give it your best effort.

With extremely good fortune and in a short period of time, Jean-Paul and Corporal Scarborough found all eight of the regiment's troop commanders. It strengthened his belief that even if you don't know how to do something exactly, setting out aggressively to accomplish it *almost always* leads to a good result. Sergeant LaCombe instructed both of them to remain standing in the back of the galley during the commander's meeting just in case the two Colonels needed them for something.

What Jean-Paul heard from Colonel Wood at that meeting was quite disturbing. The convoy's order to move out had been countermanded by Washington. It seems a U.S. Navy officer had mistaken some of the convoy's ships for being Spanish. This was reported to Washington as the sighting of Spanish warships. They responded by saying the Spanish threat had to be eliminated before the troop convoy could proceed. Thus, scout ships were sent out to find the *alleged Spanish vessels.* There was no telling how long that would take. Until the perceived threat was dealt with, the convoy would not be moving. Jean-Paul thought about the nasty food and the sweltering conditions in the cramped and smelly troop bays. Oh well, there was nothing he could do about it except add it to his ever-expanding prayer list.

While the navy was trying to find the phantom Spanish ships, the Rough Riders spent the time on the cramped ship doing the manual of arms, cleaning their weapons and equipment, telling stories, and attending training classes. Recreationally there was swimming in the bay, playing cards, singing, and listening to the army bands that were on board. The young soldiers were particularly interested in the war stories of the veterans of the Civil War, the Indian Wars, and the exotic wars of some of the foreign-born Rough Riders.

The officers were called daily to the galley to receive classes on tactics and related military subjects. Captain Allyn Capron, commander of Troop L, was the usual instructor. Jean-Paul remained impressed with the captain. He had enlisted in the army as a private in 1890. Through hard work and maximizing his talent by extensive self-study, he received an officer's commission and was now a captain commanding a troop of cavalry going to war. He had an amazing knowledge of tactics and military history. He shared many practical historical examples from the Civil War and stories he heard from his father who had fought in the Sioux Indian Wars. Jean-Paul of course, was always present at these classes in case Colonel Roosevelt needed a runner. He found that notion curious since virtually everyone to whom he would potentially be taking a message was sitting in the class. Oh well—an order was an order.

Captain Capron's presentations were always interesting as well as informative. Jean-Paul wondered where he found the time to prepare his classes. Capron was a most impressive individual. According to J.P, he looked and behaved like a combat soldier—*a warrior*. He was tall, thin, with a perfectly proportioned head and piercing eyes. He had a deep, masculine voice, and conducted himself with total self-control and complete self-confidence. Here was a natural leader who not only received instant respect but also admiration and even affection from his soldiers.

One day the topic was connecting military tactics to military strategy. Almost all the training for the unit up to this point had been tactical so this session would be quite different. Colonel Wood, the regimental commander, opened the class by saying strategy was a necessary topic but perhaps not as practical for the regiment as the previous classes on tactics. Wood said he felt the unit's officers should receive this information since all professional military men should be knowledgeable of military strategy.

The Colonel initially gave an overview of military strategy with a discussion of Prussian Major General Carl von Clausewitz's book *On War*. Captain Capron was then to pick up the discussion of military strategists by discussing *Sun Tzu* and *the Swiss born General, Baron Antoine-Henri Jomini*.

Jean-Paul was thrilled to be present at this class. Two years ago, based on his father's advice, he had started to read Clausewitz's strategy book *Vom Krieg,* or as it is titled in

English: *On War.* It was a difficult book to understand. Jean-Paul had taken copious notes and felt he had at least a basic acquaintance with the Prussian's philosophy. Clausewitz's book, according to Jean-Paul's father, was confusing because it was actually a rough first draft. Clausewitz had died of cholera while on campaign in Poland before he could revise or edit it. His wife, *the Countess Marie,* an intellectual in her own right, had it published in the form and style in which she found it. J.P. thought a large portion of it very confusing both when he read the English and French translations as well as the original German. From the German that his friend Berti had taught him, it seemed the translation of *Clausewitz's book* from the original German into English was neither precise nor accurate. Jean-Paul reconciled he felt that way because his German was not that good.

Colonel Wood began by saying the idea of strategy came from the Greek word *strategos,* which was defined as *the art of the general.* It dealt mostly with the planning and conduct of military campaigns and the movement and disposition of forces. He proceeded to *briefly* share examples of strategy from American Civil War. These included those of General Grant at Vicksburg, Sherman's March to the Sea, and Robert E. Lee at Chancellorsville.

He then transitioned to General Clausewitz's writings on strategy. Colonel Wood indicated two of Clausewitz's main ideas were misunderstood in the West because of how they had been translated from the original German. That certainly resonated as truth with Jean-Paul. Wood continued and said that the General's most well-known principle was: *"War is the continuation of politics **by** other means."* According to Wood, a more precise translation from the German should be: *"War is the continuation of policy **with** other means."*

Colonel Wood also said the other misunderstood Clausewitzian maxim was that the *moral is more important than the physical elements of war*. According to the Colonel, the correct translation was that *the intangible forces in war, such as the psychological and emotional, are more important than the quantifiable or physical elements of war*. He went on to say that there can be a huge difference in the meaning based on how an idea is translated into another language.

Colonel Wood further highlighted that Clausewitz said a war should never be started without three items being crystal clear. *First*, there must always be a clear objective of what is to be achieved; *second*, the war must always be fought to achieve that objective; and third, adequate resources must be committed to the war effort, so the objective is in fact achieved.

Colonel Wood was obviously enthralled by the subject of military strategy. He was a medical doctor by education, but a soldier by inclination. Teaching while sitting on a stool, he very casually shared one *Clausewitzian* principle after another:

strategy is an art while the tactical is more of a science; surprise, combined by speed and secrecy, were always essential; strategy is a give and take between policy benefits and military costs, i.e., the cost-benefit ratio; and finally, the commander should continually look for what Clausewitz called the *Schwerpunkt.* This is the operational center of gravity or *point of maximum effort where decisive action (and victory) will be achieved.* That means forces should always be massed at this potentially decisive point. Colonel Wood went on to say that in their upcoming campaign, taking the city of Santiago would be the *Schwerpunkt.* It was interesting thought Jean-Paul that the Colonel did not elaborate on why he thought Santiago was the *Schwerpunkt.* J.P. certainly did not understand why that would be the case. Huh....

Colonel Wood suddenly stopped talking and surveyed the room apparently to see how his discourse was being received. After what seemed like a considerable pause the Colonel asked, "Has anyone here read Clausewitz?" When no one raised a hand, Jean-Paul felt compelled to raise his. As soon as he did, he knew he had made a mistake. He was an enlisted orderly and foot messenger and not one of the regimental officers to whom the question was asked.

Colonel Wood moved his head to see whose hand had been raised. "Well," he said, "It's Lieutenant..." Then he paused when he saw that the trooper who had raised his hand was wearing corporal stripes. Colonel Roosevelt, sensing Wood's surprise and annoyance, intervened.

"Sir, that is Corporal DeBert. You remember him—he was our interpreter at Colonel Davout's party the other evening. He also gave us the overview about the Alamo battle when we were in San Antonio. We call him *Professor* because he seems to be quite knowledgeable of military history."

By his frown and the placing of his hands on his hips, Colonel Wood was clearly not impressed. With a condescending grin, he said, "Well then Professor, tell the regiment's officers what you learned from your reading of Clausewitz." This comment caused muffled laughter among the officers' present. They all turned toward Jean-Paul with great interest anticipating his discomfort, embarrassment, and potential failure.

Jean-Paul had been leaning against the galley wall. He now took two steps forward, stood at the semi-position of attention and began, "Sir, there were a number of key points that I remember from reading General von Clausewitz's book *On War*. First, there is the *friction of war* and *also the fog of war*. They have some similarities but are also quite different. In regard to friction, Clausewitz said that in war, most everything is simple, but the simplest things are difficult. Shortcomings of a plan are promptly exposed during the early phase of the battle. Leaders have an expectation of how things will go and how their units will perform, but *seldom in war do things develop as planned.* This is what General Clausewitz calls the friction in war. Clausewitz believed that friction is the factor that distinguishes the actual battlefield from the paper theory of war."

When Jean-Paul finished he noted that everyone was still staring at him. However, they had all stopped laughing.

"What else Corporal?" asked an equally surprised Colonel Wood.

Jean-Paul continued, "Well sir, General Clausewitz also wrote extensively about *the fog of war. The fog of war* or *the moonlight in war* as he also called it, deals with the unpredictability of warfare. It goes beyond the friction of war. This term refers to uncertainties such as one's fighting capabilities, the enemy's battle potential, the enemy's intent during actual combat operations, the weather, the terrain, and the many other factors that could affect the outcome of a battle. The fog also includes the commander's knowledge of his unit's actual capabilities, as well as those of his allies and his foes. This is knowledge that is generally incomplete and can therefore have a significant impact on the outcome of the fighting."

Colonel Wood, seldom to be caught at a disadvantage, wasn't quite sure what to say. Evidently, he did not think that anyone present, with the exception perhaps of Colonel Roosevelt, had read Clausewitz. With a slight frown and with his arms folded, he said in a low tone, "And what did you learn from your reading of *On War* that would be of *practical value* to our regiment of volunteers?"

Jean-Paul thought this question quite strange since this was to be a class on strategy and there was not an obvious connection between strategy and a practical tactical application to a volunteer regiment of cavalry. He quickly recognized it was a question aimed at embarrassing him. It was a *stump the chump* kind of question! Jean-Paul thought quickly and then said in an upbeat tone, "Clausewitz said that in battle, leaders must lead with great boldness and audacity. He called this style of leading *hero leadership* or in German: *held fuehrerheit*. He even quoted a figure of the French revolution, Georges Jacques Danton, who said, '*Il nous faut de l'audace, et encore de l'audace, et toujours de l'audace.*' Translated it means, '*We need audacity, and yet more audacity, and always more audacity*' Clausewitz believed that war, *unlike* most other undertakings, is settled by bloodshed. War is the province of physical exertion, hardships, suffering, and danger. Therefore, the first quality of a soldier is courage—raw, uninhibited courage. Commanders must also place heavy training demands on their soldiers in peacetime. The heavier the demands placed on them during training the more the commander can depend on them in battle. Moderation and kindness with either the enemy or one's own troops are never in order. That Clausewitzian concept has a very practical value to a regiment of volunteers."

Jean-Paul paused and waited for a response. When there was none, he added, "General Clausewitz also said that even though there are principles in war, they cannot be followed blindly. They must be interpreted and applied based on the immediate situation. *This situational application is the art of war.* He said *it is genius to do this well.* Besides an exceptional intellect, a general of genius must have both *a captivating personality and a virtuous character.*"

Jean-Paul knew he should now stop talking. It was as if he could hear his father's voice saying, *"Now sit down and be quiet."* He slowly took two steps backward. He looked at the officers in the class. They seemed to be looking at him with a combination of shock, surprise, and disbelief. He wasn't sure if their non-verbal response was good or bad. He wasn't even sure they had heard a word he had said. Oh well, Colonel Wood had asked him, a corporal of a few days, and he had responded.

Colonel Wood responded, "All very interesting, but I think you are mistaken about who made the quote regarding audacity. It was not the Frenchmen you said but it was the Prussian emperor Frederick the Great. The quote is in French because Frederick did not like the German language and made French his court's language."

Jean-Paul knew that Colonel Wood *was exactly wrong* about that. Nevertheless, he said, "Thank you sir for the correction." Wood nodded and smiled with obvious intellectual satisfaction.

Colonel Wood continued, "General Clausewitz was an intellectual in a time when what was valued was *competence on the battlefield* and not writing war theory. He fancied himself as a combat warrior and even though he was present at many major battles during the Napoleonic Wars—he never commanded. Because of his *introverted temperament, aloof personality, intellectual orientation, and apparent arrogance,* he was always on staff and never given a command. That caused him great frustration and disappointment. "

Colonel Wood looked directly at Jean-Paul and said, "The point here is that intellectuals and smarty pants don't make it in the army. Promotion and honor go to men of courage who excel on the battlefield and not in the library." The Colonel stopped talking and continued to stare at Jean-Paul. It was clear he was talking directly to the corporal—a point no one in the room had missed.

As if in defense of Jean-Paul, Colonel Roosevelt said, "Sir, I think the Army and Navy needs both thinkers and men of action. Thinkers are valuable in peacetime. In wartime the warriors take the prescriptions of the thinkers and then apply them on the battlefield."

"I suppose you are right. We probably do need both. They each have their place depending on the circumstances." There seemed to be a mumbling of agreement among those officer's present.

Colonel Wood now turned it over to Captain Capron. With that, Jean-Paul gave a sigh of relief and again leaned against the wall. The captain began by discussing the Chinese military thinker *General Sun* who lived around 500 B.C. He said the General was a recognized genius for war and as a result, was given the title of Sun Tzu—with Tzu meaning *master* in Chinese. There was a story Captain Capron told that was an excellent reflection of General Sun's temperament. The Chinese king turned over one hundred eighty of his concubines to Sun Tzu for military training. Sun divided them into two companies of ninety each, *putting the king's two favorite concubines in charge.* The first time he gave the command to turn right the women did not respond but giggled. Sun once more explained what was expected and gave the command to turn right a second time. Again, the women did not comply but proceeded to snicker. Ignoring the king's protest, he *executed* the two concubines who had been placed in charge. He explained to the group that if subordinate leaders understood the commands they had received but did not obey them, they must be removed at once. Sun Tzu added that once an officer was appointed, it was his or her *duty* to carry out the mission *regardless of the obstacles or the cost.* Sun then appointed two other women in charge of the companies. Now the women *obeyed all of the commands instantly and perfectly.* Captain Capron said there was an excellent leadership lesson in this story that was still applicable in the present age.

Capron then transitioned from Sun Tzu to *General Baron Antoine-Henri Jomini.* He said the Baron was from Switzerland and had written extensively about the Napoleonic wars. Capron noted that General Jomini's ideas had been and were still being taught to the cadets at West Point. All the leading generals in the late Civil War, to include those Colonel Wood had mentioned earlier, were influenced by General Jomini's strategic theories. According to Captain Capron, Jomini was known as the *Devin de Napoleon,* which means *the general who guessed what Napoleon was going to do.*

The example Capron shared fascinated everyone in the room to include Jean-Paul. In 1806 Napoleon asked Jomini to travel to meet him in the German city of *Mainz am Rhine.* There he was to share with him his personal and extensive knowledge of the Prussian army. So impressive was Jomini's briefing, that the emperor asked Jomini to join his staff. Jomini said he could, but *it would have to be in Bamberg in four days.* Shocked, Napoleon responded, "Who told you I was going to Bamberg?" Jomini explained from a map how he assumed, based on Napoleon's previous campaigns, the route that he would most probably be taking would place him in Bamberg. Napoleon was both astonished and impressed. He told Jomini not to say anything because at that point, not even General Berthier, Napoleon's chief of staff, knew what direction the army would be taking.

Captain Capron went on to tell another story about Jomini and Napoleon. Apparently, after Napoleon had read Jomini's writings of 1804, the emperor concluded Jomini could teach better than any of the teachers who had taught him. Napoleon said to his staff that Jomini's writings included insights few generals had, and that his writings could potentially teach his enemies his system of warfare. But then he paused and said there was really no cause for concern. He believed old generals no longer spent time reading and the younger officers who do read, had little influence because they were not at a sufficiently high level of command. Here Capron made a point emphasizing the value of continuous reading. This is something Jean-Paul's father had constantly impressed upon him. Excellent counsel!

Capron closed by highlighting Jomini's genius of understanding strategy and also his *overbearing arrogance*. That latter trait caused many of his superiors and peers to deeply dislike him. Their disdain went well beyond simple envy or jealousy. French Marshal's Berthier and Ney both fell into the category of those who detested him. Ultimately, this resulted in Jomini not being promoted in keeping with his performance or potential. Frustrated, Jomini actually left the French army in 1813 and joined Napoleon's arch enemy—the Russian army. This was similar behavior to Benedict Arnold in the American Revolution. Arnold too, felt his talents were not appreciated. That caused him to commit treason and join the British Army. Captain Capron paused and then asked if there were any questions? No one responded.

Colonel Wood stood and made a few closing remarks. Staring at Jean-Paul, he said, "The majority of Jomini's superiors did not like him because he was too smart for his own good. They seemed to think he was purposely attempting to show them up and that of course was unacceptable. To have knowledge is important—but how you share or display that knowledge is equally, if not more important. Does everyone understand that? The Colonel was still staring at Jean-Paul.

"The officers' present gave a weak *'yes sir.'*"

"Good. Excellent class and discussion. You are dismissed."

The officers filed past Jean-Paul on their way out of the galley. When Colonel Roosevelt walked by, he grabbed Jean-Paul's shoulder and said in a patronly way, "Don't worry about a thing Professor. You keep reading and studying and getting more knowledge. Do that and someday you too will be a general. *Never, ever become discouraged.* And remember, despite everything, *Jomini too was finally promoted to full general.*" Roosevelt then patted him on the shoulder with some vigor.

"Thank you, sir," said Jean-Paul weakly. When everyone had left the galley, he stood there alone. He reflected on the meeting. He had several personal learnings from Colonel Wood and Captain Capron that had value well beyond the ninety minutes invested. Regardless of Colonel Wood's comments, he really appreciated classes on military topics and his ability to share his ideas on the subject. Maybe the army life was what he was made for. He would find out once in Cuba facing the Spanish.

\*      \*      \*      \*      \*

While still anchored, Jean-Paul would check on Trooper Bell at least twice a day. He would do the manual of arms with him and if the timing was right, eat a meal with him. He also started to teach Bell the art of savate—French stick fighting. From going into the troop bay, he noted that the conditions were deteriorating daily. He wasn't sure that was even possible, but it was. Ever increasing was the stench of human sweat, filth, vomit, and the wafting odor from the droppings of the horses that were on board. This had caused everyone to hope and pray the convoy would depart as soon as possible.

After the fourth day of floating in the harbor, Jean-Paul went on his morning mission to check on Bell. As usual he took his walking cane or as his father would say—his savate fighting stick. As he walked down the stairs the smell hit him like a clenched fist. My goodness it was worse than ever. When Jean-

Paul arrived in Trooper Bell's area, he saw him hunched over on the floor sobbing. Confused, Jean-Paul asked, "Bell, what's the matter? What's going on?"

Bell turned to him and displayed two black eyes and other facial bruises and bloody cuts. He replied slowly between the choking rhythms of his crying, "They said I'm stupid and that I will for sure be killed in Cuba. When I said I was not stupid, they beat me."

Jean-Paul felt the *strong feeling* of anger in his chest. "Who beat you? Who?"

Bell looked up and pointed to four troopers who were bunked behind him. All four were looking at Jean-Paul and Bell with large satisfied and cocky smiles.

Jean-Paul said in a loud but clear voice, "Do you do this? Why did you do this? Why?"

The four simultaneously laughed out loud. One, who had apparently not shaved since getting on the transport said, "Why not? That dimwit is going to get his self killed and probably us with him. He's lucky we didn't throw his dumb self off the ship."

The others nodded and grunted in agreement.

Jean-Paul turned to Trooper Bell and said, "Get your things together. We are going to move you away from these *thugs.*"

The unshaven trooper stood up and said in a loud voice, "Thugs? Thugs are we? Did you hear that boys? This young snot nose called us thugs." At this the other three also stood up but with some difficulty because of the closeness of the quarters.

"After I resettle Bell, I am going to report all of you and we'll see who gets thrown off this ship," said Jean-Paul with some energy.

The unshaven bully stepped over Bell and *came at Jean-Paul.*

Jean-Paul, in a swift *windmill motion* hit the bully squarely on the top of the head with great force. He went down like a sack of potatoes. Sliding the cane down his hand, he thrust the head of the cane squarely into the solar plexus of the second trooper. Gasping for air, he fell directly on top of the first unshaven goon. With some agility and a loud scream, the third soldier leaped at Jean-Paul over his two downed comrades. Despite the extremely close quarters, the professor forcefully cracked him upside the head. He too went down falling between Bell and his two comrades.

After seeing what had just happened, the fourth trooper hesitated. Jean-Paul said, "Come on tough guy. What's the matter, are you like your buddies, something of a simple wit? Well? You four dumbbells will probably get each other and many others killed. Morons." Jean-Paul was so hot with anger he wanted to seriously whale on that fourth coward. Unfortunately, or fortunately, he couldn't step over the pile of semi-conscious bullies lying on the floor.

"Come on Bell, get your things and let's go, and now."

As he and Bell were starting to leave, one of the fallen bullies made a vain effort to grab Jean-Paul's leg. That resulted in him getting his hand smacked hard with the walking stick. The soldier cried out with a painful yelp. Jean-Paul bent over him and whispered, "Tell your friends that if you ever come near Trooper Bell again, I will personally hurt you to the point that the only job you will ever be able to get after that is as a freak in a circus sideshow. Do you understand?"

Jean-Paul looked at the fourth soldier who had sat down. He now repeated himself, "Do you understand?" The soldier, white faced, nodded yes. "Good. Good."

Jean-Paul took Trooper Bell to the A Troop area of the bay. To his good fortune First Sergeant Troxler was inspecting the trooper's gear. "Say First Sergeant, I was wondering if my man Trooper Bell here could bunk up with A Troop until we get to Cuba. It seems the bullyboys back yonder like to pick on folks they think inferior to themselves, and I need to make sure Bell stays safe. Can you help me out here?"

Troxler gazed at Jean-Paul and then at Bell. "Sure, he can stay here as long as he doesn't cause any trouble."

"You won't—right Bell?" Jean-Paul did not wait for him to answer.

"I will check on him at least twice daily, maybe more. Thank you, First Sergeant. "

Jean-Paul then introduced Bell to Three-Ring and Preacher Wilson. After explaining Bell's situation and ensuring he was settled, he turned to go back above deck. Trooper Bell followed him and tapped him on the shoulder.

Jean-Paul turned and somewhat surprised said, "What is it Trooper?"

"I want to thank you for sticking up for me and getting me away from those bullies. I really appreciate it and I will never forget it." Bell was actually tearing up....

Jean-Paul wasn't exactly sure what to say. "Thanks for the comment, but it wasn't really necessary. Sergeant LaCombe put me in charge of you and so it is my responsibility to take care of you. And that is what I will do. Now you stay away from those failures. When I am not around you, stay close to the men of Troop A. You got that? They will look after you when I am not here."

"Yes, Corporal DeBert, I will do that. You know, they call you Professor, but I think they should call you *Brave Heart.*"

"Brave Heart—right. Now get your gear cleaned up and I will see you later for some manual of arms practice."

Trooper Bell came to attention and saluted Jean-Paul who returned the salute. On the way out, Jean-Paul looked over at the four buffoons who had assaulted Bell. They were all bent over in a huddle as if they were plotting something. He stopped and looked at them. When they saw him, they stopped talking and straightened up. He continued to stare directly at them. He tapped his savate stick mightily on the floor twice, then smiled, and finally continued up and out of the bay. It seemed he no longer noticed the smell of the place. Once out and in the fresh air, he reflected on what had just happened. He smiled at his thought that his behavior must have been caused by a rush of blood to his head...!

### *Thought Questions for Chapter 14:*

1. Why did Jean-Paul say to Three-Ring that after six weeks in the Army, it could favorably be compared to a circus? Have you ever had similar thoughts or experiences? Please explain.

2. What were your impressions and reactions to *First Sergeant Troxler's response* to the comment that sometimes the Army can be like the circus?

3. What was Jean-Paul's philosophy about how he would handle an order received when he had absolutely no idea how to carry it out? Do you agree or disagree with him? Why?

4. According to Clausewitz, what is the difference between *the fog of war* and *the friction of war?*

5. Why did Colonel Wood seem to resent Jean-Paul when he responded to his question if anyone present had ever read Clausewitz?

6. What was your biggest learning or take away from this chapter? What can you apply from the information in this chapter? What in it did you find the most interesting? Why?

# 15

## *Landing in Cuba*

After six days sitting stagnant in the burning heat and oppressive humidity of Tampa Bay, the convoy finally departed for Cuba on the 13th of June. It had been determined there was no threat from the Spanish fleet. The naval officer who had reported it had been overcautious and *had made a mistake.* It was a mistake that caused a week of discomfort for the over 20,000 soldiers languishing on board the various transports. Jean-Paul reflected how the *simple act of one man* could have such a significant negative impact on thousands. Even in peacetime it could cause death—in this case the death of several horses that could not take the heat and humidity below deck.

He then thought about his readings in military history. One general officer, through similar incompetence, could cause the death of thousands, perhaps even tens of thousands of soldiers and civilians. Jean-Paul reflected on the idea of *responsibility*. It was one thing to be responsible for teaching routine history classes at the Jesuit school in New Hope. It was quite different to be a military leader and be responsible for others' lives in wartime. Jean-Paul then made a conscious decision to think about something else—something more pleasant.

# Chapter 15: Landing in Cuba

It was quite a spectacle when the convoy finally sailed out of Tampa Bay. The army bands on board were playing, *Old Glory* was waving proudly on all the departing vessels, and the riggings were hanging full of cheering and shouting soldiers. Everyone was in a festive mood. So much so that a number of transports nearly collided with one another in their excitement to get out into the ocean.

It was a huge relief to be out on the open sea. Being underway considerably improved the ventilation in the troop bays. The air was still foul, but not to the degree it had been while the ship was anchored. Plus, the horses on board that had died from the heat had since been tossed overboard. That also reduced some of the unwholesome stench.

It would take six days to sail to Cuba. Jean-Paul had never been on a body of water larger than a lake or a river. For him, this was a completely new experience. The thirty plus transports that were flanked by massive gray warships were something to see. There were small torpedo boats that periodically broke away from the convoy to check vessels that were not part of the convoy. J.P. found life at sea interesting, but certainly nothing he would want to be part of in the long term.

It was pleasant sailing the tropical seas in June. Watching the *flying fish* was great fun. At night the stars looked so close that one could almost reach out and touch them. All of the ship's lights were brilliant at night. Jean-Paul and the other noncoms that were in cabin #4 would stand outside at night, lean against the railing, smoke or chew, and tell stories.

Jean-Paul liked to listen to the Rough Riders standard-bearer, Sergeant Guitilias. He would be carrying the *regimental colors* into battle. He of course, was a veteran of the Civil War. He was older but he had the energy and enthusiasm of someone forty years younger.

One night, Jean-Paul told Sergeant Guitilias he looked younger than his real age. Initially Guitilias simply stared at him. He then looked away and said quietly, almost as if he was speaking to himself, "I am old in years, but I learned long ago that one's physical age in years means nothing—absolutely nothing. You can be old at 25 or young at 50. It all depends on your attitude, how you have taken care of yourself, *and whether or not you let life drag you down.* Life has the tendency to do that you know. Life is hard—very, very hard. But so what? Life is to be lived and experienced. We are in the grave much longer than we are alive. Living life to the fullest every day is what it is all about and is what keeps you young. Every day is a gift—that's why they call it the *present!* Because it is a *present.* I had a choice. I heard my country was going to war. I survived the War of the Rebellion with four wounds. My wife is dead and my six kids are grown and gone. So, I thought why not sign up? Life is to be enjoyed and is not for sitting in a drafty old farmhouse looking out the window at a snow storm. Any jack-wood can do that." Sergeant Guitilias's volume and tone had picked up as he talked. He finished with an enthusiastic crescendo.

Jean-Paul also liked to watch Guitilias roll a cigarette with one hand. That was even more interesting when he was standing by the ship's rail with the trade winds blowing. Sergeant Guitilias was still able to roll his cigarette successfully in those conditions, but most of the time that took two hands.

Jean-Paul sincerely enjoyed these times at the railings looking at the sea, the stars, and the convoy. Sometimes Sergeant Major Ernie Sacker would join the group. Sacker had been in combat in several Indian campaigns. The discussions of the group ranged from the experiences and adventures they had had, to their families, to what they were planning to do after the war, and to their thoughts about what Cuba would be like.

One night when there was a lull in the conversation, Jean-Paul asked the Sergeant Major, "How do you deal with the fear, the stress, and the anxiety of battle? What do you think about before the fight? How do you prepare for your first battle?" Jean-Paul paused, not being at all sure that what he had asked was appropriate, or that the two combat veterans present had thought about such things. He had read that most soldiers who lived through combat were simply happy to have survived. Survival seemed to be a priority equal to accomplishing the mission.

After what seemed like a considerable pause, Sergeant Major Sacker, staring out at sea and puffing on a disgustingly wet cigar began. "There is always an anxious anticipation before the fight—always. That never goes away because you don't know if these were your last hours on earth. I didn't think about combat before my first fight, but I did after it was over. At any second during the battle you could die. A single arrow or bullet can hit you square in the forehead or in your heart and there after you are pushing up daisies. There is no more whiskey, beefsteak, dancing girls, hot baths, or sunshine on your face.... None of that ever again—*it's all over*. Then too, at least in your first action, you are convinced you will survive and that all the other poor beggars in your unit *will get it*. After two or three actions that notion goes away. You then begin to see the randomness and the fickle nature of the battlefield. The best soldier gets killed or seriously wounded while the unit *screw-up* survives. Because he lived and the other sergeants were casualties, the *screw-up* then gets promoted. And he's the one who probably hid in a hole during the entire fight and didn't even fire his weapon. There is no justice or fairness in combat—it's all random chance, all seemingly arbitrary. There are things you can do to improve your survival odds, but even then, there is no guarantee you will not get it. That's what I learned and that's my answer to your question."

Jean-Paul wasn't exactly sure what to say. Finally, he blurted out, "What about praying and having faith that the Divine will protect you? In Deuteronomy 32:29 Jehovah said, '*I kill and I make alive; I wound and I heal; and there is none that can be delivered out of my hand.*' It seems to me that says there is nothing arbitrary that ever happens even on the battlefield."

Everyone leaning on the railing stopped staring out to sea and now turned and looked at Jean-Paul. Sergeant Major Sacker said gruffly, "You don't believe that stuff, do you? I never found any of that chaplain, or Good Book, or Holy Joe stuff useful or in any way helpful. What I did see is that the boys who did all the prayin' and Bible readin' and hangin' around the chaplain got killed or wounded just like everyone else. Yep, just like everyone else. And that's the truth."

That brought a pause to the discussion. Jean-Paul thought on what the Sergeant Major had said. He didn't think Sacker was at all correct. Providence promises, at least in a general way, to protect and take care of those who trust in Him. That's what both Psalm 46 and Psalm 91 are all about. Some soldiers of faith may be killed in combat, but many others are not. Jean-Paul was somewhat bewildered by what the Sergeant Major had said.

Now Color Sergeant Guitilias joined the conversation. "I agree with everything the Sergeant Major just said—particularly that point about your first combat. You don't think you will be hit. It will always be some other poor unlucky bloke. After a number of actions, you realize your *chances of not getting hit* are becoming slimmer and slimmer. Also, anyone who says they are not *diaper scared* in battle is either a liar or a complete lunatic. You are scared as holy heck from the first shot to the last. I've seen some soldiers who could not move, others who cried like a baby, vomited, and still others who out of pure terror couldn't stop screaming. *The worst was always the wait.* Consider what it would be like if your unit is just standing there waiting for orders while the battle is going on all around you. Bullets are flying, cannonballs exploding, and some of your comrades are falling. And here you are stationary, waiting for some genius to give the order to attack, retreat, move, or do something. That was absolutely the worst of all situations. I saw men go insane and run in every which direction not having any idea what they were doing or where they were going."

Sergeant Guitilias paused and started to roll a cigarette. Because of the stiff wind he was for once unsuccessful. As he put the smoking materials away and he said, "There was one other thing. I was with the Eighth Ohio Infantry in *the War*. We were called the *fighting fools.* The entire regiment came from the same area of Ohio. I knew many members of the regiment before I joined. We all knew that if we survived the war we would go back home and have to live with each other once again.

That was a huge incentive to stand and fight because if you ran away, you for sure couldn't go back home. Everyone there would know you were a run-away coward. One last thing, it was my experience that once the firing started and we started maneuvering around, *the fear was not as strong.* Moving and doing something, no matter how small, helped reduce fear. It didn't eliminate it, but to some degree, it kinda kept it under control. And of course, two other things that also seemed to cut our fear were *experience and training.* The more battle experience and training a unit had, the less the fear.

Guitilias paused and then began again, "Combat is about the worst of all human experiences. Just think about it. You are trying to kill other human beings while they are trying to kill you. Now, does that make any sense at all? And everyone is doing that for reasons they barely understand. We are told it is to preserve the nation or for the glory of the state. Really? What does that even mean? Someone has to tell me.... The reasons we are given for fighting are ones no sane person on a bright sunny day would agree to die for."

After that speech no one knew exactly what to say. Finally, Trooper Scarborough, Colonel Wood's runner, asked Sergeant Guitilias, "If that is the way you feel, then why did you sign up for this here war?"

Guitilias looked at Scarborough thoughtfully and finally said, "Because combat shows you whether or not you are a man.

You can be scared out of your wits, but if you are a man, you will still do your duty and stand and fight. And furthermore, women like that kind of man and not the effeminate, girly man who stays at home when there's fightin' going on."

Guitilias continued, "Also, there is a big physical rush when in battle. There is nothing else like it. It is kind of an elixir. I experienced it, and regardless of the dark side of combat, I want to experience it again. Even though I was wounded four times and almost bled out on three of those occasions, I am going back for more. That's right, I'm going back for more. I wear all my battle scars with pride. See?" The sergeant rolled up the sleeve of his left arm and showed everyone the nastiest scar imaginable.

"And just so you know, those wounds, every one of them, were awfully painful. Fortunately, I remained conscious each time I was hit so I able to apply a tourniquet. Had I lost consciousness I would have bled to death for sure. Almost did on one occasion anyway. There was also a time when I am certain I was shot by someone from my own unit. That was a problem we always had—shooting our own people. Some yahoos, particularly the new replacements, were so scared they had no idea what they were doing or what they were shooting at. That was a real problem when they were behind you in an attack. I think that's how I got my leg wound. It took me out of the war. It also took a long time before I could walk regular again. But that's why I like this warm weather. In the Ohio winter my old, wounded leg freezes up and pains me so bad that I can barely get around. However, in the summer heat that don't happen. But that's enough from me. You asked about going into combat, well Professor, that's my answer to your question."

Jean-Paul was not given the opportunity to respond. Sergeant Major Sacker—who had been quiet during the color sergeant's discourse—now interjected. Talking to Sergeant Guitilias directly, he began, "There are always reasons why a nation goes to war. Some are good and some not so good. Almost all the Indian wars the Army fought were because the white man had encroached on Indian lands. Naturally the Indians retaliated—who could blame them? We can make our own judgments if something like that is a good enough reason to go to war and have young men die. You implied that soldiers generally don't know why they are going to war—and that whatever the cause, it may not be something worth dying for. In my book that is absolutely false. If our country calls, if our country needs us, we must answer the call and join the colors. It's just that simple. If we want to completely understand all the causes of the war and all the reasons and the why's, then we should go into politics and stay away from soldierin'." The Sergeant Major looked at Sergeant Guitilias for a response. Guitilias was again trying to roll a cigarette and acted like he wasn't listening. But Jean-Paul was quite sure he had heard everything the Sergeant Major had said. Wisely, he did not respond to any of the Sergeant Major's comments.

Now looking at Jean-Paul, the Sergeant Major said, "To your question Corporal, there is one more thing I would like to add. It's one thing to go into battle as a private. It is quite another to go into battle as a leader—as an officer or a sergeant. Not only do you have your own safety and survival to be concerned about, but also the survival of the soldiers you are leading. That adds a completely different dimension to the situation. Furthermore, you have the mission to accomplish. The mission always takes priority over your own safety and that of your men. If you *all have to die* in order to accomplish the mission, then so be it—*you all die*. Never forget that—the mission always comes first and the troops second. That said, it is my impression that the best leaders always accomplish their mission with the minimum number of casualties. The poor leaders—because they are poor leaders—generally cause more casualties than are necessary. And the casualties may be for nothing if the mission isn't accomplished. That's my experience and I think it is an unqualified truth. Guitilias, wouldn't you agree?"

"Absolutely Sergeant Major—absolutely." Guitilias was clearly listening.

"There is one other thing about leaders that I think is critically important." The Sergeant Major took a long drag on his now short and more than disgusting wet cigar. "The leader, regardless of his level, must—*not should, but must*—be conscious of the example he is setting for those he is leading. Leaders are always being watched. Someone is *always* watching. The leaders, particularly the officers, set the tone for the unit. The behavior they model is *contagious*. If they act and talk like everything is under control—no matter how difficult the situation—then the soldiers will remain calm and fight well. The opposite is also true. When things are difficult, the leaders can't be running around yelling, '*We are all going to die.*'" That comment brought considerable laughter from the group leaning on the railing.

He continued, "The leader's behavior is the standard. It is the pattern for everyone else's conduct. The higher the leader is within the chain of command, the more powerful the impact that leader's behavior will have. Do you understand that idea? I hope so because it is about as important as anything you can learn about leadership. If you decide to stay in the army—it is something about which you must always be conscious. The Sergeant Major then threw his nasty cigar into the sea, said good night, and marched off to his quarters.

The rest of those leaning on the railing took this as their signal to also turned in. Jean-Paul went to his sleeping area and got ready for a good night's rest. As was his custom, he lit a candle to do some reading or write a letter, or both. This evening he simply lit a candle, laid down, and stared at the ceiling. He thought about the answers the Sergeant Major and the color sergeant gave to his questions about being in combat. *The fear; the waiting; the thought you would survive above the others; the actions that reduce fear; the rush of combat; the notion that being functional when under fire was the characteristic of being a man; and the example of the leader is critical.* The one thought that impressed Jean-Paul more than any other was that at any moment in combat *you could cease to exist.* That would be it. Everything would be over. Astonishing thought, just astonishing; he had never thought of it quite that way before. But then again, you would be in heaven with the Good Lord—forever! How bad could that be? With that he said his prayers, blew out the candle, and fell fast asleep.

\*          \*          \*          \*          \*

When the island of Cuba came into view on the 21st of June, there was great excitement on the convoy. From the railing it looked to the Rough Riders that the Cuban island was mostly jungle-covered mountains. All the troopers, to include Jean-Paul had been cooped up in these horrible steel hulks for almost two weeks. Many in the troops had been seasick the entire time and could not wait to get on dry land.

There was also much interest when the convoy passed Guantanamo Bay. Two weeks earlier, in one of the first actions of the war, the Marines, with significant fire support from the

Navy, had successfully stormed Guantanamo Beach. Their mission had been to secure the Bay so the navy's ships would have shelter during the upcoming summer hurricane season. Other than U.S. naval vessels floating menacingly in the Bay, Jean-Paul noted there was no sign of the bloody battle that reportedly had taken place.

As the convoy steamed closer to Santiago, the Rough Riders saw the even more majestic U.S. warships that were blockading the inlet of Santiago Harbor. Everyone in the convoy appreciated the Navy's blockade since it kept the Spanish fleet from interfering with the Americans' upcoming land invasion.

The excitement continued when on the 22nd of June the order came to land near the Cuban village of *Daiquiri.* Jean-Paul, staying ever near to Colonel Roosevelt, was astonished to hear there was neither reliable nor sufficient means to get the soldiers from the transports to the shore. Launches were in extremely short supply. There were also no harbor facilities to land near this squalid little village. Furthermore, many of the merchant marine captains refused to take their ships close to the shore for fear of enemy fire and the possibility of getting stuck in the mud flats.

Jean-Paul again noted that luck favored the Rough Riders. A converted yacht named the *Vixen* pulled up to the *Yucatan.* Its captain, a Navy lieutenant named Sharp, asked for Colonel Roosevelt. Sharp had been Roosevelt's naval aide-de-camp when he was assistant Secretary of the Navy. Surprisingly, he offered to help get the Rough Riders ashore. Since the landing was going to be a chaotic scramble and was to be managed on a *go-as-you-please* basis, Wood and Roosevelt jumped at the opportunity. Jean-Paul watched the two colonels board the *Vixen*. Lt. Sharp then sent his Black Cuban pilot aboard the *Yucatan* to safely navigate it to within a few hundred yards of land. With his knowledge of the water, he maneuvered the ship at least a mile and a half closer to the shore. Embarrassed, the other transports followed....

Observing the goings on at the railing, Jean-Paul said to Sergeant LaCombe, "I am very impressed with how everything always seems to go in the favor of our two colonels." The Sergeant looked at him and said, "Really? You think they are just lucky? Well, having worked for Colonel Roosevelt for over a year, I can tell you *he creates his own good fortune.* He never waits for things to happen. By being proactive and taking the initiative *he makes things happen.* He creates momentum and movement. And, that's what's called leadership. Colonel Wood is of the same ilk. They see a problem or a challenge and don't just sit. They act to solve the problem. They are always in the game and never on the sidelines. They are leaders who lead from the front. Because of those two, our regiment will be the first to land and probably be the first to fight the Spaniards. Just watch, we will be in action while some of these other units with their *wait and see leaders* will still be on the ships or fumbling around on the beach." Jean-Paul nodded in agreement. Everything the sergeant had just said made perfect sense. The teenager was glad to be serving under leaders who set such a shining example. In many regards they reminded him of his father Louie.

Jean-Paul then thought about the Second U.S. Infantry Regiment. It was their commander who, at the gangplank of the Yucatan, threatened to send him to prison at Fort Leavenworth. Then too, there was the deputy commander of the Second, Lieutenant Colonel Ralph Gordon Howell III, who—with contempt and arrogance—almost had a personal attack staring him down after the incident. J.P. was sure that with those leaders, the Second Infantry's regulars would probably be the last to get off the transports and also be the last to see combat. That, however, was not his problem.

Jean-Paul was extremely excited during the entire landing process. The navy's smaller vessels shelled the town of *Daiquiri* in order to dislodge any Spaniards in hiding. They also shelled other locations along the coast to confuse the enemy as to the American's intentions. In an amazing display, the horses and mules of the expedition were thrown overboard with the assumption they would swim ashore. It was clear to all that with the high surf, many of them would drown. The rumor was that over fifty had already died because of the squalid conditions on the ships—ships the soldiers were now calling *prison hulks.*

The launches that were available were generally overloaded. Each trooper was carrying his equipment as well as three days of rations and 100 rounds of ammunition. Jean-Paul thought the off-loading of the regiment's two rapid-fire colt automatic guns and the dynamite gun was American ingenuity at its best. With these heavy loads and the surf being as rough as it was, one of the boats from the Black infantry regiment capsized. Two of its soldiers could not swim and started to sink. Captain O'Neill, Jean-Paul's former commander in Troop A, jumped into the water to save them. A natural hero thought Jan-Paul.

Once ashore hundreds of Cubans approached the Americans. Some of the Americans yelled, *"Viva Cuba libre!"* The Cubans responded with *"Vivan los Americanos!"* Many of the insurgents had been fighting the Spanish for years. Regardless, Jean-Paul was shocked by their appearance. They were emaciated, barefoot, unwashed, dressed in filthy torn rags, and were carrying all sizes and types of weapons, most of which were rusted and in a complete state of disrepair. Worst of all, they had no visible military order or discipline. These rebels were to serve the American Army as guides, scouts, and to assist with reconnaissance. Even with Jean-Paul's limited military experience, he could see they would not be particularly useful.

Then another group of Cubans showed up at the beach. They were civilians looking for food. They also wanted to get away from the potential fighting. They looked just as ragged and tattered as the rebel soldiers. The Rough Riders were told to ignore them. Jean-Paul couldn't help himself and gave some hardtack and a few pieces of pork to a gaunt mother with three small children. In return she gave him six Cuban cigars and an over ripe banana. All the Cubans had to be gently shooed away from the area because in addition to begging, they would simply pick up American gear or equipment and walk away. Jean-Paul paused for a second and thought: *"These are the people we have come here to liberate from Spanish oppression? Huh...!"*

A journalist who had come ashore raised the American flag on the flagpole near an abandoned Spanish army blockhouse. This resulted in an eruption of ship sirens, music, and cheering from the convoy. There had been a company of Spanish soldiers manning that blockhouse, but they had fled prior to the anticipated landing and the naval shelling. Seeing the flag raised and the convoy's energetic response caused Jean-Paul to experience a surge of pride. He yelled the traditional military cheer: *"Huzzah! Huzzah!"*

As soon as each Rough Rider unit came ashore, they marched a short distance inland to make room for the follow-on units. By late afternoon all of the troopers of the First

Volunteer Cavalry Regiment had disembarked and thankfully were on hard ground.

Jean-Paul and the headquarters section were located next to Troop A. Even though it was not supposed to rain, the Rough Rider's built shelters out of palm leaves. This process disturbed Cuba's population of *oversized land crabs*. Those ugly creatures made Jean-Paul shiver. He heard people actually ate them. He couldn't imagine how anyone would have the courage to do so. Simply looking at them was disgusting. After a short visit with his former mates in A Troop, Jean-Paul and Trooper Bell cleaned their rifles and got ready for a good night's rest. After a short Bible read and a prayer of thanks for their safe arrival, he fell into a deep and restful sleep.

The next morning, and into the afternoon of the 23rd of June, the Rough Riders unloaded their remaining equipment from the ship. This process reinforced to everyone that a major shortcoming of the campaign was the lack of adequate transportation. Jean-Paul, Corporal Scarborough, and Trooper Bell helped unload the regiment's food, ammunition, and supplies from the launches that were about 100 feet from shore. Since much of the time was wading in the water, all the troopers had stripped down to their skivvies. This was hard work as the surf was angry and the footing poor. More than once someone fell into the water with a heavy container and got a bad bruise or a nasty cut.

When most the boxes were ashore, Colonel Roosevelt said to those near him, "It is unfortunate that the foreign observers had to witness the chaos of our disorganized disembarkment. I'm sure they think that if the landing had been opposed, we would have failed. But of course, it wasn't opposed and now we are here. Gentlemen, I do believe we are ready for anything. Bully!" Jean-Paul loved Colonel Teddy's optimism and knew he was exactly right. The Rough Riders were indeed ready....

Finished with the unloading the Rough Riders began marching toward Santiago around 4 PM. It seemed it was hotter at that time than it had been all day. Colonel Wood insisted on a fast-paced march so the regiment would get ahead of the other units. This would ensure their place in the fighting the next day. It again was clear to Jean-Paul that because of their proactive leaders, Wood and Roosevelt, their regiment was always a step ahead of the other units.

The road march was difficult and exhausting. It was because of the heat and humidity, the days on the ship, the seventy-pound pack each trooper was carrying, and the fact most of the Rough Riders were not used to walking since they usually rode everywhere. Despite those difficulties, there was little straggling. Jean-Paul noted that the officers tramped alongside the troops and encouraged them by word and example. He had no problem with the march. The only shocker was when the regiment marched through the squalid village of

*Siboney*. He had never seen such filth and poverty. It spoke volumes of how poorly the Spanish had taken care of the Cubans. At around 7 PM, the Rough Riders stopped for the evening. They halted in column and each man was instructed to sleep where they stood. The Spanish army was reported to be only four miles away, so pickets and sentries were posted.

Despite their exhaustion, Jean-Paul, Corporal Scarborough, and Trooper Bell built a fire and enjoyed a feast of hard tack fried with pork. No sooner had they finished their coffee than Sergeant LaCombe came running. Out of breath he said, "The colonels need you two right now. Take your rifles and leave everything else. They are going for a meeting with the division commander, and they need you and *NOW!* Hurry! Bell, you stay here and watch their equipment."

LaCombe then took the two of them aside and in a low tone said, "What you hear at the meeting with the generals and colonels is not to be shared with anyone—and I mean anyone. Do you two understand?"

Both nodded and said in unison, *"Yes sergeant. We understand."*

The two of them double-timed to catch up with Colonel Wood and Colonel Roosevelt. The two officers acknowledged the salutes of Jean-Paul and Scarborough with the obligatory movement and a soft grunt. They were in a deep and whispered conversation in anticipation of the meeting with General Wheeler.

The Rough Rider contingent was the last to arrive at Major General Wheeler's command tent. Everyone was standing around a handmade map of the area that was resting on a hastily constructed wooden frame. The map had only names and some lines on it but no detail. Present at the tent were General Wheeler, the Cavalry Division commander; Brigadier Sumner, the First Brigade commander; Brigadier Young, the Second Brigade Commander (and Colonel Wood's immediate superior); General Wheeler's peer Brigadier Lawton, the Second Division commander; and lastly a Cuban major, who was the liaison officer from General Garcia's Cuban rebels.

Wheeler began, "Welcome to Cuba gentlemen. I hope all you Northern boys are enjoying this Georgia style heat and humidity." He paused, smiled with satisfaction, and then began again. "Now gentlemen, this is the situation. General Shafter's Fifth Corps has a total of 22,000 troops. After two days of landings, we have approximately six thousand of those boys on shore. At that rate it will be another four or five days before all of them are on land. General Sumner, what is the status of your units?"

With noticeable embarrassment Brigadier Sumner answered, "Sir none of my units have come ashore just yet."

With a frown General Wheeler said, "Right, none on shore yet and that's after two days of unloading. General Young, what's your brigade's status?"

"Sir, I believe all of Colonel Wood's Rough Riders as well as their equipment, horses, and mules are ashore. Isn't that right Leonard?"

Without hesitation Colonel Wood replied in his usual confident fashion, "All ashore sir. We are fully operational and awaiting orders."

General Wheeler nodded with obvious approval. It was as if one warrior spirit had connected with a kindred spirit.

Brigadier Young continued, "In additional to Colonel Wood's regiment, I also have two operational squadrons of dismounted regular cavalry from the First and Tenth Cavalry. More will be ready tomorrow and the day after."

Wheeler mumbled another approval. Jean-Paul couldn't help but stare at General Wheeler. He was just over five feet tall and weighed about one hundred pounds. He was the exact opposite in appearance to his 300-pound boss, General Shafter. Jean-Paul had read about Wheeler and had heard the troopers talk about him. He was a graduate of the Military Academy at West Point. He had fought Indians in New Mexico and had been the senior cavalry commander of the Confederate's *Army of Tennessee*. He was apparently aggressive to a fault, hence his nickname of *Fightin' Joe*. Jean-Paul was interested to see if the sixty-two-year-old general would live up to his reputation.

Jean-Paul also eyed with great interest Brigadier Sam Young, the Second Brigade commander. By barracks reputation, he was yet another real *fighting man*. He had risen in the ranks from private to brigadier general of volunteers. He had been wounded at least four times in the War of the Rebellion and had also fought in several Indian campaigns. According to Sergeant LaCombe, Colonel Wood and Colonel Roosevelt had met with Young before the war. Young had apparently promised that if they got into the war, they should try to get into his brigade—because he would ensure they would see their share of fighting. He was about to make good on his word.

Also present was the Second Division's commander, Brigadier Henry Lawton. Major General Shafter, commander of the American forces had appointed Lawton, a brigadier general and a regular army officer, to be in charge of the landing operation. With that position and responsibility, he actually ranked Major General of Volunteers Wheeler, who was in charge of rear security. It wasn't exactly clear to Jean-Paul how this chain of command worked. It seemed to him the senior ranking general on the ground, Major General Wheeler, should be in charge of the landings—and not Brigadier General Lawton.

Lawton looked the part of a soldier and by reputation was also a fighting man through and through. He too had distinguished himself in the War of the Rebellion. He had earned the Medal of Honor, had received a battlefield promotion from first sergeant to captain, and had seen action in over twenty-two battles. After the war, he had fought in several Indian campaigns. Jean-Paul felt quite privileged to be in the presence of such a distinguished group of warriors. And that of course, included his regimental commander and Medal of Honor recipient—Colonel Wood.

General Wheeler began, "Gentlemen, this is the situation. *The Yankees,*" he paused, "I meant to say the Spaniards under General Linares, have approximately 1,500 soldiers four to five miles from here in the town of *Las Guasimas.* According to intelligence from the Cuban rebels," he paused as if to indicate he was not sure how credible this information was, "the enemy is set up in three successive defensive positions, all of which straddle the main road into Santiago. Today our allies, the Cuban rebels led by General Castillo, made several unsuccessful attempts to breach those enemy positions. Brigadier Lawton's advance guard also had a brief but inconclusive skirmish with the Spanish early this morning. Based on those two enemy contacts, I decided to personally recon that road. For the three miles I traveled, the road is muddy but adequate for foot movement. I saw some bodies of dead Cuban rebels but no sign of the enemy. The terrain on both sides of the road, however, is thick jungle vegetation that is impassable. It is however, excellent terrain for an enemy ambush. It has also been decided by our Fifth Corps headquarters that our forces, which are still on the ships, will be landing farther west down the coast. They will be landing about four miles south of the current Spanish positions. If the Spaniards decide to oppose those landings, it could be nothing short of a disaster. Now you all know our division has been given the mission of being the rear guard for the rest of the landings. However, I believe the tactical situation has changed since that mission order was received. Considering today's enemy contacts and the enemy's closeness to the new landing sight—*I am convinced we must act.* Therefore, tomorrow we will do a reconnaissance in force in the direction of Las Guasimas—with the objective of neutralizing the Yankee force. My goodness, did I say Yankee again? Darn it, I meant to say the Spanish force. That's right, the Spanish force."

General Wheeler paused, then looked at Brigadier Lawton. Now here is my challenge since I am the senior officer on the ground here in Cuba. Our corps commander, Major General Shafter, is still in his shipboard command post. And of course, Brigadier General Lawton has been put in charge of the landings. Our division is to provide rear area security. The orders Lawton and I have from General Shafter specifically said we were not to commence with combat operations until the entire force has landed. General Castillo, the commander of the rebels, concurs with this because he thinks we need several thousand soldiers to defeat the 1,500 entrenched Spaniards. He has advised me of that through his liaison here, *Major Batista.*" The General made that last remark in such a derisive manner that it was clear to those present he felt General Castillo did not want to attack and simply wanted to avoid a fight.

General Wheeler then paused and lit the extra-long cigar he had been waving in his hand. He inhaled deeply, exhaled the smoke mostly through his nose and then said in a louder and stronger tone, "However gentlemen, I have decided based on my own authority and by virtue of being the senior ranking officer on the ground, to take some liberties with that order. I believe *the situation demands we act.* Considering the close proximity of the Spanish to the new landing sight, I believe our main force could potentially be in serious danger. Since our mission is to provide security for the upcoming landings—what we will do is an *aggressive reconnaissance in force.* That will meet the spirit of the order I received, if not the letter. We will probe for the enemy and if contact is made—*we will* neutralize him. We will do this recon at first light tomorrow morning. I am convinced it would be foolhardy to do nothing and potentially jeopardize the entire expedition. I will advise General Shafter of my decision *after* our successful reconnaissance. Brigadier

General Lawton agrees with my decision. Isn't that right General?"

Even though Lawton did not look pleased, he nodded but said nothing. Outwardly he appeared reluctant, but Jean-Paul wondered if internally Lawton, the fighter, eagerly agreed to Wheeler's liberal interpretation of their orders.

Wheeler continued, "Brigadier Young will lead the reconnaissance. He will move forward in file formation on the main road to Santiago with his two regular squadrons of foot cavalry. Colonel Wood, your regiment will provide flank security on the high road to the north of Young's force. If contact is made with the Spanish army by any of your elements during this reconnaissance, they are to be *neutralized.* Is that understood General Young—neutralized?"

Brigadier Young said, "Yes sir." All the others present nodded and mumbled in the affirmative. Corporal DeBert caught himself doing the same.

"One last thing gentlemen. The United States has not fought a major war in over thirty years—or a war with a foreign nation in over fifty years. And oh yes, a war with a European power in over eighty years. Tomorrow, we the cavalry division will move forward and draw first blood. As always, the cavalry will lead the way. The eyes of the entire nation will be on us gentlemen. And, with the large number of journalists present, the nation will know exactly how this division of cavalry will have performed in its first battle. Gentlemen, I expect you and your officers to set the finest example of courage and gallantry and, that you will always be leading from the front. From the front gentlemen—that is outstanding battle leadership."

General Wheeler paused, took a draw from his cigar, squinted and looked around at everyone. Then he asked, "Are there any questions?" He then paused. No one said anything. "No questions? Well then gentlemen, go and make your preparations and good luck tomorrow. *Do your duty and make your country proud!*" Everyone saluted and turned to leave and prepare.

John Paul had never experienced anything like that meeting. He was quite moved by what General Wheeler had said and how he had said it. He didn't even know why exactly. For years he had been reading military history and war books. Now he saw firsthand what leaders do before a major battle. That type of meeting of commanders had probably taken place among the Spartans, the Romans, the Crusaders, and in Napoleon's Grand Armée. This gathering of war leaders was something Jean-Paul felt privileged to have observed.

Brigadier General Young said quietly to Colonel Wood and Colonel Roosevelt," I need to see the two of you."

He then began speaking with a sense of urgency. "We really don't know what we will be up against tomorrow so make sure your regiment is prepared for anything. The only intelligence we have is from General Wheeler's brief recon and from General Garcia's liaison, Major Batista. I agree with General Wheeler that Batista's intelligence is probably not credible. General Wheeler seems to think our rebel allies intentionally gave us false information to discourage us from attacking. General Garcia made it clear he wants to wait until all the Americans are ashore before going on the offensive. He believes the Spaniards are too strong for the small force that has landed so far."

Colonel Roosevelt said, "Just out of curiosity sir, what did Major Batista say about the enemy and the terrain?"

"All right, here it is. Even though it might sound credible, it may not be. The Spanish are set up in defensive positions at Las Guasimas about five miles from where we are now. The two avenues of approach our forces will be taking to that enemy location are said to be nothing more than single file mud trails. The two trails are about a mile apart separated by a deep valley and dense jungle. According to the Cubans, the jungle vegetation on these approaches will offer zero visibility to our flanks. Thus, there is no possibility of sending out flank security or any prospect of communicating with the column on the other approach. Units on these two routes will only be able to support each other when the trails merge at Las Guasimas. At that point there is some open terrain, but it is also where the Spanish trench lines begin. Because of the underbrush and poor visibility, both of the avenues would be ideal for enemy ambushes or snipers. The enemy is very familiar with the entire area and especially these trails. According to the Cubans, the Spanish have purposely chosen their positions because they know exactly where we would be approaching. Thus, they know precisely where to place their fires. They will certainly utilize the terrain and the jungle cover in a manner that it would make it difficult for us to locate them. In addition, their rifles use smokeless powder, which will not give away their immediate position. Therefore, it will be difficult to know from which direction we are receiving fire."

Brigadier Young paused, seemed to catch his breath and then began again, "They are apparently set up in three successive defensive lines. Forward of the first line they will have an advance element that includes sharpshooters and soldiers in dugout pits. Their units in the three main defensive lines are set up in trenches, blockhouses, and in the buildings of an abandoned ranch. That's what the rebels told us. Considering the easy time the Marines had at Guantanamo a week ago, I doubt if the Spaniards are anywhere as sophisticated as the rag-tag rebels say they are. We all know what we have to do. Now go and make your preparations and have a good night's rest. Tomorrow will be a full and adventure filled day. It's what we joined up for in the first place!"

On the return walk Jean-Paul overheard Roosevelt say to Colonel Wood, "The information the rebels gave us about the terrain and the Spanish sounded credible to me. How did it sit with you sir?"

Colonel Wood reflected for a second and then said, "I agree. The Cubans have been fighting the Spanish for over three years now, and I think they know how their enemy fights. Plus, they've fought over the ground around Santiago time and time again. If what was said about those parallel trails is accurate, we probably will not be able to come to Young's support if they do make contact. Nor will they be able to help us if we come under attack. Plus, we must be especially alert for snipers and ambushes."

Colonel Wood took a few more steps and then said, "That old game cock Wheeler is first and foremost a fighter, a war dog who seems to revel in combat. I think he purposely ignored the intelligence General Garcia gave him so he would be first to get into a fight and not have to wait for the entire force to come ashore."

Colonel Roosevelt said, "Just think, back in 1862, General George McClellan's Army of the Potomac had almost 170,000 soldiers. It was one of the largest land forces the world had seen in modern times. Unfortunately, McClellan was always tentative and over cautious. He consistently hesitated to engage the enemy and never took advantage of his numerical superiority. As a result, President Lincoln said he had *the slows* and relieved him. The reason I am saying this is because if *Fightin' Joe* had commanded that Yankee army, the North would probably have won the war by the end of 1863. Clearly, the General wants the cavalry division to be the first army unit to see action and in so doing, make a name for itself. Inactivity is not who or what he is."

Colonel Wood then said in a soft tone, "Yes, you could say he is a fighter and in war that is a good thing. Wars are won by audacity and by going on the attack. That's what wins wars. That said, a commander's aggressiveness must always be tempered with good judgment and common sense. If it isn't, it could be disastrous and can get many soldiers killed unnecessarily. Remember what happened to Custer at the Little Big Horn River. Even Sitting Bull said old *Yellow Hair* was a *fool*. Custer was a *glory hound*. A commander seeking glory on the battlefield is something no army needs. That kind of commander, like Custer, will get soldiers killed."

Jean-Paul noted that Colonel Teddy did not respond to Wood's comment. There had actually been newspaper articles accusing Roosevelt of being a *glory hound*. Perhaps Wood had intentionally aimed his comment at Teddy and he recognized it as such. Perhaps....

Colonel Wood then turned to Jean-Paul and Corporal Scarborough and said, "Go and round up all the troop commanders. Tell them to report immediately to my headquarters to get briefed on tomorrow's mission." The two saluted and double-timed to complete their assignment.

Jean-Paul couldn't help thinking about how General's Wheeler and Young had so casually discounted the information provided by the Cuban insurgents. Just because they were dressed in rags and did not have the same standard of discipline as the Americans, it didn't mean their information wasn't credible. Perhaps General Garcia's suggestion to wait to go on the offensive until all the Americans had landed was based on his hard experience and *not* on a reluctance to fight.

Jean-Paul had heard the Spanish forces numbered over 150,000 and the U.S. force was twenty-two thousand. That was a seven to one difference and seemed to be way out of proportion. Of course, Jean-Paul was not sure how many Cuban insurgents there were. Then he reconciled that his generals were professional military men and veterans of many battles and wars. They obviously understood more of what was going on than he did. Obviously....

The attitude his leaders had about the Cuban rebels vaguely reminded Jean-Paul of the attitude the town's people of New Hope had regarding the Chacopac tribe. For many of the locals, differences and appearances seemed to drive their attitude about the Chacs. Chacopac character or behavior was not given any consideration. That J.P. thought, was incredibly ignorant.

When all of the regiment's eight troop commanders arrived, Jean-Paul remained in the background and listened to Colonel Wood's briefing. He said with firmness, "Commencing at 6:00 AM, Brigadier General Young, who is in charge of this entire operation, will proceed along the ridgeline of the Siboney-Sevilla road with four dismounted troops of the Tenth Regular Cavalry commanded by Major Norvell. They will be accompanied by four troops of the First Regular Cavalry under Major Bell and two Hotchkiss one-pound guns under Captain Watson." All the while he was talking, Wood was pointing to a rough map that he had drawn on the ground with a stick.

Colonel Wood went on to say that the First Volunteer Cavalry Regiment's eight troops would move parallel and to the south of Young's force on a narrow hillside trail. *Their mission was to first provide flank security for Young's force.* The avenues on which the two units were moving would intersect five miles from Las Guasimas. Where these two approaches crisscrossed was where the Spanish had established their first defensive trench line. At that point the Americans were to make a flank assault and secure the area by eliminating all Spanish opposition.

Colonel Wood indicated Captain Capron's L Troop would be the lead unit. Wood emphasized Captain Capron's unit was chosen for the most dangerous and responsible mission because of their commander's military skills and leadership. That choice was something no one could challenge thought Jean-Paul. Four or five men were to be on point and a support team of twenty men would follow behind them at a close distance. These elements were to position themselves about two hundred and fifty yards in front of the main body of L Troop. Colonel Wood indicated this was a successful tactic utilized in the *War of the Rebellion*. Skirmishers had always been sent out between two hundred to three hundred yards to the front of the man body.

Colonel Wood said he and his two aides, Captain Dunn and Captain Jenkins, would follow behind L Troop. Colonel Roosevelt, who would be acting as a squadron commander of three of the troops of men, would be next in the formation. Major Brodie's squadron would follow them. The final three cavalry troops would be reserve and would bring up the rear.

Colonel Wood emphasized the route would be muddy and narrow. The troops by necessity, would march in file. The trail would also be bordered by tangled jungle—which would be very difficult for a human to negotiate. As a result, flank security would *not be put out because* the flankers would not be able to keep up because of the terrain. Since the Spanish were only five miles away, the Rough Riders had to be on the alert for snipers, ambushes, and the Spaniard's advance skirmishers. Part of the regiment would remain in the rear to guard the regiment's supplies. Because of the anticipated difficulty in marching up the mountain to the objective, Colonel Wood said they would probably go into the fight with five hundred troopers. Jean-Paul was a bit shocked by that number since that was about half the strength of the regiment and was three to four times fewer soldiers than the Spanish supposedly had in their defensive positions.

Immediately after Colonel Wood's brief of the troop commanders, there was a tropical downpour that lasted over two hours. After the rain, the troops built fires and tried to dry their uniforms and equipment. Regardless of the discomfort of being soaked and living in jungle mud, Jean-Paul noted that morale was sky high, and everyone was mentally ready to go on the attack. Jean-Paul and Trooper Bell cleaned their rifles and pistols. He wrote a couple of notes in his journal, read a chapter of Scripture, said a prayer, and then fell fast sleep. It was a sound rest despite the potential danger the next day would bring. It would be a day Jean-Paul had thought about, dreamt about, and looked forward too as far back as he could remember! It would be the day he had been anticipating all of his entire young life!

**Thought Questions for Chapter 15:**

1. Evaluate Sergeant Guitilias' philosophy about aging and life.

2. What are your impressions and reactions to what Sergeant Major Sacker and Sergeant Guitilias shared about experiencing combat? Would you add anything to what they said?

3. Why did Sergeant LaCombe say Colonel Roosevelt was always lucky and had good fortune? What can you learn from that?

4. Ignoring the orders he had received, why did Major General Fightin' Joe Wheeler decide to move on Las Guasimas with *a reconnaissance in force?* Why didn't he have confidence in the intelligence that the Cuban rebels had provided to him?

5. How did Major General Wheeler describe outstanding battle leadership?

6. What was your biggest learning or take away from this chapter? What can you apply from the information in this chapter? What in it did you find the most interesting? Why?

**Thought Questions Regarding Book 1:**

1. What did you learn about war, the craft of soldiering, and leadership in this book?

2. What can you apply from the information in this book?

3. What in it did you find the most interesting? Why?

4. What was your biggest learning/take away from this book?

5. What would you say to Corporal Jean-Paul DeBert if you met him? What would you say to Trooper Three-Ring?

6. After reading this book, what would you say to the author if you met him?

## About the Author

Lieutenant Colonel (Retired) Gene Klann, Ph.D., was most recently a member of the training faculty at the Center for Creative Leadership. Prior to joining the Center, he completed a distinguished 25-year career in the U.S. Army, serving in the Vietnam War, Cold War Germany, Panama, the Persian Gulf War, Italy, and Belgium. From 1992-1994, he served as a senior member of the U.S. military delegation to NATO in Brussels. He has earned a Ph.D. in philosophy from the Free University of Brussels.

# Other Books by Blacksmith Publishing

**Small Unit Tactics Handbook**

**Fire in the Jungle**

**Land Navigation From Start to Finish**

**Tactical Leadership**

*www.blacksmithpublishingcom*

CPSIA information can be obtained
at www.ICGtesting.com
Printed in the USA
LVHW010710191122
733278LV00023B/1340